Praise for New... USA TODAY b... GENA S...

Catch a Mate

"The versatile Showalter...once again shows that she can blend humor and poignancy while keeping readers entertained from start to finish."
—*Booklist*

"Another smart and sexy romance brimming with hilarious pickup lines, fiery banter and steamy sensuality. A wid... heroine mix wit... tremen...
—*Romantic Ti...*

"As close to a perf... ...g nonstop laughter, i... ...y true-to-life characters...the ultimate feel-good book."
—*All About Romance*

"Smart-alecky, wicked, and hilariously funny... [Showalter] captures the essence of romantic comedy as well as she writes paranormal romance. Bravo!"
—*Contemporary Romance Writers*

The Nymph King
"Gena Showalter's stories hum with fast pacing and characters that leap off the page. Pick up one of Gena's books! You won't be disappointed."
—*USA TODAY* bestselling author Julie Kenner

"A world of myth, mayhem and love under the sea!"
—*USA TODAY* bestselling author J. R. Ward

"I want to visit Atlantis! Deliciously evocative and filled with sexy men, *The Nymph King* is every woman's fantasy come to sizzling life. A must read."
—Award-winning author P.C. Cast

Gena Showalter

Catch a Mate

HQN™

Recycling programs
for this product may
not exist in your area.

ISBN 13: 978-0-373-77568-2

CATCH A MATE

Copyright © 2007 by Gena Showalter

This edition published by arrangement with Harlequin Books S.A.

® and TM are trademarks of the publisher. Trademarks indicated with ® are registered in the United States Patent and Trademark Office, the Canadian Trade Marks Office and in other countries.

www.HQNBooks.com

Printed in U.S.A.

This book could not have been written without
Jill Monroe. (Road trip + Gena Showalter +
Jill Monroe - Sanity = Trouble.)
I'll leave it to your imagination as to why.

To Merline Lovelace and Sharon Sala.
Thank you!

To Pennye and Terry Edwards and
Max and Vivian Showalter.
Much love!

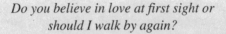

One

*Do you believe in love at first sight or
should I walk by again?*

IN LIFE, there was only one guarantee and that, Jillian
Greene hated to say, was that all men were pigs. "Will you
repeat your question?" she asked her coworker and friend,
Selene Garnett. "I'm positive I misheard."

"Nope. You didn't mishear. I asked what you would
say to a man who told you to take off your panties so he
could smell them."

Jillian gazed over at Selene, a blond goddess in black
leather, who was untouchable in a way that made men
want to touch her. And keep touching her. Over and over
again. "Is that a trick question?"

"Hardly." Selene stood in the opening of Jillian's
cubicle, slender arms braced on the blue makeshift walls.
Her hands covered the two posters Jillian had pasted up
only a short while ago. One said, Where There's a Man,
There's a Lie. The other read, Behind Every Good Man

Is a Gun. "A guy said it to me last night," Selene added. "I was so shocked, I froze."

"Do you like this man?"

"Please." Selene rolled her eyes. "He was a target."

"In that case, you tell him the only way you'll allow him to sniff your underpants is if they've been laced with the Ebola virus."

"I knew you'd have the perfect reply." Selene smiled that cool smile of hers and practically floated down the hall on a cloud of violets and jasmine, throwing over her shoulder, "Danielle owes me ten bucks."

Oh, yes. Men were pigs.

Some were piglets, all oink and no bite. Some were swine-in-training, teetering on the edge between man and boar. Some were Miss Piggies, no explanation needed. And some were hungry hogs, devouring everything in their path.

Those, Jillian hated most.

But no matter where a guy fell on the Pigometer, Jillian didn't let his bestial qualities upset her. Since men were oinkers, it was safe to say that she was the slaughter house. She quite happily cut the different breeds into bacon and served them to their owners on a silver platter.

It was her job and her greatest pleasure.

She (and Selene) worked for Catch a Mate. How deliciously romantic that sounded, right? Except Catch a Mate was the place women came to test their significant other's trustworthiness. Here's how it broke down:

Jane Doe enters the CAM office, cites three incidents that make her believe her man has cheated, then flips through a book of photos and chooses the face and form that will most appeal to her husband, boyfriend or asshole lover too cheap to fork over a ring. The woman she picks—a.k.a. the bait—is then given the man's—a.k.a. the target's—schedule and proceeds to "accidentally" meet him, laying on the charm. Of course, she's wearing a hidden camera and a microphone, recording his every transgression.

Jillian was bait.

She was paid to smile, to lie. To flirt. These already attached men ate it up, too, no spoon required, proving just how disgusting they really were.

Some people (those who were guilty) might consider what she did entrapment. Some people (those who were *very* guilty) might consider what she did wrong. But she never kissed, touched or screwed the men, just allowed them to incriminate themselves with their own words, so her conscience was safe. Besides, there wouldn't be a problem if her targets would simply send her on her way.

Instead, they returned her smiles, told her lies of their own and flirted back. They were willing to forget years of fidelity, sweep aside their honor and completely disrespect their lover for one supposed night of wildness.

To Jillian, they deserved what they got.

She never told her clients their men had cheated; that was her boss's job. However, she often watched those conversations on a monitor in another room, and what she saw was heartbreaking. Tears, curses, depression. The emotions of the victims of infidelity ran the gamut, but they all had one thing in common: a ruined life. *That's* why she so enjoyed taking these men down a peg or two. Because of them, their partners would never be the same.

And for what?

Married men pretended they were divorced—just to get a little booty. Engaged men pretended they were single—just to get a little booty. Boyfriends pretended they were unattached, just to—you guessed it—get a little booty. Not one of her targets had ever *not* tried to pick her up.

She didn't understand it, either. She was cute, sure, but not drop-dead gorgeous. Average height, a decent figure she worked very hard to maintain, long, curly black hair, big blue eyes, slightly rounded cheeks and dimples. God, she hated those tiny, innocent schoolgirl dimples.

Without a doubt, she was nothing special in the looks department. However, if a man thought she was going to ride him like a carnival pony, it didn't matter what she looked like. She suddenly represented every sex fantasy he'd ever indulged.

Bastards. Jillian had worked for CAM for six years now; she'd started when she was only twenty-one. From day one, she'd gained a perverse satisfaction in nailing a man's ass to the wall and saving a woman from further heartbreak. That sense of fulfillment had only grown over the years.

But, uh, speaking of nailing male ass…she glanced at her wristwatch and pushed out a sigh. She should have met with her boss thirty minutes ago; instead, she'd watched Anne enter her office with a tall, blond specimen of deliciousness. Jillian had gotten only the barest glimpse of him, but it was enough of a glance to know he was tanned and muscled and wearing jeans that hugged a perfectly squeezable butt.

She might think—know!—guys were pigs, but she

wasn't blind and she liked to look. Looking was all she allowed herself anymore, so when she looked, she *really* looked. X-ray vision that saw past clothes, past all hint of decency.

Sometimes she reminded herself of a window-shopper, gazing inside the store with her nose pressed to the glass, never actually buying the pretty, overpriced merchandise because she knew that she'd later experience buyer's remorse.

Why fork over hard-earned cash when the item in question undoubtedly would be stolen, tainted, stained or ripped to shreds?

Once (or twice) she'd allowed the "salesman" and his sweet, sweet sales pitch to convince her to purchase, but each of those occasions had ended at the return booth. Yep, the few boyfriends she'd permitted herself over the years had all failed CAM's test, which was especially pathetic since they knew what she did for a living. Finally, she'd cut up her credit cards (so to speak).

She sighed. What depressing thoughts. She needed to think about something else. Like her boss. Which, incidentally, led her straight back to Cute Ass. He and Anne had closed the office door and no sound had emerged since. Not even pressing her ear against the shuttered glass wall had proven useful. And yes, she freely admitted to spying. To her, there was nothing wrong with listening to private conversations, opening someone's desk drawer, sneaking a peek through their wallet, glove compartment, whatever.

Sneakiness was the best way to learn about people. To learn the *truth* about them, anyway.

Sipping her coffee, Jillian leaned back in her chair and cast her boss's door another glance. She had an assignment tonight and she always met with Anne to outline a strategy beforehand—as if it took more than a push-up bra and an I'm-so-innocent-but-I'm-not-wearing-any-panties smile to stir a man's interest. Still. She was due at the scheduled rendezvous point in four hours and she had yet to look at photos of her target.

As her feet tapped impatiently, her black spiked heels clicked into the floor tile of her very blue, very plain cubicle. Besides her posters, she had no personal items here, no pictures of family. She liked to keep business, business and—what did she care about her cube? She wanted to know what No-Nonsense Anne and Cute Ass were talking about. She wanted to know what they were *doing.*

"Did you see the guy Anne escorted into her office?"

At the sound of the husky feminine voice, Jillian pivoted in her seat. Georgia Carrington stood at the opening of Jillian's cube, the fragrance of vanilla and sugar wafting from her. Rich, silky red hair framed exquisitely delicate features.

Georgia had gentle cheekbones, a dainty nose, almond-shaped green eyes and flawless skin. Her body was a smorgasbord of naughty curves, and right now those curves were encased in a strapless, barely-there red sheath dress. Men became slaves to their hormones whenever Georgia approached, so it was no wonder she was CAM's most popular choice of bait.

That hadn't always been the case, though. Jillian had known Georgia since grade school, when Georgia had been a gangly, freckled kid. Everyone else had teased her unmercifully, but Jillian had recognized a kindred spirit when she saw one—two girls against the rest of the world.

But it hadn't been an official friendship until Thomas Fisher called Georgia a speckled carrot-head. Jillian had socked him in the nose, Georgia had bandaged her hand, and they had been best friends ever since.

"I saw him," Jillian said now. She set her coffee aside, lifted a pen and tapped it against the armrest of her chair. "Who is he and why's he here?" A client, perhaps? But they only dealt with women. Unless…did he suspect his wife was a lesbian? That was a possibility, though what woman would prefer a female to that prime, grade-A quality meat, she didn't know.

"Maybe Anne decided to give up her stance on the merits of self-gratification and take a lover." Georgia sashayed around the desk and plopped onto the edge, crinkling papers and files. The hem of the red dress rode up her thighs and revealed several inches of tanned, firm flesh.

Jillian shrugged. "Maybe he's her sister's brother-in-law's cousin's uncle and he's here to borrow money."

"Yeah, well, maybe I want a piece of her sister's brother-in-law's cousin's uncle. I almost slid out of my chair when he walked past me."

Jillian, too, had experienced a very feminine reaction: breathlessness, beaded nipples, quickened pulse. It had been a long time since she'd been intimate with a man and, well, the scent of sin—that's the only way to describe it—had followed this one, lingering in the air long after he'd stepped into the boss's office and shut the door.

"I thought you had a boyfriend," Jillian said, trying

not to frown at the image of Georgia and Cute Ass. Together. Naked.

A dark, haunted glint entered her friend's eyes but was quickly extinguished. "I did." Georgia sighed. "I do."

"Problems?"

With a dismissive—forced?—laugh, Georgia waved her hand through the air. "Of course not. Things are the same as they've been for the last several weeks. Wyatt tells me I'm beautiful and asks me to marry him every single day. And every single day I tell him I'm still thinking about it."

"If you have to think about it, he's not the man for you." Jillian didn't think he was the man for Georgia, anyway. He treated her like a queen, sure, lavishing endless compliments on her physical beauty. But where were his compliments on her witty mind and kind heart?

"I've heard your argument against him a thousand times, counselor, so no need to rehash the case. I just want to be sure we're forever, that's all." She sounded miserable.

"We could put him to the CAM test again." Every woman who worked here ended up putting her man to the test. Only two had passed. Wyatt and some guy Selene had dated—and later dumped when she found him in bed with another man.

"He'd just pass again. Since he knows what we do for a living, he's always suspicious of pretty women who approach him." Georgia crossed her legs and her skirt rode all the higher. "No more talk of Wyatt. I want to discuss, in minute detail, Anne's possible new lover. He has to be a superhero. Pleasure Man or something like that, able to cause orgasm with a single glance. No ordinary man could have charmed his way into a private meeting with Frigid Anne."

Jillian eagerly returned to the topic of Cute Ass. "Did he look at you when he passed you?" she asked pensively, replaying his hallway stride through her mind, step by sexy step. "Did he give you any sign of interest?"

Georgia's forehead furrowed and her red brows drew together. She blinked in dawning confusion. "No. He didn't."

"He ignored me, too," Selene said as she strode past Jillian's cube, head bent over a file. "Danielle, too."

"He didn't look at me, either," Jillian assured Georgia. Hadn't cast a single glance in her direction, actually, and she had been making plenty of noise as she'd struggled to pick up her jaw and draw in even a molecule of air. It wasn't that she thought she was entitled to male appreciation or anything like that. But to completely ignore the women of *this* office as if they were nothing more than asexual beings…maybe he was gay.

"What a waste if he's gay," Georgia said, confirming her thoughts.

It was telling, really, that neither one of them thought there was a chance in hell he was so devoted to a wife or girlfriend that he failed to notice other women. It wasn't even a possibility in their minds.

"But I didn't get the gay vibe," Georgia added. "Did you?"

"No." So if he wasn't gay, what was he? Jillian didn't like mysteries (they sucked), hated working puzzles (they blew), and wanted to spit on surprises (they both sucked and blew). Maybe that was one of the reasons she enjoyed working at CAM. Every night, the outcome was the same. The target cheated. End of story.

Okay, so that was a little sad.

"Do you think he's blind?"

"Come on, Detective Carrington. You can do better than that. He didn't have a Seeing Eye dog or a cane. Nor did he stumble or need Anne to lead him." She thought about it for a moment. "My guess is he's so self-absorbed, he didn't realize anyone else was in the building."

"Oh, no doubt you're right. What an ass!" Discussion over in her mind since that made Cute Ass a jerk and unworthy of their time, Georgia pushed to her feet and twirled. "So…do you like my new outfit?"

"You look like a slut. I love it." Jillian grinned. "Do you have an assignment tonight?"

Returning her grin, Georgia plopped back onto the desk. "Nope. This outfit is for Wyatt. After last night's assignment…" Her full, red lips curled in revulsion. "I may not go into the field again. I sat next to my target—at a coffeehouse, of all places—and the slimy bastard immediately tried to talk his way into my pants. *Your dad has to be a thief. That's the only way to explain those stars in your eyes.* Gag! He's married, for God's sake, and had just celebrated his sixteenth wedding anniversary."

"Let me guess. He claimed he'd just gotten a divorce, the loneliness was almost more then he could bear and a pretty girl like you could sure ease the pain in his heart."

"Bingo."

"Men can't be trusted," Jillian muttered with an appalled shake of her head; black curls swished in every direction. "Did you tell him to go fuck himself?"

Georgia rolled her eyes. "I wish. I wanted to tell him who and what I was, but couldn't bring myself to break the rules."

Telling a target the truth could lead to panic—and panic from a target could be a dangerous, even life-threatening, thing. "So what did you do?"

"I made sure he won't be getting in anyone's pants for a while, maybe not even his own."

Jillian patted her friend's knee in approval. They'd both taken self-defense lessons after joining the agency, courtesy of Anne. Anne refused to pay for bodyguards—they were too expensive—so the girls were on their own when in the field. Jillian actually preferred it that way. She didn't want to rely on a man/lying piece of swine for her safety. Her Mace acted as her hired muscle, bringing down the strongest of opponents.

"Anne showed his wife the video earlier and the woman burst into tears. I know because I stupidly watched on the screen in the conference room." Georgia expelled a slight puff of air, as dainty as the woman herself. She drummed her perfectly manicured nails against the desk.

Jillian didn't mention that she'd seen the wife, too, just as the woman was leaving the office. Those tearstained cheeks had almost made *Jillian* cry. Poor thing. She had a tough road ahead of her.

Victims were always told the day after the evidence was gathered. No reason to put it off and prolong the torture. The criers always caused Jillian's chest to ache. The punchers—well, they might hate her and the other bait now, but they'd thank them later.

Still. Maybe she and Georgia needed to start coming in late the day after an assignment.

"I despise that part of the job, you know?" Georgia said. "Just once, I'd like to see a happy ending, a man who doesn't care about a pretty face. A man who's happy with what he has at home, even if she's gained weight or acquired a few wrinkles."

"Me, too, but we both know the odds of that happening. And women are better off learning the truth now instead of later," Jillian said, her tone firm with conviction. After all, she should know. Years ago, her dad had cheated on her mom and her mom hadn't known, hadn't suspected at all. But little Jillian had known—her dad had taken her to the neighbor's house to "play with the cat." She'd chased that stupid tabby all the way into the bedroom and gotten an eyeful.

Her dad hadn't explicitly asked her to keep quiet, but he had to have known she would never speak of it to her mom, too afraid her parents would split.

The guilt of not telling her mother had eaten at her.

A few months later, the knowledge had become too much for her to bear and she'd confided in her older brother and sister. They had begged her not to tell Mom, not wanting to cause their parents' divorce, either. So she'd kept quiet. Again. Pretending her dad really was going to the grocery store when he sneaked next door.

She'd been the only seven-year-old with an ulcer.

About six months after that, her mom flew off to visit her sister. But then Evelyn decided, for whatever reason, to come home early. That's when she found Jillian's dad in bed with the neighbor. Her mom had been shocked and devastated, and the truth had finally spilled from Jillian.

The next morning, her mom tried to kill herself.

A familiar rage kindled inside of Jillian, images of her bleeding and unconscious mother flashing through her mind. *She'd* been the one to find her. Not her brother, Brent. Not her sister, Brittany. Not her dad. *She'd* been the one to cry over her mom's bloody—Jillian quickly shoved those memories away before she punched a wall. She didn't like thinking about those worry-filled weeks, her mom teetering between life and death.

Needless to say, she hadn't spoken to her dad since. Her mom had divorced him and he'd taken off. He still called Jillian about once a week, but she never picked up. Brent, the easygoing contractor, and Brittany, the tender-hearted stay-at-home mom, begged her almost daily to forgive him, but she just couldn't. Maybe one day, she thought.… No. Never, she decided in the next instant. There was simply too much pain there.

"Without us," she said now to Georgia, teeth clenched, "women would be lost in a world of lies, thinking their men loved and respected them."

Georgia pondered those words for several minutes, then shrugged. Her body glitter caught the light, making her bare shoulders shimmer. "Maybe believing the lie is the only key to happiness." Today was the first time she'd ever voiced doubts about their profession.

Anything to do with Wyatt and his marriage proposal?

"So where are you going tonight?" Georgia asked before Jillian could question her. "You look like a cheap hooker."

"Thank you," Jillian replied with a genuine smile.

She wore a skintight white tank top with a low V-neck for ultra cleavage, a barely-there jean skirt with a frayed hem, a thick silver belt and tall black boots. Her hair was a wild, untamed mass of curls, her makeup heavily applied.

At the moment, everything about her screamed "saddle up and take me for a ride." But then, the man she was supposed to "catch" later apparently liked his women dressed that way. The trashier the better, or so his girlfriend, who dressed like a dime-store prostitute herself, had said.

"I'm going to The Meat Market," Jillian explained. No lie, that was the name of the nightclub situated in the pulsing heart of downtown Oklahoma City. It was supposedly *the* place for prowling singles.

Her target's live-in girlfriend said her man had been visiting the club for weeks. For "beer." Jillian believed that one-hundred percent—if beer was the new name for T & A. If the guy was simply throwing back a few cold ones, why couldn't he take his girlfriend with him? Why did he leave her at home and insist she stay there?

Anne had suggested the girlfriend follow the guy herself before resorting to bait, but the woman had shut down that idea immediately. Jillian thought she knew why. It was one thing to believe your man was cheating; it was quite another to actually witness it yourself, live and in person. Plus, the girlfriend could be spotted and the guy could alter his behavior accordingly.

The door to Anne's office suddenly jerked open, startling her. Surprising Georgia, too, who gasped.

Jillian jolted upright as Anne stuck out her head. She caught a glimpse of the woman's graying hair and stern, wrinkled features before Anne called, "Jillian. Get in here ASAP. I've got some bad news for you."

She disappeared without another word, but left the door open.

O-kay. Jillian's heart skipped a beat. She flicked Georgia a nervous glance, and it didn't help that her friend was wide-eyed and openmouthed. Hands beginning to sweat, she eased to her feet.

"Bad news," Georgia said quietly, her attention veering between Jillian and the door. "She's usually abrupt, but that was…"

"Maybe my case has been reassigned," Jillian said, hopeful.

"Maybe."

Georgia didn't sound convinced and deep down Jillian wasn't, either. Shit. *Shit!* More than going over her assignment tonight, Jillian had hoped to talk to Anne about making her a partner, or—what she really wanted— selling her the business outright.

She'd tried to broach the subject a few times already, but each time Anne had been busy and had shooed her away with a promise of "later."

There was no one better equipped or readier to take over than Jillian. She'd been here forever (it sometimes seemed) and had many wonderful ideas, if she did say so herself, about taking CAM to the next level. Like a counseling center for victims of infidelity, support groups and even a Web site dedicated to warning women about particular men. Sort of an Internet Wall of Shame, appropriately dubbed the Swine Whine, with ratings of just how high on the Pigometer certain individuals ranked. Oklahoma's most *un*wanted.

If she had her way, CAM's clients would get the kind of help her mother hadn't.

Now that conversation would have to wait. Again.

Bad news...she gulped. Something was about to go down, that was for sure, and from the sound of Anne's voice, Jillian suspected it was herself.

Two

I miss my teddy bear. Would you sleep with me?

JILLIAN STEPPED INTO Anne's office, her heart thundering. Anne was already settled behind her desk. She was a stern, no-nonsense woman, always abrupt and demanding, but she'd never commanded Jillian's presence with such force before. Never told her she had "bad news."

What was going on? *Does she want to get rid of me?* Why? What could Jillian possibly have done? She studied her boss. Anne was of indeterminate age and refused to discuss the matter on threat of death. Jillian's guess? Two thousand, give or take a year. Deep lines bracketed her mouth, eyes and cheeks. Coarse gray hair frizzed—no. Today her hair wasn't frizzed. Today her hair was slicked back from her face, making her look almost…pretty. Huh. That was a first, too.

Anne glanced up from the papers on her desk; her hazel eyes, normally devoid of any emotion except annoyance, were now colored with guilt. "Shut the door," Anne said, returning her attention to the papers.

Without turning her back on her boss, Jillian pressed the heavy glass door closed. The blinds were drawn, so no one could see inside. She sent her nervous gaze around the spacious room. Large windows consumed the far wall and numerous dying plants were lined up in front of them. An opened bottle of Scotch rested on the wet bar.

One day, she wanted this office to be her own. Was that even a possibility now?

Cute Ass sat in one of the chairs in front of the desk. His back was to her and he didn't bother turning to acknowledge her. He remained slumped in the plush blue seat, completely relaxed. A little irreverent.

"What's going on?" Jillian asked, proud that she sounded at ease and unconcerned.

"Sit down." With a brusque chin tilt, Anne motioned to the other chair—the one beside Cute Ass.

Did Anne plan to fire her? Was the blond here to protect her in case Jillian went ballistic? Instantly her mind replayed the last few assignments she'd taken. Sure, she had kneed one target in the balls. But he could still father children. Sure, she had caused a barroom brawl. But no one had died.

She swallowed the sudden lump in her throat and strode to the chair. She eased down, smoothing her jean skirt with shaky hands. "What's going on?" she asked again.

"Jillian Greene," Anne said, "meet Marcus Brody. Marcus, Jillian."

You're breezy. Not a care. "Nice to meet you," she told him, twisting and holding out a hand.

His attention never veered in her direction. He kept his gaze fixed straight ahead, merely arching a brow in acknowledgment of her words. O-kay. So he didn't want to look at, talk to or touch her. *Bad news...*

The moisture in her mouth dried. Maybe he wasn't so cute, after all. Jillian's hand dropped to her side.

Anne propped her elbows on the desk and pinned her with a hard stare. "Marcus has joined the agency as bait."

"What?" Her jaw dropped open, but she closed it with a snap. Of all the things she'd expected to hear, that didn't even hit the bottom of the list. So many times she had heard Anne swear to God and her three bastard ex-husbands that she'd never hire anyone with a penis. Still, Jillian experienced a kernel of relief. *Not fired.* Thank the good Lord. "I thought you wanted to keep this office testosterone-free."

"I did, but I changed my mind."

What kind of response was that? Anne hated men. H. A. T. E. D. That's the reason she'd opened the agency. The fact that she'd now hired one, and would pay him to prove women were just as untrustworthy as men, boggled Jillian's mind. She couldn't even count the number of male applicants Anne had refused (with relish) over the years.

She had to be missing something here and floundered to understand. "Are we trying to draw gay clients, then?"

Marcus Brody snorted. That was it, his only reaction. Yet still she shivered. How could one little snort be so... sensual? What the hell would his voice be like, then?

"No, he's not gay," Anne said, rolling her eyes.

Jillian's confusion increased. Was this some kind of joke? She discarded the idea almost as soon as it formed. Anne had no sense of humor. Could this be—she gasped as the answer slid into place. "Anne, can I have a minute alone with you?"

"No." Anne peered at Jillian over the rim of her glasses, unbending. Stern. A familiar expression. "Time is of the essence, and I'd like to get this meeting out of the way."

Fine. She'd voice her suspicions out loud, in front of Marcus. "Is he blackmailing you?"

Finally the man in question decided to spare her a glance. At the exact moment she looked over at him. Their eyes met, her blue against his velvety brown, and her breath snagged in her throat. From behind, he was gorgeous. From the front, he was even more delicious than she'd suspected. Unbelievably delicious, actually. Tall, blond and muscled. Tanned and rugged. Almost savage looking, as if he didn't belong in this time period but with a band of bloodthirsty Vikings intent on raping and pillaging.

He was eyeing her up and down with a hint of disdain in his dark gaze.

Disdain? What had she done? *You accused him of blackmail, dummy. And don't forget you also accused this manly-man of being gay.* Oh, yeah. Still. The look in his eyes lit a fiery heat inside her. Some people might call that heat lust. She called it annoyance. He shouldn't regard her as if she were beneath him, no matter his provocation. He didn't even know her.

"What's so hard to believe about my legitimately working here?" he demanded.

It was the first time he'd spoken and his voice washed over her in rolling, erotic waves, her every cell sizzling. It was more seductive a voice than she'd suspected. Decadent. Okay, maybe she felt a *little* lust.

"Well? No response?"

He spoke in a deep, humming rhythm, a slight English accent making his words orgasmically crisp. Her nipples hardened—damn those traitors!—and it took every ounce of willpower she possessed not to cover them with her hands because her thin, too-tight tank revealed everything. *Everything.* He'd have to be blind not to notice the two-nipple salute she was giving him.

She gulped. "I'm sorry if I've offended you. That wasn't my intention. You just aren't the kind of person Anne usually hires."

His sandy brows arched. "And just what kind of person is that?"

"Someone with a vagina," she said bluntly.

"I have something better, I assure you."

Jillian blinked, took a moment to digest his words, and shook her head. "Please tell me you did not just imply what I think you just implied."

"Implied?" He chuckled, the sound rich and smooth, utterly captivating and completely mocking. "I spoke only truth, Dimples."

Dimples? Grrrr! So, not only had Anne hired a male, she'd hired one with an overinflated ego. Life would only be more perfect if Jillian scheduled a pelvic exam and gained four hundred pounds. She was kind of glad he'd revealed his true nature, though. Knowing he was a hungry hog lessened his visual appeal. Or so she told herself.

"I'm the best bait in the business," he added, "and you're lucky to have me here. You, on the other hand, are of questionable morals, questionable character and prone to extreme bouts of emotion. I've read your file."

He'd read her file? While it was okay for her to sneak around and read confidential files, it was *not* okay for someone to read hers. Double standard be damned! But something hot—very hot—washed through her blood as she thought about *him* doing it. Something very much like…desire? Oh, hell no. *You're mad that he just insulted you. You are not excited. Your stomach is clenching in anger,* not *arousal.*

"First, you shouldn't have read my file. That's for Anne's eyes only. Second, I am not of questionable morals *or* questionable character. I have never, *ever* slept with a target." It was the truth. She felt nothing but contempt for her targets, now and always. "I've punched a few in the face, yes, so I won't argue the 'extreme bouts of emotion.'"

"Gold star for Jillian, then," he muttered, "for managing to keep her clothes on at work."

That hot, fiery *something* sparked again. "Do you hear the way he's insulting me?" she demanded of Anne. "Do you realize what kind of person he is, that he can say something like that?"

Amusement flashed in Anne's hazel eyes. "I hear and I realize."

"And you're still going to hire him?"

Anne gave her an enigmatic smile. "Something like that."

She gasped. *Just shut your mouth. Act like a professional—unlike Marcus.* "You're telling me you want this…this *miva* working for you?" she found herself saying anyway. One child in the room obviously wasn't enough.

"Miva?" Anne echoed, confused.

"Male diva," Jillian replied.

"Nice," Marcus said, sarcasm dripping from that one word. "I'm right here, you know. You might save this stimulating conversation for after I've left."

"And you're fine with that?" she continued, as if Egotistical Ass hadn't spoken. Everything—well, almost everything—inside her wanted him gone. Now. He'd insulted her and rather than experiencing fury as she'd tried to convince herself, she wanted to tear off his clothes. There. She'd admitted it. This kind of thing had never happened to her before and it creeped her out. "His attitude doesn't make you want to feed his organs to your cats?"

Anne held up her index finger. "One, I don't have cats." Another finger. "Two, his attitude doesn't bother me because you're the one who has to deal with him. He's going with you tonight."

"What!"

"You heard me. He's going with you." There was no room for argument in Anne's tone and all traces of humor had vanished from her expression. Jillian barely had time to react before Anne added, "As Marcus said, he's done this type of work before. But I want him to observe how we at CAM run our operation.

"Here are photos of your newest target." She handed one to Jillian and one to Marcus. "I've got personal business for the rest of the day, so I'll be back tomorrow. You're a professional—I hope—so you should be able to handle a day without me."

What? What! "Where are you going?" Jillian gasped out. Her fingers closed shakily around the photo.

"I told you, it's personal. No more questions. Now, have a good day." And with that, Anne gathered her purse, stood, and strode to the entrance. Her starched black pantsuit crackled as she walked.

"Anne," Jillian called, shock pounding through her. Anne practically lived in the office. Why was she leaving early?

"The answer is no," Anne said, reaching for the doorknob.

"You don't even know what I was going to say."

"Doesn't matter. The answer is still no." With a tug, she opened the door. Georgia spilled inside and tumbled onto the crimson carpet. Never breaking stride, Anne stepped over her, saying, "Get back to work, Carrington." Then she disappeared down the hall.

Georgia popped to her feet, cheeks blooming as bright a red as her hair. She tugged on her strapless dress before the twins popped out. "I, uh, was just about to knock. Would anyone like a cup of coffee?"

"No, thanks," Jillian muttered. The caffeine might be the final push her heart needed to achieve full arrest. She never would have gotten out of bed this morning if she'd known *this* kind of day awaited her.

Marcus didn't utter a word.

"All righty, then." Georgia hurriedly shut the door, closing Jillian and Marcus inside. Alone. Together.

Heavy silence filled the room.

Say something. Do something. She shifted in her seat and her gaze flicked to CAM's newest employee. He was watching her, something unreadable in his eyes, something hard and soft at the same time. Something dangerous to her peace of mind. She shifted again. *Be nice so he'll stop insulting you. Then you won't get turned on anymore.*

Which, by the way, her mind added, *is ridiculous.*

When had she become such a masochist?

"How did you convince Anne to give you this job?" she asked, her voice breathless as it pushed through the sudden block of ice in her throat.

A muscle ticked in his temple. "You may not realize this, so allow me to enlighten you. That question is insulting. In fact, you've done nothing but insult me since you first entered this office. Or maybe you *do* realize it and you just don't give a shit."

She held up a hand, palm out. "Honestly, no insult intended." *Good, you're doing good.* "It's just, I know Anne, you don't. This isn't like her. You're not the only man who's wanted to work here. She's always said no in the past."

"I may not be the only man to want to work here, but I promise you I'm the best."

Jillian had no doubts about that. No woman would be able to resist that potent allure of his. Still… "There's got to be more to it than that."

"What are you getting at?" he asked through clenched, white teeth. "That I'm Anne's boy toy?"

Suddenly on the defensive, she stiffened her spine. "Well, are you?"

"FYI, Dimples. I've never been so hard up for a job that I had to sleep with the boss to get one." Tone crisper with every word, he added, "Even though you're obviously slow, I really hope you understand my next words so I won't have to bring out Happy the sock puppet. Pay attention. There might be a quiz. Anne. Wants. To. Expand. The. Business. End of story."

Her eyes narrowed. A wave of intense loathing—yes, loathing and not some other, brainless emotion—swept through her. Some people clicked at their first meeting, some people…didn't. They obviously hadn't. And every moment together made the dislike—yes, dislike and not some other, even more brainless emotion—intensify.

Be in control. Don't let him see how much he's affecting you. "My questions and concerns were legitimate," she said (somewhat) evenly.

"No, they weren't," he ground out.

"Of course you don't think so." She smiled sweetly at him. "You're unreasonable."

"I bet you're a real bundle of joy in—the job," he said, then mumbled, "I really hope I don't have to step in and douse the fire you're sure to start tonight. I hear you've caused several brawls."

"Blame the Brotherhood of the Raging Hard-on," she said, still nauseatingly sweet, "not me."

"Is that why you're so grumpy right now, Dimples? Afraid I'll cramp your style tonight and keep you from all those hard-ons?" There was more disgust in that one sentence than she'd ever heard from another person. "You probably get off on arousing your targets and walking away."

That was low. So low. It was one part of the job she didn't like, but she'd resigned herself to it because the end results were so important to the victims of infidelity. "That observation is funny, Mark. Coming from you. Did you not just take a job that requires you to arouse women and then walk away from them?"

"It's Marcus," he said tightly. "I only answer to Marcus." Was that a flash of guilt in his eyes? No, surely not. Probably pride. Most likely he was giving himself a mental high-five.

She shrugged. "Whatever you say, Markie."

A long while passed as he stared at her intently. Then, "What I said about the hard-ons was uncalled-for," he admitted grudgingly.

Jillian shook her head, blinked. Had he, dare she believe it, apologized to her? Her dad had done it. Past boyfriends had even done it. But the words had never coasted over her skin with the fervency of a caress before. They'd never affected her to the marrow of her bones and made her want to forgive.

"Let's just get to work," she said after clearing her throat, not knowing what else to say. She forced her mind off Marcus and onto the photo Anne had given her. Good distraction. The man she was to charm tonight was in his early forties. He had a slightly receding hairline, nicely fringed brown eyes, a strong jaw and sharp cheekbones. Overall, not a bad-looking swine.

By tomorrow, life as he knew it would be in ruins.

Maybe she was emotionally barren or something, because that would have made most people feel a little sad, a little guilty. Perhaps even made them back away from the job. Jillian, well, she wanted his girlfriend to know exactly what kind of loser she'd been cooking and cleaning for, sleeping with and giving all of her time and energy to.

Like Georgia, Jillian would have loved to encounter a man with honor and integrity, who wouldn't crumble under the allure of forbidden temptation. A man who placed more importance on love than sex.

That thought brought her back to the male she didn't want to think about but couldn't seem to keep from her mind, making her wonder what kind of person *he* was.

She didn't think she could have enticed him away from a steaming pile of shit. Did he have a girlfriend? Did he treat all women with such disdain or just her?

How would he treat someone he loved?

"What do you know about Darren Sawyer, tonight's target?" All business now, Marcus leaned back in his chair and folded his arms over his stomach. His shirt strained against his hard sinew and velvet skin. "I haven't had a chance to read his file yet."

"His girlfriend says he's in the middle of a midlife crisis."

Marcus paused, a lock of pale hair falling over his brow. Pretty, yet somehow wholly masculine. "The girlfriend says that? Or you do?" He propped his elbow on his upraised knee and his chin in his palm. "The tone of your voice says the man's already been tried and convicted. We're supposed to be objective, aren't we?"

"No," she scoffed. "We're not supposed to be objective."

"And why not?"

"What does objectivity matter? The man will either cheat or he won't." She waved the folder in the air. "Darren traded his Toyota for a Cobra. He spends two hours a day at the gym when he used to spend those two hours talking with his girlfriend. And he's been visiting nightclubs every weekend. He's most likely decided to trade his old girlfriend in for a new one, too, only the old girlfriend doesn't know it. Yet."

That now-familiar glaze of disgust blanketed Marcus's eyes, piercing her like a laser beam. "A new car, working out and dancing equals midlife crisis, does it, Dimples? Maybe the man just wants to improve himself."

Damn, his accent was freakishly sexy. It made her

tingle. Still, she hated, hated, *hated* the way he said the word *dimples*. Sounded like an endearment, right? Not from *his* lips. It was more of a curse. "And maybe that time I ate a large pizza on my own, in one sitting, was for medicinal purposes."

"I drive a bloody Jag. I work out. Does that mean I'm in the middle of a bloody crisis?"

Two bloodies. Had she, perhaps, hit a nerve? "Well, let's see." She tapped a finger on her chin and pretended to mull over her next words. "Did you trade your old car in for one you couldn't afford?"

"No," he said stiffly.

"Did you just get a tattoo that says I'm On Fire?"

"No," he said, a little more stiffly.

"According to his girlfriend, Darren Sawyer has done both of those things. Do you think he put himself into debt and permanently marked his skin simply to improve himself? Or—and I know this is a stretch but bear with me, Mark—maybe he's trying to nail some hot, tight ass."

Marcus ran his tongue over his teeth. He was like a banked inferno, ready to explode. He didn't need a tattoo to tell the world he was burning. "One hundred dollars says Darren doesn't hit on you tonight."

Her eyes narrowed. "Planning on sabotaging me?"

"Hardly. I simply have faith in Mr. Sawyer. I think you're wrong about him. I think he's just trying to express himself. I think he's going to take one look at you and run the other way. As a betting man, I really like my odds on this one."

What was he trying to say? That she couldn't attract a man, even one on the prowl? Her hands clenched, crinkling the photo. Oh, she would show Marcus. With great pleasure. Express himself, indeed. Run the other way? Not likely. "You're on."

"No hesitation?" he said, sandy brows arching and giving him that insolent appearance she was coming to hate. And desire, damn her hormones.

"None whatsoever."

"I'm not surprised." He shook his head, more blond locks tumbling over his forehead. "You obviously have a high opinion of yourself."

"Actually, I have a low opinion of men." *Pig,* she inwardly cursed, even as she stayed the urge to caress that hair from his face. What was wrong with her? She needed a spanking for these masochistic tendencies. A bad, naughty spanking and, oh yeah, a— *Dummy. Stop.* "Darren won't cave because he wants me specifically. He'll cave because he's a walking penis and walking penises can't even tell an anatomically correct doll no."

"I should have known you'd say something like that." Marcus uttered another dark, rich chuckle. Darker than chocolate. Richer than whipped cream. "You're a man-hater, aren't you, Dimples?"

She bit the inside of her cheek so forcefully a metallic tang flavored her tongue. "I hate liars and I hate cheaters. So yeah, I guess I am a man-hater."

"Maybe you haven't met the right man yet."

"Is that man supposed to be you, Markie-warkie?" she sneered, making it obvious how ludicrous she found the concept. God, she'd never disliked someone so much, so quickly. He was vile. Absolutely vile. And so desirable her hands were shaking with the need to touch him. She was definitely a masochist. Funny she'd never realized that before today.

"You don't have to worry about me coming on to you," he said. "You're not my type."

"And what type is that?" she couldn't help but ask.

"Cold and heartless. And my name is Marcus."

"Are you calling *me* cold and heartless or is that the kind of woman you like to date?"

"You."

Oh, how her blood boiled, white hot, consuming. She was not cold and she was not heartless. But the insult hit home and hit deep because sometimes—just sometimes— she *was* afraid that she was becoming both of those things. After all, she helped ruin people's lives and she wasn't sorry. "Why the hell are you so malicious toward me? If you don't know what malicious means, I'd be glad to borrow your Happy the sock puppet and explain it to you."

"You're a woman, Dimples." He stared over at her, a half smile, half sneer curling his delectable mouth. "That's all it takes to bloody piss me off."

She blinked. "You don't like me because I'm a woman?" Maybe he really *was* gay.

"No, I like you just fine. Parts of you, anyway." His gaze slid over her body in a leering once-over, lingering on her breasts and between her legs, slowly stripping away her already scanty clothing. Daring her to challenge him. Begging her to do it, actually.

As if she would ever, *ever* let that swine see her naked. And knead her breasts. And roll her nipples between his fingers. And lick his way down her body. And—she growled low in her throat.

"*Women* are the cheaters and the liars," he said, "not men. They blithely forget their morals when they think they're going to get an orgasm. Or a man with more money. Or a man who will stupidly do anything they ask. The list could go on and on."

She blinked again as realization slammed into her. Oh, the irony. She laughed, incredulous. Marcus Brody was the male version of *her*. This savagely beautiful specimen thought women were pigs. Unbelievable. Incomprehensible. Priceless.

"That wasn't funny," he said tightly.

"Yes, it was." Forcing herself to sober, she studied him. "Exactly how long have you worked in this business?"

He pressed his lips together in a mutinous line. Apparently sharing personal information wasn't part of their hate/hate relationship.

"Well?" she pressed.

"Eight years," he finally responded. He glanced at his wristwatch. "And now this conversation is over. I have the information I need on the target. You may go."

"I may go?" She gasped. "I may go?"

"Yes. Is there an echo in the room?"

Had she mentioned that she hated this man?

"I'll meet you at the club in three and a half hours," he said. He pushed his big, hard body out of his seat and strode around Anne's desk. He plopped into Anne's chair.

Shocked at his daring, Jillian shook her head. "What do you think you're doing?"

He gazed down at the papers. "Not that it's any of your business, but Anne told me to make myself at home."

"I can guarantee she didn't mean at her desk."

He leaned back and stretched out his legs, anchoring his ankles on the surface. He met her gaze. "Were you here? Did you hear the conversation?"

"No," she gritted out.

"So you don't know what she meant, do you?"

Smug bastard. More than puzzles, more than this man, she hated being bested. She wanted Marcus out of this office so *she* could go through Anne's desk. She wanted to read his employee file, like he'd read hers. And what the hell had Anne put in her file to make Jillian seem of questionable morals?

"Well?" he prompted. "How long do you plan to sit there?"

Fine, she decided in the next instant. *Let him stay.* It might piss Anne off when she found out, and Anne might (please, please, please!) fire him. Besides that, arguing with him was still arousing her. More so now than before. Her skin was heating and hot blood was flowing through her veins at an alarming rate.

"Leave the door open on your way out," he added smugly.

Eyes slitted, panting a little, Jillian stood. Better to leave now, before he called her a bad name—a worse name, anyway—and she jumped his bones. *What's wrong with me?* she wondered for the—what?—thousandth time?

She strode toward the door, calling with mock breeziness over her shoulder, "I'm going home to purge myself of your nastiness. I'll see you at the club, Markie. Make sure to bring that hundred dollars you're going to owe me.

I expect payment the moment you lose." She slammed the door behind her, making the glass vibrate, and sauntered down the hall.

Three

Excuse me, I need your phone number to give my friend so he'll know where he can get a hold of me in the morning.

GEORGIA CARRINGTON'S PHONE RANG just as Jillian stormed out of the building without a word or glance. O-kay. *What had happened?* She'd never seen her friend so upset.

Brrring, brrring, the phone sang as she pushed to her feet to go after Jillian.

After a momentary hesitation, she fell back into her chair. She'd have to find out later. Only one person called her at this time of day and she didn't have the strength to ignore him. Besides, Jillian would probably appreciate time to cool down.

That's lame. You're a bad friend. Still, she picked up the phone and held it to her ear, already a little breathless. "Georgia Carrington."

"Hey, you."

Hearing that deep, tender voice, her stomach instantly

clenched. Yep, she'd been right. Brent. Jillian's older brother and the bane of Georgia's entire life. "You have to stop calling me at work, Brent," she said, knowing he wouldn't.

Part of her was glad of that. The other part of her hated that part of her.

"I can't help it," Brent said in a low, whispered tone, as if they were sharing a secret. "I needed to hear your voice. It's been twenty-four hours since we last talked, and that's just too long."

Her stomach clenched again and goose bumps broke out over her skin. Contact with Brent was dangerous, even over the phone. He was the only man in the world who could tempt her away from Wyatt and the only man in the world she would never, ever allow herself to get involved with.

He hadn't wanted her when she'd wanted him, had rejected her time and time again, and now it was too late. Besides, even if she were to date him now, he'd walk away from her the moment she started aging. A wrinkle—bye-bye Brent. Gain a few pounds—where'd Brent race off to so quickly?

In school, she'd been the ugly duckling and he'd avoided her. Now that she was easy on the eyes, he pursued her relentlessly. It was insulting. *So why don't you put a stop to it?*

"Want to go to the movies later?" he asked. "Don't say no. I'm willing to see a chick flick, and if that doesn't prove my dedication to you, nothing will."

She closed her eyes, pictured sitting next to him, sharing popcorn. Wyatt hated going to the movies. Expensive dinners, galas, those were his preferences. "No, sorry," she forced herself to say. "I've got plans with Wyatt."

There was a thick, heavy pause. She used it to tamp down her regret.

Then Brent growled low in his throat. "I fucking hate that asshole."

"How do you know he's an asshole? You've never met him."

"I don't have to know him to know he's not good enough for you."

She shivered. *End this. You're just playing with fire.* "Goodbye, Brent," she said, once again forcing herself to do something she didn't want. She placed the phone in its receiver, cutting the line. *He isn't for you. Don't lead him on.*

Hell, don't lead yourself *on.*

So why did she suddenly want to cry?

The door to Anne's office opened and that blond god of deliciousness peeked out. He stared down one end of the hall, then the other.

"Looking for Jillian?" she asked. He and Jillian must have come to blows because he seemed every bit as infuriated as Jillian had.

He didn't say anything, just scowled at her and closed the door again.

"That went well," she muttered. Time to get back to work. She'd think about the Greenes later.

INSIDE ANNE'S OFFICE, Marcus stomped to the desk and plopped into the swivel chair. He crossed his arms over his chest. He stared at the door, his nose twitching at the lingering scent of luscious female. A mysterious scent he couldn't quite place. Maybe a sunset. Maybe a midnight ocean breeze. Maybe sulfur and brimstone.

Okay. So. The meeting hadn't gone as planned. He blamed Jillian, of course. Infuriating woman.

He'd worked in this strip-you-of-your-innocence business for a long time, but he'd never encountered bait quite like her. She was...unpredictable. A sweet smile one moment, a tongue-lashing the next. Mmm, tongue-lashing. He frowned. *Don't go there.*

He'd meant to behave, to show Jillian his polite side. She'd walked in, however, looking eatable in a scrap of nothing, and that intention had been blown straight to hell. At that point, the only politeness she'd have gotten from him would have been if she'd asked him to take her up on her clothing's unintentional offer and eat her. He would have said thank you.

Hence the reason he'd done everything in his power to piss her off.

If she despised him, she'd continually push him away and he'd never have to worry about giving in to temptation. Or trying to seduce temptation. Firecracker that she was, she'd ignited at every barb he'd tossed her way. That shouldn't have been such a turn-on. *Insulting* her shouldn't have been such a turn-on. But they had been. Oh, they had been.

Sadist, he berated himself. He didn't usually allow women to affect him on any level except a sexual one. But Jillian had done that and more—and she'd done it while looking at him as if he were a pus-filled wound on a horse's ass one moment and a platter of chocolate-dipped strawberries the next.

Anger? Yes, he'd felt angry. She'd accused him of

fucking the boss to land a job. Admiration? Definitely. She'd faced him nose to nose, matching him in insults and in (pretend?) disregard. Excitement? Abso-freaking-lutely. More than he'd experienced in years.

Conclusion: buying CAM from Anne without personally meeting all her employees first had been a mistake. One it was too late to rectify. He'd gone through their files, of course, but hadn't considered their actual personalities. Or clashing with their personalities. Or lusting after their personalities. In his defense, he'd simply wanted to expand his business and had been blind to everything but the profit margin.

He wasn't blind anymore.

After calling and offering him the company, then changing her mind the next day, then changing her mind yet again when he visited her, Anne had suggested Jillian Greene as his second-in-command. No way in hell he'd consider that now. One, he was attracted to the infuriating demoness. He'd never been attracted to bait before and didn't like that he was now. To this woman. Two, Jillian was a danger to society with her innocent face, killer body and forked tongue. And now she was his.

His body instantly hardened in all the right places. *Whoa, boy. Not mine personally. My* employee.

Fighting the wildfire in his blood, he leafed through the employee folders resting on the edge of the desk. When he found Jillian's, he tugged it free and flipped it open. Her deceptively innocent features stared up at him. *You want to taste me, don't you?* her half smile seemed to say.

Yeah. He did.

She had a button nose, a small scattering of freckles

barely visible—he'd had to search intensely for them when he'd met her in person—and, sweet Jesus, the cutest dimples he'd ever seen. He hadn't had to search for those. They'd snagged his attention and hadn't let go. Added up, these features were the attributes of a Sunday School teacher.

She also had glossy dark curls made for a man's hands, lush pink lips and wide blue eyes fringed by inky lashes—the attributes of a well-sated sex puppet. An exquisite combination that made him wonder which she'd be in bed. Maybe both.

Don't go there, asshole.

He coughed, shifted in the chair, hot and definitely bothered. Reading on… Under strengths, Anne had marked: *loyal, honest, determined* and *trust issues.* How was *trust issues* a strength? Under weaknesses: *gives to charity, is a closet do-gooder* and *considers her friends' well-being before she considers her own.* Those were weaknesses? He shook his head. Anne was weird.

He himself had seen no redeeming qualities from Jillian. Okay, that was a lie. She'd apologized to him the first time she'd inadvertently insulted him, after she'd asked why Anne had hired him. Also, there was her mouth. That was certainly a redeeming quality. And her legs. And her breasts, with those so-hard-I-need-a-lick nipples.

All of his blood rushed south again. *Please,* he mused in the next instant. *Like it's ever migrated north since Jillian stepped inside the office.*

What was he going to do with that woman?

I can think of something, his cock replied.

"Shut up," he muttered darkly. "You don't get a voice in this situation." Hell, no. Erections turned men into, well, dicks. Made them do stupid things. He wasn't stupid. Most of the time.

Women were vipers by nature; Jillian clearly more than most, what with her *trust issues* and all. Getting involved with an employee—especially one who wouldn't hesitate to slice and dice her opponent to shreds—would be tantamount to cutting out all his vital organs and selling them on eBay.

Not that Jillian had wanted anything to do with him.

Not that Marcus wanted anything to do with her. Really.

He was a gambling man but she was high stakes. Too high. Still, he would have liked to play naked poker with her. To have all of Jillian's passion directed at a hand of cards while she was bare-assed naked… Ah, hell. Anymore of that and he might lose all common sense and go ahead and try to seduce her.

Did she have a boyfriend? Was Jillian the type who demanded a commitment? Surely not. Like him, she probably kept her relationships strictly about sex, sex and more sex. No strings. Ever. And never with employees, he reminded himself. Or coworkers. Or other bait.

He'd probably need the reminder a few (thousand) more times because he'd been in a slump lately and wasn't getting even a little sex. Not his fault. There'd been offers—oh, there'd been some offers. Fine. There'd been two. In his defense, *again,* he hadn't been nice to anyone who approached him.

Lately he just wasn't interested and (embarrassingly enough) couldn't get hard because all he could think about was the doomed nature of the whole mating dance. Meet, screw, say goodbye or try for something lasting, then wait for failure. Then he'd seen Jillian and the slump had ended. Literally.

What have I gotten myself into? he wondered again.

Despite his need to keep Jillian at an emotional distance, to keep her mad at him so there was no chance she'd want to be friends or lovers, he had to smooth things over with her or life at the office would be hell. *Tonight* would be hell. He didn't need more hell. He'd been looking forward to relaxing, to simply watching an assignment unfold and critiquing it in his mind. Now he'd have to step in and do cleanup when Jillian messed up. And she *would* mess up. Women that emotional were volatile and out to get everyone in their path.

That wasn't a stereotype. That was simply the truth.

As dread (and anticipation) uncurled inside him, he glanced at Jillian's home address. He'd have to go over there, smooth things over while still keeping her at a distance. He'd have to use his notorious "bluff" face to cover his dread (and anticipation).

Good thing he liked a challenge.

JILLIAN stormed through her front door. *Stupid. Idiot!* she seethed, not sure if she meant herself or that smart-ass Marcus Brody. She couldn't recall having been this mad in a long, long time. How could one person be so rude? So diabolical?

So damn sexy?

She tossed her keys and purse on the side table in the foyer and pounded to her bedroom. Usually her home was her place of comfort, her refuge from the maddening, always disappointing outside world. Lush tawny-colored (fake) plants abounded, spilling from every corner. She'd painted them herself. Her walls were caramel, the color of coffee—her biggest weakness. The floors were wood and polished to a high gloss. Nothing was out of place, every surface was clean.

Jillian was a woman who despised clutter and messiness.

Marcus Brody was total chaos.

"The man must die!" she told the bronze lamp hanging from her hallway ceiling. "But first, he must experience pain and suffering," she told her bedroom.

With a screech, she fell onto her sleigh bed. The velvety brown comforter—too close in color to Marcus's eyes for her peace of mind—puffed around her. She punched it once, twice, then let loose a storm of fury, determined to release her temper so that she wouldn't bite her target's head off before she even tested him. By the time she finished, she was panting and tired, but she felt better.

"I can, too, control my emotions," she muttered, despite her outburst. *Sometimes.*

Everything would have been fine if Marcus hadn't awakened such potent desires inside her with his lame-ass insults. She hadn't wanted a man in a long time, and to want him…now…. Grrrr!

She'd stopped dating, damn it, had stopped feeling anything but disgust when it came to males and relationships. Then Marcus had walked past her cubicle and her nerve endings had sparked to life—no one should smell that good *and* look like heaven in a pair of jeans—and that was one very good reason to despise him more than most.

Except, she hadn't hated him. Not right away. Then he'd opened his mouth and said rude things and looked at her with loathing—and it should have been enough to remind her of her own predisposition toward hatred, as well as to turn off any sane girl. Instead, his attitude had excited her. Intrigued her. No one had ever treated her like that before. Men flirted with her, damn it.

"Maybe I'm becoming my mother," she muttered. Hating something one moment, loving it the next. Happy one moment, depressed the next. "God save me." She sighed. Marcus Brody should be illegal in fifty states and three countries. "Pig."

As she expounded on the reasons he belonged in a pen, rolling in mud and fattening up so he could be carved into thick strips of bacon, her phone rang, startling her. She jolted upright and glanced at her caller ID. *Carrington, Georgia.* Brow furrowed, Jillian picked up the line and held it to her ear. "What's up?"

"Oh, good. You're home," Georgia said. She was whispering. "You have to tell me what happened between you and the blond."

"Where are you?"

"A bathroom stall. Not important. Concentrate and spill. He saw that you'd left, went back into the office, then stormed out a few minutes later."

She experienced a prickle of satisfaction that he'd left in a huff, too. He'd probably needed a little alone time to stroke his overinflated…ego. Jerk. "Did he leave the building or just Anne's office?"

"The building." Georgia expelled a frustrated breath. "I couldn't hear you guys through the door. What did he say? What did *Anne* say?"

Jillian explained Anne's odd behavior, the way she'd

commanded Jillian to work with Marcus and then abandoned her, her voice clipped with irritation. Of all the men Anne could have chosen to work at CAM, she'd had to pick that one. That... "Ass," she muttered.

"That's not possible."

"You didn't hear the way he insulted me." *And aroused me with those very insults.* Idiot. "He's an ass, I assure you."

"No, I mean Anne actually hired him? A man?"

"That's right." See? Jillian wasn't the only one to be astonished by such a happening. Her reaction had been justifiable. She only wished Marcus were here so she could hold the phone to his ear and shout, "Did you hear that? I did nothing wrong!"

"Dear God, why?" Georgia said.

"Your guess is as good as mine."

"She could have a brain tumor that's making her do weird things."

"An alien being could have taken over her body," Jillian suggested.

"She could have stopped her medication and is now listening to the voices in her head."

True, so true. "Whatever her reason, *we* will be the ones to suffer. Marcus actually thinks women are untrustworthy, that we'll do or say anything for an orgasm."

"Well..."

"Georgia!"

"I haven't had one in a while," she said, defensive, "and I'm feeling a little desperate."

Jillian pinched the bridge of her nose. "An hour ago, you told me everything was great with Wyatt."

"It is." An unspoken *kind of* hung in the air. "I just, well, I stopped sleeping with him when he asked me to marry him that first time and I miss his Jerry Seinfeld clockwise swirl with a twist."

What the hell was wrong with the world? Georgia was the optimist who wished on stars for love, and Jillian was the coldhearted bitch who didn't believe in happily-ever-afters. It wasn't like Georgia to *stop* sleeping with a man because he wanted to marry her. "Are you trying to drive him away?"

"No, of course not," Georgia said, but again there was doubt in her tone. "I just want to be sure he's the man for me."

"What are you so unsure about? You tested him and he passed."

"I don't know, okay. He tells me how beautiful I am. He tells me how much he loves looking at me. But what happens when I gain a few pounds or, God forbid, get wrinkles? Will he still love me or will he be like B— boys?" she rushed out. "*Be like other boys?* I mean, Jill, I don't let the man come around me when I get a pimple."

"So let him."

"I'm scared," she whispered with a desperate edge.

Jillian massaged the back of her neck. She had no real answer for her friend. "If you're not sure about Wyatt, date my brother. You know he's in love with you and he won't mind if you're a fat, pimply, wrinkled old hag."

"Not true," she said. With longing? "Even though he doesn't tell me I'm pretty, I know Brent is just as in love with my appearance as Wyatt is. He wasn't interested in me in junior high or high school, when I was the ugly girl everyone loved to tease. Only when I developed breasts did he even glance in my direction."

Georgia was right. Brent hadn't looked twice at her back then. He'd treated her like a pesky sister and had even left the house on the weekends he'd known Georgia was staying the night. Maybe he *didn't* deserve her—even if he was one of the best guys Jillian knew.

"So tell me the rest about our newest coworker," Georgia said.

Deciding to ignore that earlier longing and what it possibly meant—she would not get Brent's hopes up, only to have them dashed—Jillian explained their bet about whether or not her target would come on to her and Marcus's assurance that he wouldn't. "Honestly, I didn't know whether he was cheering for his fellow man or insulting my appearance."

"What a waste of chiseled features and movie-star muscles," Georgia said with a sigh. "Is this a cold shoulder situation or an all-out war?"

God, she loved her friend. Besides her brother and sister, there was no one else in the world who would automatically take her side and be willing to do anything necessary to help her. "War," she answered without hesitation. Marcus and his sexy rudeness had to go.

"Cool. We haven't gone to war together since we convinced that bitch Judie Holt to quit."

Jillian grinned. Ah, good times. From day one, Judie had caused nothing but dissent. She'd gossiped, lied, slept with her targets and gotten a friend of theirs fired. At that point, they'd snapped. They'd laxatized a cake and thrown her a birthday party. They'd moved her computer to a stall in the bathroom at least once a week. They'd taped "kick me" signs to her back as often as possible. Childish? Yes. Did they care? No. Even Anne had found the whole thing amusing.

"Hang on." Georgia's breath cackled over the line. "Someone just entered the bathroom." A long pause. "Uh-oh," she whispered, then gagged. "I think they'll be in here a while." She didn't wait for Jillian's response. "I'll call you later." *Click.*

Jillian stared at the phone for a moment before shaking her head. She pressed the cordless off and tossed it aside. What should she do now? She didn't want to think about Marcus anymore—not if she hoped to stay calm. She could worry and think and dream about his demise tomorrow.

Sighing the same way Georgia had, she labored to her feet. What to do, what to do? She had wasted half an hour and now had three more to go. Maybe she should write a few pick-up lines for her newest target. Nah, she decided in the next instant. She'd have him at "hello, let's get freaky." Maybe she should add a little more gloss to her lips and cut a few inches from her already short skirt. That'd waste a whole five minutes and then she'd only have one hundred and seventy-five more to go.

The doorbell rang.

Her mouth dipped into a frown. She didn't want to deal with a visitor. It could very well be her mother—who adored impromptu visits to check on her. Her grandmother—who liked to borrow her sluttiest clothing so she could peruse cemeteries looking for widowers. Her sister—who loved to expound on the bliss of married life. Her brother—who enjoyed showing her charts and statistics on the wonderful creation known as man (to "prove" what she saw on the job wasn't the norm) before asking about Georgia.

Jillian strode to the front door, her heels clicking against the wood floors. She glanced through the peephole, froze, cursed under her breath, peeked again, cursed again, then pulled the door open. There stood the devil himself. Marcus Brody.

Her heart immediately kicked into overdrive; her breath burned her lungs. Once again, just being near him caused her nipples to harden. "What are you doing here?" she demanded, the question flowing from her mouth as soon as it formed in her mind.

"Hello to you, too, Dimples."

They were playing nice, were they? "Oh, my. Where are my manners? Hello, Mark," she said, sugar-sweet this time. "Whatever are you doing here?"

"It's Marcus." A muscle ticked below his eye and he regarded her with a scowl before leaning against the door frame, a mockingly casual pose. "I came to apologize."

"Really? What for? Living? Breathing? Having a penis?"

"Do you respond this way to everyone who apologizes to you?"

A wave of guilt hit her. She *was* being rude, but she couldn't seem to help herself.

"Can I come in?" he asked.

"No. Now isn't a good time."

"Great. Thanks." He barreled past the door *and* her. His shoulder brushed hers and she bit back a gasp at the electric sensation. At the live-wire jolt that zinged through her entire body.

She stood in place for several seconds, eyes narrowing, mouth opening in astonishment. In arousal. In anger. That man... Oh, that man! Fuming, she turned. "I have Mace," she told his retreating back.

"I'm not surprised," he replied over his shoulder, striding into her living room and disappearing from view.

"You're not welcome here." She remained where she was, holding the door open, determined to make him leave. She *had* to stay away from him and that freaky body chemistry playing Russian roulette with her common sense.

"You want to get rid of me," he said, "you have to talk to me first."

"Or I can call the police and report a break-in."

He chuckled, the sound warm and rich and filled with challenge. "Tell Chief Higgins I said hi. I've been meaning to go see him, but haven't had time."

"You do *not* know the police chief," she said, her back stiffening. What was Marcus doing in there? She could hear shuffling.

"I always make friends with the local law enforcement. Plus, he plays poker." Heavy pause. "Is this picture of a naked baby on a bearskin rug you? I bet it is. Same blue eyes, same dimples. I'll have to check your ass for the heart-shaped birthmark to be sure, though." He sighed. "Oh, the things I do to assuage my curiosity."

She saw red. "Put that photo album back!"

"But it's so pretty." Another pause, the swish of a page. "Ah, look at you in this one. Ten years old, is my guess, and you're wearing rain boots, a leather duster and a cowboy hat. Not smiling, big surprise. I like the one beside it better. Still not smiling, but you have panty hose on your head, which I'm assuming is supposed to be braids. Liked to play dress up, did you?"

I will not respond. I will not respond.

He chuckled again, and this time the sound was filled with genuine amusement. "Well, now. These just get better and better as you get older."

"I'll count to three," she said. Her jaw was clenched so tightly, her teeth throbbed. "You better be walking toward this door by the time I reach the end or you'll regret it. One."

"Your prom date looks constipated. What'd you say to him before Daddy snapped the picture?"

Bastard! "Two."

"Three," he said helpfully. "Please tell me you still own this…can something comprised solely of bows and ruffles be called a dress?"

Argh! Fists clenching, Jillian abandoned her post and stormed into the living room. She'd never killed anyone, but there was a first time for everything.

Four

There are two-hundred-and-sixty-five bones in the human body. How'd you like one more?

MARCUS HAD SETTLED on Jillian's sofa and now glanced around her home with unabashed curiosity. Not what he'd expected. Everything was color-coordinated. From the tan couch that matched the beige walls to the bronze rug that matched the amber vases spilling with gold-sprayed plants. Also, everything was clean. Precise. *Too* precise.

Seemed Little Miss Sex Puppet Sunday School Teacher was a neat freak. The glass coffee table was speck-free. The floral portraits on the pristine walls were hung in perfect alignment. Not a hint of dirt or lint marred the glossy perfection of the wood floors.

Foolishly, the neatness aroused him. Didn't take much today, it seemed. Still. He wanted to mess everything up. While having sex on it. Dirty sex. With sweat and body oil and handcuffs. *Mind out of the gutter, Brody. You're dealing with a sexual piranha. She'll smell any hint of arousal and attack.* He didn't need to know the woman herself to know that for a fact—he just needed to know her type.

Female.

But damn it, he shouldn't have looked through her photo album. She'd been a cute kid, a little sad—which made his chest ache—with a head full of curls and huge blue eyes that had dominated her face, and now he wanted to know if the birthmark on her butt had faded or gotten darker.

She stomped into the living room, a cloud of that let's-go-to-bed fragrance accompanying her. He held his breath as long as he could. He didn't want to smell her, didn't want to be attracted to her anymore. He'd come here to smooth things over—not that he'd had any success, but that didn't mean he had to enjoy it. That didn't mean he had to be friends with her. Far from it.

Stopping in front of him, she grabbed the album from his lap—fingers brushing his thigh and making his penis stand at (higher) attention, which made him scowl. She tossed the book behind her. Oblivious to anything except her own anger—he hoped—she anchored her hands on her hips. "I told you that you aren't welcome here."

Happy as he was to be back in the me-man, you-woman game and out of his sexual slump, he folded his hands in his lap to cover his erection. It irked him that Jillian had been the one to bring back his desire, making him want to forget that all relationships, even those based solely on sex, were doomed.

"You also told me I needed to be gone by the time you counted to three. You lied then, too."

Her blue eyes glittered and snapped. Steam might very well have curled from her nostrils. What a little fireball she was, which was sexy as hell. Damn it! He liked passive, take-whatever-he-dished-out women. Didn't he? He definitely liked women who wanted to sleep with him. Right? Jillian was neither of those things, or so he told himself because he didn't think he would be able to control himself if he knew she wanted him.

But he liked her more and more each time she opened her smart mouth. He could see her doing a thousand different things with that mouth and none of them involved talking.

Gutter, he reminded himself. *Don't go there.* Not with her. But he liked her wit. If her insults hadn't been directed at him, he would have thought they were funny.

"Get. Out," she said.

"Just zip it and listen, Dimples. I told you I came to—" He ground his teeth together. God, this was difficult, saying it again when she'd probably reject it again. "Apologize." He didn't mean it this time, but he'd said it all the same.

"Apologize?" she said, incredulous, as if he hadn't just apologized a few minutes ago.

"That's right. Apologize. For your attitude," he couldn't resist adding under his breath.

"Hey." She frowned. "I heard that."

"Well, yeah." He frowned right back. "That's because I said it out loud."

She stepped on his foot, hard, her spiked heel digging into his big toe. "You aren't truly sorry. Admit it."

Grimacing, he looked up at her and spread his arms wide. "So?" He didn't comment on the toe. That'd give her a sense of power and right now he needed all the power he could get. "Does that matter?"

Her mouth opened and closed; a gurgling sound escaped her throat. At least she removed the heel. "Yes, it matters. You could have the decency to lie about meaning it."

"Now wait just a second." He frowned again. "You accused my apology of being a lie—something that obviously pissed you off since you tried to impale my favorite toe—and now you're mad that I didn't lie again." His brows arched in sardonic amusement. "Typical."

He could tell she wanted to yell at him, at the very least offer a stinging retort. But she took a deep breath, then another. Her expression smoothed, but her color remained high and pink. Pretty. "I do believe I've forgotten my manners again," she said sweetly. "Can I get you something to drink? Arsenic? Bleach?" She batted her lashes at him, all innocence.

He had to admit he often had that effect on women. Not the innocence, the death threat. But those usually weren't made until after he'd dated them. According to his mother, he was lucky someone hadn't murdered him in his sleep. According to his father, who'd divorced his mom years ago, women didn't really want to kill him, they wanted to reform him.

He didn't need reforming. He liked himself just fine.

He'd rather be considered cold and emotionally unavailable than a sappy romantic who would tolerate anything for love. Morons. That's what lovesick people were. They were also cheat-on-me targets. Something he would never be again. He'd done the whole marriage thing and it'd been nothing but a waste of his time.

"Beer will be fine," he said graciously.

Jillian ran her pretty pink tongue over her pretty white teeth and stepped away from him, but she didn't venture into the kitchen. She plopped into the chair across from him. "There's beer at the convenience store down the street. You can show yourself out."

Yep. If she'd said it to someone else, he would have laughed. "Despite what you might think, I didn't come here to argue with you. We work for the same agency now. We need to get along." Just not too well, he silently added. They needed to be able to tolerate each other while secretly cursing each other to everlasting hell and *not* ripping each other's clothes off. Not that she looked willing to rip his clothes off. She did look perfectly willing to rip out his heart and eat it in front of him, though.

His erection, which had begun to behave and act like a mature adult, jumped to attention once more. He scowled. How the hell was the thought of her feasting on his organs—well, any organ except his favorite—exciting?

Jillian lifted her dainty shoulders in a shrug. "You're right. I admit it. We need to get along. Feel free to leave now that we've established that."

"So," he said, because he was a bad, bad boy who had a gambling problem. Five dollars said she'd stab him in the thigh with this next jab, but he just couldn't resist. "Your rudeness in the office obviously wasn't an aberration of character."

Her eyes narrowed to tiny slits. She was probably planning his death in her mind. But she didn't stab him. He owed himself a five spot.

"I can totally tell you want to get along with me," she said darkly.

He rested an ankle on his knee and regarded her intently. "Fine. You want the truth? We bring out the worst in each other."

"I can't argue with that."

"Finally," he muttered. "Something you won't argue about."

Jillian's nostrils flared and he had to press his lips together to keep from smiling. He really hadn't meant to say that aloud. It was just that she provoked the beast inside him. Something about her fired him up and set his every nerve on alert.

"I shouldn't have said that," he admitted. He'd come to smooth things over with her, but so far he'd only managed to make things worse. "Listen, do you need any help setting up for tonight's job?" There. That was a safe enough topic.

"No." Her tone was clipped. "Everything's in order."

"Good."

"Yep. Good."

They looked at each other, looked away. He didn't know what else to say at that point and for a long while silence slithered between them, a poisonous snake ready to bite, so uncomfortable it was almost painful. The ticking of the wall clock became audible, a time bomb. Detonation imminent.

Should he leave? Try and stick it out?

Things still weren't amicable between them, so he should probably stay. At least he wasn't hard anymore.

"So," he said, just to break the silence.

"So," she said.

"Oklahoma has had warm weather lately."

"Yep."

"I haven't been here long. Is it always this warm?"

"No. It can change in an instant," she said, glancing anywhere but him. "Hot one minute, bone-chilling the next."

Like Jillian herself, he thought, but didn't say that out loud. This had, without a doubt, developed into the most blah, boring conversation he'd ever experienced. Or maybe he just wished it was boring, because talking about the weather should have been a fucking nightmare. And would have been, with any other woman. But here he was, on the edge of his seat, wanting to hear Jillian's husky voice again, even if she told him more about the goddamn weather.

If he'd been on top of his game lately, he never would have reacted to her this strongly. At least, that's what he told himself. But…why had she broken through his lack of interest when no one else had been able to?

He almost wished she'd yell at him. *That* he understood. Yelling equaled anger and anger equaled passion. Passion he liked. Passion he could control. Wait. He liked those things with anyone except her. No passion with Jillian. Too dangerous.

"Maybe tomorrow will bring rain," she said.

Argh. How had they gone from snipping at each other, which was exciting and wrong and practically foreplay, to this, a fucking weather forecast—which still wasn't boring the way he wanted it to be, but instead was exciting and wrong and practically foreplay. He pictured her naked in the rain and hello, Marcus Jr.

"So," he said.

"So," she reiterated.

Why the hell did he need to get along with her, anyway? At the moment, he couldn't recall. They worked together—so the hell what. She'd make life at the office uncomfortable—that didn't seem so bad now.

"You still want that beer?" she asked, casting a wistful glance toward the kitchen.

That eager to get away from him, was she? Either she found the direction of their conversation as disturbing as he did or she just found him boring. "Yes," he said and thought, *I'm not boring!* "Thank you."

With a relieved breath, she popped to her feet and beat a hasty retreat out of the living room. Sweet solitude— he wished. He was tempted to make his own escape out the front door, maybe a window, just so he would stop weirding himself out about what was going on here.

She had him so turned on he couldn't think straight. If she'd started talking about snowflakes, he might have been able to come. Leaving now would mean Jillian won, though, and he refused to let her win even this minor skirmish.

Marcus had a long time to think about the skirmish and its victor and what would happen during said skirmish if things got a little out of control—calling each other dirty names and breathing hard and liking it way more than he should—because Jillian was gone way longer than necessary. That seriously irritated him. Like *he* was the problem in their little tête-à-tête of weather and insults and horniness.

"Here you go," she said when she finally returned, holding out an uncapped amber-colored bottle.

He didn't take it at first, just stared at it suspiciously. "Will I need to be rushed to the E.R. if I drink this?"

Her eyes flashed that delicious blue fire at him. What a shame so much sexiness was wasted on someone completely off-limits to him. "No," she snapped. "Unfortunately."

Oh, good. Anger again. That was more like it. But he could feel his excitement mounting, his pretend boredom receding. He took the bottle without further comment, careful not to touch her. One touch and he might push for another. Then another, until they were naked. Until they were writhing together, panting, part of a wild dance that would damn them both to hell.

She reclaimed her seat across from him. Her jean skirt rode up her thighs, revealing several delectable inches of pure temptation. He gulped back a drink, but the cool liquid did little to douse the raging fire in his blood.

Stupid hormones. Stupid chemistry. Stupid penis. If he weren't so attached to it, he would punish it until it screamed for mercy. Mmm, screaming. He frowned and shook his head. *Dumbass.*

"So," he said.

"So," Jillian reiterated. She hooked several silky curls behind her ear.

He caught a glimpse of multiple diamond studs. They circled the shell of her ear. The effect was surprisingly erotic and he wondered what it would feel like to run his tongue over each of those earrings.

"What agency did you used to work for?" she asked. She studied her cuticles as if she didn't care about the answer.

"The Ultimate Test in Dallas."

"Why'd you leave?" She brushed a piece of lint from her leg. "Or were you fired for pissing off your coworkers?"

He shrugged. He wasn't ready to tell her the truth yet, that he owned TUT and had wanted to expand. That he was now her boss. Was it wrong of him to so anticipate her violent response when he did tell her? If she played her cards right, he might just introduce naked Tuesdays to the company. "I wanted a change of scenery," he finally said. "And no, I wasn't fired."

"You're from England, right?"

"Manchester."

"Cool." She twirled a denim string around her finger.

She didn't sound impressed by his origins the way most women were, just curious—and even that, not so much. Maybe he'd done what he'd set out to do in the first place: made her dislike him so much she'd never be tempted to sleep with him. Which was exactly what he'd wanted. Really.

"I've lived in the States half of my life, though," he said, just to expand the conversation.

"Cool," she repeated, clearly still not really caring.

I'm not fucking boring. He chugged another gulp of beer and glanced at his wristwatch. One hour and forty-seven minutes before they were due at the club. Surely he could spark her fury again—uh, continue to smooth things over—in that time.

"Well," she said. She, too, glanced at her watch, a silver chain that looped around her small wrist bone. "I guess I should start getting ready for tonight's assignment...."

A roundabout way of saying get the hell out. Funny, she'd been more forthright earlier. "I thought you were already prepared." He should want to leave. He did want to leave. She was trouble, their conversation had the potential of becoming even more boring—weather, for God's sake; he still couldn't get over that—and things were probably as smooth as they'd ever be between them. "That's why you turned down my offer of aid, remember?"

"I—well." She leaned forward, black curls falling over her face as she rested her elbow on her knee. He was given a spectacular glimpse of her cleavage. Round breasts, absolutely perfect. No bra. His favorite. "Look," she said. "We got off to a bad start. You apologized," she added dryly, "and I accepted. Sitting around chatting isn't doing either one of us any good. Let's cut our losses now, before we drive each other to suicide."

Okay. That pissed him off royally. Drive her to suicide, indeed. He was allowed to feel boredom; she wasn't. Not that he'd felt any, damn it.

"Since you so sweetly patched things up between us," Jillian continued, "we'll now be cordial to each other at the office. That doesn't mean we need to socialize after hours."

"I didn't ask you to socialize after hours, now, did I?" There was more heat and anger in his tone than he'd intended.

"Good." She popped her jaw, silent for a moment. "Because I'd rather crochet oven mitts with my depressed mother than spend another second in your company."

The excitement that ignited every time they fought returned full force. "I'm going to make you eat your words," he said, praying he was bluffing because he truly couldn't afford to sleep with her, which was a damn shame, but still. "And you're going to find every one of them delicious. You'll even beg me for a second helping."

She shivered. A shiver of dread? Or anticipation? "The only thing I'll be begging for," she said, "is your absence."

"I wouldn't say anything else if I were you. The more you say, the more you'll regret later."

She yawned. "Your accent is annoying."

"Liar." He hoped. "Do you like to gamble?"

"No," she said, brow furrowed with confusion over the sudden change in topics.

Too bad. Would have made her irresistible, so maybe he should be happy about that. Already he wanted her, which wasn't necessarily a newsflash. Stripping her, throwing her on the ground and penetrating her would be a bonus.

"Don't look at me like that," she growled.

"Like what?"

"Like I'm dinner."

"Want to be?" he couldn't help but ask. *You can't have her, idiot!*

"No," she gasped.

Good. He was glad about that. Really. "I guess you do know something about poker. You're a good bluffer."

"I never bluff."

"Please. You're all about the bluff, Dimples. And FYI, you're going to lose our bet tonight." He said it just to bring them back on track, even though he wanted to continue down the slippery slope of temptation. "I have every faith that Darren Sawyer will see you for the walking heartbreak you are and send you on your way." Marcus stretched to his feet and strode to the door. Better to leave now before he did something more stupid than getting a hard-on while discussing sunshine and cool breezes.

Was there anything more stupid than that, though?

God, he was tempted to turn around, leap across the room and kiss those lush, pink lips of hers, drinking in her breath until she could only gasp his name. Hell, maybe he *should* do it, just to get it out of his system. He was primed and ready. Kissing wasn't sex, and as long as they didn't have sex, they'd be fine.

Yeah. Right.

If he started kissing her, he wouldn't stop until he'd kissed every inch of her. No kissing. He quickened his steps to the nearest exit.

"I have every faith someone's going to murder you while you sleep," she called after him.

He grinned. Yep, it was a damn shame she was off-limits.

Five

*If it's true that we are what we eat,
then I could be you by morning.*

MUSIC BLASTED from large speakers that hung overhead. Smoke billowed in every direction, cutting through the darkness. Waiters and waitresses pranced back and forth, serving drinks and smiles. A strobe light swirled from the center of the two-story structure, illuminating the throng of writhing, dancing patrons in a multitude of colors. There was more skin displayed here than was usually found between the pages of *Playboy*. More breasts and thighs than the good Colonel served on any given day.

Ah, yes. It was Friday night and The Meat Market was open for business.

Jillian worked her way through the gyrating, sweating crowd. Her camera and mic were in place, pinned at the cleavage of her tank in the form of a bejeweled flower. Everything was being transmitted to and monitored on Anne's computer. Tomorrow, she'd review the feed with

Anne, who would then meet with Darren Sawyer's girl-friend. Poor thing.

Jillian wouldn't be there for the meeting—to avoid outbursts of jealousy, bait was never allowed in the room when the victim was told. But if she chose, she could watch from the screen as Georgia had this morning. Sometimes she did that, too, sometimes she didn't. She didn't think she would this time. This girlfriend was a crier; she knew it, felt it and didn't think she could stand to see another woman cry.

As Jillian sauntered toward the bar, her purse bounced at her side. In it, she carried Mace, lip gloss, a little cash and a slightly tampered-with ID. She never wanted a target to locate her home address, therefore all of her identification listed CAM's. From the corner of her eye, she spotted a table of twentysomething women. All but one laughed and chatted. The one who didn't looked… sad as she stared into a margarita glass.

Had she been cheated on? Was this the girls' night out that was supposed to cheer her up? How many of those had Jillian witnessed over the years?

"Hey, gorgeous," someone said, drawing her attention. "I'm fighting the urge to make you the happiest woman on earth tonight."

She ignored him. Lord save her from cheesy come-ons.

She found herself scanning the masses for Marcus rather than her target. Was he here yet? Had he changed out of his sinful jeans? After all, those jeans had proudly showcased his very large erection the entire time he'd been inside her house. Wrong, that's what it was. He should wear a tent to keep that thing hidden. No woman should be subjected to that and no man should be that well-endowed *and* gorgeous. And what the hell had excited him? A discussion about the freaking weather?

No doubt about it. Marcus was strange.

Never mind that she'd felt white-hot embers of desire the whole time he'd been there. Never mind that fighting with him had aroused her. Again. *I hate that man.*

Wherever he was, whatever he was wearing, he was damn well going to watch her win their bet. She would rub it in his face for the rest of his life. Not that she planned to know him that long. She wanted him fired ASAP. He was too dangerous to her peace of mind. Too dangerous, period.

When she reached the bar, a man in his mid-to-late fifties offered her an eager grin. Or was that a scowl? Hard to tell with Botox. He held out a chair for her as he looked her up and down, lingering on her breasts, between her legs. He had thick silver hair, a plastic face and a suit-clad body that shouted wealth. He even smelled expensive. And he was wearing a wedding ring.

"My name's Ted but you can call me anything you want, as long as you call me," he said. "I hope you don't mind my saying so, but your body is exquisite."

"Thanks, grandpa," she muttered, taking the seat. She was in a bad mood. Which could totally be blamed on Marcus. All men were on her shit list just then. *Aren't they always?*

"Grandpa?" His frozen expression didn't change, though his eyes glinted with affront. Jillian often had that effect on people. Without another word, he slinked away. If he hadn't been wearing a ring, she would have felt guilty for insulting him. *Am I becoming cruel and heartless like Marcus said?*

"Ginger ale," she told the bartender, a stacked little bleached blonde with bright orange streaks in her hair. Jillian would have liked a beer, but drinking on the job only caused mistakes, so she never indulged.

Her drink arrived a moment later and she sipped from the straw. The coolness wet her too-dry mouth, the sweetness teased her tongue. God, would this night—

"Screwdriver," a sexy voice said, suddenly beside her. The speaker didn't touch her, but she felt his luscious heat, smelled pure sin. Wanted. Yes, she wanted.

Marcus.

She shivered and sipped again at her soda, the sugary carbonation now like acid in her throat. She forced her attention to remain straight ahead—even though she felt Marcus's eyes on her, burning bright, burning…burning… Time to concentrate and find her target.

"Make it two," he added, his accent suddenly thick and richly erotic, as if he'd just gotten off a plane from England. "One for me and one for the special lady next to me."

Obviously they didn't share the same beliefs about drinking on the job.

"Aren't you just the prettiest thing," he said then. Gone was all hint of his earlier disdain and in its place was smooth charm. Seduction. Persuasion. His warm breath caressed the back of her neck and she once again found her nipples hardening in his presence, her blood sizzling. Her heart even skipped a beat as provocative tingles moved over her skin.

Jillian pressed her lips together. What did he think he

was doing, talking to her like this? After the way he'd treated her today, she had expected him to arrive with a pitchfork and a one-way ticket to hell with her name on it. This had to be some sort of game to throw her off guard, to make her lose their bet.

Yes, that's exactly what he meant to do, she realized, hand clenching on her drink. Well, she would show him.

Drawing in a deep breath, she turned toward him and, starting at his feet, gradually moved her gaze up his body. He hadn't bothered changing, was still wearing those butt-hugging, erection-showing jeans and that muscle-kissing T-shirt. The only difference in his appearance was the very masculine, black stone necklace he now wore, which she suspected was actually a camera.

His eyes were dark and luminous, at half-mast, radiating a single word: orgasm. His hair was disheveled and fell over his forehead. His lips were lush and slightly parted. *Kiss me,* they said. She loved—hated!—the way the strobe light surrounded him in a bright multicolored halo. An angel. A fallen angel.

"Is that the best pick-up line you've got?" she asked, her voice more breathless than she'd planned. "Because it sucks."

"Oh, sorry. I wasn't talking to you." He grabbed his drinks, swirling the ice, and moved around her, only to skirt up to the woman on her left.

Jillian's jaw dropped open and she gasped. Why, that rat bastard! He'd done that on purpose. Payback for telling him she'd rather kill herself than talk to him? When she took over CAM, he was *soooo* fired.

The woman's cheeks bloomed with a pretty blush as

he leaned over and whispered in her ear. Her ash-blond hair was teased and sprayed, her makeup just a little too thick. Her look-at-me dress could have earned her the title of Whore of Babylon if Jillian hadn't already held that title herself.

"What's your name, love?" Marcus asked her, his back to Jillian. His accent was even heavier than before. And he'd called the woman "love." She suspected his soft, lush lips were curled in a devastating smile. And he'd called the woman "love." She had no doubt his brown eyes were glowing with a knowing, wicked intent. And he'd called the freaking woman "love."

Why do you even care?

I don't, she assured herself. She certainly didn't want him for herself. No way. No thanks. He probably hadn't had all his shots.

The woman giggled like a schoolgirl. But Jillian was willing to bet the only class that female had attended lately was Slut 101. And no, she wasn't jealous. She was merely stating a fact. *Don't be cruel. You're pro-female, remember?*

"I'm Rhonda, but my friends call me Ronnie. With an *i e.*"

"Well, Ronnie with an *i e,* I'm Mark and I've bought you a drink. I saw you and just had to approach."

Another giggle. "I'm so glad. I've been eyeing you since the moment you walked inside and I would have cried if you'd ignored me."

Jillian practically threw up in her mouth. He was letting Ronnie with an *i e* call him Mark and *she would have freaking cried if he had ignored her.* Please. Again her hands clenched around her ginger ale.

"Are you married, Ronnie with an *i e?*" he asked.

Jillian watched unabashedly as Ronnie lost her grin and dropped her left hand behind her back—as if her two-caret rock hadn't been visible during the beginning of the conversation. "Oh, uh. No. Just divorced."

"Have the intelligence to take it off before you go out, at least," Jillian muttered.

Marcus tossed Jillian a pointed glance. And wouldn't you know it was a quick *I told you so?* His features gleamed with victory.

Jillian flipped him off. His lips twitched into a smile. Enjoying himself, was he?

Ronnie with an *i e* hurried to change the subject, tracing her right hand along his shirt to regain his attention. "Where're you from, Mark? I can't place your accent. Wait, let me guess. Somewhere with sun, right? Australia?" She paused. "I'm right, aren't I? You're so tan."

"You should ask him about the weather there," Jillian said and turned away. "He really likes that." The man wasn't just a pig, he was bacon, already sliced and ready to be served. So he'd made his point. So what. Some females were as nefarious as males. Big deal. That didn't change the fact that on the scales of immorality, men won. Every time.

She downed the rest of her soda, wishing it were a (double) shot of tequila. The giggling continued. The nauseating *love* endearment was used several more times and Marcus was blatantly propositioned each time, which he expertly sidestepped with compliments about her hair, eyes and "amazing" curves.

It was pure torture, listening to the sickening exchange.

"Hey, Ronnie with an *i e*," she found herself saying as she slammed her glass onto the counter. She turned back to the happy couple, expression purposefully concerned as she peeked over Markie's shoulder.

Marcus scowled at her, but there was only devilry in his eyes as he leaned forward to—smell her hair? She frowned. Ronnie frowned, too, not liking that she'd been interrupted.

"I wouldn't get too attached to this one," Jillian said, patting Marcus's shoulder. "I hear he's a premature ejaculator."

Marcus choked on his drink. Ronnie's mouth fell open. When Marcus was able to breathe, he stiffened and glared at Jillian, all hint of devilry gone.

She flashed him an innocent eyelash flutter. A second later, she caught a glimpse of a muscle-bound hulk entering the club. Familiar receding hairline. Familiar strong jaw. Darren Sawyer. Her target. Thank God.

When she first started working for CAM, nervousness had hit her every time she initially spotted her target. Not anymore. The nerves had soon turned to righteous indignation. Tonight, however, she felt pure, undiluted anticipation.

Let the games begin.

"Oh, dear," she said. "Will you two excuse me? I've just spotted a little slice of heaven right here on this earth and I've *got* to meet him or *I'll cry*." She strolled away, swaying her hips, knowing Marcus had to watch her in action as Anne wanted.

Her steps lighter than they'd been all day, her pointed heels clicking on painted concrete, she closed the distance between her and Darren. He was here with two of his friends and they were all grinning like idiots as they surveyed tonight's selection of booty. They found an empty table in the back, eased into their chairs and ordered drinks. Darren didn't order the beer he supposedly couldn't live without, she noticed when the waitress brought him three shots of tequila.

Jillian couldn't help it; she allowed herself a single backward glance through the thickening crowd to the bar, where Marcus stood peering at her through narrowed eyes. Ronnie (with an *i e*) was tugging on his arm, but he didn't look at her.

Now Jillian had his full attention and the thought made her shiver. Hell, the heat in his dark, dark eyes made her shiver. "Watch and learn," she mouthed.

"Good luck," he mouthed back with a smug expression.

I don't need it. She turned back to Darren and, having reached her target, "accidentally" bumped into him, skidding his chair backward. His arms wrapped around her to keep her from tumbling the rest of the way into their table. She was careful to hide her revulsion. "Watch where you're—" he began.

"I'm so sorry," she said, layering her voice with equal measures of embarrassment and naughtiness. "How clumsy of me."

He lost his anger when his gaze locked on her cleavage, so proudly displayed by her V-neck. When Marcus had looked at her like that, she'd wanted to jump him. Darren, she just wanted to knee in the balls.

"No problem," he said leeringly.

"That last pink nipple must have really gotten to me. Oh, my." She squeezed his biceps and willed herself to blush—

a skill that had taken her more than a year to master. "Thank you for catching me. You probably saved my life."

He puffed up like a peacock. "Well, then, I guess that means you owe me."

"Guess so." She smiled, secretly gagging.

His companions laughed and one of them said, "Why don't you join us, honey?"

"I'm not sure if I should." She batted her heavily mascaraed eyelashes, going for an I'm-so-innocent-but-I'm-such-a-naughty-tramp aura. "You're strangers."

"Then allow me to make introductions so you *will* know us," Darren said, his gaze *still* on her breasts. "I'm Darren and these two clowns are leaving."

The two men groaned, but they didn't protest as they pushed to their feet and slinked to the bar. They were obviously used to helping each other with the ladies. Like Georgia, Jillian sometimes wanted to tell men like these who and what she was so badly she could taste it. Oh, the satisfaction she'd feel…

But she couldn't say a word, not even if the target passed the CAM test. Admitting such a thing truly would lead to trouble. Men freaked when they knew their sins had been filmed. Years ago, Jillian had heard about a woman, bait, who had been killed by a target, murdered so that she couldn't tell his wife what he'd done.

"I'm Jane," she said. She offered Darren a hand and he twined his fingers around her palm, holding her longer than necessary. Forcing another smile, she settled atop one of the now-vacant seats. "You want to buy me a drink?" It was a standard agency question, used to test the waters.

He hesitated for several seconds and for an agonizing

moment Jillian thought she might actually lose her bet with Marcus. He studied her, gauging…what? Her easiness? Finally, he motioned the waitress over. "So what can I get you, sweet little Jane?"

She was both relieved and depressed. "I'll have a ginger ale. I really shouldn't have any more alcohol. Already I feel so loopy."

"One more won't hurt," he cajoled.

"Well, maybe just one. I'll have another pink nipple." She giggled. God, she hated giggling.

He ate it up, like she'd spoon-fed him sugar.

The waitress hurried off to get the drink and as she moved away, Marcus and Ronnie claimed the table next to Darren's. Of course, that table was already occupied by a group of loud, cackling women…who didn't mind Marcus's company at all. They practically drooled on him as introductions were made. Ronnie wanted to claw their eyes out, Jillian could tell.

"So what's a sweet little thing like you doing in a place like this?" Darren asked Jillian, oblivious to the newcomers.

She barely refrained from sighing. How many times would she have to hear that line? "Well," she said, leaning forward and letting her arms rest on the table surface. "I just finished work—I'm a dancer—but I wasn't ready to go home." Usually she said "librarian." Most men liked the innocent-turned-wildcat fantasy, but Jillian knew from Darren's file that he wasn't into innocence. "I thought it might be fun to, I don't know, be a little wild."

"Nothing wrong with that," he said, grinning happily.

His knee purposefully brushed hers. "A dancer. Wow. So you like…strip and stuff?"

"Strip and all kinds of stuff." She didn't jerk away, but she wanted to. Crap like that always pissed her off. She didn't want to be touched by cheating scum. Expression rapt, she scooted back in her chair. A few more minutes and she'd have the evidence his girlfriend wanted, then she could get out of here. Away from Darren, away from the crowd. Away from Marcus and his dangerous appeal.

She was opening her mouth to ask Darren if he was married when she heard Marcus say, "Ronnie, you saucy wench. I've never met a more beautiful woman."

Giggle, giggle.

Jillian's hands squeezed at her sides. "Darren," she said, making sure her voice was loud enough to carry and oh, so eager, "you did save my life, and you mentioned I owed you a favor. What kind of favor are we talking?"

He leaned toward her, brows wiggling. "What kind are you willing to give?"

"Ronnie, you're driving me crazy. You smell so good."

"Darren, what would you say if I told you I was willing to do *anything?*"

He gulped. "Anything?"

"Anything."

"Let's see…" He tapped a finger against his chin. His green eyes gleamed with triumph, as if he already had her in bed. He reached out and clasped her hand. "I have something in mind, but I don't want to seem forward."

"Ronnie, you're everything I've ever dreamed of in a woman."

"Darren, you delicious thing, you can't be too forward

with me. Tell me what you want and I'll— Oh, wait. You're not taken, are you? Please tell me you're not married."

"Hell, no, I'm not," he said. "No girlfriend, either. You?"

"No girlfriend." She leaned into him and grinned slowly, even though she really wanted to scratch his eyes out. He'd be the first to go up on her Internet Wall of Shame. Rating: pig shit. "Why don't you come home with me? I'll put on a little music, model my lingerie collection for you and thank you properly. And just so there isn't any misunderstanding, I'm talking about sex." *Say no. For your girlfriend's sake, say no.*

She'd only seen his girlfriend once and that at a distance, but she easily recalled the nervous tension the girl had radiated. The hope that she was wrong. Jillian realized in that moment that she would happily lose her bet with Marcus if only she could go to CAM tomorrow and hear Anne tell the girlfriend that her man had passed the test.

"I'd love to," Darren said, nearly stuttering in his haste. He whipped to a stand. "Just let me tell my friends goodbye."

Disappointment slammed into her, hard. "Don't bother," she said, losing her grin. There. She had the proof his girlfriend wanted. She'd won her bet with Marcus. But she'd never felt so lousy.

Good things had come of the night, she told herself. Darren's significant other would now know what a loser she was saddled with and would hopefully leave him. Jillian had earned a hundred bucks proving Marcus wrong. Still, somehow neither of those prospects lifted her spirits.

She wanted to grab Marcus by the hair and shout, "I

told you so!" *Then kiss him,* her hormones added, *and lose yourself for a little while.*

No, she told them firmly, *and collect my money.* Dumb hormones. Marcus was an enigma, that was all. Men like Darren, she understood. They saw something they wanted and they took it, no matter the damage it would cause. Marcus had done nothing but the unexpected. Surely that was the only reason he was affecting her so badly. Once she figured him out, he'd be exactly like every other male she'd known and the wanting would stop.

She hoped.

Frowning, she twisted toward him. Their eyes met, locked. Jolts of electricity trekked along her spine. "I believe I mentioned that I don't take checks," she said, hopping to her feet.

"Hey, where are you going?" Darren asked, confused. "Do you want me to follow you or something?"

"I've changed my mind." Pig. "I'm going home. Alone."

"Hey!" Darren said. "You can't change your mind."

Jillian anchored her hands on her hips. "Well, I just did."

He latched onto her arm, a little too firmly for her peace of mind. She dug in her purse with her free hand and whipped out the Mace. She held it in his face. From the corner of her eye, she saw Marcus tense, as if gearing for a fight.

Darren's jaw dropped and he released her so quickly she almost fell.

Jillian suppressed a smirk. And a shudder. She hadn't had to threaten anyone with the spray in months. Wouldn't you know fate would choose tonight to make her job more difficult than usual?

"You're pressing your luck," Marcus snarled to Darren, who paled and backed up a step. To Jillian, he said more calmly, "Are you okay?"

"Of course I am," she said, trying to sound strong and assured but not quite managing it.

He studied her a moment. Trying to read her? "Double or nothing says you won't get on that dance floor with me," he said.

She was tempted to dance with him. Oh, was she tempted. To let him wrap his arms around her. To let him hold her close. And it had nothing to do with money and everything to do with seeking comfort. A man had just threatened her. Not with words, but with force, all because his toy had been taken away. Jillian liked to think she was tough, but perhaps it would have been nice to let someone else take care of her, just once. Which was silly. Relying on a man for anything was bad, bad, bad.

"You win that bet. I don't dance with pigs," she said, then she strode away without another word. For once insulting Marcus felt wrong—he'd genuinely wanted to know if she was okay—yet it was the only way she could think to keep him at a distance. More than anything, she needed to escape the club, escape the dangerous things Marcus made her feel, escape everything, but his next words stopped her.

"You know what? There are only three kinds of women in the world, Dimples," he called over the music. He'd never sounded more mocking.

She didn't want to, but she found herself pivoting and facing him, somehow needing to hear what he had to say more than she needed to leave. He was standing beside the table. Both Darren and Ronnie were looking from him to Jillian and Jillian to him, their faces puckered in angry confusion.

"And?" Jillian prompted, tapping her foot. God, he was sexy. He looked dangerous just then, capable of anything. If he'd been any other man—besides Darren, that is—she might have thrown herself at him. Anything to taste all that dark exhilaration, to forget her own fears and the heartbreak Darren's girlfriend would experience tomorrow.

Watching Marcus, need and desire continued to spiral through her, sinking…sinking her resolve, and that angered her. She shouldn't want him. Shouldn't have wanted him earlier today, shouldn't want him now. *Leave. Leave, damn it.*

"I'm waiting," she told him, and thought, *Say something that will make me truly hate you so I can stop wanting you.*

"Some are cock teasers." Marcus held up one finger. "Some are cock junkies." Another finger. "And some are cock haters. You're a hater, Dimples. You'd rather bite a man's head off than trust one even a little. No wonder Anne wrote such glowing things in your file. And by the way," he added on a growl, turning to Darren. "You really let the team down tonight. Thanks a whole fucking lot."

Damn this. And damn Marcus. Somehow his words only made her want him more, made her want to prove him wrong. *If I'm such a cock hater,* she thought, spinning on her heel and striding away for real, *why do I want yours buried deep inside me?*

Shaking her head, she quickened her step and let the door of the club slam behind her.

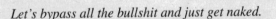

Six

Let's bypass all the bullshit and just get naked.

ANNE COMMINGS-BAKER-MOSSEY (damn those three marriages!) sat propped on her decadent bed of silks and satins, gazing at her laptop and trying not to laugh. She didn't want to wake the sex toy snoring beside her. Okay, he wasn't a sex toy. But he was too young for her, too sexy. Still, he made her shiver every time he looked at her, so she'd decided to have a go at him, however long he'd let her.

Marcus had just called Jillian a cock hater and Jillian had just given him a look that said "you're disgusting, kiss me," and they had both looked as if they'd enjoyed the sparring a little too much and hated themselves for it.

Now they were separated.

Anne watched the whole thing transpire on two different sides of the computer screen, one view from Jillian's camera, one from Marcus's.

On the right side of the screen, Jillian was getting into her car. On the left, Marcus moved through the bar—to follow Jillian? Anne might never know because he stopped himself before he'd made it halfway. *Why stop? You obviously want her. And I want to see one of you throw a punch.*

"What's going on?" the cupcake hanging on to Marcus's arm demanded.

"Yeah," Jillian's target, Darren Sawyer, said. "What the hell is going on? She wanted to go home with me, then nearly peppers me? That's some crazy shit. And I didn't let the team down! I'm not even on a team." He took one look at what Anne guessed was Marcus's murderous expression, lost his nerve and raced away to find his friends.

"Go home to your husband," Marcus told Cupcake. "It's not nice to cheat."

"What? I don't know what you're talking about." She laughed nervously. "I'm not married."

"Yes, you are, and you should be ashamed of yourself."

Cupcake gasped in shock, outrage, indignation and disappointment. Outrage won. She glared up at him. "There's nothing wrong with having a little fun."

"And that," Marcus said dryly, "is why I gave up relationships years ago. Thanks for the reminder."

"Hey." Scowling, she jabbed a finger into his shoulder. Her wedding ring glinted in the multihued light, pink one second, yellow the next. "You're a dickhead, you know that? *You* flirted with *me*. *You* came on to *me!*"

"For your husband's sake, you should have sent me on my way, now shouldn't you?" He walked away from her then, pushing past dancers and talkers, and strode outside just in time for Anne to see the sedan Jillian drove—one of the few company cars every bait used when on assignment so no one would know their real plate numbers—whip from the parking lot, gravel spewing from the rear tires.

Marcus cursed under his breath, froze for several seconds, then ripped the camera from around his neck. He turned the lens to himself and Anne caught a glimpse of narrowed eyes, thinned lips and fury. Total fury. A luscious sight, to be sure. "I hope you enjoyed that," he growled, then his side of the screen went blank.

Oh, I did. Anne laughed wickedly.

Jillian, meanwhile, was slamming her fist into the steering wheel. "I am a stupid, stupid woman and I should be shot to save the world from myself. That was not a turn-on! He is rude and insufferable and just because he fills out his jeans every time he looks at you does not mean you should get excited when he calls you bad names. You are not a masochist. You didn't used to be, anyway," she muttered darkly.

She hit the steering wheel again. "Oh, this sucks!" she said, sounding mortified. She ripped off her camera and threw it on the floorboard. Her side of the screen went blank.

Anne laughed again. She didn't normally watch the feed live. Since this was the last assignment she'd ever get to observe, however, she'd decided to make an exception. Thank God she had! Jillian's life needed a little shaking up. The girl was becoming too jaded, too closed off.

Too much like Anne herself. And Anne didn't want that for Jillian. Yes, she'd once found kindness and caring to be weaknesses, and had done her best to leech them from Jillian. Now…

Anne sighed. She'd had good reason, she'd thought. She'd endured three no-good, cheating husbands. After kicking out number three, bitterness took root and she'd decided to start CAM. Women had a right to know what they were getting—or had gotten—themselves into. At the time, the business had also been good therapy, allowing her to take out her frustrations on the targets.

Over the years, though, as she watched more and more men cheat on their women, she'd grown to hate them. That hate had soon consumed her life. All day, every day, she'd thought of nothing except ways to castrate and maim the male species.

Then, a few weeks ago, she'd gotten a phone call. Husband number two had died of a heart attack. He'd been a year younger than Anne.

Even though she'd often fantasized about his death, it had rocked her. She wasn't promised a tomorrow, she'd realized, and she'd wasted most of her life already. Wasted it on hate and loneliness and despair. That realization had been a defining moment for her. No more would she cut herself off from the opposite sex. No more would she allow cynicism to color her every move. She'd live in the moment; she'd enjoy everything thrown her way.

She'd do it now, before it was too late.

Her companion rolled toward her and exhaled softly. A moment passed in silence, then he was reaching out and caressing her bare arm. "Ready for another round?" he asked huskily.

She was fifty-one and in her prime—a prime she'd denied herself for the past fifteen years. During her marriages, she'd been a woman who liked her sex often and hard. After the third one, she'd pushed sex from her life completely. Her body was delighted to finally be back in the game.

That's why she'd left work early today. "Personal business"—a.k.a. Operation Orgasm—was now a priority. She was through denying herself.

Picking this guy up at the supermarket—all right, liquor store—had been an aberration for her. One, he worked the cash register at the aforementioned liquor store. He wasn't the corporate type she'd been attracted to in the past. Two, she was twenty-five years older than he was.

Three, she was twenty-five freaking years older than he was.

He had to think she was an alcoholic, as many times as she'd come into the store lately. But he was always sweet to her, always flirted. Before, she'd treated him like dirt to mask her attraction. This time, she hadn't. This time, she'd invited him over for shots of the vodka she'd just bought from him.

What Anne wanted, Anne now went after.

To her surprise, he'd happily accepted.

"Well?" he prompted, already hard.

She set her laptop aside and sank into his waiting embrace. The chemistry between Marcus and Jillian was enough to light a fire inside any woman with a clitoris. Anne definitely had one. And her lover knew just where to find it.…

THE PHONE RANG, and Jillian was startled out of tossing and turning and imagining Marcus hovering over her, his mouth taped shut so he couldn't say anything while he pleasured her, and then imagining his death because he had no business pleasuring her, in dreamland or otherwise, and disrupting a peaceful night of rest—the phone rang again—a peaceful night of rest she was never going to get, it seemed. Dreams or no dreams.

Another ring.

She grabbed for the phone, missed, but managed to knock it down. Cursing under her breath, she rooted around on the floor. Her eyes burned, she was aroused, it was dark inside her bedroom and she was cranky, so it took her a while to find the little bastard. When she finally held it to her ear, she rolled to her back and snarled, "What?"

"Just making sure you arrived home safely."

Marcus. She sucked in a heated breath. Hearing his voice after all that imagining was like having her legs spread, Marcus crawling on top of her. Moving, moving so wickedly, hammering hard, so hard, and pushing her all the way to orgasm. Shivering, she glanced at the alarm clock on her dresser. 1:03 a.m. Why was he calling?

"Jillian?" he said.

"What?" she repeated, breathless this time. Her nipples pearled and her stomach quivered. The (seemingly never-ending) ache between her legs intensified.

"You did make it home okay, didn't you?"

"You're talking to me, aren't you?"

"Sounds more like snapping to me," he pointed out. *He* sounded happy about that. Too happy. Excited, even.

Her eyes narrowed suspiciously. "Are you turned on?"

"Maybe," he said after a long pause. "You?"

"How dare you ask me something like that, you don't even know me."

"You asked, I answered. I asked, so you had better answer. Are you turned on?"

"Hell. No."

He chuckled. "Liar."

Yes, she was. "You called me a cock hater and you're right. You're a cock and I hate you."

"You want to know something?"

"No," she said, breathless again. What was he going to tell her? Something sexy, judging by his tone. "No, I don't."

"I'll tell you anyway. Arguing with you turns me on. It's stupid, but there it is."

Dear Lord. Their arguing affected him the same awful way it affected her. They were doomed. Doomed! Unless… No, no, no! But there was no help for it. She had to be sweet to him. So sweet he'd gag from a sugar high. She'd do it, though. Anything to stop the madness.

Tomorrow, she'd tell Georgia to forget the war, to forget doing horrible, mean things to Marcus. In Jillian's current state of insanity, that might seem like foreplay. She did not need more foreplay. She might jump him.

"Did you and Ronnie with an *i e* have fun tonight?" she asked in a syrupy tone. "She seemed like such a nice girl."

"Jealous?"

"Please. You're such a—" *egotistical pig, I can see why you'd think so* "—nice boy for helping her with her obvious self-esteem issues and being *nice* to her. Yep, we women love it when men are *nice* to us."

"So what are you?" he asked, confusing her.

"Excuse me?"

"You aren't really a cock hater, since you're lying about being turned on right now. Are you a junkie or a teaser?"

"You'll never know," she gritted out.

"Great. A teaser." He sighed. "What a pity."

Her blood boiled. "This conversation is boring and so are you. Next you'll be asking me about the weather forecast. Goodbye."

"Wait," he said in a rush. "Don't hang up. I have to tell you something."

She paused, stupidly happy that he wanted to keep her on the line. "What?"

"Double or nothing, remember? You didn't dance with me. Don't forget to bring my two hundred dollars to the office tomorrow," he said. "Like you, I don't take checks." *Click.*

Openmouthed, she stared at the phone. Then, scowling, she pressed *69. Marcus answered right away. "I won the first bet and you owed me one hundred dollars," she said. "You won the second, so you just keep your money. I owe you nothing. If you need me to use Happy the sock puppet and explain it in simpler language, just let me know." *Click.*

A second later, her phone rang. "What?"

His drugging laughter caressed her ear. "We aren't playing the American way, baby. We're playing British. The right way. You owe me two hundred dollars." *Click.*

Again she found herself staring at the phone. Unethical, that's what he was. No way the British rules for gambling were different than the American rules; he'd made that up.

The phone rang again a second later and Jillian grinned. She was tempted to let it ring all night, but found herself eager for round four. She pressed talk and said, "Don't ever hang up on me again or I'll—" *stab you in the heart* "—bake you chocolate-chip cookies and bring them to you in a pretty, decorative basket." There. That was sweet. Well, sweet as long as it wasn't Jillian's mom doing the baking…but that didn't bear thinking about right now. "Now admit it. I don't owe you a cent."

"What are you talking about? I didn't hang up on you, and I know you don't owe me any money. And why are you threatening me with chocolate-chip cookies? What'd I ever do to you?" her sister, Brittany, said. Without waiting for Jillian's response, she added, "Listen, Mom just called me. She's having one of her breakdowns."

"What? Why?" Suddenly serious, Jillian jolted upright. Dark curls cascaded down her temples and back.

"She's decided to try the dating scene."

"No, no, no," Jillian groaned. "Why would she put herself through that again? Why would she put *us* through that again?"

"Because she has *needs,*" Brittany said, her tone dripping with disgust.

"Gross. Don't ever, ever, *ever* say that to me."

"Hey, I'm just repeating what she told me."

"Well, don't."

Brittany sighed, loud and long and frustrated. "What are we going to do? We—" Pause. "Apple, Cherry, what are you doing up? It's way past your bedtime."

Jillian heard giggling and pictured her ten-year-old twin nieces running around Brittany's bedroom. They might look like angels with their sweet, round faces but they were devils in their souls.

The chance of Jillian settling down and having kids was very remote, so she lavished all her attention on her nieces.

"Go. To. Bed. Or I'll tell Daddy you misbehaved." Pause. "Thank you." Pause. "She refuses to take her anti-depressants," Brittany said, picking up their conversation as if it had never stopped, "so she'll end up crying on the shoulder of every man who approaches her, those men will drop her and then she'll become even more depressed because no one wants her. I feel a suicide attempt coming on—and it won't be Mom's!"

The phone beeped and Jillian sat up straighter as a wave of excitement swept through her. "Hang on. I'm getting another call." It had to be Marcus, and she could hardly wait to hear his voice—uh, could hardly wait to tell him off, the pig. Amid Brittany's protests, Jillian clicked over. "What? This had better be an apology."

"Has Mom called you yet?" her brother Brent—Brittany's twin—asked. "And why would I apologize to you? I haven't done a damn thing wrong."

She sighed with disappointment. "No, Mom hasn't called me, and don't worry about the apology. I'm on the other line with Brit, who's telling me all about the situation."

"Mom never calls you with her problems," he grumbled. "It's not fair. I think she likes you best."

"She just wants someone to think of her as normal, and the someone she picked is me. Remember what the therapist said?"

"Wants someone to think of her as normal," he mocked. "I just wish her revelations and breakdowns happened during the day."

"Again, remember what the therapist said? She's alone

at night with nothing to distract her." Jillian paused. "Maybe we should buy her a dog."

"She's allergic, dummy. So, have you talked to Georgia lately?"

Jillian fell back onto the softness of her mattress. God save her from her family. "She's dating someone else. You know that, so stop stalking me about her. You should have asked her out when we were teenagers."

"How serious is she about the boyfriend? I asked her to a movie earlier today, but she said she had plans with him. What kind of plans?"

"She's practically engaged, so leave her alone. Now, goodbye, Brent," she said and clicked over.

"—to bed," Brittany was saying over loud giggles. "I'm serious, girls. This is your last warning. Steven! Steven, the girls won't go to bed."

The giggling stopped and murmuring took its place, then Steven's deep voice drifted over the line. "All right, my little fruit pies, let's give your mommy some privacy." Static, kissing noises. "Love you, bunnybear."

"Love you, too, sugarbutt," Brittany said.

Jillian gagged. Thankfully, her other line beeped again, saving her from having to hear the rest. She clicked over. "What now, Brent."

Silence.

"Brent. Please. No heavy breathing or I'll have to hurt you."

"Uh, Jillian?"

Everything inside of Jillian froze. Hatred filled her, as did longing and need and all the tears she hadn't shed over him these many years. "I told you not to call here, Dad."

"Brent told me you were up. I just wanted—"

Hand shaking, she clicked over. "—cutest man I've ever seen," Brittany was cooing.

"And you're—" Steven began.

"I'm here, I'm here," Jillian said hastily. She forced her dad's phone call from her mind. Just like she always did. He would not affect her in any way. "Brent called me," she said. "Mom called him, too."

"Why does she always call us in the middle of the night?"

Instead of giving her the same answer she'd given Brent, Jillian said, "Here's a better question—why do you always call me in the middle of the night after she's called you?"

"Well, duh. If I have to suffer, so do you. So what are we going to do about Mom?"

"Let's buy her a cat."

"She's allergic, silly."

Sighing, Jillian gazed through the slit between the beige curtains draping the bedroom's only window and out at the moonlit night, soaking in the gently swaying trees. "Don't worry. I'll think of something." Brent and Brittany got to hear about the problems and Jillian got to fix them. At least it would take her mind off Marcus.

She hoped.

BACK AT HIS APARTMENT, Marcus sat in his recliner, staring at his magnificent poker table—the felt was the color of money and the base was intricately carved, high-glossed maple. It was his altar. His place of worship.

He glanced over at his weights and the boxes scattered across the living-room floor, each one filled with his stuff.

Clothing, dishes and basically everything he needed to survive. He hadn't unpacked yet, though he'd had several weeks. He didn't think he would for several more. He'd been too busy trying to buy CAM and now he was too busy trying to make it a success. Not to mention, too busy annoying Jillian.

He should call her again.

He frowned. No, he shouldn't. He'd acted unprofessional all night, which was very unlike him, and it was time to put a stop to it. He blamed Jillian. He needed to stay away from her. Far, far away. That woman irritated and excited him on levels he'd never experienced before. Every time he was near her or heard her voice or thought about her, he became primed.

He needed her gone, out of the company. But...

She'd made him laugh. She'd gotten the better of him. He wanted her to get the better of him again.

Shit. Frustrated, he tangled a hand through his hair. Yes, he needed her gone, but if she went to another agency he wouldn't be able to control her assignments. Annoying as she was, the woman needed a protector. One day she was going to piss off some poor sap and the poor sap was going to snap, hurting her. At least Marcus could keep an eye on her if she worked for him.

When Darren had grabbed Jillian's arm to keep her in place, Marcus had nearly broken the man's nose. Of course, that wouldn't have been painful enough, so he then would have ripped off the man's arms and legs and beaten him over the head with them. But Jillian had shoved Mace in the guy's face before Marcus could make a move and all had ended well.

But what if it hadn't? Jillian could have been hurt, beaten. *That* was enough to make him sick to his stomach. Women were cheaters by nature, but they didn't deserve physical pain.

He'd never worried about female bait before, but he was worried now. Jillian was such a delicate little thing—okay, she was average height and probably packed a punch like a linebacker. She was self-reliant, tough and fearless. Still. Men *were* stronger. The fact that Jillian and the other female bait usually went on assignments alone, placing themselves in the line of fire without any true means of escape, froze his blood and he vowed then and there to make sure it never happened again.

Of all of them, Jillian would need the most protection. He didn't need a reason for that assessment, he just wanted it to be true. She had an appeal that drew all kinds of immoral attention. Just sitting at the bar, he'd watched man after horny man scope her out and contemplate making a play for her. She'd looked aloof, untouchable, yet still utterly willing to try any sexual act suggested, the more depraved the better.

He himself had wanted to do wicked things to her. Wild things. Illegal in thirty-two states things. He blamed her let-me-suck-you mouth. And if he, an upstanding citizen (when he wanted to be), had yearned to do such wicked things to her, what had the other men wanted?

Nothing good, that was for sure.

Yep, he was going to be her new partner. Whether she liked it or not. Whether *he* liked it or not. So much for staying far, far away from her.

He picked up the phone and dialed his best friend's

number. It rang and rang and rang until— "This better be good," Jake said in a scratchy sleep-rumble.

Marcus didn't bother identifying himself. "Can you and the others come to the new office tomorrow? I need you earlier than planned."

"What the hell for?" Jake yawned. "I was looking forward to relaxing on a Saturday for once. You know I've always hated working weekends."

"One, you know Saturdays are the best time to test targets, and two, that's the time when most clients are available to meet with us. Besides, you can relax at the office."

"That's hard to do since my boss is an asshole, demanding I come in early."

Marcus snorted. "Funny. I want to assign the female bait partners and you guys are it."

"Partners. I like the sound of that."

"Strictly business, my friend."

Jake mumbled something under his breath that sounded like "you aren't any fun anymore." As if Jake would develop a thing for one of the women. The man had been celibate for two years. "We still on for poker tomorrow night?"

Marcus hated to reschedule; he usually planned his life around their late-night poker games. "No, we'll have to do it the night after. Something's come up tomorrow. Don't be late for work," he said and hung up. He tossed the cordless onto the nearest box. No way he'd explain about Jillian. *He* didn't understand the need to protect and guard her. Or argue with her. Especially since he hadn't even known her for twenty-four hours.

All he knew was that he was going to have to be nice

to her from now on. That was the only time he felt halfway in control around her. Otherwise, he'd end up dipping his pen in the company ink because Jillian liked their fighting as much as he did, the little liar. She'd gone all breathy when he'd insulted her.

Thank God he wasn't the only crazy one.

He guessed that meant if she upset, snubbed or offended him, he'd smile and thank her. If she slapped him, he'd smile and thank her. If she chained him to a bed and stole all his clothes and money, he'd smile and thank her. Maybe he'd ask her to climb on top of him, too, but that would be a wait-and-see situation.

Dumbass.

Frowning, he pushed to his feet and strode into the kitchen to get a beer. No, two beers. In all honesty, being nice was starting to sound fun and deep down he knew that wasn't a good sign. Not good at all.

You're so beautiful, baby. I was looking forward to showing you off to all my friends tonight, but I'm working late, Wyatt had said a few hours ago when he'd called.

Georgia hadn't been upset that Wyatt broke their date. Damn it! She should have been upset. She *wanted* to be upset—and that want was driving her crazy, making her brood and mope and worry about what the hell was *wrong with her.* They'd been dating for a year now. He treated her wonderfully. Not a day went by that he didn't compliment her appearance. *Let me look at you. God, if there's another woman more perfect, I haven't seen her.* Despite the way she'd complained to Jillian, she did like those compliments. Except…

I just want to be loved for who I am, she thought, depressed. *I just want to be loved for the woman I am inside.* Once she'd thought Wyatt was capable of that, but lately she wasn't so sure...

What would Wyatt do if he saw her without makeup? Would he still want to show her off to his friends? What would he do if she wore sweatpants to dinner? Would he still claim there was no one prettier? The prospect might not have bothered her quite so much when they'd first started dating, but now just the thought of his reaction made sickness churn inside her stomach.

She could easily picture him running away from her the same way Brent had run all those years ago. Brent. Just his name made her shiver. She didn't have to wonder what would happen if *he* saw her as anything less than perfect. He'd run again, as fast as his feet could carry him. *And that'd be a good thing,* she told herself firmly.

She recalled how, several years ago, she'd had dinner with Jillian and her family. During the course of the meal, Georgia had managed to dump spaghetti all over herself, covering herself in thick red sauce and noodles. Brent had taken one look at her, jumped up and raced from the dining room. Even though the imperfection had been temporary, he hadn't been able to get away from her fast enough.

Maybe Jillian had had the right idea all along. Maybe men really *were* pigs and incapable of giving a woman—*her*—everything she needed. And yet, that didn't stop Georgia from longing for that elusive dream-come-true romance.

"I just want to be loved," she shouted, throwing herself atop her bed. She cried until there was nothing left inside her.

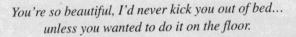

Seven

You're so beautiful, I'd never kick you out of bed...
unless you wanted to do it on the floor.

"THE WAR IS OFF," Jillian said.

"What?" Georgia, whose eyes were rimmed with red, frowned at her. They stood in the CAM parking lot beside their respective cars as traffic whizzed past on Oak Street. The sun was high and hot, but a cool breeze wafted around them. Magnolias fragranced the air, sweet, so sweet. Mocking. "Why?"

For six years, five days a week, Jillian had come to this large, white building with its pristine, virginal-looking walls and emerald-green trees splashed along the border. She'd always loved those five days and would have lived here if possible. Now, though, she found no comfort. She only wanted to leave.

Marcus was inside.

"I can't deal with our new coworker right now," she replied. Truth. The entire night had proven unproductive, which was totally and completely Marcus's fault. Even after all the phone calls about her mom, she hadn't been able to get him out of her mind and, in turn, hadn't figured out a way to deal with her depressed mother trying to score.

Yech. Mom…scoring. She shuddered.

"Why not?" Georgia insisted. Tendrils of dark-red hair swept across her eyes and over the elegant slope of her nose. She brushed the locks aside. The sunlight usually paid her creamy skin nothing but tribute. Today she looked like hell.

"What's wrong with you?" Jillian asked her.

"Nothing's wrong with me." She waved a dismissive hand through the air. "Now tell me why we can't go to war with Marcus."

"Because," Jillian said, switching back to the original subject without protest. Georgia would talk when she was ready.

Jillian leaned against the sedan she'd returned, her own car just a few spaces down, and looked away, toward the busy intersection. She mourned the loss of her uncomplicated, predictable life. No matter what happened today, she was going to talk to Anne about buying CAM or at least becoming partner. She'd borrow and beg for the money, if necessary—anything to get rid of Marcus and at last realize her dream. "Just because."

"That's not really an answer, but it doesn't matter. *I* can deal with him." Georgia crossed her arms over her chest. "I'm anti-man right now."

Brow puckering, Jillian faced her friend. "Why?"

A glint of insecurity slid over Georgia's perfect features. "Wyatt stood me up last night. Said he had to work late," she added, a sad, wistful note to her voice. Apparently she was ready to talk. "Do you think he did it to punish me? For not giving him an answer to his proposal?" She didn't wait for Jillian's response. "Well, he can punish me all he wants. I don't have an answer! I thought about it all night and still couldn't decide."

"I'm sorry, I really am, but you can't leave him hanging forever." Jillian wasn't sure how many more problems she could deal with. It seemed to her that if you couldn't decide whether to marry the man you were dating, then the answer was probably no—not that she'd tell Georgia that. She made enough mistakes in her own life and didn't want to be responsible for Georgia's.

"I know, I know." Georgia chewed on her bottom lip. "I'll figure it out sooner or later. In the meantime, I need a distraction. Hurting the guy who hurt my best friend is a good place to start."

Jillian sighed. "He didn't hurt me, not really." Infuriated and excited her, yes. "Take your frustrations out on Marcus if you want. Just…don't expect me to help." She couldn't. Not if she wanted to resist Marcus and his wicked, naughty mouth, his let-me-pleasure-you body.

"But why?" Georgia pouted. "And don't tell me you can't deal with him because I know better. Yesterday he called you incompetent and you hated him. Something had to have happened between now and then to change your mind. I want to know what it is."

Yesterday I didn't realize how much fighting with him turned me—him—on. She didn't tell her friend that, even though they usually discussed everything. She was just too…embarrassed by her feelings. "I've found religion, that's all, and I'm going to try something new. It's called forgiveness."

She snorted. "*You* found religion? In one night?"

"Hey, I believe in God. It's just, well, now I've seen the depths of hell," Jillian said dryly, "and I don't want to visit there ever again." Truth.

Before Georgia could reply, Selene pushed open the front door of the building and peeked outside. Her long blond tresses floated around her temples like angel's wings. "Anne's called a meeting," she said.

"We'll be right there," Jillian told her. A meeting? About what? Wait, she knew the answer. *Marcus.* She turned back to Georgia and smoothed her jeans. "How do I look?"

Her friend gave her a once-over and frowned. "Honestly?"

"Always."

"Like shit."

"Oh. Good." Jillian grinned. She'd purposefully dressed to un-impress in ripped jeans, a blue shirt and flip-flops. If being nice to Marcus didn't put a damper on her sex drive, she would need some sort of shield against him. Case in point: if he thought she was ugly just because she wasn't dressed provocatively, she could hate him forever. No problem. *Please let it be no problem.*

"You *want* to look bad?" Georgia shook her head. "You are so bizarre sometimes."

Jillian shrugged.

"I wonder what Anne wants."

Together they walked toward the building. "She probably wants to introduce Marcus to the rest of the staff," Jillian said and opened the front door. Georgia sailed past her. When she entered behind her friend, she frowned.

"Look," she said.

Georgia stopped mid-stride and spun around. "What?"

"Look at the walls."

Her friend did as commanded, and her mouth fell open. "All of our posters are gone."

A few weeks ago, they'd designed and hung male-bashing posters along the walls—like the ones in her cube—laughing all the while. Her favorite had been the one that read, You Know a Man Is Lying When His Lips Are Moving.

Why had they been taken down?

"After working with us, the clients fell in love with those posters," Georgia said with a frown of her own. "Anne even suggested we make more."

"Marcus," Jillian said through a clenched jaw. "If he thinks he can make this a man-friendly business just because he's now an employee, he can think again."

Georgia scowled. "Bastard."

"Who does he think he is, messing with our walls? Really, he's worked here less than a day. I'll… I'll—" *Be nice to him, that's what.* Jillian gnashed her teeth, fighting a tide of desire already working through her.

Georgia arched a red brow. "Still determined to forget the war?"

No. "Yes." There had to be a way to punish him without outwardly fighting with him.

"Stubborn. Come on." Georgia grabbed her hand and tugged her down the hall. They turned a corner and passed a table piled high with doughnuts and coffee. The scent of caffeine wafted through the air and made Jillian's mouth water.

"At least tell me you won the bet with Marcus last night," Georgia said, not slowing her steps. "Tell me you proved to him that men are pigs and women are superior."

"Let's just say I'm one step closer." She hoped. Yes, she had won their bet about Darren Sawyer, but Ronnie with an *i e* had done a lot of damage to the girls' team.

Lapsing into silence, they swept past open glass doors and entered the conference room. CAM only boasted a handful of employees and every one of them was present. Except Marcus, thankfully. She wasn't ready to face him yet.

Each woman Anne had hired was lovely and desirable, but in different ways. Jillian had always thought that seeing them together was like looking at a painting come to life. There was something for everyone. A temptation for every palette.

While Georgia usually attracted the art collectors, the men who liked fine wine and sophistication, Jillian usually attracted the ones with innocent schoolgirl fantasies (Darren the bastard being one less-than-memorable exception). Selene, of course, was the quintessential blond goddess. Cool. Aloof. Untouchable.

Men who liked a challenge went crazy for her.

Then there was Danielle, the resident bubbly blonde. She was tanned and toned with a smile that said *let's jump into bed right now.* She was also extremely intelligent but loved playing dumb so her targets would feel superior and underestimate her capabilities.

Becky was a mocha-colored beauty with long legs and

breasts any *Playboy* centerfold would envy. Amelia was the dominatrix. She had straight, dark-brown hair, always wore black and had wild, exotic features that appealed to men who wanted a spanking.

Currently, they were standing around the long, square table, sipping coffee and chatting. Jillian liked them all. Not many others outside this room understood her Pig Scale. Not many others eschewed love and marriage with such unmitigated determination.

Anne, leader of this sensual buffet of womanhood, sat at the head of the table, attention centered on a stack of papers. Jillian opened her mouth to get Anne's attention, to request a private meeting before she told everyone about Marcus, but Georgia's next words stopped her.

"The conference walls are bare, too," her friend muttered.

Jillian looked and…yep. Plain-blue walls stared back at her, the posters gone, vanished as if they'd never been there. She ran her tongue over her teeth and clenched her hands at her sides. Marcus! Maybe, if God truly loved her, Marcus would have a heart attack and need to be rushed to the hospital.

Really, when did you become such a bitch?

"Good afternoon, everyone."

Jillian felt every nerve in her body sizzle at the sound of *that* voice. Crisp. Slightly accented. Deep, husky. Lethal. No heart attack, then. (Maybe he didn't have a heart.) She bit the inside of her cheek in disgust. Disgust with him. And herself. The devil's favorite spawn shouldn't sound like an angel. Truly, if he kept talking like that, *she'd* have a heart attack.

Just then, Marcus brushed past her. On purpose? Their

shoulders touched briefly and the contact singed her, all the way to the core of her cells. She pressed her lips together to hold in a gasp. Pinpricks of electricity dotted her skin, spreading, weaving together and forming a blanket of heat.

It's disgust, she told herself. *Not lust.* Absolutely not. Uh-uh. No way. *He's mean and hateful and smug and egotistical and he took down our posters.*

Everyone began to whisper.

Georgia squeezed her arm and sucked in a breath. "I hate him, but he's a decadent slice of cake, isn't he? How could I have forgotten that?" she asked softly. "Have you ever seen a more perfect specimen?"

"Honestly?" Jillian said, giving Marcus a once-over as he scooted around the table and eased beside Anne. He wore blue jeans and a tight white T-shirt. His sandy hair was in disarray, as if he'd plowed his hands through it repeatedly—or a woman had plowed *her* hands through it repeatedly. During sex.

First Jillian shivered at the thought. Then she frowned. Had he slept with someone last night after flirting with her? Pig!

He had a masculine, beaded necklace wrapped around his neck. Tight enough to choke, she hoped. "I've never seen a more perfect example of a human pig."

Anne and Marcus shook hands and engaged in a quiet conversation. Jillian wanted to demand everyone be quiet so she could listen. Turned out, she didn't have to. Conversation throughout the room tapered to silence as every woman present feasted her gaze on the eye candy that was Marcus Brody. Speculating. Wondering. Hoping…

Despite the sudden hush, Jillian still couldn't hear what he and Anne were saying. Her hands clenched.

"Who is he?" Danielle whispered to Selene.

Selene shrugged. "He was here yesterday, remember?"

"I know what I'd like him to be," Amelia said. Jillian didn't have to guess: her tied-up bitch with a racket ball taped inside his mouth and a chain replacing the necklace around his neck. Maybe Jillian wasn't the only one who wanted to choke him.

"Couldn't you just lick him up?" Becky asked. "Mmm, mmm. Vanilla ice cream."

Their admiration was a little irritating. They didn't know him. If they did, they'd stop staring at him and break out their Mace. "Bastard," Jillian muttered.

"What was that?" Georgia asked with a laugh.

Everyone turned and looked at her expectantly. Even Marcus. Jillian felt her cheeks heat. "Nothing," she said sweetly, giving Marcus a saccharine smile. "Absolutely nothing."

He blinked in surprise, confusion—desire?—in his eyes as he gazed at her grinning lips.

Anne clapped her hands, gaining everyone's attention. "Have a seat, ladies. There are some things we need to discuss."

The girls milled to their respective chairs around the table, some of them hurrying to sit closest to Marcus. Most of them, Jillian noticed, had to wipe the drool from their mouths. Including Georgia, the traitor. Jillian claimed a seat at the end, as far from Marcus as possible.

He was still watching her, she realized when their gazes locked in the next instant. Brown against blue. Excitement against...damn it! Excitement. She felt it sparking to life, heating her blood. Felt it radiating from him. Great. Now he didn't need to insult her to turn her on. He just needed to look at her. Freaking great.

She raised her hand, intending to flip him off. Thankfully, she caught herself in time. *Don't make it worse. Stick to the plan. Be nice.* Jillian forced herself to wave at him, forced her features to relax. Forced her mouth to curve in another welcoming smile.

"Hey, Marcus," she said in greeting. Gag. Someone kill her now. "It's nice to see you again."

Once more, he blinked in surprise. Once more, confusion darkened his velvety brown eyes. "Nice to see you, too," he said, unsure.

Everyone looked from Marcus to her, her to Marcus. "You two know each other?" Danielle asked.

Unfortunately. "Yes."

"Yes," he echoed. *Unfortunately* hung in the air unsaid.

"Marcus," Anne said. "Are you ready?"

He nodded, stood and anchored his hands behind his back, his mouth slightly curled at the corners. Suddenly he looked ready for battle. For a riot. Something. But he tore his gaze away from Jillian, walked to the back wall, leaned against it and remained silent.

"I want to begin by saying how proud I am of each and every one of you," Anne said. There was an odd inflection in her voice. A hint of sadness.

Jillian frowned. Usually Anne began her speeches and lectures by telling them they were ingrates and should fall on their knees, thanking her for allowing them to work for her. Anne, proud of them? Possibly sad?

This can't be good, she thought, tensing.

"There were times you wanted to kill me, I'm sure," Anne added. Was that a tear in her eye? "But none of you ever did. Not many women would show such restraint."

"Anne?" Becky said. Her voice was shaking. "What are you trying to tell us? Are you...dying or something?"

Anne wagged a finger at her. "I'm getting to that, you ingrate, and I'd like silence until I do."

Finally. Anne sounded like, well, Anne again. Jillian expelled a relieved breath. Her attention veered to Marcus, to see how he was responding to the speech, the girls. *Everything.*

His gaze was locked on Jillian's mouth. Again. Unbidden, her lips parted as she tried to catch her breath. Her lungs burned for air. Marcus raised his eyes, dark pools, and for a split second they stared at each other and she was drowning...drowning.

His eyes devoured her, undressed her right there in the conference room. Blistered her from head to toe. Anne's voice faded from her ears and in that suspended moment, her entire world seemed to revolve around Marcus.

Her skin grew hot, her stomach flip-flopped. *Look away, look away, look away.* But she couldn't. He'd trapped her. Held her captive. She didn't want him. Really. She wasn't attracted to him.

Thankfully, for whatever reason, he tore his gaze away from her and she was able to do the same. She focused on the far wall. Its bareness irritated her. At least, she wanted it to be irritation she was feeling. Her heart was hammering inside her chest, all of her pulse points like little drums. *Boom, boom, boom,* knocking against her ribs. She could breathe, could hear Anne again.

"—should just say it." Anne paused, squared her shoulders. "Change was inevitable. Change is always inevitable. And I can't say I'm sorry. It was…time."

Change. How Jillian hated it. Marcus meant change, and she wanted things back to the way they were.

Treat him as a friend, she told herself. *The attraction will go away if you're nice.* Yes. Nice. She straightened in her seat and, drawing on her determination, faced Marcus for the third time. For the third time, he was watching her. Pulled, perhaps, by the same invisible cord that beckoned her to take another look, no matter the excuse. She felt her body reacting as heatedly as before, but forced herself to smile sweetly, as if she hadn't a care.

He frowned in return. Looked away.

What kind of game was she playing? Marcus wondered. Her sex-kitten features radiated all kinds of different emotions. Lust—his favorite, though it shouldn't be. Hate—something he expected from her. Sweetness—a shocking development and surely a lie. Innocence—also a lie. Had to be.

The sweet smile was giving him a hard-on.

What didn't, nowadays? He was really beginning to miss his sexual slump. He'd thought—hoped—only Jillian's anger turned him on so potently. No such luck. Great. He'd have to be nice to her without making her smile.

That wasn't even the worst of it. She sat a good distance away from him, but he could still smell her from when he'd brushed against her a few moments ago. Not her perfume, but *her.* She smelled too good, like a tropical, hedonistic island catering to the pleasures of the flesh. *Stop breathing,* he told himself.

His mind kept flashing images of himself and Jillian, in bed. Naked. Tangled together. Writhing. And he kept finding himself watching her, studying. Wanting. Okay, so, to recap: he'd have to be nice to her without making her smile while standing far enough away from her that he couldn't smell her.

Totally doable.

Women like her should be caged. And thrown into a dark, never-ending tunnel. And then the tunnel should be permanently blocked from the rest of the world. A menace, that's what she was. A menace to his piece of mind. His good sense. His work ethic. His sex drive.

He couldn't help himself; he faced Jillian and studied her for the thousandth damn time. Hoping that this time she would not affect him. Hoping that this time the desire wouldn't make an appearance. Her hair curled down her shoulders and back. Black, silky. Pure sex appeal. She toyed with one of the strands, winding the end around her finger. When she released it, the tendril curled around her nipple.

Dear God. The agony. His mouth watered. Had she done that on purpose?

She didn't appear guilty, though. She appeared aroused. And worried. And angry. And then determined. But she smiled at him again. His stomach tightened into a hard knot and he stuffed his hands into his pockets to keep from strangling that sexy, wouldn't-you-like-to-spank-me smile right off her.

Anne's next words penetrated the fog enveloping his

mind. "I'm going to take a chance for once," she said. "I've wanted to do this for a while, but held on, unsure. Well, I can't hang on anymore. I want a life outside of this office before it's too late. And so, I—I sold the business."

Jillian's eyes widened.

"There," Anne continued. "Now you know. I'm sure you knew it was coming, or at least suspected."

Jillian's eyes widened even more, nearly popping out of her head.

"Ladies, I'd like you to meet your new boss, the new owner of Catch a Mate, Marcus Brody."

He didn't expect applause and he didn't get any. Horror splashed over Jillian's face. She paled and focused all her attention on Anne. "What! What? No, no, no. Tell me you're lying. Damn it, Anne. You told me he was bait."

"And I didn't lie. Marcus still plans to be active in the field. But he wanted a chance to meet everyone on equal footing, so I gave it to him."

Stay where you are. Don't react. If he displayed an ounce of smugness or triumph, it would piss her off and then he'd barely be able to control himself. He teetered precariously as it was.

Ah, hell. Who was he kidding? This was one hand he wasn't going to fold. Later, he could regret it. Later, he *would* regret it. Now he'd simply enjoy.

Marcus strode to the end of the table and flattened his hands on the surface. He leaned toward Jillian, her scent stronger, more arousing than before. Sexy as it wrapped around him, lulling, begging for a touch, a caress.

He resisted as he opened his mouth to speak; Jillian beat him to it. "Double or nothing says you won't shut up and walk away from me right now," she whispered quietly, menacingly.

With no hesitation, he whispered just as softly, "You win, because someone needs to say it. *You* are now a puppet, and *I* get to pull your strings. Dance, little puppet." He grinned. "Dance."

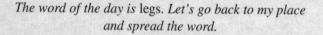

Eight

The word of the day is legs. *Let's go back to my place and spread the word.*

No. No! Amid feminine twitters of confusion and delight, Jillian felt her safe, happy world crumbling around her. Leaving her destitute. Miserable. Of all the things she'd expected to hear from Anne, that had been nowhere on the list. For a moment, she forgot that Marcus was still leaning into her, still poised above her, and simply wallowed in the hell in which she now found herself.

Marcus was her boss.

Marcus was her freaking boss. *Dance, little puppet, dance.*

Dear Lord. That meant he now called the shots, controlled her cases, would fill out her employee reviews. This, after she'd called him a pig and accused him of sleeping with Anne to get a job. This, after she'd insulted him time and again. *This,* after she'd offered to feed him poison. The knowledge hit her with devastating force, nearly doubling her over.

No, no, no. No!

CAM would not be hers. Not now, not later. Jillian felt like she was at a funeral, mourning the death of her dreams. The conference room was suddenly too bright, too hot. No, too cold. Her skin was like ice, her blood like fire.

Marcus was her boss. Ugh. Just…ugh.

Before Anne's announcement, she'd known her attraction to him had been bad. Now it was suicide. *Now* making him angry wouldn't just turn her on, it would get her fired.

Fuck, she thought. *Well, your plan is still good. Be nice to him and he won't arouse* or *fire you.* But she didn't want to be nice to him anymore. She wanted to scream at him, to rant, to slap. The bastard had ruined everything!

Marcus was living her dream. He'd be in control. He'd get to try new things and expand the business. He'd get to choose the cases they took on. He'd—

Not yet moved away, she realized. He was still leaning toward her, his nose almost touching hers, his sinful scent enveloping her. She narrowed her gaze up at him. *Get out of my face,* she wanted to snap. At the moment, she truly did feel capable of murder.

Heat invaded his brown eyes, darkening them to that rich velvet. *Kiss me,* his eyes seemed to say, *and all your troubles will go away.* He licked his lips and she felt her anger draining as she melted under a strange, erotic spell. Her traitorous mind was shouting that he could comfort her. That he could soothe the hurt and depression suddenly washing through her.

Oh, no, no, no. *He's evil. He's the devil. He's destroyed*

your life. She gave him a sweet smile. *Bastard.* "Congratulations. I'm sure you'll do a wonderful job." *Running the company into the ground.*

Frowning, he straightened and pulled his attention from her. He even walked around the room. The distance between them was not enough. No distance would be enough, she suspected.

After clearing his throat, Marcus said, "I'm happy to be here and I want you to know I feel it's an honor to join the CAM team. I've worked in this type of business for a long time. Together, we're going to do great things for our clients." He paused, avoiding Jillian's general direction. "But as Anne said, change is inevitable. Things are going to be different around here, ladies."

"I like change," Danielle said happily.

"Me, too," Becky agreed.

God, what a nightmare this was. Jillian glared at them, these women who should hate Marcus simply on principle.

"We'll miss you, of course," Georgia said to Anne, a little sad.

Anne snorted. "I'm not your boss anymore. You don't have to kiss my ass."

Selene's smile was radiant. "Thank God for that."

"Good riddance," Becky said.

"Don't think you have to visit," Amelia said with a wink.

Danielle added, "I'm allergic to water, so don't even think about inviting me to your lake house."

A smile curled the edges of Anne's mouth and for a moment it appeared as if her eyes misted. "I love you girls, too."

Jillian couldn't bring herself to say anything, though

she really would miss the old bat. She respected her—well, she'd respected her until now. What a horrible decision, selling the business to Marcus. Customers would hate that razor-sharp tongue of his. *I should have forced her to acknowledge my request to buy CAM.*

That sense of depression skated through her, stronger than before because it was now laced with betrayal and insecurity. Why hadn't Anne given her a chance to run the place? She'd proven herself, hadn't she?

"Jillian, be a dear and get me some coffee," Marcus said then, cutting through the goodbyes and pinning Jillian with an intense stare.

Silence filled the room.

Everyone turned to watch her, clearly speculating on what she'd say and do. They were used to her directness and probably expected her to verbally cut Marcus into a million tiny pieces, boss or not. Oh, how she would have loved to do it. To cuss at him, to refuse.

If she refused, what would he do?

Her eyes narrowed as realization hit her. He wanted to push her past the edge of her tolerance so she'd blow up and he could wash his hands of her. Well, he wouldn't get rid of her that easily. Her friends worked here and she was on the high end of the pay scale. She didn't want to make new friends somewhere else and she couldn't afford a pay cut. And if she switched agencies, she'd definitely have to take a cut—a big one.

"Sure thing," she said airily. She stood. "Sugar? Cream?"

His mouth fell open in surprise, but he quickly snapped it closed. "Uh, black."

"Black it is, then." Jillian sashayed into the hallway, all

eyes on her. As if she hadn't a care in the world, she stopped at the snack table just outside the conference room. She poured the desired beverage and with her back to him added three scoops of sugar and several splashes of mocha flavoring, then sashayed right back to Marcus. She handed him the cup without a word, only a smile. *I hate you.*

How could she fight him? How could she make. Him. Leave. Forever?

The room was still silent and everyone still watched her, including Marcus, who claimed the offered drink, careful not to touch her. She was glad. She didn't want to know if their fingers would generate electricity again. Especially now. Her boss. Her goddamn boss!

"Thank you for the coffee," he said, his voice strained. He hadn't expected her to do it, and he most assuredly hadn't expected her to do it with a smile, but he obviously wasn't going to drink it. He just held the cup.

"My pleasure," she forced herself to say. She remained in place and eyed the coffee expectantly. "Is it too hot for you, Mr. Brody?"

He looked at her lips, and her stomach quivered. "I happen to like it hot, *Miss Greene.*"

"Are you sure? You're just holding it, not enjoying it to its fullest."

He ran his tongue over his teeth before taking that first sip. His eyes widened when he tasted the sweetness. "Mmm, just how I like it."

She crossed her arms over her chest. "Really?"

"Oh, yes. Sweet."

"I thought you took it black," she said stiffly.

He leaned close to her and whispered smugly, "I lied."

The fire inside her blazed all the hotter and she quickly sat down, just to get away from him. Everyone breathed a sigh of relief because disaster had been averted. She hadn't punched him.

Only Anne seemed disappointed. She rolled her eyes. "If you two get any more sincere, I'm going to need a tissue. Or a barf bag," she muttered.

Becky said, "So, uh, what's your policy on interoffice romance, Mr. Brody?"

Several girls chuckled. Some giggled like schoolgirls, reminding her of Ronnie with an *i e.* But all of them watched Marcus with hawk-like stillness, predators stalking their prey. Did they think Jillian was dating him? Or did they want to date him themselves? Probably the latter.

Jillian wanted to gag. Did they know nothing about men and the horrible personalities that came with them? They should after working here, of all places. But the girls were soaking Marcus up, giving him a good eye-fuck, even though he'd just treated her like a lowly gofer. How could they not realize he was poisonous?

"Please, call me Marcus. And we'll get to office policy in a moment," he assured them.

I'll just bet you will. Jerk. He probably wanted to check everyone's teeth and survey the merchandise first. No doubt he'd have an open-bedroom policy.

"Anne," he prompted.

"I guess that's my cue to leave." Anne stood. She looked both happy and sad. Her eyes glowed brightly and there was rosy color in her cheeks. "We've had a good run together, girls. Stay in touch and don't take any crap.

Do what you want, when you want." A long pause ensued. "Truly, let yourselves have a life. Don't hide, don't regret." Her voice had cracked as she cast a meaningful glance at Jillian. A tear slipped from her eye, traveling along her cheek. She hurried out of the room before anyone could respond.

Jillian almost chased after her. She wanted to know why Anne had done this terrible thing. She wanted to know why Anne hadn't given her a chance. When she stood, Marcus said, "Uh, uh, uh, Jillian," and shook his head.

She sat without a show of emotion. Later, she assured herself. Later she'd track Anne down.

For the moment she'd focus on Marcus.

"Now, down to business. I've read over each of your files and I'm very impressed with your work," he said. Everyone but Jillian chirped happily until he added, "But…with the new rules and policies I'm about to outline, you'll all be starting with a fresh slate. No pros. No cons."

When he said *cons,* he leveled Jillian with a pointed frown.

Yes, she hated him. Could the day get any worse?

"One mistake," he added, "and you're out."

At that point, the girls lost all hint of amusement and happiness. One mistake. The legal system was more forgiving to hard-core criminals. And like he'd really wipe Jillian's slate clean. Please. He still looked at her with heat in his gaze. Angry heat. Lustful heat.

"That's a little strict, don't you think?" she asked.

"Rule one," he said, as if she hadn't spoken. He paced around the table, arms locked behind his back. Of course, the position displayed his pecs and abs to utter perfection. Totally unfair. "There will be no arguing with my orders."

"What, we're in the military now?" She rolled her eyes.

"Yes," he said, taking her words seriously. "*My* military."

She couldn't help herself. "Whatever you say, sir," she said, saluting him.

"Do you have a problem with me, Greene?" He stated the question quietly. Hopefully. A dare, a challenge. He stared at her, expectant. "If so, you can pack your things right now and leave."

You'd like that, wouldn't you? "Nope. No problem, sir."

"Is that so?"

Her jaw clenched. "Yep. That's so."

"You sure?" His brows arched and he never once removed his attention from her. The challenge in his eyes intensified.

"I'm sure," she bit out. *Be nice,* she reminded herself, no matter what the provocation. When his brown eyes darkened further, the challenge becoming desire, she forced her expression to soften. "I don't ever plan to argue with you, so I think rule number one is a winner." She gave him a thumbs-up.

He rolled his eyes. "Rule two."

He paused and she said, "I'm writhing in anticipation," maintaining her sweetest voice, careful to remove all traces of sarcasm. The devil was inside her, no doubt about it. Marcus brought out her worst.

His hands fisted at his sides and he deliberately moved behind her. She didn't have to turn to know he curled his fingers around the top of her chair. She *felt* the heat of him, reaching for her, wrapping around her. Unbidden, she pictured his fingers caressing her back. Lower, lower, winding around. Right where she needed them most. Her breath emerged choppily, shallowly.

She shifted in her seat. *That's what you get for making him mad.* He deserved it, though.

"As I was saying," he began. But he paused. Waiting for her to speak up so he could strangle her? A moment later, his fingertip brushed a lock of her hair. A gentle caress, almost a shadow, but effective nonetheless. She shivered. Had he done that on purpose?

"Rule two. There will be no relationships of any kind with a target or a client. Or an employee," he added, almost as an afterthought. "Understand? That is my policy on interoffice romance."

The girls nodded solemnly. Jillian remained absolutely still, too afraid she'd come into contact with Marcus again. "Anne already had that rule," she stated.

"Wait. I'm sorry." He leaned down until his breath trickled over her hair, making another shiver dance through her. Damn it. She gritted her teeth. "I must have failed to make rule number one clear. No. Interrupting. Me."

"You said no *arguing* with you," she reminded him stiffly.

"And what are you doing now?"

Danielle and Becky cast her sympathetic glances. Selene, Amelia and Georgia pressed their lips together to keep from laughing.

"Let's just say rule one is no arguing with and no interrupting me and leave it at that. Rule three," Marcus continued, staying behind her. "No gossiping amongst the hens."

Hens? Did that make him the cock? She knew he'd

said it to piss her off, but she laughed. The entire situation was simply too surreal and it was better to find amusement where she could than to wallow in depression.

His hands hovered over her shoulders, then fell away. "Rule four. No complaining. I know women like to do that, so if you feel that you absolutely must, I'll put out a suggestion box. Just don't expect me to read your suggestions."

I will not interrupt, I will not interrupt, I will not interrupt. Did he truly expect them to sit at their desks, silent? Utterly still? Maybe raise their hands when they had a question? Robots who obeyed his every command? Her hatred for him intensified. Apparently the others had begun to dislike him, as well. They'd finally lost their air of excitement.

"Does anyone need a notebook?" he asked. "You might want to write all this down. Or is everyone following along?"

"We aren't stupid," Jillian told him.

All eyes locked on her. "Well," she said. "We aren't."

Next, all eyes shifted to Marcus, gauging his reaction to her rule-breaking. Technically, though, she wasn't really breaking his rules. She hadn't interrupted him— there had been a slight pause as he stopped for breath.

What the hell, Jillian thought in the next instant. So what if she broke some rules. If he got the upper hand now, they'd never be able to get it back. They'd be forced to obey, always living in fear that he'd fire them. "Marcus," she said, "you really are being rude. To, what? Teach me a lesson?"

"Do you like working here, Jillian?" he asked. He sounded casual, at ease.

She turned in her seat and looked up at him. "You know I do." She matched his tone.

He didn't say anything more, but his threat was clear. Okay, so. Her defiance had done no good. She hadn't shamed him, embarrassed him or softened him. At least she hadn't been fired. Finally he moved away from her, circling the table. A hawk, a panther, ready to attack.

Selene kicked her feet up on the table. There was a glacial glaze in her blue eyes. Good. She wasn't fooled by his looks. "I'd like a notebook. I haven't doodled in a while."

Jillian chuckled, bravado returning. "Me, either."

"Ladies, I am perfectly willing to make an example of you. This isn't a game we're playing." His voice was stern. His gaze returned to Jillian. "Much as some people might think so. This is my business and I want it to be a success. I'll be a bastard if I have to be to ensure things are done professionally."

That sobered everyone. Selene lowered her legs, Jillian gazed down at her hands. She understood his need to make the business a success. She'd wanted to do that, too. Back when she'd planned to own CAM herself—which happened to be about ten minutes ago.

"Rule five," he said. "Spa day is a thing of the past."

The sober, somber air of the room was also a thing of the past.

"What?" Becky demanded, outraged.

"What!" Amelia gasped out, equally pissed.

"You can't do that." Georgia banged her fist on the table, the picture of feminine pique. "We need to look our best or we aren't effective in the field."

"Spa day is the only employee perk we have," Danielle said.

"Are you trying to ruin our lives to make yours a success?" Selene demanded.

Taking away their day at the spa really was a low blow. Once a week Anne had paid for their trip to Body Image, where they were massaged, pampered, manicured, and oiled down. To take that away from them... Even Marcus's sexy face and bedroom body couldn't save him now.

He threw his arms in the air, the last sane man in existence. "I've worked in this business for a long time and, frankly, I've never needed a manicure, pedicure or hair highlights on company time, on the company's dime. Women in every profession manage to keep up their appearance without the aid of a spa day."

"Cruel *and* cheap. Isn't this our lucky day," Jillian said before she could stop herself. She didn't whisper, either. Self-sabotage at its finest.

A collective gasp filled the room.

Marcus stalked to her. He grabbed her hand and tugged her to her feet. "May I speak with you privately?" He didn't wait for her response, but jerked her from the room.

As she passed her friends, she saw that Georgia had gone pale, Selene winked, and the others mouthed *good luck*. Marcus was probably going to fire her. Good, she thought defiantly. She'd never have to see him again, never have to speak with him again, never have to *deal* with him again. So what that she'd have to start on the bottom of the ladder somewhere else and make new friends. So what that her paycheck would take a dive and her bills would pile up.

It would be worth it just to be rid of him.

Liar. About all of it.

He marched to Anne's—nope, *his* office now—and slammed the door shut. Bright light streamed in from the wide wall of windows, the blinds open and raised. He released his vise-like grip on her hand. She felt cold all of a sudden. Bereft. He whirled on her. "Do you want to take me on, Jillian? Is that what this is about?"

She straightened her spine, tilted her chin and strove for a strong, brave tone. But when he looked at her like that, she wanted to throw herself at him, rip off his clothes. Taste him. Despite everything. "Actually, *Mr. Brody,* this is about rule two. You want us to act professionally, but you can't seem to do the same. You called me last night, for God's sake, and asked me if I was turned on. Isn't that dipping your hands in the company cookie jar?"

Fury—at himself or at her?—blanketed his expression. "That was a mistake."

"Yes, it was." With barely a breath, she added, "Where's my cash? You didn't get out of my face in the conference, so *you* now owe *me.*"

He got in her face again, until they were nose to nose. His eyes flashed dark fire. Ominous fire. His color was high, his accent more pronounced. His warm breath fanned her cheeks. "You are the most infuriating woman I've ever met," he snapped. "You're rude, obnoxious and cold."

"Yeah, well, you're the most annoying man *I've* ever met. You're egotistical, a sadist and pure evil." The more she spoke, the hotter her blood became, rushing through her veins, sizzling, blistering. "It's sad that my day would have been better if you'd been in a car accident on your way to the office."

They stared at each other for a long while, each panting with the force of their fury. "I could shake you right now," he said.

She stepped even closer to him, meshing their chests together. Her nipples pearled, the traitors. "Do it. I dare you. Shake me."

"You don't think I will?" He wrapped his fingers around her shoulders, his grip firm, searing. He shook her once, and her breasts rasped his shirt. They stared at each other.

"That's it?" she taunted. "That's all you've got?"

He shook her a second time, her breasts rasped his shirt again and then they were kissing. Wild and untamed. His tongue plunged into her mouth. She was already open for him, totally willing—stupid, stupid—their teeth scraping together. His decadent flavor filled her mouth. Claimed her. Her hands tangled in his hair, holding him captive.

He gripped her ass and jerked her pelvis into his erection, hitting her exactly where she needed him. Pleasure jolted through her. She moaned. He groaned. *I can't believe I'm doing this. I can't believe*—he tastes so good. Her thoughts tapered to total sexual enjoyment as he angled his head and took more of her mouth, feeding her kiss after delicious kiss.

"More?" he said on a harsh gasp of air.

"More."

He backed her into the wall and her excitement spiked. When her back hit the cool stucco, she hissed at the ecstasy. Good, so good. One of her knees bent up, pressing Marcus deeper into her. She gave another gasp. Oh, God. He gripped her calf, spread it wide. Oh, God, Oh, God, Oh, God. And when he began rubbing against her, the long, thick length of him hitting the center of her world, when she began to edge closer and closer to orgasm, panic should have hit her. They were fully clothed. Inside an office that should have been hers, but instead belonged to him. He was her worst enemy—and her new boss. He shouldn't be able to excite her this much. Yet…she didn't care.

"I dreamed about you last night," he said huskily. He ran his tongue over the rings in her ear. "The things you did…you should have woken up ashamed of yourself."

She shivered. "What'd I do?"

"Bad things. Amazing things."

The kiss became hard. Savage, just like his appearance promised. She yearned to bite him, to scratch him, to erupt, not in fury but in passion. *Don't,* she commanded herself. *Don't.* She'd never fallen apart for a man, and so easily. She couldn't—wouldn't—start now. Not with this one. Control mattered. Control was everything. Already she clung to a thin thread of it.

These needs, these desires were new, unwelcome. Kissing was fine. But to totally let go, giving him the sharp bite of her teeth, the passionate sting of her nails… he'd know just how much she wanted him. That, she couldn't allow.

"Stop pretending you don't like it," Marcus suddenly growled, pulling away from her slightly. His lips hovered above hers. "You want more, you know you do."

Come back. Kiss me. She couldn't raise her gaze from his lips. "I can't stand you. Why would I want more?"

"You may not like me, but you want me."

Want him… Oh, yes. Never had a man tasted so good.

Never had a man made her so excited, stolen her common sense. Consumed her. Unable to help herself, she meshed her lips to his and his tongue thrust against hers without protest.

He tugged on her shirt, lifting it up. His fingers settled on her bare midriff. The contact was electric. Amazing. And her resolve faded to the background, to be indulged later. She pulled at *his* shirt, wanting all the pleasure he could give now, wanting skin-to-skin contact. Wanting to touch the ropes of his stomach.

Her hands coasted over him. Oh, the strength. So wonderful, almost drugging. She wanted to touch forever—there was a knock on the window—and never let go, never give up the excitement and passion she found in Marcus's arms—another knock—and take more, give more, so much more, not worrying about letting go completely—and there was another freaking knock on the window!

Someone wanted their attention.

Panicking, she flattened her palms against Marcus's chest and pushed. She didn't push as forcefully as she could—should—have, but he stumbled away from her. They were both panting. His eyes were glittering, alive.

She jerked her attention away from him and looked to the window. Her eyes widened. A man stood outside, staring in and grinning. She gasped. Marcus whipped around. When he saw the intruder, he stiffened and held up a finger. Not the middle one, she noticed.

"Damn it, I need a minute," he growled.

The man nodded and turned away reluctantly.

What were you doing? The rational part of her brain spoke up again. *What the hell were you doing?*

Making out, her body answered happily.

With Marcus Brody, you moron.

Her blood chilled as she realized the depths of her stupidity. Her clothes were in total disarray. Her shirt bunched under her bra, wrinkled from the press of him. The imprint of a button was visible on her stomach.

"Who's that?" she asked, hating how breathless she sounded. His taste was still in her mouth. She didn't mention the kiss. Avoided the subject entirely.

"A friend." Marcus returned his attention to her and ran his hand down his face.

That was worse than if he'd said it was a stranger. "Don't you dare tell anyone what happened," she said. And yeah, she knew the guy had already seen everything.

"Like I want to admit to something like that. And for the record, nothing happened."

"That's right." She straightened her chin. "Nothing happened. And nothing will ever happen again. Understand?"

"Oh, I understand and I'm grateful." His voice was rough. "So…"

Get lost, was the unspoken command. "So." She cleared her throat, turned away from him to right her clothing. *Idiot. Moron.* She wished she knew whether she was referring to Marcus or to herself. "There goes rule number two, I guess."

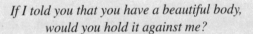

Nine

*If I told you that you have a beautiful body,
would you hold it against me?*

WHAT THE HELL was rule number two?

Marcus couldn't remember. He'd been making them up as he'd gone along. Could be *no office relationships*. Could be *obey my every command*. He didn't know. All he could think about now was the perfect way Jillian had erupted in his arms. How her lush, perfect breasts had felt plastered to his chest, how perfect the juncture between her sexy thighs was—the perfect cradle for him.

How Jake had ruined it all. He gritted his teeth.

He and Jillian should not have felt so...perfect together. Nor should such a viper taste like perfect heaven. Perfect, how he hated the word. He'd known she was trouble the first time he saw her. He'd known she would bring about his downfall. He'd known, and yet he'd brought her into his office for a private "chat," anyway.

Why not invite her over to his apartment for a night of wild sex while he was at it?

A heathen, that's what his mother would call him. And he'd deserve it.

His hands actually shook with need. For Jillian. Only her. He would have liked to tell himself it was because she was close enough to strangle, but...that would have been a lie. He knew it. *I have got to get laid.* That's why she affected him so strongly, because it had been so long for him. No other reason. He smoothed his fingers over his shirt, trying to brush away the wrinkles she'd caused by fisting the material.

He looked at her, even though it was a foolish thing to do. He was officially a foolish man, so the action didn't surprise him. Jillian was facing him again and her eyes glowed brightly. Her lips were red, swollen. Moist. He'd expected her to leave after she'd smoothed her clothes, but she hadn't. She'd raised her chin stubbornly.

"Why are you still here?" he said, more for his benefit than hers.

"You plan on firing me?" Her black brows arched and the spark died in her eyes. If not for the high, rosy color on her cheeks, she would have appeared totally unaffected just then. She crossed her arms over her chest. "I broke a rule and your employees only get one chance. Just one," she said, mimicking him.

A muscle ticked below his eye. "I'll make an exception, but only this once. Next time you attack me, though..."

Her mouth fell open, giving him a glimpse of the tongue he'd just tasted. The tongue he wanted to keep tasting. "Me? Attack you? You practically swallowed me!"

"Whatever you need to tell yourself to sleep at night, Dimples." He had to get her out of here, couldn't be alone with her a moment more. Just looking at her was making him hard. Well, harder. Sparring with her was as stimulating as kissing her. "Go back to the conference room," he commanded. "I'll be there soon."

Her eyes regained their sparkle, snapping and crackling with heat. "Be a good little boy, Mr. Brody, and choke yourself." She whipped around and stalked away from him.

Good thing, too. He might have kissed her again if she'd stayed a single second more.

Drawing in a deep breath—and catching an unwelcome hint of her exotic scent—he walked to the front of the building. Jake and the others waited just outside. He opened the door, letting in a warm breeze and light.

A few seconds later, he learned that letting his friends inside was a mistake, one of many he seemed destined to make that day. They filed past him, grinning wide, tooth-baring grins.

"Who was she?"

"How'd her lungs taste?"

"Do we get one of those, too?"

The rapid-fire questions pounded at him as they turned and faced him, still giving him those knowing smiles. He ignored them. "Just…wait in the hall. Quietly. Give me ten minutes, then come into the conference room." He'd given them an after-hours tour of the building the day the lease had been signed over to him.

A few of them snickered.

"What?" he demanded.

"Nothing," Jake said. He pressed his lips together. "Nothing at all."

Marcus shook his head. "Whatever. Ten minutes." He didn't wait for their replies, but turned and stalked away. His friends scoffed and laughed behind him. They'd tease him unmercifully later, he was sure.

The office, he thought, striding past the bare blue walls, needed some fixing up. Something totally nonsexual. Religious statues, perhaps. Maybe some antiwomen posters to replace the blatantly false anti-man decor he'd removed.

No, that would probably piss Jillian off and then she'd storm into his office… She'd be angry, so of course she'd be stripping off her clothes along the way. Anger—with him, at least—aroused her, no matter how much she denied it. She had too many tells. Shortness of breath, raised voice, hard nipples. Back to the fantasy. He'd be sitting at his desk, innocent, and she would approach him, chest heaving, push him back in his chair and straddle his lap. And, uh, there was no way he wanted that.

Was it hot in here? Had someone turned on the heater?

God, this day was so not going as planned. He'd wanted to tell Jillian he was her new boss, maybe gloat a little, but not enough to anger her. Well, he'd told her and he'd gloated. A lot. She'd gotten angry. A lot. They'd kissed—a lot—and it had been good. The hottest kiss of his life and better than most of the sex he'd had. Shit. *Shit.*

She was his forbidden fruit, and he needed to do a better job of resisting.

Marcus wasn't sure what he'd find when he entered the conference room. He knew it wouldn't be Jillian, naked

and on the table, a wicked smile on her face as she
beckoned him over and demanded he swallow her
again—which he would flat-out refuse to do, her being
forbidden and all—so he kind of wished he could just go
home and start over tomorrow.

Can't you think of anything besides sex? He stopped
just before he reached the turn, hidden from his friends,
hidden from the conference room. He pressed his
forehead against the wall and adjusted his pants. First
chance he got, he was going to find a willing woman, take
her as many ways and times as he could in one night and
get sex out of his system. Maybe then he could look at,
yell at and think of Jillian without becoming a perverted
sex addict. *Hello, my name is Marcus and I'm addicted
to sexual thoughts about an employee.*

Yep, he definitely needed to find a willing woman
outside of the office. But wouldn't you know, the
thought of being with someone else fucking depressed
him. *Well, hell.* He reminded himself that he couldn't
fire Jillian and end his misery that way. No, as evi-
denced by that asshole Darren, she needed a protector
when on assignment. And he was it. But he *could*
continue to make her fetch his coffee. That had been
fun. Her hips had swayed deliciously as she'd walked
to the table.

Well, hell, he thought again.

"WHAT HAPPENED?" Georgia asked the moment Jillian
stepped back into the conference room. "Have you
been..." She gasped. "Crying? Your face is red."

"We're dying here," Becky added. "Tell us!"

"Did he fire you?" Worry blanketed Danielle's pretty face; her blue eyes gleamed with concern.

"Should I put a contract out on him?" Selene demanded.

"Should I whip that naughty boy until he cries?" Amelia asked eagerly.

"Everything's fine," Jillian replied. Her cheeks flushed with hotter color. If they found out she'd just kissed the boss…if they discovered she still wanted his mouth pressed against hers, his hands all over her body… God, her humiliation would know no bounds.

Damn it! Why had she given into temptation and enjoyed that (sexy) disgusting, (sexy) vile, (sexy) power-hungry egomaniac anyway? Now she'd have to get a tetanus shot. The man probably subsisted on one-night stands.

"Everything's not fine," Georgia said. "Something happened. I can tell. Your clothes are wrinkled."

"I twisted them. I was worried about losing my job, after all." She forced a laugh, claimed the seat she'd abandoned and folded her hands over her stomach, the picture of demure. She'd act calm, prim, absolutely unaffected. "Thankfully, he didn't fire me."

Georgia's eyes narrowed suspiciously, all concern suddenly gone. "Did you twist your lips, too? Because they're swollen."

Her stomach rolled. "I, uh, bit them. From worry. Like I said, I was worried."

"Did you lick them from worry, as well? They're awfully moist," Danielle said, her tone dripping with amusement. Gone was her concern, as well.

Jillian sighed. "Yes, I licked them. End of subject."

All the girls stood then and closed the space around

her. "Please, girl," Becky said. She rolled her eyes. "We've been worried about you and you were out there making babies, weren't you?"

"Or maybe she's been out there welcoming the new boss on her knees," Danielle said, brows wagging suggestively.

"As if," Jillian retorted.

"Have a seat, ladies," a familiar male voice suddenly said, cutting through the speculation. Everyone stiffened. One by one, the girls plopped into their seats.

Marcus entered the room, the door snapping closed behind him. He strode past her chair, wafting a breeze of sin in her direction. Jillian's lungs constricted as memories flooded her. Lips, wandering hands, arousal. Attack him, indeed. The only way she'd attack him was if she were wearing brass knuckles and had razors attached to her boots.

Liar. How could one man be so potent? So…lethal to her common sense? That kiss had been a moment of insanity, surely. *You stopped being nice to him, and that's when the trouble started. Stick to the plan, genius, and you just might make it out of this building with some dignity.*

Well, what little dignity she had left, anyway.

"So." Marcus clapped his hands together. His features were hard, unreadable, his tone even more so. He hadn't straightened his hair and the short locks were tangled together in disarray. "Let's get back to the meeting," he said, glancing at her.

Jillian looked away from him. Cowardly, yes, but she simply couldn't face him right now. He'd had his tongue down her throat and she'd liked it.

Silence. Dead silence.

"You, uh…" Georgia paused, gazed around helplessly.

"You have lipstick on," Amelia finished for her. With relish.

Oh, dear God. Jillian felt the color drain from her face. *No!* Her horrified gaze whipped back to Marcus and dropped to his lips. And there it was. A pretty smear of pink. Calypso Coral, to be exact—she should know, since she applied that exact shade every day. It rimmed the edges of his lips. Mortified, Marcus flushed a bright, bright red. The color was a lovely contrast to the coral.

Their eyes met in the next instant. She shook her head. *Don't tell them. Please don't tell them,* she beseeched silently. His eyelids slitted, low, so low she could barely see his dark irises. His mouth floundered open and closed.

He didn't have a ready response. Would maybe blurt out the truth if he couldn't think of a lie. She couldn't let him do it. They'd tease her; they'd ask her about him. Questions she wasn't prepared to answer.

"He's a cross-dresser," she said, spewing the first answer that came to mind. What the hell, she spewed the second, too. "And he's gay!"

Another silence slithered through the room. This one heavier, a phantom reaching out and choking the life from them. Finally Becky said, "A gay cross-dresser. Huh. I never would have believed it if I hadn't seen the lipstick for myself."

"I never would have believed it, either," Georgia said, and she didn't sound like she believed it now. "I mean, you weren't wearing lipstick before your *private meeting* with Jillian."

"It was sweet of her to let you borrow her lipstick," Danielle said, all innocence. "Pink is a good color on you."

Jillian thought she saw steam curl from Marcus's ears.

"My personal life is my business, ladies," he barked, grabbing a tissue from the tabletop and wiping his mouth.

"It's nothing to be ashamed of," Selene told him. "I actually think it's cute. And if you ever see me wearing a shade of lipstick you'd like to try out for yourself, just let me know."

Marcus pinned Jillian with a fierce stare that said *You'll pay for this.* "Let's get back to business. It's time for a little test. Who here remembers rule number two?"

Jillian's cheeks heated again. He was doing this on purpose. Rubbing it in, blaming her for what had happened.

Amelia raised her hand, the amber rings on each of her fingers winking in the light. Becky, too, raised her hand and even said, "I know, I know."

Slowly Jillian raised her hand in the air, as well, unwilling to be cowed.

"You." Marcus pointed to Amelia. His eyes avoided Jillian altogether.

"No relationships with anyone. Ever."

"And specifically no relationship with a client, target or employee," Jillian added pointedly.

"That's right." Marcus flicked her an unhappy glance. "That rule still applies. In fact, for those of you who wrote it down, put a star next to it and circle it."

"It's not like you have to worry about us laying the moves on each other," Jillian said. "None of us are gay. Like you," she added, just to be mean.

His left eye twitched. His irises swirled with velvety fury. *Those eyes of his are the color of mud,* she told herself. *Not rich, glossy wood. Not chocolate. Not gold.*

They are not sexy. He *is not sexy.* "Don't make me pull you aside for another private meeting, Jillian."

The moment he spoke her name, everyone turned to face her, watching her, gauging her reaction. She bit the inside of her cheek. She couldn't respond the way she wanted: *You'd like that, wouldn't you?* They'd end up kissing again, in front of everyone this time. She knew it, felt it. His chest was heaving, his nostrils were flared, his eyes dilated. Challenge radiated from him.

A knock sounded at the door.

Finally, the heavy burden of attention was removed from her as the women focused on the conference room's entrance. Beyond the glass stood an army of men. Of gods. They were powerful, rugged and undeniably handsome. Pure seduction. Her brows furrowed in confusion. What was going on?

One of them—Jillian recognized him as the tall, lean Peeping Tom who'd watched her kiss Marcus—peeked his head inside. "You ready for us?"

Marcus smiled with more satisfaction than she'd ever seen from a man. Even after hard-core, sweaty sex. "Absolutely. You're just on time."

Her insides twisted and knotted. Obviously, these men were about to upset her. Nothing else would put such a smile on her enemy's face.

The door opened completely and those five godlike creatures entered the room. Peeping Tom, followed by a blond Adonis and a mocha-colored muscleman. After him was a redheaded guy who was burly and rugged. Last, there was a dark-haired, blue-eyed platter of deliciousness.

The men filed inside and stood at the far wall. Her

friends, Jillian noticed, were drooling. Even Amelia, who liked to dominate, to be in control and normally did not reveal the slightest hint of her thoughts to the opposite sex, was starry-eyed.

As the males surveyed the females, they smiled with delight.

"Ladies, meet your new partners," Marcus said, his tone dripping with relish.

"What?" Jillian shouted. No, no, no. She was supposed to saddle up with one of these pigs? Hell, no. "We've never had partners and we've always done a good job."

He peered down at her smugly. "Like Anne said, things change. And it's time we started having male employees."

"Why?" she insisted.

"You need protectors."

Grrr! "No one here has ever gotten hurt on the job. We don't need protectors."

"I've been scared a few times," Danielle spoke up.

Jillian glared at her. *Not a good time, Danny.*

"Well," Danielle said, splaying her arms wide, "it's true."

"Do the men need protectors, then?" Jillian asked through gritted teeth.

"Hell, no. But you *will* be needed when the men go on their own assignments. You'll act as cling control, keeping other women from distracting them while they do their job. That's just as important."

Jillian opened her mouth to respond, but Marcus cut her off with a shake of his head. "It's going to happen whether you like it or not, Jillian. I've already decided. After the way Darren grabbed your arm last night, I realized I didn't like how vulnerable you were."

"I took care of myself."

"Doesn't matter. Each one of you will be accompanied by a male partner on every assignment. This man will remain close by but out of the way and the pair of you will need to work up a signal for when you're feeling threatened or even uncomfortable." He lifted a sheet of paper from the table. "Georgia, you'll be with Jake."

Peeping Tom stepped forward. Georgia nodded in welcome.

"Danielle, you'll be with Joe." The gorgeous black man stepped forward, and Danielle practically melted into a puddle. "Becky, you're with Kyle." Adonis gave a finger wave and Becky returned the greeting.

Jillian's stomach knotted further, twisting painfully. Her name hadn't been called yet, and she was beginning to worry about what that meant. Only three men were left and one of those was Marcus.

"Selene," Marcus continued, "you'll be with Rafe." The redhead gave a tilt of his chin and Selene gave him a cool nod. "Amelia, you're with…" Marcus paused.

Jillian almost threw up. He had better say—

"Matt." The dark-headed, blue-eyed platter stepped forward. Amelia smiled wickedly at him.

"I hope you enjoy pain," she said.

Matt licked his lips and winked. "I hope you enjoy feathers."

"Rule number two," Marcus said with a frown. "Let's not forget. I'll switch you around if I have to."

The two of them flushed and hastily glanced away from each other.

Ohmygod, ohmygod, ohmygod. Jillian swallowed past

the lump in her throat. She knew what was coming next and wanted to scream. Wanted to cry. This wasn't happening, couldn't possibly be happening. The man was diabolical, doing everything in his power to make her miserable. To punish her. She'd suspected he wanted her to quit, but this proved it beyond a doubt.

"Jillian," Marcus said, drawing out the word, as if her name was a caress to his senses. "You're with me. Before you dance with joy, I should tell you that I've already procured our first assignment. It's tonight at eight. Be ready."

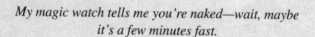

Ten

My magic watch tells me you're naked—wait, maybe it's a few minutes fast.

HE NEEDED a poker table in here, Marcus thought, surveying his new office. Maybe a foosball table, as well. The place looked boring. He pursed his lips; he couldn't have Jillian thinking he was boring, especially after all that talk about the weather yesterday. And speaking of Jillian, maybe he'd bring in a monitor—with the camera pointed at her cube—so he could keep an eye on her, make sure she was really typing case notes or reading about her next assignment. Otherwise she might be looking for ways to sabotage him.

You're with me, he had told her. *Before you dance with joy, I should tell you that I've already procured our first assignment. It's tonight at eight. Be ready.* He would have loved to have seen her reaction to those parting words, but he'd left, too afraid they'd start kissing again. There had been fire in her eyes and the need to taste her—again—had nearly consumed him.

Like a coward, he'd run away from her as if his feet were engulfed in flames.

"What's up with you and Curls?" Matt asked now as the men congregated in Marcus's office.

Marcus wasn't surprised that Matt was the first to bring up such a dangerous topic. Matt was a reckless man who lived for danger and liked all things fast. Fast cars, fast women, fast living.

With a sigh, Marcus leaned back in his chair. He crossed his hands over his stomach and stared up at the boxed ceiling, away from the guys milling around the (boring) office, picking up papers, leafing through cabinets. They'd wanted to know about Jillian. He'd known this conversation would come up soon. But he'd hoped for a day's reprieve at least.

"She's a nuisance, that's what she is. And the only thing that's up is my blood pressure." With barely a breath, he added, "So why the hell didn't you tell me I was wearing lipstick earlier?"

"Because it was funny," Jake said with a laugh, "and I didn't want you to take it off."

"You were sporting a stiffy when you told her she was your new partner," Kyle said. "I was embarrassed for you."

Male chuckles abounded. Marcus ground his teeth together. Having friends sucked ass. "You guys are welcome to find new jobs."

Jake rolled his eyes. "Not a good bluff, Markie, since you make that threat at least once a day."

The nickname reminded him of Jillian, the way she tossed it at him in the heat of pique. His ex-wife had called him Markie, the reason he couldn't stand it—

something Jake knew. To chastise Jake, though, was to invite all the men to call him by the hated name.

"Do we all get to make out with our partners or what?" Matt asked. His eyes were gleaming.

Rafe dropped to his knees and laced his fingers together. "Say yes and I'll work this job for free."

"No." Marcus snarled the word, a reminder more for himself than for the men. But he wanted to, God, he wanted to. Jillian's sweet taste lingered in his mouth; her moans still echoed in his ears. "What you witnessed was a mistake that will never happen again." Unfortunately.

Slowly Joe grinned. "Mistakes that look that good are always worth repeating. Guaranteed."

"No, they're not," he insisted.

"I think you're lying," Jake said, lips twitching. "I think you like her and want to make another mistake with her. A harder mistake. A longer mistake."

The guys chuckled.

"Wrong," Marcus gritted out. "She's my employee."

Kyle crossed his arms over his chest. "What would you do if you were stranded on a deserted island with her and work didn't matter?"

"Commit murder-suicide," Marcus answered. Or make love for days and days and days without stopping. Frowning, he gathered the folders he'd already sorted on his desk and began tossing them at his friends, one at a time. "This is your partner's schedule for the week. Memorize it."

"What about *our* schedules?" Jake asked with an arched brow, finally accepting the change of subject.

"The previous owner had a strict policy against testing

wives, so I've only had one male client approach me. I'm taking that case myself." He wanted to prove a point to Jillian—that women were as nefarious as men when it came to the game of sex, lies and more sex. "For the time being, you guys are simply acting as bodyguards. Soon you'll have more cases than you know what to do with, I hope."

Guarding Jillian's body would be fun, he thought. Pounding in and out of it would be more fun. *No. Stop! Don't think like that. Bad Marcus. Bad.* He scowled.

"What's the death-glare for?" Jake asked, palms up. "I didn't say anything."

"Nothing," he grumbled. Jake was loyal, trustworthy and Marcus shouldn't glare at him. He and Jake had grown up in the same neighborhood after his move to the States. Their moms had been friends and they themselves had been inseparable, always in trouble. Of course, he'd been responsible for most of that trouble, but Jake had never complained.

He'd met his other employees at various agencies. He'd always liked them, admired them, had fun with them. They'd all just clicked. Then, three years ago, he'd bought his own company and offered the guys a job. They'd happily signed on.

When Anne first contacted him about buying CAM, then called and changed her mind, he'd flown here and spent several days convincing her of his worthiness. Expansion had always been his dream. Finally, the old warhorse had agreed. He'd promoted his younger brother, Farris, leaving him in charge of the Dallas office, and moved here.

Single and always up for a challenge, his friends had

readily packed up and followed him to Oklahoma City. One day Marcus hoped to have offices all over the States, with each of these men in charge. After all, people were willing to pay massive amounts of money to test their significant other; he was just happy to oblige.

"The crop is exquisite," Matt said, cutting into his thoughts. He was peeking out of the blinds, gazing into the cubicles beyond. The others closed in around him, looking over his shoulder.

"That redhead, what's her name, Georgia?" Kyle looked around for confirmation. "She's a juicy peach in need of plucking."

"That's lame. Who calls a woman a peach? I like Selene," Rafe said. "She's—"

"A white grape," Kyle interjected. "Sink your teeth into her and her juices will pour down your throat."

"Moron. You and your fruit. She's ice. My favorite. The cool ones always melt when you make them hot enough."

Marcus pinched the bridge of his nose. His crew smelled fresh meat—or fruit, in Kyle's case. They were just like him; he'd taken one whiff of Jillian's delectable scent and begun foaming like a rabid beast. Hopefully everyone—himself included—would settle down soon.

"What do you think Curls is saying to Georgia?" Matt asked. "She sat down so I can't see her mouth anymore."

Curls, the magic word. Though he knew he shouldn't, Marcus joined his friends at the window. He was pulled by an invisible force, compelled. Forced by a need greater than himself, damn it, to look and see for himself what Jillian was doing. Georgia and Selene stood just in front of Jillian's cube, their backs to him. They were now talking animatedly, hands waving through the air, hair swishing down their backs. He could only see the top of Jillian's head.

Marcus willed her to stand back up so he could see her. She didn't, so he forced himself to turn away. His eagerness was embarrassing, anyway.

"I'll have your cubicles set up by the end of next week," he said, getting them back to business. What would it take to purge Jillian from his system?

He was afraid of the answer.

"Right now," he said, "we're going to sit on the floor and play a game of cards." He needed to relax and get his mind off his least favorite employee. "Loser buys the entire office lunch."

AFTER GEORGIA AND SELENE tired of her nonresponsive "yeahs" and "uh-huhs" and flounced away—she didn't want to talk about Marcus's favorite shade of lipstick and whether she'd "helped" him apply it—Jillian leaned back in her chair and stretched her legs under her desk. For several minutes, she simply simmered. Simmered and cringed and battled a need to cry, to scream. A familiar sensation lately.

Marcus was her partner.

He wasn't just her boss, wasn't just her greatest foe. Wasn't simply the man she'd kissed and almost screwed against a wall. *Would* have screwed, if they hadn't been interrupted. He was her freaking partner. Why had he chosen her? To make her miserable? Done! To make her quit? She was on the verge.

God, if only Anne had given her a chance instead of

shooing her away. By taking over CAM, Jillian would have had a ready-made income and a solid reputation to build on. If she opened her own place, however, she'd have to go into debt and would have no clientele for weeks, possibly months. That would be even worse than starting over at another agency and taking a pay cut. No, her reasons for staying were still valid, which meant quitting still wasn't an option.

Stuck, that's what she was. With Marcus. As her partner.

What the hell was she going to do?

How was she going to survive both days and nights with him? He'd be tempting other women or watching Jillian's every move. He might breathe on her, that sweet, warm breath that tickled her skin. Brush against her, a gentle caress, a hard touch. Already her heart rate quickened and her body warmed. Readied itself.

He'd ruin her, that was for sure. Ruin her concentration, her peace of mind. Her good sense. Not that she'd demonstrated any of those things lately, she thought, shoulders slumping.

Just then, her phone rang. Not wanting to talk to anyone but knowing she had to be professional, she placed the receiver to her ear. "Jillian Greene."

"Mom just called me," Brittany said in lieu of a hello. "She was crying."

Not again. Jillian sighed and lowered her head onto her desk, pressing her forehead into the cool wood. "What's wrong with her now?"

"She put her profile on a dating site and so far no one has contacted her. She thinks all men hate her and no one finds her attractive."

"When did she post the profile?"

"An hour ago" was the exasperated reply.

"Dear God." Inside her purse, her cell phone burst into a high-pitched crescendo. It was her brother's ring tone. "Brent's calling my cell. I'm not going to answer."

"He probably wants to talk about Georgia."

"No doubt." Thankfully, the ringing stopped.

A moment later, Brittany said, "Hang on. Someone's on my other line."

"It's probably Brent."

Brittany clicked over anyway. Silence claimed the line for over fifteen minutes. Jillian's ear began to throb. She tried to work, to flip through the folder Marcus had thrown at her just before he'd entered his office. She tried to study the woman he was supposed to flirt with tonight, but her concentration was shot.

Finally, Brittany came back onto the line. "Crisis averted," she said happily.

"What happened?"

"You were right. That was Brent. Mom called him and he pointed out that she hadn't pressed upload, so her profile never actually went live." With barely a breath, she added, "Brent wants you to call him. He wants to know what Georgia's wearing today."

Jillian's lips twitched into a smile. "He's such a perv."

Brittany laughed. "Yeah, but a cute perv. I just wish he'd get over Georgia and focus all that lechery on someone who's actually available. She's a nice girl and I like her, but I want him to have some stability, you know?"

"Yeah, I know. Me, too." They ended the conversation soon after and Jillian's gaze slid to the wall clock. She sighed with relief. Lunchtime. Well, lunch for her. Since CAM employees didn't arrive at work until late morning, they didn't take lunch until later in the afternoon.

Jillian stood, determined to hit the nearest restaurant even though she wasn't hungry. Any excuse to leave. No way in hell she'd ask Marcus's permission, though. Going into his office (which should have been hers), the very place she'd first tasted him, in front of the very men who'd witnessed her journey into ultimate stupidity/paradise… not going to happen.

She stalked to Georgia's cube, careful not to look toward the office. The blinds were closed, anyway. Her friend was talking on the phone while peering at her computer and frowning fiercely. She was muttering about "this stupid job."

"Let's go to lunch," Jillian whispered when Georgia paused for breath. She braced her hands on the side walls. "I've got to get out of here."

Georgia gasped and looked up. One hand clenched around the cell, the other fluttered over her chest. "You scared me."

"Sorry."

"Hang on," she said into the phone. To Jillian she said, "Should I gather the others?" She began closing down the file she'd been reading.

Jillian nodded. "Let's go to Café Maxwell."

"Cool," Georgia said, her frown easing into a grin. "It'll be good to escape our cross-dressing boss." Then her grin lost a little of its dazzle. "You do realize I can't go to war with him now. He'd fire me."

"Yeah. He's such a bastard."

"Should we tell him we're leaving?"

"I'm sure he ate his Smart Boy puffs for breakfast and can figure it out on his own when he sees our empty desks. Besides, informing him when we go on break isn't one of his rules."

Georgia's green eyes twinkled with wickedness. "I like how your mind works. See you there once I've rounded up the troops, then."

Jillian returned to her cubby, pausing a moment to see if she could hear what Georgia was saying to the person on the other end of her cell. Something like, "I didn't answer my work line for a reason. I'm not going out with you."

Brent, she realized.

She sighed and gathered her purse, clicked off her computer—thought she heard male laughter from Marcus's office and flipped off the door—then quickly exited the building. She didn't bother getting into her car; the café was just across the street. When the road cleared, she raced across, her flip-flops clacking rhythmically. The more distance she put between herself and CAM, the more relaxed she finally felt.

This late in the day, between lunch and dinner and on a Saturday, to boot, she was able to snag a large empty table in back. The café was spacious, with square wooden tables, mosaic floor tiles in a dizzying array of colors and walls painted with murals of ancient Greek gods and goddesses. Jillian had always liked it here. A place of whimsy and art, of beauty and serenity.

Georgia and the others arrived ten minutes later and all of them looked guilty.

"What's wrong?" Jillian demanded.

Without a word, Georgia kicked out a chair beside her and plopped down. She crossed her arms over her ample chest. Selene, Becky, Danielle and Amelia did the same, expressions unreadable. And that's when Jillian encountered a horrendous sight straight from her darkest nightmares.

Marcus and his henchmen had come, as well.

They were lined up, grinning wide, ridiculous grins. Even Marcus appeared happy. Had he been drinking? Jillian hopped to her feet, glaring at him. "What are you doing here?"

"I invited us," Marcus stated unashamedly. He stalked around the table and claimed the seat on her left, careful not to touch her. "Now, I want everyone to sit boy/girl, boy/girl. This is going to be a get-to-know-your-partner lunch."

Instantly a round of musical chairs ensued as everyone found their place. No one protested. Someone male said, "I prefer to do my getting-to-know-you horizontally." The men laughed. The women pretended to be offended, but Jillian could tell they were amused. Grrr!

"Since this is business, the company better pay the bill," Jillian snapped. She'd needed time away from him, damn it, time to breathe without taking in his sinful scent. Time to just…*be,* without feeling his heat. Without imagining his hands on her body. But noooo. He'd managed to ruin that, too.

"I'll pay," he said. "Happy?"

She shrugged. *She* wasn't happy, no, but her body sure was. Being next to him again stimulated every nerve ending.

The men, she noticed, clapped and cheered and immediately ordered a round of beer. "Don't let his generosity fool you," Jake said. "He would have had to pay no matter what. He lost our poker game."

"Yeah, but I was going to pick up McDonald's," he grumbled.

They'd been playing poker instead of working? So much for Marcus's strict business ethic! Jillian waved the waitress over. "I'll have a glass of Hpnotiq. No, I'll have two. As soon as possible."

Marcus frowned at her, then held up his hand, stopping the waitress before she could flounce away. "She'll have a ginger ale."

"I'll have Hpnotiq," Jillian insisted.

His frown deepened. "You're on the clock, Jillian, and we have an assignment tonight. You shouldn't be drinking."

"You drank beer before our assignment yesterday and you didn't complain about your friends ordering beer just now. I'm sure you believe in equality. If not, we can talk about a lawsuit." She gazed pointedly at the harried waitress. "Make it three Hpnotiqs. And hurry. Please."

The gray-haired woman raced away before Marcus could stop her. She returned a short while later with the requested drinks. The requested *alcoholic* drinks. Jillian's Hpnotiqs, and the men's beers. The women placed their orders for diet sodas, then everyone ordered their meal.

"You should like it that I'm drinking," Jillian told Marcus. "Alcohol makes a woman easy, doesn't it?"

He only snorted.

She drained the first glass in record time, followed quickly by the second, loving the taste of the bright-blue liquid as it burned through her. Ah, sweet relief. Maybe

now she could be in Marcus's presence without kissing—
damn it, *killing*—him.

After a few minutes passed, she propped her elbows
on the tabletop and leaned forward. Her gaze circled the
unwanted guests, keeping her attention off Marcus. "So.
Are any of you married?" The question escaped her out
of habit. She uttered it at least once a day, it seemed.

"Hell, no," said Adonis. She thought his name might be
Kyle. "No," said someone else. "Dear God, no," said
another. Rafe, the redhead, bellowed, "Not in this lifetime."

Jake didn't say anything, but his expression was sad.

"No bloody way," said Marcus.

She rolled her eyes. "A hazard of the business, I guess.
None of the girls are married, either."

"I'm considering it," Georgia offered in a soft,
hesitant voice.

"Is that a proposal?" Kyle asked, leaning toward her
eagerly. "'Cause I accept."

"Hardly." Grinning, she shook her head. "Who knows?
I might decide to eschew the institution altogether."

He stabbed at his heart with his fist. "Just kill me,
then. I no longer have a reason to live."

Georgia chuckled behind her hand before turning to
Marcus. There was an evil glint in her eyes. "Oh, hey.
I'm having a Heather Rae party next Wednesday. We're
going to do facials and apply makeup. Are you interested
in coming?"

"No," he said, his voice heavy with self-derision.
"I'm busy."

"Ah, but you'd look so good wearing cranberry eye
shadow," Jillian told him with an innocent smile.

"I did like you in that lipstick," Jake said.

"Thank you, everyone. You're too good to me." Marcus winked at Jillian, his features completely relaxed, true humor in his eyes.

The action surprised her. Feeling as if she'd been transported to another dimension, Jillian drained her last glass of Hpnotiq. Why couldn't he have been this nice, this charming, when they had first met? He could have been, but he'd chosen not to and that knowledge made her irritation grow. "So who's ready to break the ice? Anyone want to share their most recent bad kiss?" she asked, just to strike at him.

"I have one," Marcus muttered, losing his good humor.

His friends snickered.

Oh, God. She'd forgotten for a moment that they knew, that they'd seen her lip-lock with Marcus. Her cheeks heated. The waitress returned, thankfully, gaining everyone's attention as she set down their meals. Jillian dug into her hamburger. She'd wanted a relaxing lunch; now she just wanted it to end.

Silence passed between her and Marcus for a long while. Finally he said, "You shouldn't have left the office without my permission."

"That wasn't in your rules," she reminded him without sparing him a glance.

"It is now."

Of course it was. "Do I need your permission to go the bathroom?"

"I'll let you know," he said, leaning into her. He didn't say anything else.

How could he smell so good? Jillian wondered.

How could she look so bloody lovely? Marcus wondered. She was driving him insane! But, he had to admit, she challenged him as no one else ever had. She excited him, too.

And wasn't that just a pain in the ass? Why couldn't she be like other women? Push him away completely or fall in love with his "aloofness" and, in turn, think that meant they were supposed to be together? He could forget her then. He could stop thinking about her at foolish times— like during a poker game with his friends, where he'd forgotten about his cards and folded with a full house.

"What are you thinking about?" Jillian asked him quietly. For once, her tone was curious rather than infuriated. "Your face is all pinched with disgust."

"You," he answered honestly, just as quiet as she was. "I'm thinking about you."

"Well, that's nice." She rolled her eyes—trying not to show just how much that hurt? "At least we feel the same way about each other." He opened his mouth to comment, but she beat him to it. "So, what's our assignment tonight?"

"Did you not read the file I gave you?" He was annoyed by the way she spat the word *our*.

"I meant to read it, but I got caught up in something else."

"Like what?"

"Like family."

She probably expected him to complain, to tell her not to deal with family issues on company time. But he didn't. He understood family and couldn't help but wonder what problems hers was having. Irritating that he cared. "Our case is simple. The client suspects that his wife is going to bars and flirting with other men. I'm going to test her and see if she'll pick me up."

"Well, well. I'll finally get to see you in action. And not the Ronnie with an *i e* kind of action." She popped a fry into her mouth. "Were you just blowing smoke in the conference room or do you really need a female partner to…I can't even remember what you said we were supposed to do."

"Yes, I really do need a female partner." He swiped one of her fries. "If I encounter a clinger, like Ronnie, you're going to distract her so I can do my job. Believe me, you're going to save me a lot of grief. I'm just pissed I didn't think of this sooner."

"Oh, yeah. A clinger. I remember now." She grinned, a true, genuine grin of amusement. "Had to deal with a lot of those, then?"

"Too many to count." He really did like her smile. Pretty, sweet, warm. And yeah, once again it turned him on. He was beginning to realize everything about Jillian turned him on. Angry, calm, humorous, didn't matter. "It's always been the worst part of the job. Well, besides telling the spouse what happened."

Just then, Georgia laughed and the sound of it floated across the table. He flicked her a quick glance. She was leaning into Jake, smiling up into his face as if he were her favorite brother in the whole wide world. Jake appeared highly amused, admiring, but not enslaved.

The love of Jake's life had died in a car accident a few years ago and Jake had yet to get over it. That's why Marcus had paired him with Georgia. She was a beautiful woman. Exquisite, even, like the goddess paintings on the walls. Men fell at the altar of her beauty every day— her file said as much.

He'd paired her with someone who could resist her.

Marcus, too, would have been a good choice for Georgia's partner. She did nothing for him. Once, she might have. But she lacked the intensity Jillian possessed, the…wow factor. And now that he'd encountered that intensity, that *wow,* nothing less would do for him. He focused once more on Jillian. Trying to do otherwise usually proved pointless.

"Are you dating anyone?" The stupid question slipped from him before he could stop it.

"No!" Jillian looked insulted that he'd even ask. A few of the others glanced over at them, but her dark glare had them turning away. "I wouldn't have kiss—" She cut herself off and her cheeks reddened. She whispered, "I wouldn't have let you borrow my lipstick if I were."

He liked that about her, such integrity—until he realized she didn't plan to return the question. Did she assume he'd have kissed her even if he was seeing another woman? "I'm not, either," he said stiffly.

She didn't respond.

"Have you ever been married?" he pressed.

"No." She wrapped her delicate fingers around a water glass, sipped, didn't face him. "Have you?"

Finally, some interest. Except it was in a topic he didn't want to explore further. "Yes." He loathed the subject of his marriage and rarely discussed it. Not even with Jake. Why had he even brought it up? It wasn't like Jillian's answer had mattered to him. What did he care if she'd been married?

His jaw clenched. Okay, so it did matter. He didn't like the thought of her with another man. In fact, every possessive bone in his body seemed to stretch, awakening from a lifelong slumber. *Mine,* they said.

Stop, he commanded. *Not mine. Never mine.*

As he fought with himself, she eyed him, trying to appear bored, trying to appear nonchalant, but there was a sharpness to her gaze that she couldn't hide. "Didn't work out, I take it."

"Hardly," he said.

"I'll never take the marriage plunge." Her voice was strong with conviction. "It's just too risky."

"Hear, hear." He lifted his water glass, and she did the same. They clinked them together.

She settled back in her chair and gazed at him as if he were the only person in the room with her. Something almost—dare he say it—vulnerable clouded her eyes. In the next instant, both of them seemed to realize that they weren't shouting at each other, bickering or hurling insults. Shock blanketed her pretty face, probably a mirror of his own expression.

"Truce?" he asked. "For now?"

She hesitated, then nodded. "Truce."

He wondered how long it would last.

"Do you think people like us ever have a happy ending?" she asked softly.

His brows furrowed. "What do you mean, people like us?"

She thought about it, shrugged. "People who know exactly what the opposite sex is capable of."

He thought about it, too, rolling the question through his mind. "No," he finally answered. "I don't. People like us are destined to grow old alone. Wise, but alone."

Funny, the thought of being alone had never depressed him until now.

"Yeah," she said wistfully, turning back to her lunch. "You're probably right."

Eleven

*Do you live on a chicken farm? No? Well, you sure do
know how to raise cocks.*

AFTER SHE FINISHED UP at the office, Jillian drove to
Anne's. It was a thirty-minute commute and she wouldn't
be able to stay long since she had to prepare for tonight's
assignment. But she only had one question.

Why?

The drive proved surprisingly smooth, relaxing, with
lush-green trees scattered along the sides of the road,
climbing toward the darkening sky. Pink, purple and
yellow flowers bloomed prettily, swaying with a slight
breeze. Jillian listened to rock music pound from the
speakers, tapping her foot as she drove. At least she was
able to keep Marcus from her mind. Kind of. Sexy bastard.

He'd once been married. Shock. They'd shared a
lunchtime truce. Shock. *You're keeping him from your
mind, remember?* Oh, yeah.

Anne's house finally came into view, a spacious cabin

made from both light and dark woods. White shutters adorned the windows; knowing Anne, they should have been black. The driveway was gravel and the small rocks crunched beneath her tires. Overall, it was a place of tranquility. She'd been here before, but was always surprised that the serene home belonged to no-nonsense Anne.

Jillian parked. Outside, warm air enveloped her. A fragrant bouquet of roses and crisp lake water filled her nose. Having heard her approach, Anne waited in the open doorway. She was puffing a cigarette. "I know I told you to visit, Greene, but damn, girl. Not even I expected it this quickly."

"Maybe I missed you," Jillian said, stopping just in front of her former boss. *Just say it. Get it over with.* "I would have bought CAM from you, Anne." There. "You knew that, didn't you?"

"Yes, I knew." Anne's tone was unrepentant.

She tried not to show any emotion. "Why didn't you offer it to me?"

Anne remained silent for a long while, returning Jillian's searching gaze with one of her own. Then she turned, smoke wafting around her. "Come in. We'll talk."

She didn't want to; she wanted to go home and curl up and hit something and maybe cry. But she followed Anne. The doorway opened into a clean, breezy room where white drapes swayed from gaping windows. Stiff but pretty furniture in dark browns and off-whites formed a circle in the center.

"Sit," Anne said, motioning to a barely padded chair.

She sat. Anne claimed the couch across from her. For the first time, Jillian noticed her appearance. She wore a black silk robe and her gray hair was brushed to a shine. Expecting company?

"You want to know why." Anne took a drag of her cigarette, then smashed it into an ashtray. "Nasty habit," she said. "I'm trying to stop."

"Yes. I want to know."

"What if I told you that you weren't right for the job?"

Jillian's eyes narrowed. "I'd know you were lying."

Anne's lips twitched with humor. "Fine. I'd be lying."

"Why?" Jillian insisted. "I deserve the truth."

"You want the truth? I'll give it to you, but you're not going to like it." Anne settled deep into the couch and with a sigh, peered up at the slatted ceiling. "You would have ended up like me and I didn't want that for you."

She blinked in surprise. She didn't know what she'd expected to hear, but that wasn't it. "So what?" she said, incredulous. "That's not for you to decide."

"Your bitterness toward men grows daily, Jillian. If you don't do something about it while you're still young, you are going to end up alone and miserable, more so than you are now. You'd always have wondered what could have been. You'd always have wondered where the years had gone."

To mask the fury in her eyes, Jillian gazed down at her hands. "Is that what you do?"

"Not anymore. I'm living now. Finally living. You should try it."

"My future isn't your concern, Anne." Her lashes swept up of their own accord, and she pinned her former boss with a fierce frown. "At the very least, you owed me a chance. I helped make CAM what it is, getting us ads in all the local papers, placing fliers around town, expanding our client base. You owed me a chance," she repeated. Her chin trembled. She wouldn't cry. She wouldn't fucking cry.

"Maybe I gave you one," Anne said softly.

"What? When?" she demanded. She would have remembered; she would have pounced on it. "Every time I tried to talk to you, you told me we'd discuss it later."

Anne rolled her eyes. "Obviously, we're not talking about the same kind of chance. But I don't feel like explaining myself at the moment. You're not ready to hear me yet. Hopefully, you'll come to understand on your own." Her voice was dry, a little scolding. "The other girls, well, they aren't as closed off as you. They, at least, take chances."

I take chances, Jillian thought, hurt. Sure, she couldn't think of one at the moment, but that didn't mean anything.

A knock sounded at the door, saving Anne from further explanation. She straightened and smoothed the crinkles from her robe. "My date is here."

Jillian's eyes widened. Her date? *Anne's?* Anne, who hated men more than anyone Jillian knew? "You're seeing someone?"

"Seeing…debauching…whatever you want to call it."

O-kay. She shook her head. God, had she ever really known her boss? Anne had sold the business to Marcus when she could have sold it to a woman, someone she knew and trusted. Why not have a lover, too, even though she'd often claimed there was no better partner than a vibrator (it couldn't talk and would never betray).

"Come in," Anne called.

The door creaked open and a young, lean and very handsome man—a boy, really, when compared to Anne—strolled inside. He appeared eager, happy to be there. How old was he? He didn't even have a shadow beard to prove he'd hit puberty. He saw Anne and gave her a sexy, come-hither grin. "Hey, baby."

Ew. *My cue to leave.*

But Jillian found herself looking at Anne, trying to see what the man-child saw. Pretty hazel eyes that were a perfect blend of green and brown. Intelligence in every line of her face. Gray hair that appeared soft and thick. A compact body. And…zest. It radiated from her. She fairly pulsed with life and vitality.

Had she always looked that way and Jillian just hadn't noticed?

The man-child slid his arm around Anne's waist and kissed her neck. "This is Hugh," Anne said. "Hugh, Jillian."

"Hey," he said, barely able to tear his gaze from Anne long enough to greet Jillian.

"Hey." Oddly jealous of the pair, Jillian pushed to her feet. She didn't have the answers she craved, but she was done here. The diabolical woman and her cryptic "I gave you a chance" would probably haunt her for days. Weeks. Hell, the rest of her life.

How? Damn it, how had she given Jillian a chance?

"I have an assignment tonight. I'd better go." She strode to the front door, giving the couple a pondering look over her shoulder. Maybe she needed to take a lover, too. Maybe that would finally get Marcus out of her head. The idea of getting naked with anyone else was abhorrent to her, though.

"Jillian," Anne called, stopping her.

She didn't turn, just stood where she was and waited.

"You'll thank me one day. I promise you."

"No, I won't." Nothing good would come of her time with Marcus. How could it? They might have called a truce, but they were bad for each other. "Goodbye, Anne. Have a nice life."

"Oh, I will. It's you I'm worried about."

It's you I'm worried about.

As Jillian dressed for the night's assignment, Anne's parting shot echoed through her mind. There was no reason to worry about her; she'd be just fine, her life would be just fine. All she had to do was get her hormones under control.

Desperate to at last shove Marcus out of her mind, she flipped through the mental file she'd compiled about their case. A thirty-three-year-old male, married for less than a year, had found several handwritten phone numbers in his wife's purse—not in his wife's writing, either. He feared she was flirting with men to get them.

Tonight, the wife supposedly planned to sing karaoke at Mary's Bad Idea, a bar a few miles from Jillian's house. Sometimes—okay, a *lot* of times—a client's spouse wasn't where he claimed to be, so CAM usually tried to run into him at his office building. A lost and lonely woman in need of a strong man to help her find her way. But lately, people were so blatant with their cheating. So…unconcerned. Was there something in the air? Was getting caught the new black?

Jillian was simply supposed to show up tonight at the bar and observe, not speak with anyone at any time or leave Marcus's sight, even to go to the bathroom. The only time she was to approach him was if he signaled her over and then she was to extract him from a clinger.

Marcus had told her all of this on a Post-it note he'd attached to the inside of the folder. She'd been oddly pleased that he'd written such a chauvinistic message. It had helped wipe away the memory of the truce they'd shared at lunch. A truce that, she admitted, scared her. It made him irresistible. Almost likeable.

But she did not want to like that man. She couldn't. To do so even for a moment was to remember their passionate kiss. To think about their passionate kiss was to desire him. To desire him was to make a complete fool of herself. Again.

Sighing, she withdrew a tight black dress from her closet. It had thin silver straps and a choker collar. Perfect. Not too flashy, but just sexy enough that she would blend in with the crowd. Blend…it was odd. She usually had to dress to stand out.

She quickly shimmied into the material, anchored her curls haphazardly atop her head, letting several tendrils escape, and tugged on her knee-high boots. She pinned a silver flower to her right strap; the camera hidden inside its center would capture the night's escapades and catch anything Marcus's didn't.

Finished, she glanced in the mirror. Not bad. But as she studied her appearance, she couldn't help but wonder what Marcus's wife had looked like. Blonde? A redhead like Georgia? Beautiful, no doubt. A man like Marcus would want a stunner by his side. Had he loved her?

From there, Jillian's thoughts spiraled, spreading poisonous branches. What had the wifey-poo been like personality-wise? Why had they divorced? Infidelity? Most likely. If so, the wife's? Or his? Definitely the wife's, judging from the tone of Marcus's voice when he'd spoken of the marriage. What kind of woman would cheat on a guy as magnetic as Marcus? A *smart woman,* she forced herself to answer. He was a pig. Had he cheated, too?

Her wall clock chimed the hour, saving her mind from having to produce an answer she knew she wouldn't like. If he hadn't, he was a better man than she wanted to give him credit for being. As Jillian gathered her purse and keys, her phone rang. Groaning, she rushed to her nightstand and glanced at the unit. There was a flashing red light because her dad had left a message the other day. *Call me, please. I miss you.* And she hadn't erased it yet.

Caller ID showed this call was from Greene, Evelyn. Guess it was finally Jillian's turn to hear firsthand about her mom's (mis)adventures in the dating world. She was glad, she'd always wanted honesty from her mother, but she didn't have time for this. Still, she answered. If she didn't, her mom would call her cell all damn night, maybe even sink into a major depression that Brittany and Brent would have to deal with.

Jillian picked up the phone and tried to sound happy. "Hello, Mom. How are you?"

"Hi, sugar. I'm good. I started missing you and decided to call so I could hear my baby's sweet voice. How are you?"

Okay, no mention of dating. She wasn't surprised; in fact, she didn't know why she'd expected her mom to spill. Mom cried and moaned to Brent and Brittany, but only ever showed Jillian her happy side. She and her siblings had spent countless hours with a therapist, learning how to deal with their mother's depressed personality. They'd been told to expect denial, but Jillian hated the happy facade.

"I'm good, too," she said, being dishonest herself. *Hypocrite.* In her defense, her mom couldn't even deal with her own problems. No way she could deal with Jillian's.

But she loved the woman, she really did, and even understood where the depression and mood swings had originated: her dad's affair. "I hear you're dating again."

"Yes," her mom said hesitantly.

"You want to talk about it?" Jillian eased onto her mattress and rested her elbow on her knee.

"Nothing to tell, really." She laughed, and there was a nervous edge to the sound. "No one has responded to my profile, but I'm totally okay with that."

No, she wasn't. She'd cried to both Brittany and Brent. Wanted to cry again now, Jillian was sure. "Men are pigs, Mom, you know that. But sooner or later someone will recognize how special you are."

"Yes, men are pigs. Except your brother, of course. He's actually a decent human being. Almost a woman," she added as an afterthought.

"I'm sure he'd love to hear that," Jillian said dryly. Brent was actually total man. A little chauvinistic, a lot wild, but he was the one male Jillian loved and could always count on. He never lied, never let her down. He'd kick Marcus's ass if she asked him to.

Hmm… Food for thought.

"Brent told me I was too emotional," her mom suddenly burst out. "You don't think that, do you, baby?

You love me, right? You think I'm perfect just the way I am, right?"

Lord, how was she supposed to answer that? Jillian gulped. "I do love you."

"Brittany told you about the man I e-mailed on that dating Web site, didn't she?" Her mom tried to laugh. "He was my perfect match, you know, because we liked the same things. Golfing, sailing, Cajun food."

"Mom, you don't like golfing and you don't like sailing. You don't even like swimming. And you hate spicy food. It gives you indigestion."

"But I could have liked those things! He didn't e-mail me back, he didn't even give me a chance, so I e-mailed him again."

A chance! How she was coming to hate that phrase. Jillian covered her eyes with her hand, blocking out the light. "How soon did you e-mail him again?"

"I don't know, ten minutes. It seemed like an eternity."

"Mom," she groaned.

"I might have called him a bastard for ignoring me, I can't remember. Then he finally e-mailed me back and told me to leave him alone. Then he blocked me. That was cruel, right? I cried a little, but just a little. You would have done the same, right?"

And she'd wanted honesty. More fool her. "Mom, maybe Internet dating isn't for you." Jillian could remember a time, as a little girl, when she herself had been fascinated by love and romance. Cinderella and her prince. Her favorite bedtime story.

Reality had a way of destroying those illusions, though. Hurt had a way of obliterating everything else.

She'd thought her mom was long past the need for such things. She'd thought her mom was smarter. "The men on the market are no prizes," she added.

"Brittany says there's a man out there for me. Just waiting for me like Steven waited for her," her mom said. "I'm a woman and I have needs, you know."

"Please." She almost groaned. "Don't tell me about your needs."

Her mom drew in a shuddering breath, probably trying to get herself—and keep herself—under control. She uttered a forced laugh. "Of course I won't, baby. I didn't call to whine. I truly did just want to hear your voice. Everything always seems better when I talk to my sugar. You think I'm wonderful, right? Right?" she insisted, desperate, when Jillian didn't respond right away.

"Of course I think you're wonderful. I love you. Just… rethink the dating thing. Okay?"

"Okay," was the still-forced, still-happy reply.

"I'd love to see you tomorrow afternoon, as well as Brent and Brittany and Granny," Jillian said. "We can have a little party. Will you call them?" That would give her mom something to do. "You took that cooking class and I haven't had a chance to test your new skills."

"Oh, I'd love to cook for you! We could all get together and talk and laugh. No one comes to see me anymore." She clapped after the guilt-inducing words, her happiness no longer forced. "I'll cook your favorite, roasted pork chops and corn bread dressing."

"I'll see you tomorrow, then." Hopefully, the lunch would lift her mom's spirits and put her in a good frame of mind. "Love you, Mom."

"Love you, too, sugar." *Click.*

Confident her mom would be okay, for the night at least, Jillian threw the phone aside and raced out the front door, locking it behind her. She was going to be late. Was already late. Anticipation whipped through her. She couldn't wait to see Marcus in action with a target. Yes, she'd seen him with Ronnie with an *i e,* but his actions had been born of revenge. How would he treat a true target? Touch the small of her back? Would his eyes dip to half-mast as they'd done just before he'd kissed her?

She shivered, then spent the entire drive to the bar thinking about him, picturing his face, eager to see him and chastising herself for it. When she was parked, she checked the driver-side mirror, gave her lips another swipe of gloss, then exited. The gravel parking lot teemed with cars and people—some already drunk.

One guy grabbed his crotch when he spotted her and slurred an invitation to join him for a late-night snack. She could guess what the snack was. Him. Ew. She ignored the invite, but quickened her step toward the shadowed red-and-black building.

Muted music seeped from the walls. The air was cool, fragranced with beer and exhaust and wafts of cigarette smoke. She'd once had to proposition a target at a horse race with manure all around her. Once at a convenience store while eating a warmed-up burrito. Twice at a used-car lot while a salesman tried to pair her with the "perfect" vehicle for her (a convertible for easy access, naturally). This was no worse, she supposed.

Just before she reached the door, a hand shot out from

the darkness and latched onto her arm. She was jerked against a hard, hot body of steel. Jillian gasped. Her heart pounded erratically. Mace—had she remembered her freaking Mace? Didn't matter, really. She'd dropped her purse when the man had grabbed her. What should she do, what should she do?

Acting on pure instinct, she elbowed her captor in the stomach. He hissed out a breath. Spinning, she balled her fist and planted it in his face, hard.

A howl. Then, "Bloody hell."

At the sound of that harsh, sexy voice, she stilled. "Marcus?"

"As if you didn't know," he grumbled. "That hurt!"

"Of course it did. I punched you. Don't ever grab me like that again." Her heart had yet to slow down and had, in fact, sped up with the realization of who held her. His spicy male scent enveloped her, driving away the noxious odors she'd lamented only moments before. She bent down and grabbed her purse strap.

"I think you blackened my eye," he growled. He was angry, yes, but he also sounded grudgingly impressed.

"Big baby." She latched onto his hand and ushered him aside, into the streetlight. Rays of gold ribboned over him, illuminating his savage beauty. His brown eyes were narrowed, the lashes so thick they intertwined. His lips were thinned in pain. And yes, there was a definite circle of red around his left eye.

"Oopsie," she said, trying hard not to laugh.

"Laugh it up, Chuckles. Just remember I now sign your paychecks." He rubbed the slightly swollen bone. "God, beaten up by a girl."

"I told you I could take care of myself. Why did you grab me?"

"I wasn't trying to hurt you. I called out, but you didn't answer. You were about to slam into the door, woman."

"No, I wasn't." Her gaze strayed to the door, closer than she'd realized. Okay, maybe she had been.

His gaze traveled over her dress. "Nice, but unnecessary," he said, his anger seeming to intensify. "You're not supposed to flirt with anyone tonight."

She scowled. "The dress is to help me blend in so I can stay out of the way as my new boss, the office Nazi, has ordered."

"One, I doubt you could ever blend in and two, I'm offended by that description, Dimples. It so happens I'm very easy to work with."

She snorted.

"You didn't let me finish." He faced off with her and their noses almost touched. Their chests *did* touch. "I'm very easy to work with when the employees are reasonable and not prone to violent fits."

Her breath began to come in shallow pants and her blood was heating inside her veins. His warmth was intoxicating. His banter…more so. Beyond them, she could hear the hum of speeding cars, the giddiness of drunken laughter, and somehow they only added to the sensuality of the moment.

Then Marcus cleared his throat and stepped away from her. She took a minute to study the rest of him, desperate to release herself from his magnetic pull. Black button-down shirt, black slacks. Each fit him perfectly and emphasized his delicious muscles. Her mouth suddenly watered. She, too, stepped back.

"Let's go inside," he said, "and get this over with."

He walked away without another word, forcing her to follow him inside the building that was as dark and dim as the night. The moment he opened the doors, music blasted, a *bump, bump,* grind; people strolled past, laughing, talking, drinking.

The intelligent part of Jillian's brain—which was barely functioning lately—told her to run. Run as fast as she could. Go home. Instead, she found herself increasing her pace to keep up with Marcus.

"Pig," she muttered. But this time she was talking about herself.

Twelve

If I were you, I'd have sex with me.

THE WOMAN WAS A MENACE, Marcus thought, but then, he'd already known that. She was too sexy to be loose on the streets and too poisonous to be around without common sense dying a quick, painful death.

Well, that wasn't true. She wasn't always poisonous. Sometimes she was nice, sweet…vulnerable. He still remembered the way she'd looked at him during lunch, her features soft, her eyes needy. Impossibly, he'd liked their easy camaraderie as much as he liked fighting with her.

According to his hormones, she could do no wrong.

He wanted to kiss her again—wanted to do more, really—and almost had while they'd stood outside, shadows and light fighting for dominance around her. Breathtaking, that's what she'd been. She'd punched him, for Christ's sake, and he'd still wanted her.

Do people like us ever get a happy ending? she'd asked him earlier. He'd said no and he'd meant it. He'd tried for a happy ending once, had fought for it with no thought to pride. All he'd gotten was a painful divorce and another lesson in distrust. No thanks, not again. Yet…

Jillian was starting to make him want things. Impossible things. Foolish things. Starting? Ha. He'd wanted impossible things from her the first moment he'd seen her. She was so wrong for him, though, wrong in every way imaginable.

Unfortunately, that made no difference to his dick.

He didn't have to look behind him to know she followed him through the smoke and darkness; he could feel her. His body was hyperaware of her every move, every breath. *Touch me,* he wanted to say to her.

Eye still throbbing, he showed the bouncer who waited at the register his stamped hand, then paid Jillian's cover charge. Without a backward glance, he maneuvered through the thick crowd of dancers, singles and not-so-singles, each looking for a good time. Rock music boomed, so loud his ears rang in protest. Manufactured smoke wafted through the perfumed air, giving off too many clashing scents. He wrinkled his nose.

He'd been here half an hour already. His target was here, too, but he'd been too worried about Jillian to approach the woman. He'd had such stupid thoughts. Had she been in a car accident? Had she decided to quit? Had someone grabbed her and hurt her? Finally he'd gone outside to wait—only to be clocked in the eye for his good deed when she finally did appear.

Disgusted with himself, he found two empty seats at the bar, claimed one for himself, then patted the other.

"Thought we weren't supposed to have contact with each other," she said, but she sat down beside him.

They weren't. He just didn't want to leave her. "Stay." He ordered a beer.

"A beer?" Jillian *tsked* under her tongue. "How interesting."

He frowned at her. When the beer arrived, he turned and faced the dancing, hedonistic crowd. He didn't drink, just watched…waited.

"Ginger ale," Jillian told the bartender, then flicked Marcus a half smile.

His blood hummed, rushing faster, wanting her all the more. He forced his gaze to remain straight ahead, searching for Amy, the night's target. He spotted his prey quickly enough; she was exactly where he'd left her, except now she was seated on the leg of a young man who didn't look old enough to be here. She was licking salt off his lips. Marcus sighed. Looked like he wouldn't have to flirt with her, after all.

"I'm going to film." Beer in hand, Marcus straightened and approached Amy's table. He could feel Jillian's eyes on him, burning deep, so deep.

Amy kissed the boy, a twenty-second Frencher that had the rest of the kids at the table cheering. So much for singing karaoke. The camera hidden in the Buddha necklace he wore captured everything as Marcus pretended to watch the dancers just beyond them. He wouldn't have to flirt or proposition to prove to Jillian that women were as treacherous as she considered men. Amy was proving that quite nicely. Her husband was going to be devastated and Marcus felt a wave of pity for him. *Been there, done that.*

"Hey gorgeous," a sultry voice said beside him. She

purred the words loudly over the music, keeping her face close to his as she stroked her hand down his back. Her perfume was heavy, a little spicy. "Would you like to dance? I promise not to bite you...unless you ask. But then again, you look like a man who likes it rough. Mmm, want me to kiss that eye better?"

He faced her without moving the camera from Amy. The new woman was a delectable blonde with big blue eyes and enough cleavage to lose a small army in. He'd decided to find a willing, easy woman, hadn't he? He'd decided to sleep with someone other than Jillian and rid his body of its constant ache. Hadn't he? He couldn't remember. All he knew was that he wasn't interested in this one. Her hair wasn't dark enough, wasn't curly enough. Her eyes weren't blue enough. She didn't have a smattering of freckles, nor did she have dimples.

"No thanks," he said. "I'm waiting for someone." He twisted toward the bar, about to motion Jillian over, but she was already walking toward him, her expression determined. No, not walking, he realized in the next second. She was sashaying, a temptress. Every man she passed watched her; he had to swallow the sudden lump in his throat.

When she reached Marcus, she draped her arms around his shoulders. Even kissed the side of his neck. Holy hell!

"He's taken, *sweetie,*" she snapped. "And I don't share."

"Yeah, well, maybe he prefers—"

"Get lost before I unstuff your bra. Understand?"

Paling, the clinger scampered away.

Jillian released him, but stayed at his side. She sipped her drink and kept her gaze straight ahead, as though she were reeling from what she'd done and said. Multicolored lights from the strobe took turns highlighting her lovely face.

"You're welcome," she finally said.

"Yeah. Thanks." Seriously. That had turned him on.

Her gaze latched on to Amy, who was still going at it with loverboy, and she shook her head. "I don't care what the target's doing. Women still aren't as bad as men and you still owe me a lot of money."

She was too stiff, too serious and he was suddenly filled with the need to loosen her up. With his free hand, he cupped his ear and pretended he couldn't hear her. "What was that?"

She frowned and repeated her words.

"What?" he said again.

Rather than relax, she scowled and leaned into him, breathing her comment straight into his ear. The side of her sweet, sweet breast meshed into his chest, the decadent scent of her teased his nose and wisps of her soft hair brushed his cheek. The heat of her, always that dangerous heat, enveloped him. He experienced an instant and unwanted hard-on.

Didn't he always when she was near?

Teasing her, he realized, had been a stupid idea. But then, he'd been very stupid lately, especially where she was concerned. When she finished speaking, she didn't move. She stayed just where she was, close to him. Too close, not close enough. Her nose brushed his ear, almost…nuzzling? Maybe not so stupid, after all.

Unbidden, he found his arm reaching for her, wrapping around her waist. His hand gripped the curve of her hip, his palm grazing the top of her ass. Holy hell, it was heaven. A perfect fit, as if her body had been made just for him. He couldn't help himself; he inched his fingers lower. Still she didn't back away, but she did draw in a sharp breath. For more…or did she want him to stop?

She worried her bottom lip, stepped closer. *More.*

The music faded from his ears. The crowd disappeared. There was only Jillian, her lush sexiness, her vivid sapphire eyes. God had done the male population a huge disservice, unleashing this woman into the world. He couldn't move, though. Couldn't find the will. *Mistake. Trouble. Rule two.* The words echoed through his mind, but he ignored them.

As if her thoughts mirrored his, Jillian's cheeks flushed a pretty pink. Her eyelids dipped. The need to kiss her again grew, intensified. Just one more taste and he could sate himself. Just one more…

"I was looking forward to watching you in action," she said breathlessly.

Not the best words to say to an aroused man. He'd have to remember to turn off the volume when he showed the client the video feed. Or maybe he wouldn't have to since the music was so loud.

Someone bumped into Jillian, shoving her forward. They lost eye contact and the spell between them was shattered. Her cheeks reddened, no longer an aroused flush but now an embarrassed crimson.

You can't stand this woman, remember? She's evil. A heartbreaker. At least he'd always know where he stood with her. Still. *Push her away.* "You were about to kiss me again," he said. "We agreed you weren't going to do that anymore."

Slowly her eyes narrowed to tiny slits, blocking the blue irises from his view and revealing only dark, spiky lashes, yet somehow he could see the fire glowing inside. "If I let you keep the cash you owe me, will you swear to jump off a bridge and break your neck?"

"I don't owe you any money. But if I did, I'm sure you'd lose every cent soon enough. You're a terrible gambler." Marcus glanced at his target. Amy was in the process of giving her boyfriend a lap dance, seemingly invigorated by the crowd around her. The guy had his fingers spread over her waist, an I'm-gonna-get-me-some smile on his face.

Yes, the husband's safe, happy world was going to be shattered because of this. It was depressing. What made people cheat? Marcus knew the standard response: *I'm not getting what I need at home.* Why commit, then? Why not leave? Or try harder to make a relationship work?

"I've filmed enough," he said to Jillian.

She nodded, spun on her spiked heels and walked away from him, leaving him confused. She strode to an empty booth in back and eased down, sliding her half-full drink to the side as if she were done with it. Her features were blank, devoid of emotion. Ah. Playtime.

Without asking permission, Marcus joined her and slipped his beer next to her forgotten glass. He wasn't ready to go home. To be brutally honest with himself, he wasn't ready to leave her. Making sure Jillian watched him, he tugged off his necklace and stuffed it into his pocket. "Now you know I'm not trying to film you."

"I don't remember asking you to join me," she said,

brows arched. She removed the flower pinned to her dress and dropped it in her purse. "But just so you know, I'm not filming you, either."

He waved a waitress over. A few seconds later, a bubbly brunette stood in front of them, notepad in hand.

"What can I get you?" she asked.

"Screwdriver," he said and Jillian raised her chin and echoed his order. The waitress nodded and hurried off. "No Hpnotiq?"

She shrugged and her bare shoulders glinted in the light. Pure cream. Totally lickable. "I'm no longer on the clock and I feel like drinking something stronger."

Marcus stretched out his legs and his knees accidentally-on-purpose brushed Jillian's. She jumped. He almost smiled. "That aware of me, are you?"

"That cautious," she stated blandly. She thought about it for a moment, then added, "Maybe disgusted is a better word."

He wasn't offended; he saw the aroused shimmer in her eyes. A shimmer, he was sure, that was reflected in his own. "What happened to our truce?"

"You happened."

"You know, Jillian, I'm really not a bad guy."

"Except for a few rare instances, all I've seen since we met yesterday is a bad guy," she grumbled.

"Your fault, I assure you. And has it only been a day? Seems like a lifetime."

"That's the typical response of a bad person, blaming someone else. And yes, only one day."

"You just gave me the typical response of a woman. Can't accept blame to save her life. And I didn't mean any insult by the forever thing. Quite the opposite. So there's no reason to sound so offended."

Their drinks arrived and for a long while neither spoke. They just sipped and looked out at the crowd of dancers. Their banter had, as always, invigorated him. He wanted it to continue, but knew it had to stop.

Finally Jillian said, "Do your male employees only get one chance to screw up or does that honor go strictly to the women?"

"I've worked with the men before." He gulped the rest of his drink. "They won't screw up."

"You can't know that for sure."

"Yes, I can."

"Double or nothing?"

He didn't hesitate, was actually thrilled to bet. "Done."

Another silence ensued. Why couldn't he bring himself to leave her? "Why'd you choose this line of work?" he found himself asking as he settled deeper into the booth.

A shadow played over her face. "I saw an ad and I needed a job. It…fit my personality. What about you?"

He shrugged. "My father owns a similar agency in Manchester. My mother hated him so much—he liked to dabble with the bait himself—that she moved us to the States when I was just a boy. But I visited him once a year and began to realize it was the perfect job for me."

"Have you ever regretted it?" she asked softly, looking down at the table. She traced a figure eight with her fingertip. "Becoming bait, I mean?"

He could have lied. He *should* lie. Strangely, he felt compelled to give her the truth. "A few times over the years I've questioned my decision to enter this line of work. I saw the kind of person my dad was, saw how alone he was, but I also saw the victims, the ones affected by betrayal, like my mom. I never wanted to be in their place and wanted to help them as best as I could."

"I feel the same," she said, still using that soft tone.

"Ah, a second thing we agree on."

Her lips twitched as she fought a smile. "What was the first thing?"

"You know, I've already forgotten." He signaled for another screwdriver. The waitress quickly delivered the desired drink, but Jillian swiped it. Her fingers brushed his, sending an electric jolt through him. "That's mine."

"People with slow reflexes usually lose," she said, then drained the tangy-sweet liquid and slammed the glass onto the table.

His stomach clenched. There was a droplet on her lip and he wanted so badly to lick it away, to savor her flavor in his mouth. He ordered another drink, half-hoping she'd steal it, too. But she didn't. She only watched him. As he drained the glass, his throat burning, his eyes never left her. She looked so pretty in the dim lighting, smoke wafting around her.

As always, his body responded to her as if she were naked, in his bed, beckoning him to join her.

"I'll have two more," Jillian told the waitress.

By this time, the brunette was no longer bubbly.

"I'll have three," he said.

"Why don't I bring you a dozen?" was the weary response. "That way, I don't have to keep coming over here."

"Good idea," he said at the same moment Jillian said, "Excellent."

"Think you can hold your liquor better than me?" Jillian asked him.

"Think?" All of his gambling genes clapped happily. "Baby, I *know* I can drink you under the table."

The screwdrivers arrived and the waitress slid them onto the table one at a time. She sighed, shook her head. "If you hadn't already planned on calling a cab when you're done here, you should start planning now," she said, then walked away to fill someone else's order.

"We'll call a cab for sure," Jillian said, claiming three of the glasses. Marcus did the same. She downed one; he downed two. She downed two more and he finished off another. When he slammed the empty glass on the table, she laughed.

To Marcus, the sound of her laughter was magical. Husky and wine-rich. Her entire face lit with her amusement. He had to kiss her again, he mused, before the night was over. Had to hold her in his arms, feel her breasts straining against his chest. Hear her moans in his ears.

Yes, his foggy mind said. *Yes.*

"Technically some people would consider this a date," she said. Already her words were slightly slurred. "Just out of curiosity, what do you think is a woman's biggest mistake on the first date? I want to make sure I do it."

"Putting out," he answered immediately. His words were a little slurred, too. "Usually I'd say not putting out, but I'm making an exception tonight."

She chuckled. "You're cute, you know that?" Once she realized what she'd said, she shook her head, froze, lost her smile. She pressed her fingers into her temples. "Wrong action. Dizzy. Wrong words. Stupid."

"Well, I think you're sexy as hell," he admitted darkly.

She blinked over at him. "You do?"

"Yeah."

"Really?"

"Yes. Okay? Yes."

"You shouldn't," she admonished without heat.

"I know," he grumbled. "Just like you shouldn't think I'm cute."

Her shoulders slumped. "I know. We should hate each other right now. You're my enemy."

He shrugged and offered, "Enemies sometimes sleep together."

She actually thought about it for several long, protracted minutes. "If you were nice, I could…" She shook her head, frowned and closed her eyes against another wave of dizziness. "No, I can't."

"I can be nice," he rushed out. An image of the two of them in bed once again flashed through his mind. Why not? he wondered suddenly. They both knew the rules of the game. Nothing serious. No marriage. No babies. Sure, he might want those things in his weakest moments, but not with Jillian. Her, he just plain wanted. Hard and long and forever.

No, not forever, he reminded himself sternly.

"You can't be nice," she said, earnest. "I don't believe you."

"Let me prove it." Before he could stop himself, he reached out and laced their fingers together. Her skin was smooth where his was calloused. "While we're having sex, I'll be so nice you'll think I'm pumping you full of sugar."

She ran her bottom lip between her teeth. "Are you going to do the clockwise swirl with a twist?"

His brow furrowed in confusion. "I honestly have no idea what the hell that is." Had she done that with someone else? And why did the thought infuriate him? Make him seethe with jealousy?

A laugh escaped her, a little nervous, a lot excited. "You really want to do this?" she whispered, a scandalized edge to the words. "Won't it break your precious rules?"

"I'm the boss and I say we forget the rules. They're stupid and I'm nice."

For a moment, she eyed him up and down like he was her favorite candy. He'd long since lost power over his own mind, his own body, his own words. He knew this was wrong, but he didn't care. He wanted her, had to have her. His head swam dizzily with the knowledge.

"You'll leave immediately afterward?" she asked.

"Without cuddling."

"Promise?"

"Promise."

Her lips parted with a heated breath. "Okay. Let's go to my place."

Thirteen

Let's do breakfast tomorrow.
Shall I call you or nudge you?

This is the first intelligent thing I've done all week, Jillian thought the entire cab ride home.

As predicted, neither she nor Marcus had felt sober enough to drive, so they'd called a cab from the club. That they'd had to do such a thing should have given her pause. But she couldn't stop thinking that with this act, with sex—with Marcus—she would finally rid her body of its infatuation with the man. Finally gain some perspective where he was concerned.

Finally be at peace. Sweet peace.

After tonight, she could be in his presence and not desire him. She would have been there and done that, would have tasted him fully. Since it was bound to be a disappointment—surely it couldn't be as good as her body expected it to be, *nothing* could—she wouldn't have to wonder anymore. The mystery of him would be dead.

At least, that's what her fuzzy mind kept telling her.

Lord, she wanted him. All evening, she'd watched him. She'd wanted to shove that blond clinger away from him, not just snap at her. The force of her jealousy had surprised her.

Right now she craved another kiss. Craved so much more than a kiss, actually. A tremor slid down her spine, delicious, a prelude to what was to come. *Get your mind off Marcus before you jump him right here.* Vision fogging, she pulled her gaze to the window.

First the scenery provided a view of wide-open spaces, then lush-green trees began to whiz past, interspersed with other cars. Her head swam. Bright streetlights illuminated Marcus's face—when had she turned her attention back to him?—followed quickly by darkness, then light, then darkness. Just behind him, stars twinkled like fresh-cut diamonds in the black silk sky.

Jillian's blood was on fire.

Eager, needy, she could barely sit still, was even leaning toward him. Or was her world simply tilting? She didn't think she'd ever wanted a man this much. Naked. Inside her. Shouting her name.

"Wanting a kiss, Dimples?" Marcus asked, a seductive whisper.

She shook her head, then cursed herself for the dizzying action. The nickname didn't seem so bad just then. It almost sounded…affectionate. Playful. "No kiss. Not now. If we start, we won't stop."

"That's a bad thing?"

Her eyes wandered to his lips, his pink, pleasure-giving lips. Deliciously bad…and delicious was dangerous. The night *had* to be a disappointment. "Are you into anything kinky?" When she realized she was talking loud enough for the cabbie to hear—the man was grinning at them in the rearview mirror—she leaned into Marcus and whispered the same question in his ear. For some reason, the words emerged just as loudly.

He licked his lips. "I guess you'll find out."

"I hope you're not," she told him adamantly.

His eyelids dropped to half-mast, but she saw the confusion in his gaze. "Silly. Why?"

"Need it to be bad," she admitted, "very bad, so we'll never want to do this again."

"But bad can be good," he said, his voice dipping huskily. "So good." His arms wrapped around her waist and he tugged her onto his lap. Oopsie. She must have forgotten to buckle. "Mmm, your nipples are hard. Your skin is soft." His warm breath caressed her neck; his hands slid up her back and tangled in her hair. "No devil horns," he said, massaging her scalp.

Chuckling, she leaned further into him and licked her tongue into his white-hot mouth. "No fangs."

He barked out an unrestrained laugh. "What about a tail?" His fingers skimmed her ass and she shivered.

"No tail." The statement gasped breathlessly from her. How much longer until they reached her house?

"Nope, no tail."

She glanced out the window again and was pleasantly surprised to realize they were winding through her neighborhood. Redbrick houses, wraparound porches, well-kept lawns, parked sedans and minivans. Finally the cab eased to a stop in her driveway.

Without dislodging her, Marcus withdrew his wallet and paid the fare. She opened the door and toppled out. She laughed, he laughed. How long had it been since she'd felt this playful? This happy? Excited?

Jillian twirled, her arms splayed wide. "I could dance."

Marcus swooped her up in his arms and she wound her hand through his silky hair. "Dance later."

"Later," she agreed, because she was thrilled to be where she was.

"We're going to regret this," he said, but he didn't sound upset. He carried her to the porch and only tripped twice.

"Regret—do you care?" She skimmed down his body, absorbing his strength, his animal heat. *Soooo* good.

"Hell, no."

She rooted through her purse for her keys. "It's not like we're flying to Vegas to get married," she rationalized.

"We're just two people having no-strings sex."

"Wild, raunchy, no-strings sex." A frown pulled at her mouth. "No, no. Not wild. Not raunchy. Bad sex. We're having bad sex." She found the key at long last. As she inserted it into the knob, Marcus closed in behind her. His breath fanned her neck before his lips scorched her skin with a kiss. His tongue flicked out, branding her.

Oh. More. Please. The door opened, but she didn't step inside. Not yet. She turned and gave Marcus her mouth. Tasting him became the most important thing in her world, her sole reason for living. Immediately his tongue thrust deep and his decadent flavor filled her. She tugged at his shirt, ripping it from his pants.

He backed her into the house and tore his mouth slightly away. "Do you have a roommate?"

"No." The word panted from her.

Ziiiip. Down went her zipper, open went the choke collar of her dress, then Marcus was shoving the material down her hips. It soon pooled at her feet. "Step out of it," he commanded.

She did. He stopped moving, stopped breathing perhaps. She stood in her black lace bra and matching panties, her black boots riding the curves of her legs. "Well?"

"Bloody hell," he said in a reverent whisper.

Her lips curled into a smile. "Take off your clothes. Wait. First close the door!"

After he'd locked them inside, he reached behind and tugged his shirt over his head. Or tried to. The buttons were too tight and caught on his jaw. Jillian bit several off, spitting them out as she moved on. Finally he was able to toss the thing aside. He unsnapped his pants in record time and, wavering slightly, kicked them off, leaving him in tight black briefs, bronzed skin and sexy muscles. Her mouth watered for him.

His body was a work of art. His nipples were small, brown and puckered, his stomach total washboard perfection, ripped with rope after rope of strength. The muscles that tapered from his waistline... *Hmmm. I'll have to lick that line.* A fine sprinkling of blond hair trailed below his navel, leading straight to a long, thick erection.

"Where's your bedroom?" he asked, his tone strained.

She pointed without taking her gaze from him. Her hand was shaky. Her body was needy.

"Too far a walk." He grabbed her, dragged her into the

living room and tumbled her onto the couch. His weight pinned her down deliciously, soft suede providing a perfect cushion.

Instinctively, she spread her legs, welcoming him close. "If you say someone else's name at any time, I'll kill you. I want this to be bad, but not *that* bad."

"Someone else's name?" He snorted. "Baby, you're all I've been able to think about since the first moment I met you."

"That's because you hate me," she said as she arched her back and meshed the core of herself against his erection. Her eyes closed in sweet surrender and she chewed on her bottom lip. "Mmm."

He sucked in a breath. "I like you right now."

She arched again, moaned again. "That's because I'm underneath you and I'm practically naked."

"Completely naked very soon." There was a pause, heavy and laden with tension. "If you say another man's name, I'll kill *him*."

"Deal."

He licked her ear, the one with the earrings, then licked her neck and pressed his erection between her legs. "You taste good."

"You feel good." Her fingers gripped his back, pinching the skin. "My head is spinning and my body is burning."

"Mine, too." He palmed her breast. "Do you have four breasts or am I seeing things?"

"Seeing things. Lick them. All four of them." The words emerged as a desperate moan.

He shoved the cup of her bra down and anchored it under her breast, plumping the flesh higher for his view.

For his sampling. Then his mouth descended. Hot, so hot, like his body. He sucked. Hard, so hard. Like his body. He swirled his tongue expertly.

"Oh, God." Her hips came off the couch at the sharp sensation and ground into his penis. "Yes, yes." She had to remind herself that this was one night, that she didn't even like this man, that she'd experienced better sex at some point in her life. Surely she had. "This means nothing," she gasped out.

"Less than nothing. Your breasts are heaven."

He gave the other one his full attention, biting until she cried out, then he licked the sting away. That sting nearly undid her…but not the way she expected. She liked it. Oh, how she liked it. Wanted more. It made her feel alive, on fire. Like a wire was connected to her nipples and every time Marcus bit them, a jolt of electricity traveled through her.

"I don't want to be gentle," he growled. He squeezed her hip in a vise-like grip.

"No. Not gentle." She wanted to be taken, ravished. The desire embarrassed her, frightened her. Hard, forceful, animalistic, that's how she wanted it. What was wrong with her?

Wasn't she supposed to want it soft? Tender?

"Hard," Marcus said. But he was torn. Usually he took his time with a woman, enjoyed her. He rarely did relationships, which meant he got one shot to get the sex right. Right now he was on fire, and the fire was demanding fast and rough, even though he knew he should slow down—no, never slow—but the need…it was so dark, he couldn't fight it, didn't want to fight it anymore.

Everything about this moment was seductive. Passion was clamoring for release, hot and heavy. He felt violent, erotic, and he knew it was wrong, but oh, he could eat this woman up, one tasty bite at a time. *Would* eat her up. *No, you'll hurt her. Don't hurt her.*

"Jillian," he managed to get out between clenched teeth. He couldn't give in to those dark desires, couldn't give in…please give in.

"Marcus," she panted. Eyes closed, she ground against him.

He loved when she did that, but every time she moved she pushed him closer to the edge. Soon he might lose control, might do something that would scare her. But… "Jillian," he said again. He had to make her understand, had to slow things down.

"Don't stop" was her only reply.

Though it required intense concentration, he forced his body to still and stared down at Jillian. Her dark curls had come undone and they spilled over the couch pillows. Her skin was flushed with pink desire. She was ecstasy, a goddess of pleasure, and if he didn't make her feel as wild as he did… Soon, soon. Please soon.

He needed her writhing, his name on her lips, his name in her mind. His name on her every cell, branded deep. He was like a caveman, possessive, primitive. Her breasts overflowed in his hands. Her stomach was soft and flat. Perfect. Her legs were tapered. He considered asking her to wear those boots all night long.

Still holding himself back, still trying to regain some semblance of restraint, he said, "How rough can you take it?" His voice was a growl.

She didn't look scared. In fact, his words seemed to excite her. "As rough as you can give it. Just…make me scream."

"Are you sure?" A bead of sweat trickled down his temple and splashed onto his shoulder. He was practically humming with the force of his need.

In lieu of an answer, Jillian smiled wickedly and sank her nails into his back. She clawed him, drawing blood. He hissed in a breath as his cock jerked in arousal. Yes, yes, that was exactly what he craved. Motions jerky, he ripped off her bra, then reached between them and ripped off her panties. The flimsy material tore easily.

She fisted his hair and tugged him to her mouth. Their teeth banged together. Her taste flooded him, tangy like orange juice, smooth like vodka, both urging him to take more of her. He tunneled his fingers through the fine hair between her legs and shoved two fingers deep inside her.

"Yes!" she shouted.

She was wet, but he wanted her wetter. As he worked her, she gasped and moaned and writhed. "Come," he demanded. "Come for me."

"Mar-Marcus." She struggled for breath as her inner walls clenched tight, clasping onto his fingers and holding them captive. She threw back her head, black curls tumbling in every direction. "Marcus!" she shouted as she came.

He could have come, too, just hearing his name on her lips. Her nails sank into his back again, then clawed their way to his chest. Even when her spasms stopped, she continued to scratch him and he continued to work her with his fingers, keeping up the frantic rhythm. Maybe she liked the darkness, too. Maybe she truly wanted it as rough as he could give it.

"We're not done," she said.

"No. Not done."

"More." She gripped his underwear and pushed it down his legs.

He grabbed her hands and pinned them above her head. "Wrap your legs around my waist."

She did so without protest and he felt the heavy weight of her boots. Cool, an erotic contrast to her hot skin. She was panting and her breasts rose and fell with every intake of breath. Her pink nipples were pearled, begging for attention. Muted beams of light slithered in from the windows and poured over her naked skin.

She was beauty.

His cock reached for her. Arching up, she bit his collarbone. He growled in ecstasy. "Harder."

Her sharp little teeth drew blood.

Only then did he slam inside her. The entire couch rocked with the motion. Jillian screamed his name. His eyes squeezed closed at the heady bliss. This was heaven. Paradise. Hot, tight, soaking wet.

He moved in and out of her, fast, faster. Hard, harder. He couldn't hold back and knew she didn't want him to. She was as wild as he was, bucking, just like he'd wanted. She nipped her way up his neck. He released her wrists with one hand, still holding them captive with the other. He used his free hand to cant her face to the side. And then he was biting the cord of her neck.

She came.

He bit and sucked and moved his hand to her ass,

squeezing, kneading, spreading her wider. The convulsions of her orgasm intensified; she clenched and clenched around him. Wet beyond his wildest dreams. She screamed, loud and long. That was all he needed to send him over the edge. His muscles tightened and a roar spilled from his lips.

"Marcus," she gasped. Sweat was pouring from her skin, maybe his.

"Jillian." He struggled to draw in a breath, struggled to get his heartbeat under control.

She didn't try to move away. "Good."

He held her tight, not wanting to leave. "So good."

Fourteen

*How about you sit on my lap and we'll talk about the
first thing that pops up?*

GEORGIA CARRINGTON wanted to cry (again), to sob
(again), to *scream* (finally!), but not for the right reason.

A few hours ago, Wyatt had picked her up and taken
her to drinks with his colleagues, then to dinner alone,
where he'd promptly dumped her flat on her ass. She
should have known, should have expected.

For the first time in their yearlong relationship, she'd
let him see her without makeup and had not used tanning
cream. Seemed like such a little thing, but it had been
major for her. She'd wanted to test him, to see how Wyatt
would react to her less-than-immaculate appearance. And
what had he done the first time she had looked less than
perfect? First he'd cringed and asked her if she wanted
to reschedule. He then apologized to his friends, saying
she was "under the weather." Then, at dinner he'd been
quiet, brooding.

"What, no marriage proposal?" she'd asked sarcastically.

He'd flushed. "We'll talk about it when you're feeling better."

That's when she'd snapped. "I feel fine! This is me, Wyatt. The real me. Warts and all. Look. Really look and see."

His cheeks had reddened further. "Are you *trying* to embarrass me? To punish me? Well, you've done a damn good job. Georgia, all I've ever wanted to do is worship you, but you won't let me. Hell, you won't even let me show you off. I try and you come looking like a…like *that*." He waved a hand in her direction.

"I'm not a show pony, Wyatt. I don't want my teeth and hair checked every time I step out of the house. I just want to be loved."

Of course, he'd then decided they had different ideas of what love meant and needed to go their separate ways.

"Bastard," she muttered, wanting to cry because she'd been proven right. Men only cared about her face and body. They didn't care about *her*. Well, she didn't want to be on a pedestal any longer.

Her eyes burned, but she held back the tears. She wanted love, marriage and babies, damn it. She wanted happily-ever-after. She wanted…more. And she wanted to know it wouldn't crumble at the first sign of trouble or ugliness.

Ugly. Just the word haunted her. She'd been an ugly child and an even uglier teenager. Too tall, too thin, too pale, hair too different and certainly too *red*. Weird, asymmetric features. Her mouthful of silver braces hadn't helped. Her thick eyeglasses hadn't either.

She'd been unpopular, noticed only by those who needed someone to taunt. And not a single boy had asked her out. Not even the nerdiest of the nerds had found her appealing. So of course Brent Greene, Jillian's older brother, had steered clear of her. He'd been one of the popular boys and all the girls had lusted for him.

Even her.

Every time she remembered the way he'd run from her, avoided her, she hurt. Bad. To this day she couldn't look at spaghetti without crying about him.

Georgia expelled a shaky breath. She hadn't gone on her first date until the advanced age of nineteen, when her breasts had finally developed, her facial features rounded, she'd put on a little weight and had doused her skin with tanning cream. What's more, her braces had been removed and she'd bought contacts.

That first date, a guy named Harper, had talked his way into her pants without any real effort. She'd been so desperate for affection, so needy, the memory still embarrassed her. He'd complimented her loveliness a few times and hadn't been able to look away from her. The sex had been…okay. Uneventful. Nothing to giggle or sigh over.

Afterward, he'd never called her again. She'd been too easy, she had realized. But she'd learned a valuable lesson that night. Look pretty, but remain aloof. And so, with that new knowledge, she'd embarked on a dating odyssey. She'd dated constantly, so many different men. They'd only ever seen her at her best and they were never allowed to touch her.

Each one of them had worshipped her, just as Wyatt claimed he wanted to do. They couldn't compliment her enough on her figure, her face, her hair. Her confidence had bloomed and bloomed and bloomed. Then she'd met Wyatt, a financial advisor. While he'd seemed supremely interested in her face and body, just like all the others, she'd fallen for him because he'd also seemed interested in her mind. He'd taken the time to find out her likes and dislikes. He'd asked her opinion on everything from politics to dessert. Maybe they hadn't had all that much in common, but at least he'd made the effort to get to know her.

Finally, she'd let another man take her to bed. It had been wonderful. Very satisfying physically, but emotionally… She rubbed her temples to ward off the sudden ache.

Then, a few months ago, everything had changed. Wyatt had asked her to marry him. Almost instantly, he seemed to stop caring about her as a person. She'd become an object, a thing, a *possession,* just as she'd been for everyone else.

So more and more she'd worried and fretted about the day Wyatt would see her as the less-than-perfect woman she really was. She'd wondered what would happen if he saw past her outer shell to the ugly, needy little girl inside. Now she knew.

Why did forever seem possible for everyone but her?

Georgia lay in bed, staring up at the wispy white canopy that draped from the four posters of her bed. Even through the material, she could see the plastic glow-in-the-dark stars she'd pasted on the ceiling. A little while ago, she'd downed her sixth glass of wine, so the stars were spinning. She sighed again. She should have stopped at two, but she'd thought of Wyatt and drank, thought of Brent and drank even more.

During the day, she could pretend to be carefree and lust after handsome men, but here, now, the truth shone too brightly to be denied. Ironic, considering how dark it was. Nights were always bad for her, alone with her thoughts, alone with her stress. Tonight was worse than usual. Could she ever have the happily-ever-after she craved?

Her doorbell suddenly rang, and she bolted upright.

The action caused her head to spin. Georgia groaned and glanced at the clock on her nightstand. It was eleven o'clock. Who would be visiting her at this hour? Wyatt? Had he come to apologize? Did he want to get back together? Well, the answer was no!

The bell rang again.

Out of habit, she studied herself in the far mirror above the dresser. The pretty pink nightgown and matching robe she wore were a little wrinkled. Makeup—check. Streaked with tears, but still in place. She'd applied it before lying down, spackling her shield in place. Again, out of habit—a habit she'd fallen into when she and Wyatt had first started dating, just in case he stopped by at night. Even after they'd stopped sleeping together, she'd kept her mask in place. A girl never knew when she'd need to look her best.

Hair—a little messy. She scrambled up and grabbed her nearest brush. Let Wyatt see the woman he'd once wanted to marry—the woman he'd never have again. Scowling, she jerked the bristles through her hair. She tossed the brush on the couch as she stumbled to the front door. Her living room was a plethora of colors and textures. Violet, sapphire, ruby. Wicker, velvet, silk. Everything that complemented her skin tone.

Ding dong. "I can see your shadow, Georgia. I know you're there," a male voice said. A sexy male voice that did not belong to Wyatt. A sexy male voice that in fact belonged to Brent Greene. A shiver stole through her; his was a voice she'd recognize anywhere, anytime.

She was immensely glad it was him—and she shouldn't be. Not now. "What are you doing here, Brent?" But she already knew the answer.

"I wanted to see you. Open up."

"I could have company."

"You don't," he said. His voice was tight.

"I've had too much to drink. You don't want to be around me right now."

"Sweetheart, that makes me want to be around you even more."

Sweetheart... Everyone had a pet name for her (Wyatt had called her Pumpkin because of her hair), but only Brent made her feel...cherished. "Brent," she said, leaning her forehead against the cool wood of the door. *Send him away. Before you forget your pride.*

More than talking to him, looking at him always made her chest hurt. She had to constantly remind herself that he wasn't the man for her, that he had rejected her over and over again. That he *could* have had her at one time but had found her repulsive.

"Georgia," he said. "Please."

She swayed, a little dizzy. She loved it when he said her name, even more than she liked it when he called her sweetheart. She'd told her friends that she'd stopped sleeping with Wyatt because she hadn't decided about his marriage proposal. But she knew the real reason, the reason she would not have admitted even to herself if she hadn't been tipsy. She'd begun to feel like she was cheating on Brent. Which was silly. Absolutely foolish.

"I just want to talk," he said softly.

Hand shaky, unable to help herself, she unlocked the door and opened it. Brent leaned against the frame, one arm braced over his head. So masculine, so alluring. The porch light spilled over his features, reverent, golden. His dark hair was in total disarray, hanging just over his brows. His lips were curled in a welcoming smile.

While she had to fight for perfection, he exuded it effortlessly.

He wore faded Levis and a white T-shirt. The sight of those clothes hugging his strength made her mouth water. "What do you want to talk about?" she asked, striving for a casual tone.

"Can I come in?"

"No." She spread her arms, blocking the entrance. If he came inside, she might kiss him. Or ask him for more. Now, as vulnerable and wine-drenched as she was, she would not be able to resist his potent allure. "Now, again, what do you want to talk about?"

"Anything." He shook his head, self-deprecating. "I couldn't sleep. I kept thinking about you, about the sadness I heard in your tone today, and decided to come over."

"I'm seeing someone, Brent," she lied, the words practically ripped from her. She couldn't tell him the truth; he would pounce on her—and she would let him. "You can't keep contacting me like this." As always, it *hurt* to tell him no, but he was wrong for her, so wrong. He didn't want the real her any more than Wyatt had.

"I don't want you to see him anymore," Brent bit out. "He's not right for you. I feel it in my soul."

"And you are? Right for me, that is?"

"Yes." There was not a single shred of doubt in his tone. He stepped forward, crowding her, drowning her in his hot scent. "You're mine."

Air sizzled in her lungs at the possessive proclamation. As flirtatious as he was, he didn't usually speak to her like that.

"Just give me a chance to show you how good it could be between us." His features were intense, beseeching.

"No." With him, she'd worry about her appearance more than she ever had with Wyatt or anyone else. *Him,* she would lose with the first gray hair or the first pound she gained. And losing him would kill her—she knew that, too.

"Why not?" he demanded. "And don't you dare tell me you love that son-of-a-bitch Wyatt. He's wrong for you and deep down you know it, too."

"You want the truth?" she found herself lashing out. Without the wine in her system, she might never have told him. Now, the words seemed to pour from her. "Fine, I'll tell you. You thought I was ugly in school. You—"

"I never thought you were ugly," he interrupted harshly. Fire blazed in his eyes.

She continued as if he hadn't spoken. "You couldn't get out of your house fast enough when I stayed the night with Jillian. You only want me now because you finally think I'm pretty. Well, what happens if I change for the worse, huh? What then?" She poked him in the chest with the tip of her nail. "Will you still want me?"

"Yes." He sounded confident.

"Prove it."

His lids narrowed to thin slits, but somehow she could still see that his dark eyes were swirling and churning. "I wanted you in school. *That's* why I always ran from you. You were too young for me and you were my kid sister's friend. If I'd stayed around you, I would have done something about the attraction. And I wouldn't have been able to live with the guilt."

Liar! But oh, the words were potent. Beguiling. She almost sank into his open arms. Almost pressed her lips against his. "I'm still younger than you and I'm still your sister's friend."

"Yes, but now you're a woman." He growled low in his throat, like an animal. "What's it going to take to prove to you that I love you, to prove that I love who you are, not what you look like? This?" He grabbed her shoulders and hauled her to him.

Her chest banged into his, her breasts suddenly meshed against him. His mouth swooped down on hers, his tongue plundering deep and sweet and just right. She moaned, she couldn't help herself.

Without her permission, her arms reached up and wound around his neck, locking him in place. As their tongues battled, she realized she'd never tasted anything more decadent, anything more intoxicating.

He didn't slow, didn't give her time to think. With one hand, he cupped the back of her neck and angled her head for more of her mouth. He tangled the other hand in her hair, squeezing, tightening on the locks as if he feared letting go. He fed her kiss after amazing kiss.

Here it is; here's your dream. Here's more.

His heat invaded her blood, her every cell, and it was both ecstasy and torture. Heaven and hell. Because she knew, good as it was, she could never have it again. Being perfect was too stressful. *No more,* she thought. No more stress. No more Brent. But, but…

She wanted him so badly. Always had. Wanted him in every way imaginable. There was no denying it now. The kiss deepened and pleasure speared her, such intense pleasure. Only then did Georgia realize she was rubbing against him, arching her pubis into his thick, hard erection, mimicking sex. Her hands had abandoned his silky hair and were clenching his ass.

She jerked away, not touching him in any way. "No!"

Brent scrubbed a hand over his face. "I love you, Georgia," he said, panting. "I've always loved you."

She shook her head and backed up three steps. Her breathing was as choppy, erratic, and shallow as his. Her body ached for another kiss, a caress. Something, anything from him. Only him. "No. You love perfection."

A muscle ticked beneath his right eye. "Love perfection? When I'd never measure up?" he scoffed. "I love the freckles underneath that makeup. I love the high-pitched sound of your voice when you're happy. I love—"

"No," she insisted, afraid to believe. "No."

He ran his tongue over his teeth. "Show me your worst, then, sweetheart. Let me prove that I don't want you for your pretty face. At least give me a chance."

At his words, a wonderful, horrible idea drifted through her mind. Her eyes widened as she contemplated the only thing she could do to prove her appearance meant nothing to him. Maybe it was the wine…

maybe it was desperation…either way, she blinked up at Brent.

"Okay. I'll show you my worst tomorrow," she said, and shut the door in his face.

WHAT WAS she planning to do?

Brent remained at her door for a long while, grinning like an idiot. What she planned didn't matter, he supposed. Right now, all he cared about was what had just happened.

He'd almost made love to her right there in the doorway. Outside, under her porch light, for anyone to see. She probably had no idea how close he'd come to jerking off her gown and tumbling her onto the cold cement. But he'd kept his hands in her hair, ever the gentleman, not wanting to scare her away. Not when he was finally making progress.

And what sweet progress it was!

He'd known her forever, it seemed, but tonight had been a first. In the past, she'd always rebuffed him, always pushed him away. This time, however, she had let him kiss her, let him taste and touch her like a lover. And she'd responded!

Brent had waited for this moment for more years than he could remember and it had surpassed his every dream, every fantasy. What he'd told her was the truth. When they were younger, he'd craved her. He'd wanted. They were only a few years apart in age, but back then she had seemed infinitely younger. Still, she'd been the cutest little thing he'd ever seen. Her glasses had constantly slid off her nose and her smile… those silver braces had been adorable.

Her hair hadn't changed, was still the same silky red mass he'd always wanted to plow his fingers through. She was no longer the shy pixie who tugged at his heart, but he found that didn't lessen his attraction. He liked the memory of who she'd been and the knowledge of who she was: assertive, strong, undeniably sexy. Except…

Brent traced a finger over his lips. There at the end, right before Georgia had closed the door, there'd been an unholy gleam in her eyes. Yes, that was the best word to describe it. *Unholy.* What was she up to?

At first, she'd been unsteady on her feet and so vulnerable and sad that his heart had squeezed painfully. Perversely, he hoped there was trouble in paradise. Hoped she was beginning to realize that idiot Wyatt, whom he'd never met but hated on principle, was wrong for her. He didn't feel guilty for that thought. Georgia was his; she belonged to him. No one else. After that kiss, he was through being nice and playing things safe. Through being afraid of scaring her away. Through trying to win her slowly but surely.

Brent was going on full attack.

"Bring it on," he whispered to her door. "Show me your worst." He could hardly wait.

GEORGIA WOBBLED to her bathroom and stared at her reflection, a pair of scissors in her hand. She's already drunk another glass of wine and her head was spinning more than before. *Let me prove I don't want you for your pretty face,* he'd said.

If she did this, he'd leave her alone; she knew he would. But…*I'm so tired of pretending to be perfect,* she thought again. Better to have him repulsed by her than to endure another moment of worry. Was her hair in place? Her makeup on smoothly? Her body free of lines and cellulite? Ugh! She felt like a rubber band, stretched so tightly she could snap at any moment.

"Just do it," she growled. "He wants to see your worst, so show him your worst."

Before she could talk herself out of it, Georgia began cutting. And cutting. And cutting.

Fifteen

That outfit looks good on you…but it would look a lot better in a crumpled heap next to my bed.

JILLIAN'S WHOLE BODY ACHED. Her head pounded with the force of a war drum. Her arms throbbed. Her neck throbbed. Her legs throbbed. She felt as if she had gone a few (thousand) rounds with a heavyweight boxer.

Was she sick? Dying?

Lord, what had happened last night? It'd been Saturday, a workday for everyone at CAM, and she'd gone to a club, had a few drinks—hey, what was thumping under her chest? And why was she so hot? It was like a heating blanket had been wrapped around her and turned on high.

Go back to sleep, her mind beseeched. *Dream and fantasize.* "Can't," she mumbled, smacking her dry lips together. She had to go to work and…wait, she didn't work today. Last night—Saturday. Today—Sunday. Her day off. She did have a lunch date with her mom, though.

Groaning, Jillian cracked open her eyelids, gradually

allowing light to seep into her consciousness. The sun was bright, too bright, and orange-gold spots clouded her vision. After a few seconds, she was able to make out lots and lots of bronzed, bruised and bitten skin—and it wasn't hers. This skin had been poured over lean, hard muscle.

"What the—" A sharp pain tore through her head and she expelled another groan. Even her stomach hurt, twisting and churning with nausea. Her mouth was cottony. How much had she drunk last night?

She stared down at the man she'd obviously slept with, a tantalizing image flashing through her head. An image of her new boss, naked, pounding into her. Sweet Christ. Horror slithered through her. She'd slept with Marcus, and those images were actually memories. And they were delicious. Her horror intensified.

How was she supposed to handle this?

"Wake up," she said, her voice shaky.

He moaned and said, "Quiet. Head hurts."

Husky voice, slightly accented. Last night that voice had told her sexy things. What would it tell her now? She gulped. Marcus was draped across her couch on his stomach, his head turned to the side, his back lined with scratches. Both of his arms were thrown over his head. He had messy hair, lush pink lips and light beard stubble. His lashes were long and spiky, black.

His hot, male scent—a fragrance made only for sin—drenched her, already fused with her skin, her cells. Oh, there was going to be trouble now. She'd never look at him the same way again. Now, every time she was in his presence, she'd think of his penis pumping inside her. Freaking great!

She jolted to her feet, away from him. Big mistake. Her stomach rolled and she wobbled. She raced to the bathroom, but never actually threw up. Just gagged. Shaking, she brushed her teeth and studied her reflection.

"Dear God," she rasped out. She was naked (except for the boots), and there were bruises and bite marks all over her skin, just like there'd been on M—*him*. Could she die of embarrassment? Please!

"I'll never drink again," she muttered. Apparently when she did, she jumped good-looking men and let them do all kinds of naughty things to her. Bite her—sure. Spank her—where's the paddle? How could she have slept with her boss and sworn enemy? How?

Her hair was a mass of black tangles. Her lips were swollen and her mascara was smeared down her cheeks. With an unsteady hand, she grabbed her bathrobe from its hook and tied the white material around herself. She washed her face, but the cold water did nothing to cool her overheated skin.

Never had she experienced as many intense orgasms as she had last night. And Marcus had been the one to give them to her. "You don't even like him," she reminded herself.

Jillian frowned as she pulled off the boots. Last night, Marcus had been charming, solicitous. Irresistible. She'd actually had fun with him. For the first time in years, she'd relaxed with a man. Talked to a man who wasn't a target.

What's a woman's biggest mistake on a first date? I want to make sure I do it.

Putting out.

The conversation played through her mind. He'd had

a wicked twinkle in his eyes when he said it, a seductive devil come to lure her, tempt her.

You'll leave immediately afterward?

Without cuddling.

They'd both come; they'd both gotten off. He should have left. Instead, he'd lured her into his arms and she'd let him. Even wrapped her arms around him, content, and drifted into a sated sleep. And a part of her was *glad* for it.

Had he woken up by now? What was he thinking? Tentative, she strode into the living room. He was already up and pulling on his briefs and jeans. She caught a flash of his ass, then he was zipping. Acting nonchalant, she leaned against the wall and crossed her arms over her middle. Her cheeks heated when she spied the torn heap of her panties and bra.

What if he was wallowing in regret? What if he hated himself for being with her? The very things she *should* be feeling. "We probably shouldn't talk about this," she said as breezily as possible.

He flicked her a quick glance over his shoulder. His brown eyes were hard, almost black, and his expression was stern. There was a red circle under his left eye. "That's what you really want?"

No. "Yes." Conversing about what they'd done would be too embarrassing, would make things too…raw.

Frowning, silent, he bent down and retrieved his shirt. His muscles jumped beneath his skin, yet he still managed to move with fluid grace.

"Am I fired?" she asked, still trying to sound casual. "I did break another rule."

For a long while, he didn't speak. Just silently buttoned

up his shirt—minus a few buttons. "You don't want to quit?" he asked softly.

He sounded half hopeful and half...scared? "No."

"No, you're not fired. I broke the rule, too, and I'm not going to fire myself."

Her eyes narrowed. She heard something in his tone, an unspoken *I think sleeping together was punishment enough.* "After this," she found herself saying, "I'm sure I'll have to have therapy to combat post-traumatic stress disorder."

"Don't try to tell me you didn't have a good time," he gritted out. "I know for a fact that you did. I've got the marks to prove it."

Yes, she'd enjoyed every moment in his arms. She'd even begged him for more. *Harder. Don't stop.* Stubbornly, she refused to reply.

"Obviously, our lapse in judgment was because of the alcohol," he said.

"Yes." Relief pounded through her—at least, that's the only emotion she would admit to. Having him think she harbored feelings for him...even more embarrassing than sleeping with him. If he had liked her, well, that would have been a different story. Maybe.

He plopped onto the couch and anchored his elbows on his knees. He dropped his head into his upraised palms. "You do know I didn't wear a condom, right?"

She closed her eyes. Shit!

"Tell me you're on the pill."

"I am on the pill, but what about the other thing?" How much more stupid could she have been? She always insisted her partner wear a condom. Always! She hadn't even given it a second thought last night.

"I'm clean." He faced her, one brow arched. "Are you?"

"Yes."

He expelled a labored breath. She took a moment to breathe, as well, but she failed to calm herself. No condom. No freaking condom. If she hadn't gotten wrapped up in proving she could drink him under the table, they wouldn't be in this situation. She would *not* have given into the temptation of him—she hoped.

"Jillian," he said, then paused. His face had softened, yet he appeared tortured.

"Look," she said. "We're both on edge right now. We both want to forget what happened. No reason to snap at each other now, right?"

"I can't believe we were so stupid." Shaking his head, he leaned forward, grabbed his shoes and tugged them on. He stood. "I'll—" He shrugged. "I was going to say I'll call you, but I think we'd both prefer it if I didn't. I'll see you at the office." With that, he strode to the front door, opened it and stepped outside. The door banged closed behind him.

Finally. Alone with her thoughts. "I'll never be the same again," she muttered, letting her head fall forward. Her chin pressed into her sternum. Life at work was going to be strained, heavy with tension. She'd tasted forbidden fruit. And once tasted…

"Where's my car?" Suddenly Marcus was back inside her living room. Frowning, he threw his arms in the air. "It's not in your driveway. Neither is your car."

Jillian started to panic—until she recalled the cab ride where she'd sat in his lap and kissed him. She rubbed her temples. "I'll call a cab. We can go back to the bar and get them."

His frown deepened. "I'll call the cab."

"I'll…" What? Kiss you again if you ask nicely? That's what she foolishly wanted to do. He'd reappeared and the urge had quickened inside her. Yep, forbidden fruit. "I'll go get cleaned up." She sailed into the bathroom and quickly showered, her gaze lingering on the love-play marks Marcus had given her.

Why, why, why had he been the one to bring out her most primal instincts?

Why couldn't another man, at some other point in her life, have pleasured her as expertly? Why had she given in to temptation?

She recalled her rationale: they'd be horrible together and she would stop wanting him. Wrong. Now she wanted him all the more. Wanted to spend more time exploring his body, tasting him, enjoying him. Wanted to give him more time to explore, taste, and enjoy her.

He made it very clear he wants nothing else to do with you.

Clean, she dressed in jeans and an I'm With Stupid tee that pointed to the right. She'd have to make sure she stood on Marcus's left.

There wasn't time to dry her hair—heat made it frizz anyway—so she pulled the curls into a wet knot on top of her head. She was about to apply makeup when Marcus called, "Cab's here."

She grabbed her purse and keys and trudged into the living room. Beige pillows were strewn across the floor and she hopped over them. Her bra and panties, her dress, were still crumpled pools of black fabric and lace. Her cheeks heated.

Marcus stood at the front door, holding it open. She didn't meet his gaze. When she stepped onto the porch, she did a quick perimeter check to make sure none of her neighbors were out. Especially Georgia, who lived a few houses down.

Mrs. Franklin, the quintessential silver-haired old woman who lived on her right, was sitting on her porch rocker. Jillian's cheeks heated for, what, the third—fourth—time this morning? Mrs. Franklin would call Jillian's granny and Jillian's granny would call her mom. And the family lunch was just a few hours away.

Shit! she thought again.

Mrs. Franklin was staring at her, as if she'd been waiting all morning for someone to come out. "Your car's not in your driveway, Jillian," her weathered voice cackled. "I thought you were out partying all night."

"Hello, Mrs. Franklin," Jillian replied. She wanted to shove Marcus back inside her house. "I'm not a party girl, you know that. I just left my car…at a friend's house."

Marcus wasn't content to wait behind her and circled around. "Nice to meet you, Mrs. Franklin."

The old woman's wrinkled lips curled into a sly smile. "Who's your man friend, Jillian?"

"No one. I've really got to run." She raced to the yellow cab.

Marcus didn't hold open her door. No, he waved at Mrs. Franklin, flashed her a wicked smile, then slid into the back seat. Jillian climbed in beside him and slammed the door closed.

"You could have ignored her," she grumbled.

Marcus told the cabbie where to go and the car eased

into motion. "Now, that would have been rude of me, wouldn't it? And, as you've pointed out numerous times, you don't like it when I'm rude."

"That's never stopped you before."

"One more insult from you and I'll visit your neighbor later and show her what you did to my back."

The cabdriver chortled.

Jillian shot him a death-ray glare before turning back to Marcus. His expression was as hard as a rock. And yet, if she didn't know better, she'd suspect he was…hurt. Surely not. "Do you want me to kill you?" she said. "Is that what this is about?"

"It's about getting a little respect from you," he said darkly.

"Respect?"

"That's right."

"Please. Enlighten me. Why should I respect you?"

"I'm—" he paused, obviously having to think it over "—your boss."

"You didn't act like it last night," she mumbled.

His jaw clenched. "I thought we were never going to bring that up again. I thought we were going to pretend it didn't happen."

"That's right. Consider it forgotten. Just like that." She snapped her fingers and gave him her back, only to glare out the window. Sunlight glowed brightly, illuminating the wood-frame houses. Green trees soon came into view and whipped past, followed by tall redbrick buildings circled by lovely blue sky.

You are such a bitch sometimes, she chastised herself. There was no reason to snap at him. *He* is *your boss.*

Despite everything that's happened, he does deserve respect. Or maybe *because* of everything that had happened. Not once had he gloated. Not once had he smirked or made her feel cheap. He'd simply agreed with her, stating they'd made a mistake, one they couldn't make again.

"I'm sorry," she found herself saying. "You're…right. I do owe you respect. Just because I made a mistake last night, doesn't—"

"We."

"What?"

"*We* made a mistake last night," he said, his tone dark.

"Right." She cleared her throat and continued. "That doesn't mean I should treat you like dirt. After all, you're as miserable as I am about this." She paused. "Aren't you?" A part of her hoped he'd deny it and tell her that he was glad it had happened.

He didn't speak for a long while, then said softly, "Right. Miserable."

Something inside her chest plummeted.

"Thank you for the apology," he added.

"You're welcome." Would she ever understand herself around Marcus? He constantly tied her into knots and beat against her resolve, all with a look, a word. One moment she hated him, the next she wanted him, and now she wanted… what? A relationship? Promises? No, no. Of course not.

But she'd gotten a taste of him and, God help her, she only wanted more.

Sixteen

*Do you have a map? Because I keep getting
lost in your eyes.*

MARCUS HAD JUST MADE the biggest mistake of his life, but he couldn't bring himself to regret it. Which made him a stupid asshole, but there it was. He was a stupid asshole, in a cab with a woman who was all wrong for him. She'd given him the best sex of his life and he only wanted more.

And he'd forgotten to check to see if the birthmark on Jillian's ass had faded or gotten darker. That's what he regretted.

Oh, yes. He'd liked making love to Jillian. Rough and wild, uninhibited, nothing-held-back, crazy sex. And yet, she'd tasted so sweet, so innocent, a combination of the Sunday School teacher and sex kitten he'd so admired when they'd first met. Right now, he could smell her. Soap and woman. *His* woman—no, no thoughts like that. Yet…

So badly he craved another sampling. His mouth watered for it, in fact.

Gravel crunching under tires, the cab eased to a stop at the place of his doom. The darkly paneled building appeared abandoned; there was no else in the parking lot, no traffic nearby.

Marcus paid the driver and exited the cab. Jillian followed suit on her side and the taxi sped away. They were suddenly alone. Again. Not a good thing for them. They stood in place for several uncomfortable seconds, not glancing at each other, the only noise between them the occasional tweet of a bird, the gentle sway of wind.

"Well," Jillian said. "Goodbye." She walked to her car, only a few feet away from his Jag.

"Goodbye," he said curtly. He strode to the driver-side door.

They faced off. She stared at something beyond his shoulder. The sun caressed her lovingly. She was breathtaking. She wore no makeup, yet she appeared prettier than ever. Her cheeks bloomed a bright pink and her eyes were glittering, her lids heavy, sated.

"I'd say thank you for last night," she said, repeating his earlier words, "but we both know that'd be a lie."

Last night... He couldn't stop picturing her as she'd been. Sultry, seductive. Passionate. Naked in his arms, she'd come alive. She'd been wet and hot and for several hours she'd been the center of his universe. Only she had existed.

Last night, it had seemed that he'd given a checklist to God and the big guy had granted his every wish. Nipples that tasted like berries—check. Legs that were long and lean and wrapped around him tightly—check. Silky hair that twirled around his fingers—check. A primal fragrance that roused the beast inside him—check. Feminine walls that squeezed and milked him—check.

"Well, goodbye. Again." She palmed her keys and rocked back on her heels.

"Yeah, goodbye." Except he wasn't ready to leave her. Things had ended badly between them and he wanted to fix it. A part of him wished they'd woken up, wrapped in each other, smiled, talked, laughed, then made love again. Perhaps slowly this time, lingering.

She wants to forget it happened, moron. Just let her go. It was hard, though. So hard.

She cleared her throat. "I think we should forget about the bet, too. We're even, no money owed."

"Good idea."

She looked down at her feet. "Good."

He didn't respond, because the words he wanted to speak were not words he *should* speak.

"Okay, then. Goodbye for real this time." She slid into her car.

He did the same, then waited until she'd eased out of the lot before keying the ignition. "Damn it!" He slammed a fist into the wheel.

Already he wanted to chase after her.

But he forced the car into motion, purposefully driving in the opposite direction of her. One hand on the wheel, an elbow propped on the door, head resting in open palm, Marcus sighed. It irked his pride that she'd kicked him out this morning. It also irked his pride that she wanted to forget their night together, a night he would never be able to burn from his mind.

Most of all, it irked his pride that he'd wanted to start

anew and she hadn't. *We probably shouldn't talk about this* had been her first words to him. There'd been desperation in her voice, as if she feared he *would* bring it up.

Last night should have gotten her out of his system, but he desired her more now than before. He banged another fist into the wheel. Weren't women supposed to go all soft and mushy after sex? So far, Jillian had proven to be different from every woman he'd ever met.

He needed a hobby, something besides work and thinking about Jillian. Poker wouldn't do anymore; he'd just think of Jillian and how much he liked to gamble with her. Maybe he'd start gardening or knitting or some other shit like that. He was acting like a woman, wanting more than his partner was willing to give, so he might as well have a hobby a woman would, too.

Grim, Marcus exited the highway and turned onto the service road that led to his apartment. Two more turns, another block and he spied the building, a brown-and-white stucco, expensive, pristine, with windowed porches on every story. Jillian would appreciate the color coordination of the place, he thought, then frowned. *Stop thinking about her, you ass.*

Maybe he just needed a girlfriend. He'd thought about sleeping with someone else, but maybe he needed an actual relationship to protect him from Jillian. A soft and feminine woman he could lose himself in, over and over again, until he forgot everything else.

Nah, no relationship. That was too drastic. Relationships were too close to marriage and he never wanted to relive that disaster again.

He didn't wave or speak to anyone milling about as he

strode to his apartment, where he showered—mourning the loss of Jillian's scent on his skin—changed and left again. If he stayed, he'd sleep. His head still hurt, but he didn't want to lie down. If he slept, he'd dream of Jillian.

He wanted that woman out of his mind. Finally. Once and for all.

Jake lived just down the hall, so he went there. If anyone could distract him, it was Jake. His best friend answered on the second round of banging. Jake was wearing a red kimono… thing. His hair was in spikes and sleep lines marred his face.

"You're wearing women's clothing now?" Marcus greeted him.

"It's for men, asswipe. You want to tell me why you're waking me up at ten in the morning?" Jake asked with a yawn. "That's just barbaric."

Marcus brushed past him. Like Marcus, Jake had only been in Oklahoma City a few weeks, but unlike Marcus, he was already unpacked, his apartment decorated to perfection. Framed pictures of his wife, Claire, covered the walls, her plain, happy face smiling down on everyone who entered. She'd been dead for two years, but Jake had not yet gotten over it. Maybe he never would. The pair had been married four years and Claire had totally trusted Jake to do his job and not cheat. And Jake hadn't cheated. Not once.

They'd been in love. True love.

Marcus had never had that with Kayla, his ex-wife. She'd left and he'd wanted her back for pride's sake. Not because he missed her or couldn't live without her. What he felt for Jillian was already more intense than anything he'd ever felt for his wife.

That scared him. Everything fucking scared him lately. *Big baby!*

He moved his gaze over the plush furniture, for the first time noticing that each piece was a different color. The couch—navy blue. The love seat—dark red. The coffee table—forest green. What would Jillian say about the place?

His jaw clenched. "I messed up," he said. Rubbing a hand down his face, he fell on top of the couch.

As Jake settled across from him, the entire story poured from Marcus. The club, Jillian, drinking, sex. Incredible sex. Jake's expression flashed concern, then amusement, then incredulity. A few times he even muttered, "You are so dumb."

"What should I do?" he asked, tortured. If anyone could help him wade out of this mess, it was Jake. As teenagers, Marcus had been the muscle and Jake the brains. Marcus had beat up the kids who'd made fun of skinny Jake; Jake had convinced their teachers not to punish him.

Since then, Marcus had grown a brain (kind of) and Jake had developed muscles. But habits died hard.

"First, let me recap." Jake massaged two fingers over his slightly stubbled chin. "You screwed an employee—"

"Don't talk about her like that," he found himself growling.

Jake blinked. "Then you didn't screw her?"

"No, I didn't screw her. I made—slept with her." He'd almost said *made love,* but managed to stop himself in time. That was so *not* what they'd done.

"O-kay. You *slept with her* and now you're looking for a girlfriend so you won't be tempted to scre—uh, sleep with Jillian again."

"Yes."

"Well, it's official. You're a dumbass."

"Why?" He popped to his feet and paced in front of the wide bay window that looked down onto the pulsing heart of the city. Tall buildings. Redbrick roads. A few people strolling down the sidewalks.

"Do you know nothing about women? I haven't dated in a long time, but even I can tell you're headed straight for trouble. If you date someone else now, you'll only be using her. She'll get hurt and Jillian will see you as the pathetic, slobbering fool you're becoming and—are those bite marks on your neck?"

Marcus felt his cheeks heat. Blushing like a goddamn schoolgirl. He scrubbed at his neck, wishing the marks would just fade away. "Stay on track. You were calling me a pathetic, slobbering fool."

Jake's eyes widened. "Sweet Christ, they are!" he said with a laugh.

Defeated, Marcus fell back onto the couch. He lay down and stretched out, staring up at the ceiling. "Your humor is uncalled-for."

"No, it's not."

"Yes, it is."

"No, it's not."

"Yes the fuck it is."

Jake snorted. "I've never seen you this worked up over a woman. Even Kayla."

His stomach clenched with a familiar knot of anger when he heard his ex-wife's name. He'd married her when he'd been young, stupid and vulnerable, wishing for the fabled happily-ever-after his parents hadn't gotten.

He hadn't gotten it, either. In the beginning, Kayla had loved him. He believed that much. After all, he'd tested her with bait and she'd passed. But a year later, seemingly for no reason, her entire demeanor toward him changed. She became withdrawn, moody, even hateful. He still wasn't clear on the details; all he knew was that twelve months after they'd pledged to love, honor and cherish each other, she'd left him for another man.

Not just any other man: their family physician. A man who had a belly paunch and thinning hair. He'd made the same kind of money as Marcus, so Marcus had never—even to this day—understood the man's appeal to a beauty like Kayla.

When he'd asked, Kayla had said, "I don't expect you to understand. I love him. He's kind and gentle and… sweet. Things you've never been and will never be. He makes me feel cherished."

Marcus had vowed to be those things for her. He'd even begged. Fucking begged her to stay with him. Just the memories mortified him. Pride was a bitch.

Soon afterward, Kayla had left without ever looking back. After their divorce had been finalized, he'd heard that she had married the ugly doctor and they now had two kids. But Marcus wasn't bitter. He just hoped they both rotted in hell for all eternity.

Women—they didn't know what they really wanted and they were never satisfied with what they had. He'd learned that lesson well.

But then there was Jillian. If she ever fell in love, he suspected it would be forever. She was just too passionate, too honest, and no kind, gentle, *cherishing* doctor would be able to turn her head. She'd knee a man like that in the balls.

While Marcus didn't want her love, he still wanted her ripe little body. If only she would have asked him to stay this morning… He was still upset that she'd been in such a hurry to get rid of him.

"You look ready to kill someone," Jake said, breaking into his thoughts.

Marcus blinked. For a moment, he'd forgotten where he was and who he was with. He glanced down and saw his hands were fisted on his pants. He released the material, forced himself to relax.

"Why don't you ask her out on a date?" Jake suggested.

"Who?"

"Your mother, dummy. Who do you think? Christ, did I mention that you can be such an asswipe sometimes? Ask Jillian out and save yourself this mental anguish."

"I have two very good reasons for not dating Jillian. One—" he held up a finger "—she'd say no and two—" he held up another finger "—I don't want to."

"Bullshit. You want to do more than scr—sleep with her. You want to spend time with her, talk with her, laugh with her and all that crap."

His body jerked in agreement, even as his mind shouted a denial. "No, I don't."

"Yes, you do. Here's a news flash. It's not really crap. It's actually…nice." Jake sounded wistful.

"If I tried to talk with her, we'd snip and yell the entire time." And then have the most amazing sex of his life, he thought, trying to dismiss the longing pouring through him.

Jake waved a hand through the air. "The snipping and yelling is foreplay, apparently."

"No," Marcus grumbled, "it's premeditation for murder."

"You're dumb and I'm tired. Look. Life is short. You're wasting yours. You never know when someone's going to die and you won't get to see them anymore. Take my word for it."

Marcus wished he could cover his ears and block the sound of his friend's regret.

"If you want Jillian, fight for her. This might be your only chance. If she's not here tomorrow…" Jake cleared his throat. "So stop treating her like she's a fungus growing on your favorite shoes. Play nice and I guarantee she'll stop hating you."

His eyes narrowed. Being told he'd treated Jillian like shit cut deeply.

"Don't look at me like that," Jake said. "You know you've treated her badly."

"Yeah," he admitted with no small amount of guilt, "but she liked it."

"Did she really or do you just think she did? Wait. Don't answer that." Jake shook his head in disgust. "We're acting like women, discussing all your problems like this. Next you'll ask me to paint your toenails or buy you some of that lipstick you like to wear."

Marcus flipped him off. "I'm not the one wearing a kimono."

Jake barked out a laugh. "Listen. You're overcomplicating things. You slept with her and, whether you admit it or not, you want to sleep with her again. Treat this day like it's your last and go get her."

Yes, he did want to sleep with her again. Badly. She'd awakened something inside him, a beast that had been caged all these years.

He'd tried to be kind and gentle for Kayla because that's what she'd wanted, but he wasn't either of those things. Not really. And Jillian seemed to like—or rather, *desire*—him just as he was.

The two women were different in every possible way, he mused. Kayla had been all smiles, a social butterfly who fluttered from party to party. She smiled even when she was pissed. Well, she smiled to your face then cut you up behind your back. Jillian didn't seem to give a damn about the social scene. She was more likely to flip you off than smile at you. She always spoke her mind, no matter how harsh her opinion.

Kayla had frustrated the hell out of him. Jillian...delighted him.

"Thanks," he said to Jake, standing.

"Anytime. Except in the morning. And maybe not at night either."

"Funny." He strode into the hall and dug his keys from his pocket. Jake's advice played through his mind. Should he push Jillian out of his life as she seemed to want—or try to develop something with her before it was too late?

A few steps from his door Marcus stopped and leaned his forehead against the cool wall. The fact that Jillian was his employee had ceased to matter last night. But if he made a play for her, she'd probably reject him. How humiliating, letting her know just how badly he desired her when she didn't feel the same way.

Why did she have to be so sexy?

Why did her body have to be so responsive to him?

Damn, but he needed something to do, something to get his mind off her until he figured this out. The office was closed on Sundays, so he'd have nothing to keep him occupied if he went in. Maybe Jake was wrong. Maybe he *did* need to turn his attentions to another woman. He could find a woman who *wanted* to be used.

Suddenly determined to do just that, Marcus unlocked his door and strode into his kitchen. It was modern, mostly silver, and Jillian would probably want to paint it beige.

He picked up the phone and dialed a former lover's number. She lived in Dallas, but he'd make the three-hour drive to see her. They both liked sex and easily said goodbye afterward. No tears. No "I love you's."

She answered, though, and her voice wasn't Jillian's. His determination drained.

"Sorry, wrong number," he said and hung up. Bloody damn hell! He tried again with an older woman he'd taken to dinner a few weeks ago, hoping to end his slump. She was gone and he didn't leave a message. He couldn't work up a single ounce of excitement about her, either.

Only Jillian would do, it seemed.

How did you get yourself into this mess? First you did everything you could to make Jillian hate you, then you slept with her, and now you're actually thinking about dating her.

He didn't do serious, he reminded himself. He preferred short, no-strings relationships where everyone knew the rules of the game and no one wanted more than the moment. Jillian was obviously as cynical about relationships and as slow to trust as he was, so she probably wouldn't want to do serious, either. Maybe they could continue sleeping together, an affair without emotion, without ties.

Life is short, Jake had said. *Live this day like it's your last.*

Marcus strode to the fridge and poured a glass of apple juice. He popped two painkillers and chased them with the cold liquid. The hangover was messing with his brain. Surely that was the reason for his stupid thoughts, his stupid desires and his stupid cravings. Jillian. In bed. Naked. Now. Grrr.

But he looked at the phone again. Hangover or not, he still wanted the woman. There was no denying it. Employee or not. Rules or not. He didn't want anyone else. Deep down, he knew only she would do and that scared him. He'd admitted to fear earlier but hadn't confronted it. If he did confront it, he'd give Jillian power over him and he hated, *hated* giving a woman any type of hold. They took advantage. Extorted. Yet…

He wanted Jillian.

You're going to do it, you know you are. Yes, he was. *Don't waste any more time.* He was going to propose a sexual relationship. At work, they'd be boss and employee, nothing more. But after hours, when either of them had a need, they could help each other out. Friends (kind of) with benefits.

If she'd agree… He had to get her to agree. He'd go crazy otherwise.

Ready to see her—and begin—he grabbed his keys and strode outside. He was grinning for the first time that morning.

Seventeen

What do you say we go back to my room and do
some math. Add a bed, subtract our clothes,
divide your legs and multiply.

JILLIAN SPENT THE MORNING sitting on her couch and staring off into space, trying to rid her mind of Marcus. But he was there, refusing to leave. Naked, beckoning. Seemingly a part of her DNA, like there was no Jillian without Marcus.

It was beyond frustrating!

What's worse, she suspected he'd be an even better lover when he was sober. Any better, though, and she would have died of pleasure. She sighed. When they'd stood in the parking lot, just looking at each other, she'd felt the urge to throw herself at him, to keep him with her and try for something more than sex.

"That's just craziness," she muttered as she toyed with the ends of the decorative scarf she'd wrapped around her neck to hide the bruises.

Think of something else, damn it! Think of Anne. The

woman had called about an hour ago to see if they were square. In lieu of an answer, Jillian had asked what chance Anne had given her, the one she'd alluded to yesterday. Anne had replied, "I gave you a chance to find happiness, girl. You're not chained to CAM. You can break the cycle of mistrust and rejection."

But happiness was far from what Jillian felt.

Thankfully, the clock chose that moment to chime the noon hour, *forcing* her to forget Anne…and Marcus. Jillian grabbed her keys and purse and headed to the front door. It was time to visit her mother and her granny and her brother and her sister and her nieces. Last time they'd all gotten together, they'd nearly killed each other. She'd mentioned a work case and the next thing she knew, they were arguing about infidelity. Her mom had run away to cry in private, Jillian had yelled at Brent, Brittany had yelled at her and Granny had slept with the pool boy to escape the volatile scene.

Ah, good times.

The phone rang, startling her. She paused, hand on the doorknob, about to lock up. Heart picking up speed, she rushed forward and grabbed the phone from the end table. Was it…could it be… "Hello."

"You bringing Georgia?" her brother asked.

Her shoulders slumped in disappointment. No—relief! "No. Sorry."

"Why not?"

"You'd just bother her."

He snorted. "I never bother her."

"Puh-lease."

"Okay, I bother her, but she likes it. Whether she admits it or not. Just…call her and ask her to come."

"No."

"You're a bad sister."

"I'm not your pimp," she told him.

"I drove over to her place last night, okay, and she was upset about something."

Jillian frowned. "Upset? About what?"

"I don't know. Just bring her," he said and hung up.

Jillian rolled her eyes. She phoned Georgia, but there was no answer. She walked to her house, saw Georgia's sedan in the driveway and pounded on the door. Still no answer. Most likely, Wyatt had picked her up and Georgia had stayed the night with him. Jillian sighed, knowing Brent would be upset about that.

As she walked to her own car, the sun glared hotly. For a moment, only a silly, wistful moment, she wanted to talk to Marcus about the weather again. How was it possible that she missed him so soon? Scowling, she pressed unlock on her key pad and the driver-side door snapped open.

"Headed out?" a husky male voice said.

Gasping, Jillian whirled. There he was, standing on her porch as if she'd conjured him. The sight made her feel like she'd fallen flat on her face, the air knocked from her lungs. Her heart drummed in her chest, a fluttery rhythm. *Marcus.* He'd changed his clothes and now sported a faded pair of jeans and a muscle-hugging black T-shirt.

She knew what he looked like underneath those clothes and the knowledge teased her mind and body. Her nipples hardened; her stomach quivered. Shit. What was he doing here?

"Headed out?" he repeated.

"Yes," she answered on a wispy catch of air. He looked good. Too good. Blond hair slightly damp, brown eyes darkened with…something unreadable. Determination, maybe. Desire? Hope? Why hope? Perhaps that was simply a reflection of *her* eyes.

A slight breeze swirled between them. The lush emerald trees that were sprinkled around the front of her house provided the perfect frame for him. Both were gifts from Mother Nature, she thought wryly. Outdoors suited Marcus's ruggedness, made him appear all the more savage.

His gaze slid over her, lingering on all the places he'd licked and pinched and nibbled. "You look nice."

Surely that hadn't been a compliment. Surely she had misheard. "I'm sorry, what?"

"You look nice, Jillian," he said softly, genuinely. "Very pretty."

Nope. Hadn't misheard. "Th-thank you." What was going on? Why was he being so…sweet? A long while passed. They were staring at each other, she realized, silence thick between them. Her gaze was hungry, she was sure. His was now blank. *Say something, idiot!* "Uh, what are you doing here?" she asked.

"There's something I need to say to you."

"Okay." Like what? Fighting an intense surge of curiosity, she hefted her purse strap over her shoulder.

Wait. Better to be curious than to spend more time with him. Already her mouth watered. Already her fingers itched to tangle into his hair. "Unfortunately," she said, "now really isn't a good time to chat."

Break the cycle of mistrust.... Anne's voice filled her head.

"Where are you going? Maybe I can, I don't know, come with you."

Her eyes widened with incredulity. "You want to come with me?"

He shrugged. "Why not?"

"No, I'm sorry." This entire conversation was a dream, right? It was too surreal. She turned back to her car. "I'm having lunch with my family."

With five quick steps, Marcus was at her car and grasping the rim of the door, his fingers smudging the window. Suddenly she felt his heat, so much more potent than the sun. She smelled his sinful aroma and the memories she'd fought all morning flooded her. Her ears filled with the sounds of his moans; her mouth tasted the salty flavor of his skin.

"I doubt they'd mind if you brought a guest," he said, his breath fanning her ear. He might have licked the shell of her ear, riding the ridges of her earrings, but she couldn't be sure.

Jillian stilled, frowned. A curl blew in front of her eyes and she brushed it back. "They might not mind, but I would." All she needed was for her family to see how she reacted to this man. *Break the cycle....*

"I need to talk to you, Jillian. It's important."

He sounded grave, as if it were life and death. Her death, more specifically. "What's this about?"

"I'll tell you inside the car or inside your house, but not out here."

She didn't want to go inside with him, not with a bed

(and a couch) nearby. More than that, she simply didn't have time. If she were late, her mom would freak or sink into a depression because Jillian didn't love her enough to rush over—not that she'd ever say that to Jillian, but Brent and Brittany would call her all night long, complaining.

Shit. It was either take Marcus along or agonize until tomorrow about what he had to say. *Break the cycle....* "You drive," she told him, shutting the door to her car. Let him pay for the gas, since he'd insisted on coming.

A look of relief flashed over his features and he nodded. He turned on his heel and practically skipped to his silver Jag. What did he have to be so happy about? She frowned. The news must be freakishly terrible if he was *that* happy to give it to her. Her stomach knotted painfully, a perfect mimic of the pain she'd felt the first day she'd met him, when she'd stepped into Anne's office thinking she was going to be fired. Had that really only been two days ago?

Jillian tentatively walked to Marcus's car and settled into the plush leather passenger seat. Buckled. Breathed. Gave him her mother's address. To distract herself, she looked around. Everything was clean. Not a speck of dust on the dash, not a blade of grass on the floorboard.

"And you called *me* a clean freak," she said.

He grinned wryly. "I guess we're more alike than either of us wants to admit." He started the car. Surprisingly, classical music blared from the speakers. Sheepish, he turned down the volume. She would have expected rock from someone so in-your-face masculine (the time he'd worn her lipstick not withstanding).

"Since opposites attract, I guess that means we're safe."

"Opposites aren't the only ones who attract," he admonished.

True. "So…what did you want to talk to me about?"

"Give me a moment to collect my thoughts."

They lapsed into silence. Not wanting to seem too eager, she waited until they were soaring along the highway and headed toward Rivendell, an exclusive neighborhood for those with money to burn. Her mom had grown up middleclass, but married Jillian's very wealthy father. In the divorce, her mom had gotten the house and a huge settlement.

The neighbor who had spent more time in her dad's bed than her mom did had long since moved. For a while, breaking the woman's windows, keying her car and poisoning her plants had been Evelyn Greene's only joy.

"So…" she prompted for a second time. Her hands were sweating.

"We're both jaded," he began, then paused.

O-kay, not how she expected him to start. *I lied to you earlier and I haven't had a checkup in years.* Maybe something like that. Or, *I'm still married and now my wife wants to meet you and show you the gun she just purchased.* "That was so important you crashed my family lunch to tell me?"

He tossed her a frown. "Give me a moment."

"I've given you plenty of moments, Mark. You don't go to someone's house, tell them you have a matter of life and death to discuss, then take an eternity to sort through your thoughts. It *is* a matter of life and death now because I'm dying of curiosity." So much for not seeming too eager.

"I never said it was a matter of life and death, Dimples, and the name is Marcus."

"You let Ronnie with an *i e* call you Mark," she pointed out.

"Because she was nothing. Not even a blip on my radar." Pause. "Jealous?"

"Hardly." She snorted, felt her cheeks burn brightly and turned toward the window.

"Tell you what. When you're naked, you can call me anything you want."

Oh, that was...that was... "Just—tell me what you came to tell me. If you're waiting for Happy the sock puppet to help you explain, don't. He'll just confuse me."

"Now you're pissed about Happy." Exasperated, he shook his head. "Go ahead. I don't mind. Insult me. Hit me."

"No. You'll like it too much," she muttered.

"Probably," he agreed with a heavy amount of self-deprecation.

Her blood pressure spiked. Not with fury, but with that damn desire she couldn't seem to shake. Hearing he might become aroused if she beat on him...her nipples hardened. An ache throbbed between her legs. Damn, damn, damn! "What. Do. You. Want. To. Talk. To. Me. About?"

His hands tightened on the wheel and his breathing was choppy as he said, "I hope you're ready for this."

"Just say it!"

"Fine. Here it is. You're single and I'm single. I think we should start sleeping together."

"What!" Incredulous, she turned in her seat, the belt buckle pulling tight around her middle. "Would you mind repeating that? I think I had a brain aneurysm while you were speaking."

"It makes sense. Neither of us wants a relationship, so

we'll never have to worry about the other hoping for more than sex. And the sex was good, you can't deny it."

Shock held her immobile. He was serious. He wasn't smiling. Lines of tension bracketed his mouth and his back was ramrod straight with…hope? Dread?

"We work together," she managed to get out.

"I considered that," he said with a nod, a lock of pale hair dancing at his temple. He didn't face her. "I think we're mature enough to act professionally at work."

"And sleep together afterward?" Her voice was barely audible.

"Exactly."

Her nipples tightened eagerly. She ached at her very core. "This is a joke, right?"

"No joke."

"I thought…" Dear God. "I thought we'd agreed to forget last night happened."

"I can't," he admitted sheepishly.

Neither could she. When he'd entered her body, he'd become a permanent part of her. An image that would haunt her for the rest of her life, a sizzling reminder of the one time she'd let go completely. The one time the pieces of her life had clicked together and formed a cohesive whole, no thoughts of infidelity, no thoughts of emotional pain.

"This is the perfect solution," he rushed on, as if he feared she was gearing up to reject him. "Both of us have needs and like I said, we don't want to have to deal with commitment. And we obviously have similar…passions."

"Marcus." She paused, not really knowing what to say. Her body wanted to agree, right now, no hesitation. Her mind had yet to jump on board. "We're barely able to tolerate each other."

"Yes, but we're perfectly compatible in bed."

"That was the alcohol."

"I highly doubt that. But," he said, shrugging, "there *is* a way to find out for sure."

Her eyes narrowed on him. She already knew the answer, but she said, "How?"

His lips twitched into a smile. "We'll have to sleep together again. Sober, this time."

Tempted, but still fighting it, Jillian scrubbed a hand down her face. "Do you realize how insulting this is? You're basically asking me to whore for you anytime you get the urge."

"It's not like that," he growled. "However, I'd be willing to whore for *you* anytime. Anywhere."

Marcus at her beck and call, naked, doing anything and everything she desired… Her skin prickled with need. What a heady, powerful thought. *You're crazy to consider this.* There were so many complications.

Break the cycle.…

Would they be exclusive, which was tantamount to the relationship neither of them wanted, or would they be free to date other people? Not that she dated anymore, but every muscle in her body clenched at the thought of Marcus taking another woman out, buying her—fat, lazy cow that she was—dinner, then dropping her off, driving to Jillian's and sleeping with *her*.

She told Marcus as much, leaving out the part about the fat, lazy cow.

"I agree," he said, surprising her with his easy compliance. "That wouldn't be fair to either of us. While we're...together, we won't see anyone else."

Hearing him agree just added massive amounts of fuel to an already blazing fire. "This is crazy! Would you call me? Would I call you? Would we see each other on holidays? How long would our arrangement last? What happens if you meet someone else? What if *I* meet someone else? How do we end things? How often would we sleep together? What if one of us decides the arrangement isn't working?" She paused, a single thought slamming into her. "What if one of us does, despite everything, want more?" What if *she* wanted more and he didn't?

Sighing, he tangled a hand through his hair. "This seemed so simple when I was alone." There was accusation in his voice.

"That's because men think about sex but never consequences," she told him dryly.

"As if women are innocent of that crime." He steered the car off the highway and onto an exit ramp.

"Hey, what are you doing? Where are you going?" She straightened in her seat and frowned. "This isn't our exit."

He whipped into the parking lot of a strip mall and threw the car into park. He unbuckled and pinned her with a stare. "Enough arguing. You want me, and don't even try to deny it. You don't like how you feel. Well, guess what? Neither do I, but at least I'm willing to do something about it."

"What happens if one of us wants out of the arrangement?" she reiterated. What happened if *he* wanted out, but she fell hard? What a nightmare that would be.

"I think we're big enough to handle it," he said.

Catch a Mate

She met his gaze, desire and anticipation washing through her. "You are so irritating, you know that? You have an answer for everything."

"No more stalling. Say it, Jillian. Agree." He leaned forward, placing them nose to nose. "I'm waiting."

His warm breath mingled with hers, both shaky, both raw. "I'm thinking."

"Think faster." He inched forward a little more and their mouths almost touched.

"You're crowding me," she said, the sound of her voice so smoky it was barely audible.

"You like it."

"No."

"Yes."

"Kiss," she breathed, unable to help herself.

His lips swooped down on hers completely. Her nerve endings erupted into live wires of sensation. Of pleasure. He tasted good, decadent. Exactly how she remembered.

"More," he said. She tasted good, like fire, Marcus thought, plunging his tongue into her mouth. He couldn't touch her enough, so he let himself touch her everywhere. His hands kneaded her breasts, so full they overflowed. Her nipples were rock hard. He even dipped a hand between her legs, rubbing. Rubbing.

"Mmm," she moaned, arching against him. She wound her arms around his neck and fisted several handfuls of hair. Only her seat belt kept her from his lap.

He was hard and ready for her, as if he hadn't indulged last night. The woman flat out turned him on, no matter what she did, no matter what she said. And when he'd realized she was seriously considering his offer, that she wanted more of him, he had almost come.

He wasn't psychic, but he predicted they were going to have lots and lots and lots of sex in the very near future. This arrangement would be good for both of them. They would have exclusive sex, not worry about emotions, not worry about cheating.

It was odd, really, trusting someone he wasn't sure he liked. But somehow he knew he could trust Jillian. She was unlike any woman he'd ever met. Working at CAM, she had to understand the trauma of infidelity. She'd better— the thought of her with another man infuriated him.

He pulled away from her, a difficult task since all he wanted to do was bask in her. Strip her. Take her. He had trouble catching his breath. "So," he said.

"So," she repeated shakily. She straightened, righted her clothing. She looked away from him, out the window. Black curls tumbled down her back.

I want those curls twined around my wrist. I want those curls caressing my chest as she rides me. I want those curls spilled over my thighs as she sucks me. His cock jerked and he had to adjust its position inside his pants. "You sure we need to go to your family's?"

"I'm sure," she said, breathless.

He pulled his focus off Jillian before he dove in for another kiss. Outside, cars surrounded them. In fact, the woman next to them was staring into their car with unabashed amusement. She flashed him a thumbs-up.

Marcus twirled his finger tersely, motioning for her to turn around. He shouldn't have kissed Jillian in public, but he'd been helpless to stop. Tasting her was a compulsion. A drug. A rush. "So you want to give this thing a try or not?"

Jillian cleared her throat, but still didn't face him. "We'll give this thing a try." And hope they didn't kill each in the process.

Eighteen

Do you wash your pants with Windex?
Because I can really see myself in them.

What the hell have I gotten myself into?

Jillian knocked on her mom's front door, a towering maple with etched glass circling the center. Marcus stood beside her. She could feel the heat radiating off him, heat that had enveloped her only a short while ago. Try as she might, she couldn't forget.

He'd touched her and kissed her as if she were his entire reason for living. How tempted she was to blow off today's lunch and go back to her house with Marcus—right now—for a round of sober, raunchy sex. Only a sense of self-preservation saved her—a sense that had deserted her quite often lately, she thought with a wry grin.

"My mother is going to hate you," she told him, keeping her gaze on the red and white roses climbing the walls of the house. "She's currently looking for a man of her own, but don't let that fool you. She almost killed herself when my sister, Brittany, brought home Steven."

"Wow. Your mom sounds…fun."

"Just…I don't know. Be nice to her no matter what she says. She's fragile and any little thing can thrust her into a depression."

"Like I'd be rude to your mother," he said, offended.

"You're rude to everyone." This was going to be a disaster. Unlike Brittany, Jillian had never brought a man to meet her family before. Why hadn't she considered the consequences?

"Are you trying to start an argument with me, Dimples?" He ran a fingertip down the ridges of her spine, then paused. "You're nervous."

Her mouth fell open. "No, I'm not."

His lips lifted in a wide smile, as if he were supremely proud of himself. "You're nervous and you're lashing out. Nasty habit, that. Do you want me to kiss you again? That always gets your mind off things."

"Okay, I'm nervous. But for the love of God, no kissing!" With just the thought, delicious sparks branched from each of her vertebrae and trekked throughout her entire body. She really did not want to make out with him in front of her family. And where the hell were they? She rang the doorbell. Their cars were in the driveway.

"This is a nice neighborhood," Marcus said, gazing around. The white, five-thousand-square-foot monstrosity of a house formed a half circle around an immaculate lawn of lush greens and rich browns. Beside the door, twisted columns stretched high and emerald ivy climbed their lengths. Potted plants spilled from the archway, the porch swing and the large French windows.

"Thank you," she said.

His brows furrowed together. "You grew up here?"

"Yes. Not what you expected, I take it?"

"No."

When he didn't elaborate, she threw up her arms. "Well, what did you expect?" The sound of laughter floated on the wind and she straightened. Her ears perked. "They're in the back. Come on."

She hopped off the porch and strolled to the side of the house, sweeping around blooming flowers and stone fairies caught in mid-flight. Marcus kept pace beside her.

"Well?" she prompted.

"I guess I expected something less...expensive. You drink beer, curse and, well, you work for CAM."

She grinned. "And only poor people can do that?"

"Not at all. I guess, in my mind, children who grow up in a neighborhood like this become doctors, lawyers or professional shoppers."

"Hey!"

"What? It's true."

She stopped at the end of the iron gate and faced him. Sunlight couched his features and crowned him in a delicate halo, giving him an almost angelic appearance. Her throat constricted. "What about you? What kind of place did you grow up in?"

"Before my parents split, something very similar to this." He lifted his shoulders in a stiff shrug. "After my mom brought me to the States, something quite different."

Unlike Evelyn Greene, his mother obviously hadn't

gotten a nice settlement. The thought of him enduring a childhood of poverty tugged at her heart. She could imagine the blond cherub he'd probably been, staring longingly at a toy his mom would never be able to afford. Her stomach clenched.

Marcus tapped the end of her nose. "Why are you looking at me like that?"

She shook her head, pulling herself from the sad images. "Like what?"

"Like I'm a beggar in the street and you have spare change for me. Feeling sorry for me, Dimples?"

"No, certainly not," she sputtered.

Grinning, he tapped her nose again. "You are too cute. I never would have suspected a soft core lurked underneath that she-warrior personality."

Jillian, a she-warrior? She laughed with delight. "Look at us. We're not drunk, but we're getting along."

"That's because you're behaving yourself." There was a twinkle in his dark eyes and a smile twitching at his lips.

She found herself grinning, too, unable to stop. "You must have eaten your Nice Boy puffs today."

More laughter drifted on the breeze, then the sound of her sister's voice. "No running, Cherry. The deck is slippery. You could fall, crack your head open and die."

Marcus made a face. "Cherry?"

"My ten-year-old niece."

"She's named after a piece of fruit?"

Jillian nodded. "So is her twin sister, Apple."

"You're kidding me."

"Unfortunately, I'm serious. Their father is fond of fruit pies and thought it would be cute."

"And their mother didn't protest?"

"She thinks Steven's cute, so she gives him whatever he wants."

There was an electrically-charged pause, then, "Do you think *I'm* cute?" He reached out and shifted one of her curls between his fingers before hooking it behind her ear. The action was so tender, so lover-like, she backed away from him.

Thick silence wormed its way between them, different this time, a little uncomfortable.

Marcus frowned and dropped his arm to his side. "Sorry," he muttered. "I didn't mean to ruin the moment by getting too serious."

"You don't have to be nice to me," she said, not knowing what to make of what had just happened. "I already said I'd sleep with you."

A dark cloud descended over his features, and he pinned her with a lethal glare. "I'll be nice if I bloody well want to be nice."

"So we're going to argue about being nice now?" She breathed in a sigh of relief. This was more like it. When he was nice, when they laughed together, she felt horrible urges to hug him and never let go.

She could justify sleeping with him as a direct result of her body's overabundance of hormones. But she could not justify the strange pitter-patter of her heartbeat when his fingers had accidentally brushed her face to get to her hair.

Her past relationships had ended in disaster, so she was beginning to like the straightforwardness of what she had, or would have, with Marcus. No surprises. No…affection.

So why did she want to gnash her teeth?

"We should, uh, probably let everyone know we're here," she said.

"First, tell me what you want from me so there are no mistakes on my part. Do you want me to treat you badly? Is that it?"

"Jillian?" she heard her mom call before she could think of a response. "Is that you?"

"Yes, Mom," she answered, never taking her gaze off Marcus. To him, she said, "I don't know what I want from you." And she didn't. She was confused and scared and *excited* about what was happening between them. "I don't know anything right now."

He nodded, his expression growing tender. "I don't, either. We'll figure it out as we go along, I guess, because I want you and I'll do whatever it takes to have you." He winked at her. "Now let's go meet your mother so I can charm her."

Not knowing what else to say, Jillian pulled open the gate and sauntered into the backyard. Why was he so determined to have her? Because sex like theirs was rare and wonderful and for once neither of them would have to worry about a cheating partner. Marcus, she was sure, would simply tell her to her face when he wanted out. *I don't want you anymore, Dimples.*

Her hands clenched at her sides and her stride became clipped. "If you're rude to anyone in my family, I'll make you hold my hand," she warned him.

He intertwined their fingers. "There. Now I can be as rude as I want."

That almost made her laugh. Almost. His hand was

warm and calloused and dwarfed hers. He was total strength, yet he could be gentle when he desired. *Danger zone! Danger zone!* It was happening again, that pitter-patter of mushy gushy *need.* She tried to slip free of his grasp, but he tightened his hold.

"You wanted to hold hands," he said, "so we're holding hands."

"I did not want to hold your hand."

"Please. I know a hint when I hear one."

"Whatever," she scoffed, but she liked that he maintained the contact. Not that she'd ever admit that aloud. They rounded the side of the house, the scent of grilled meat making her mouth water.

Clear, dappled water—no, rippled water—came into view. Cherry had done a cannonball and now came up giggling and spitting. Jillian spotted her mother off to the side. Pretty in a fragile sort of way, with dark-brown hair and pale-blue eyes.

"Hey, baby," she said with a too-bright smile.

Jillian knew that smile well. It was the expression her mother reserved solely for her, so Jillian would never know she was depressed. When her mom spotted Marcus, however, her smile faded.

"Who's he?"

"A friend," Jillian answered. "Only a friend."

Her mother didn't ask the "friend's" name as her gaze dipped to their joined hands. She didn't say anything. She simply jerked her attention to the pool.

"Mom—" Jillian began, then stopped herself. Whatever she said would only make it worse. She did release Marcus's hand, though, and this time he let her.

Brittany sat under a large green umbrella and waved to her. Her hair was black and straight—something Jillian had always envied. Her legs were long and naturally lean—something else Jillian had always envied. She had to work out to keep her own shorter legs toned. A lot. Not that she'd done any exercise lately, though she needed to. Her T-Tapp program kept her mind alert and her body strong.

Steven was cuddled into Brittany's side. He was a tall, skinny man with thinning brown hair and a plain, undistinguished face that could blend into any background. He'd taken one look at Brittany, fallen hard and pursued her relentlessly. Brittany had been unable to resist. They'd married eleven years ago and were still madly in love—yet another thing Jillian envied.

Sometimes, when she watched them together, she wished she could love like that, so carefree and sure. Then she'd think about her dad and all the targets she'd encountered and the longing would pass.

Brittany frowned at her. "It's hot out there. Why are you wearing a scarf?"

Her cheeks heated and she reached up to finger the material. "Where's Granny?" she asked, ignoring the question.

"She couldn't make it," Brittany answered. "She's attending a funeral."

"Did one of her friends pass?" Marcus asked gently, reclaiming Jillian's hand and squeezing in comfort.

Brittany shook her head. "Nothing like that. She planned to ask out the deceased's husband."

Marcus sputtered for a moment before recovering with a polite "I see."

"That's my granny," Jillian said with a fond smile. "Always looking to nail some ass."

"If she's anything like you," Marcus whispered, "she's good at it."

Brent peeked from around the grill, tall, dark-haired and frowning. Smoke billowed around him. "Where's Georgia?" he asked.

Jillian almost groaned. "She wasn't home." She didn't mention that Georgia had probably spent the night with Wyatt.

Her brother ran his tongue over his teeth, impassively absorbing the information. "Who's the guy?" He pointed to Marcus with a spatula. "Don't tell us he's your friend again, because we won't believe you."

"You can ask him yourself, you know." With Marcus at her side, Jillian stopped in front of the patio table and eyed her family, one at a time.

"I don't mind if you tell them who I am to you," Marcus said. He regarded her intently, waiting, as if he wanted to know her answer, too.

Fine. But what should she say? Marcus wasn't her boyfriend, wasn't really her friend as they'd guessed, and she didn't want them to know she was holding hands with her new boss. "His name is Marcus" was all she ended up saying.

"Nice to meet you, Ms. Gr—Jillian's mom." Marcus held out his free hand to Evelyn.

"She's still a Greene," Jillian muttered.

"Ms. Greene," he said.

Her mother just stared at his hand as if it were a snake, poised to bite her.

"I'll only bite if you ask nicely," Marcus told her, all smooth, polished charm.

Evelyn recoiled further.

Brent padded from the grill and reached out. The two men shook hands. "Nice to meet you. I'm Brent, the older brother." He tossed Jillian a you-are-going-to-pay-for-leaving-Georgia-behind grin. "You're the first man Jillian's ever brought here. You two planning on getting married or something?"

She nearly choked.

Marcus did choke.

Her mom covered her mouth with her hands, as if she were about to vomit.

Her sister clapped excitedly. "Ohmygod, are you?"

"No," she gasped out. "No marriage."

Brent mouthed, "You really should have brought Georgia," before heading back to the grill.

"She's dating someone, you turd," Jillian responded. "You are such a bad brother."

He turned and blew her a kiss.

"I'm glad I'm not the only one on the receiving end of your tongue," Marcus said. Then his gaze latched on to her mouth and he tugged at his shirt collar. He released her. "Never mind. Forget I said that."

Yes, she would. Or she'd attack him with said tongue, thrusting it past his teeth and into his mouth, where it would worship his taste for hours. She cleared her throat. "Marcus, that's my mom, Evelyn, my sister Brittany and the man beside her is Steven, her husband." Steven waved. "The little girl in the pool is Cherry and Cherry's twin Apple is—where's Apple?"

"Inside," Brittany answered, fanning herself with a napkin. "Mom bought doughnuts."

Ah. Apple would not return until every doughnut was consumed. They were her biggest weakness.

"Hey, Aunt Jill," Cherry said. She was as precocious as Jillian had been at ten. She had Jillian's curls, too, and her big blue eyes. She ran to her and wrapped wet, dripping arms around Jillian's waist. "I missed you."

Jillian hugged her back with a laugh. "I missed you, too, squirt." Sometimes, when she looked at Cherry and Apple, she was reminded of a time when she'd wanted kids of her own. A family. Before she'd realized just how painful a family could be.

"Your boyfriend's cute," Cherry said, smiling at Marcus.

Jillian's cheeks heated. Marcus took it in stride, smiling back and saying, "You're the smart twin, I can tell."

Laughing, Cherry raced back to the pool and dove in, spraying water in every direction.

"Walk," Brittany called, "or I'll crack open your head myself."

Marcus chuckled.

Still not quite used to it, Jillian shivered at the rumbling sound. If they'd been alone… *Don't go there. Not yet.*

"Why don't you both have a seat," her mom said, her tone formal. She moved to Brittany's side, making room. Still she didn't face Marcus.

As if he hadn't a care in the world, Marcus eased right beside her mom. Evelyn scooted away from him. There was a definite twinkle in his eyes as he inched closer. Not knowing what else to do, Jillian plopped beside him.

What have I gotten myself into? she wondered again.

"Lunch will be ready soon," Brent said. "You like hamburgers, don't you, Mark?"

"Yes."

When he didn't scold her brother for calling him something other than his name, Jillian frowned. He always threw a hissy fit when she did it. "Markie, Mark, Mark," she said, just to see what he'd do.

He reached under the table and squeezed her thigh. Okay, maybe she'd call him Mark for the rest of the day. Jillian smothered a grin and glanced at her mom. "I thought you were cooking pork chops and corn bread dressing."

From the corner of her eye, she saw her sister make a slashing motion across her neck. Her mom teared up and jolted to her feet. "Excuse me for a moment." She raced inside the house.

"Uh, what was that about?" Jillian demanded.

"She burned the pork chops," Steven said, "and she, well, broke down about it."

"She really needs help." A blanket of sadness fell over Brittany's features. "Even more than usual."

Jillian sighed, loud and long. "I'm sorry. I shouldn't have brought it up without making sure everything had gone well." She wondered, embarrassed, what Marcus thought of the whole situation.

"You didn't know," Brent said. "But I, for one, have decided to stop treating her like a delicate flower. I can't take it anymore. I've wanted to do this for a while, but was waiting until I had the cojones. She's just getting worse, so today I'm forcing myself to grow a pair. So just get ready, because I'm not holding back."

Uh-oh. This could not be good. But Jillian was at the

end of her rope, too, and decided to follow Brent's lead. God knows, coddling the woman hadn't helped.

A short while later, her mom opened the glass door and emerged, once again wearing her high-wattage smile. "So," she said, sitting at the table, "what are we discussing?"

Brittany flashed an overly-bright smile of her own. "I was just about to ask Marcus how long he and Jillian have been seeing each other. I've spoken with Jill several times over the last few days and she never mentioned him."

"Yes, why didn't you mention him?" her mom asked, clearly disappointed that she was dating him at all.

"She probably thought you'd kill yourself," Brent replied.

Brittany gasped. "Brent!"

"What?" He shrugged. "It's true. Mom would rather Jillian become a lesbian than risk having her heart broken by some guy. She's not in the market for a son-in-law."

"Whatever." Evelyn rolled her eyes, doing her imitation of a cool mom. "I'm handling Steven just fine."

Steven grimaced.

"You didn't at first," Jillian reminded her.

"I *can* handle men," Evelyn insisted.

"Well, men can't handle your multiple personalities."

"Brent!" Brittany repeated, fury in her tone. "Stop that."

"What? It's true."

"Jillian thinks I'm perfect just the way I am, don't you baby?" Evelyn said, gazing expectantly at her.

"I think…I think…" This was harder than she'd anticipated. But she drew strength from Marcus's presence, as if he were injecting it right into her veins, and forged ahead. "I think you'd have a chance at a stable relationship if you controlled your emotions better." God, had she just said that? She'd always blamed her dad for her fear of relationships, but she was beginning to see that her mom had played a role, as well.

There was a heavy pause.

"Will you excuse me for a moment? I need to use the ladies' room." Her mom jumped up and ran back into the house.

"Brent, I'm very close to kicking your ass!" Brittany seethed. "What do you think you're doing? And Jillian. How could you say that?"

"I told you," Brent said. "She needs a wake-up call. It's past time she admitted that she has a problem and needs to take her medications."

Jillian nodded. "He has a point, Brit. It's worth a shot, at least. Nothing else has worked."

"I guess," Brittany hedged, losing the heat of her anger. "But what if it backfires?"

"Can't get any worse," Brent said grimly.

Marcus squeezed Jillian's thigh again. "You okay?" he whispered with genuine concern.

She bit her bottom lip and nodded. What a...*boyfriend-like* thing to ask. He'd sounded as if he'd sweep her up in his arms and carry her away if needed. What's more, he hadn't seemed disgusted by her mom's emotional displays.

Evelyn returned, her lower lip trembling as she reclaimed her seat. "There's nothing wrong with embracing one's emotions," she said, as if she'd thought of the words inside the house and wasn't able to hold them back a moment longer.

"Mom." Incredulity danced over Brittany's face. She closed her mouth, opened it, closed it. Gulped. She shared a long look with Brent, who nodded in encouragement. She straightened her shoulders with determination. "You don't just embrace your emotions, you make love to them hard-core."

Evelyn gasped. "That's not true!" But at least she didn't cry.

As her mom and Brittany faced off, Jillian chanced a peek at Marcus. He was watching her, his thumb tracing circles over her leg. Even through her clothes, she could feel the seductive power of his skin.

"Sorry about this," she mouthed.

"No problem."

"Hamburgers are done," Brent called. "Buns are on the counter in the kitchen. Be a dear and go get them, Jill."

"Be a sweetie and go get them, Brit," she said. No way was she going to leave Marcus alone with her family. No telling what stories they'd tell about her or what they'd ask him.

Brittany stood. "You two are so lazy."

"I'll help you, bunnybaby." Steven pushed to his feet. He wrapped his arm around his wife's waist. They cooed to each other for a full minute before going inside the house. All the while, Jillian gagged. She might be envious of their relationship but she *never* wanted to act like that.

"Don't forget the plates," Brent called. "Hey, Jill. After lunch I've got a few charts I'd like to show you. I did a little research. Did you know that more men give to charity than women?"

"I don't believe you," she said. He was always trying to prove how wonderful his brethren were.

"I believe it," Marcus said.

"Does the chart list what kind of charity?" She arched her brows. "I mean, I can see the validity of such a claim if we're talking about Bigger Breasts for Bunnies or something like that."

Brent was about to snort, but caught himself and nodded. "Yeah, I'd give to that charity."

The screen door creaked open and Brittany and her crew stepped onto the porch. Brittany's arms were filled with plates. Packages of buns dangled from Steven's hands. Apple, an exact replica of Cherry—except for the sugar glazing her lips—stood beside her mom, holding a pitcher of lemonade.

"If you aren't careful, I'm going to put your face on my Web site," Jillian told her brother. When she got the site up and running, that is.

"You don't have a Web site," Marcus and Brent said at the same time.

"One day I will. I'm going to create a site where women can post pictures of their exes on a Most Unwanted list so other women know who to avoid."

Marcus's expression became pensive. "Actually, that's not a bad idea. Make it a coed site and it's genius."

Brittany smiled at Steven. "You'd never go up on a site like that. You're too wonderful."

"We know how wonderful sugarbutt is," Jillian, her brother and her mom said in unison.

Silence.

"Sugarbutt?" Marcus's brows arched into his hairline. "Seriously?"

Steven gave a sheepish shrug and Brittany slapped his butt. "That's right."

Everyone looked at everyone else, then burst out laughing, the tension broken.

"Cherry, out of the pool," Brittany called. "It's time to eat."

Nineteen

*There are a lot of fish in the sea, but you're the only
one I'd like to catch and mount back at my place.*

BRENT GREENE stood inside his mother's kitchen, staring
out the large French windows that overlooked the
backyard. While he was trying to get his mind off
Georgia—where was she?—the twins were once again
swimming in the pool, soaking up the sun as Brittany and
Steven sat at the edge, watching them intently. His mother
was pretending to pick flowers along the iron fence, but
in reality was watching Jillian and Marcus. Jillian and
Marcus were oblivious to everyone but each other, while
trying to appear as if they didn't know the other was there.

He'd been surprised when his younger sister had
shown up with a man. Truly a first. Jillian usually kept
her love life completely separate from her family life. In
fact, they all had for many, many years, not wanting to
upset their mother—and for good reason.

When Brittany had decided to marry Steven, Evelyn

had sunk into a deep depression that had put her in the hospital on suicide watch. She'd been certain, she claimed, that her oldest daughter was now destined for misery, disappointment and divorce. Evelyn eventually came to accept Brittany's marriage, but it had been a rocky couple of years.

And now Evelyn was on the prowl for her own man, despite her hatred of the entire species. Perhaps that was why she hadn't threatened to plunge a knife into her heart when she first spied Marcus.

Ah, sweet progress, he thought wryly.

Just then, he watched as Jillian stole a quick peek at Marcus. Marcus, who had been watching her, turned away. With his movement, his shoulder accidentally brushed Jillian's and the two jumped apart. Obviously they hadn't been dating long, but the heat between them couldn't be denied.

Brent already liked Marcus. The man did not silently endure the male put-downs that came out of Jillian's mouth, and that was something his little sister needed. It was long past time she was shaken out of her belief that all men were pigs, liars, cheaters and prime candidates for castration.

Georgia needed the same shaking, though not to the same degree—and not in the same way. God, he wanted that woman. He'd always wanted her, *would* always want her. Somehow, she completed him. He should have snatched her up all those years ago, despite the age difference; he should have pursued her harder these past few years instead of trying to woo her gently.

They were mistakes he wouldn't make again.

He'd tried dating other women, but they weren't Georgia and his body, mind and heart always knew the difference. He couldn't get hard anymore unless he thought of Georgia.

Where was she? Worse, who was she with?

Brent pounded a fist into the counter and the vibration clanged plates and dishes together. He rubbed a hand over his face. If she was with that asshole Wyatt…

Brittany chose that moment to glance into the house, her gaze landing directly on Brent. A frown pulled at her lips. She stood, kissed Steven on the forehead, told the twins something and strolled toward the screen door. She said a quick word to Jillian as she passed. Jillian's cheeks reddened. Marcus snorted and then Brittany was entering the kitchen.

Their eyes met, each the same shade of blue. "Spying on everyone?" she asked him as she sauntered to his side.

"Of course." He wasn't ashamed and didn't try to deny it.

Her frown disappeared, spreading into a wide smile. "That's why I came in. I don't have a good view of Jillian and Marcus."

"Please. You came in because you saw me, thought I looked pissed and wanted to calm me down. You're my twin. I know you."

Brittany ground her fist into the top of his head, giving him a noogie that pulled at his hair. "Thinking about Georgia?"

"Yeah. So?"

"Brent—"

"I know you think I'm wasting my time trying to win her, but she'll come around. I'm a great guy."

"And you're not egotistical in the least," she said with a laugh.

"So what'd you say to Jillian?" He didn't want to talk about Georgia right now. He'd have to wonder, again, where she was and who she was with and what she was doing and if she was enjoying it. His teeth ground together so forcefully a sharp pain tore through his jaw.

Brittany squeezed his hand. "I told our darling little sister that she and Marcus would make pretty babies together."

Brent barked out a laugh. "That was pure evil."

"I know." She leaned onto the counter, propping up her elbows. "There's something…odd about those two."

"Agreed."

"They've got the hots for each other, there's no question of that, but they're so strained and polite. He calls her Dimples, but I swear I hear the word *witch*. She calls him Mark, but I swear I hear the word *bastard*."

"Whatever is going on between them, Mom seems to be taking it pretty well. We haven't had to stuff her full of Xanax or rush her to the hospital."

"Probably because it's gotten her mind off the—I can't even say it." She shuddered, her pretty face scrunching in disgust.

"Internet stud search," he finished for her.

Another shudder racked his sister. "Has anyone e-mailed her? I haven't questioned her about it. I was too afraid that she'd break into tears the moment the subject came up."

"Actually, yes. I came over early to make sure her

computer was working—because God knows if she's not getting e-mail from horny guys looking to score, a crashed modem is the reason. I was going to send her a few e-mails myself, under an alias, of course. Just to boost her spirits. Turns out I didn't have to. A little gem who goes by the screen name Iwannagetsome asked her to dinner tonight, and, if she's lucky, breakfast."

Brittany's mouth fell open. "That is so wrong. Tell me she declined."

"I wish I could."

"God," she moaned. "What are we going to do with that woman? We need to get her on meds ASAP."

"Especially with Dad's upcoming wedding."

Quick as a snap, Brittany slapped a hand over his mouth. "Don't say that word. Not here."

"Which one?" he mumbled, the words distorted.

"Both—Dad and wedding." Her arm dropped to her side and she bit her bottom lip. "Mom doesn't know."

"She'll find out soon enough. She always does when it comes to D—that man."

"Does Jillian know?"

Brent shook his head. "I don't think so."

In unison, they gazed out the window at their little sister. As if she sensed their scrutiny, she glanced over her shoulder, right at them, and frowned. She stood.

"Uh-oh," Brent said. "Red alert."

The door popped open a moment later and Jillian stepped inside. "What are you guys doing in here? It doesn't take half an hour to get Marcus a glass of water, Brit."

She shrugged, all innocence.

Jillian anchored her hands on her hips, her expression

determined. She would deny it and slap Brent if he said this, but their father often wore the same expression. "What's going on?"

"Tell us why you're wearing that scarf and we'll tell you what's going on," Brent countered with a wicked surge of amusement. He could already guess.

Jillian's face heated with a blush and she fingered the material. "I just want to look pretty. Is that a crime?"

"You succeeded. You look fabulous. But, lookit, we were talking about Dad," Brittany answered honestly. "Still interested?"

"No." Jillian's lips pressed into a thin line. "You can start again when I leave." She strode to the cabinet and withdrew a cup.

"He wants to have a relationship with you, Jill," Brittany said. "I don't know why you hate him so much. We've forgiven him and if you'd just give him a chance, you'd see that he's actually a good person."

"He's getting married," Brent said bluntly. Brittany hit him and he shrugged. Like their mother, little Jilly needed a dose of tough love.

Jillian froze, a look of shock and disappointment falling over her face.

"He'd love it if you came," Brittany said. "He wants us to be bridesmaids."

"You know how I feel about him," she said through clenched teeth.

Brent pinned her with a hard stare. "Don't you think it's time to bury the hatchet? Or do you want to end up like Mom, bitter and alone?"

"And crazy," Brittany added sadly.

"I'm not going to end up like Mom and I don't have to listen to this." Jillian sidestepped her siblings, tugged open the fridge and grabbed a bottle of water. Her back was perfectly aligned, her shoulders stiff as she filled the cup. "But I'll say this. He has no right to start another family when he couldn't take care of this one."

"Jill—"

"No," she snapped, stopping her sister. "You didn't see Mom the day she…you just didn't see her. You didn't see how sweetly he cared for his girlfriend, while he treated Mom like a leper. So excuse me if I don't want to attend his wedding and paste a happy smile on my face." She tossed the bottle in the recycling bin and marched outside. The screen door slammed shut behind her.

"That went well," Brittany muttered. "Think she'll ever give Daddy a chance?"

Brent lifted his shoulders in a shrug. "Probably not. She was so young when Dad cheated, and she *was* the one to find Mom."

"True. She didn't speak for months afterward. Not to anyone. And her nightmares… Sometimes I can still hear her screams."

"Her bitterness has only grown over the years, I guess."

"Well, Marcus doesn't seem to be taking any of her crap," Brittany said, smiling as they watched Jillian thrust the cup of water at him. Marcus set the cup aside, palmed Jillian's jaw and tugged her face close to his. He spoke heatedly. "I wonder what he's saying to her."

"Let's find out." Grinning, Brent reached behind the microwave and held up Cherry and Apple's old baby monitor. "I found this earlier, when I was working on

Mom's computer, and taped the mic under the table before anyone got here. I had hoped Georgia would be here…."

"Eavesdropping is wrong and you should be ashamed." Brittany clapped. "So turn it on already."

"I was waiting until we could enjoy it together." He flipped the switch.

"—don't deserve the attitude," Marcus was saying.

"All I said was that men were pigs."

"I happen to be a man, and I take offense at being labeled a bloody swine."

"I seem to recall a certain man lumping all women into three categories. Shall I name them?"

"Why don't you tell me what this is really about? You were fine until you came out of the house. Did something happen or did you start this argument so I would kiss you?"

Jillian gasped, but her color deepened, became rosy. There was a gleam in her eyes Brent could see even from a distance. "You wish."

"Maybe I do," Marcus said and then he was kissing her. A deep, thrusting kiss that bellowed from the monitor.

"Turn it off, turn it off!" Brittany said.

"Not yet," Brent said, laughing.

Evelyn finally stopped pretending to pick flowers and watched the two with open abandon, with longing. With anger. The twins, too, watched. They giggled behind their hands. Steven smiled. Brent tried to control his own laughter.

"I wasn't sure about him when they first got here and Jill looked like she wanted to murder him," Brent said. "But he grew on me when I realized he wasn't going to let her male-bash. Now I think I freaking love him."

His amusement faded quickly, though, when Evelyn stepped up to the table and slapped her hands on the surface, startling the kissing couple. They pulled apart and an embarrassed silence slithered over them. Brent sighed. If his mom was going to slip into a fit of depression or rage, *he* just might kill himself.

"Marcus." Satisfied she had his attention, Evelyn straightened, adding sweetly, "Would you like a cookie?"

Brent blinked. Brittany gasped.

"No," Brittany shouted, running outside.

Brent raced behind her. Warm air enveloped him as he grabbed his mom by the shoulders and drew her away from the table.

"Mom!" Jillian frowned up at her. "I can't believe you would do that."

A look of confusion passed over Marcus's features. "A cookie sounds…good. Thank you."

"No." Jillian stomped her foot. "Mother, you will apologize to Marcus right now."

"Really, Mom." Brent shook his head. "I thought you'd learned your lesson about the cookies."

"What's wrong with the cookies?" Marcus asked, unsure.

"Nothing, if you don't mind weeklong hospital stays with your chocolate chips," Jillian answered dryly, but Brent could tell she was troubled. "Mother, this is the last straw. I've tolerated your happy facade for years while you tortured Brent and Brittany with enough ups and downs to drive anyone crazy. And you want to know something? I would have loved you no matter what you did or said. I *do* love you no matter what you do or say. But I will not let you threaten my date. That's right, my date."

Evelyn's face fell. "But...but..."

Jillian held up her hand. "No. No more excuses. Other people have emotional problems, but they don't threaten murder. They deal with their issues and lead normal, happy lives. Don't you want to put the past behind you and take charge of your life? Don't you want a little happiness for yourself?"

Go Jillian, Brent thought.

Evelyn raced inside the house and Jillian turned a tortured gaze to Marcus. Brent watched with satisfaction as Marcus wrapped his arm around her. Maybe Jill would take her own advice. He grinned. Maybe.

Twenty

Screw me if I'm wrong, but have we met before?

MISERY, that's what he should have felt.

But surprisingly, Marcus had a good time with Jillian's family. Well, except for Jillian's mom trying to poison him, something she'd apparently once done to her neighbor and ex-husband. Other than that little setback, the day had been a nice blend of fun, excitement and desire. A tad uncomfortable at times, but invigorating all the same.

The Greene clan obviously loved each other. They were a little quick on the emotional trigger, but then, who wasn't? They laughed, they teased, they argued. And Jillian adored the little fruit girls, Cherry and Apple. He'd felt a pang in his chest every time she had ruffled their hair or flashed them a smile.

That scared him more than anything else ever had. He'd experienced an inexorable urge to give her *his* children. And he'd reacted by snapping at Jillian a few times. When he'd realized what he was doing, being rude to her because he was afraid of what she made him feel, he'd begun to think that maybe she was doing the same thing. Maybe she, too, was afraid and was simply reacting to that fear.

That scared him, as well, but it hadn't stopped him from kissing her. Right in front of her mom, her nieces and anyone else watching. He didn't regret it, either.

Besides Kayla's, he'd never met a woman's family before. It took a relationship to a level he'd always resisted. But he'd been filled with curiosity about who—what—had raised Jillian. Now he knew.

Jillian's guarded yet fiery personality made a bit more sense.

He glanced over at her. She really was a beautiful woman, filled with passion and, of all things, sugar. Right now they were in his car on their way back to her place. She hadn't spoken since they'd left her mom's. Nerves? They both knew he'd be going inside the house with her and what would happen the moment they closed the door.

That's all it took to make his cock stand at attention. He could hardly wait to have Jillian again. To feel her softness. To taste her, inch by delectable inch.

His cell phone rang, dragging him from his thoughts. Jillian turned to him, curious, as he fished it out of his pocket and flipped it open. "This is Marcus."

"We still on for tonight?" Jake asked.

"Tonight?" He almost groaned.

"Poker, asshole. Are we still on or not?"

He'd forgotten about their game. A quick glance at the dashboard clock showed it was five. If he went to Jillian's, made love to her the way he'd wanted—no less than two hours of foreplay before the main event—he'd have to leave immediately afterward. While she'd claimed before to want no cuddling, he thought she'd want it now, with their new arrangement. *He* wanted it now.

He wanted to savor her, before and after.

"Let's reschedule," he told Jake. And he was startled to realize he wasn't disappointed. Poker was his game, his favorite hobby. His religion. The excitement of winning, the anticipation of the flip and discovering what cards his opponents held…he lived for it. Usually. Right now, Jillian was more important.

"This *is* the rescheduled game," Jake pointed out, "and I've been looking forward to it all day. So have the others."

"We'll reschedule again."

"No, we won't. We'll play without you and you can wonder how much money you *could* have won." A long pause ensued and the line crackled with static. Then, "You're with Jillian, aren't you?" Jake whooped out a laugh. "Finally decided to seize the day, didn't you, you dirty, perverted—"

Marcus closed his phone, hanging up on his friend.

"Do you have plans tonight?" Jillian asked, speaking up for the first time. Her tone held no hint of her thoughts.

"Only with you," he said. He turned the ringer off and stuffed his phone back into his pocket. No more distractions.

Relief washed over her expression. "So," she said, her voice unsure, "you met my family."

"I won't try to deny it."

"You're hysterical." She rolled her eyes. "That was… odd for me."

"How so?"

"Like my brother told you, I don't usually take men to meet my mom."

"You mentioned she was a man-hater and she proved it. What I don't know is why?"

Jillian returned her attention to the window, as if the tall, green trees and brown flatlands were fascinating. After a long pause, she finally said, "When I was seven, she found my dad in bed with another woman. That pissed her off. But when she found out he'd taken me to play with the woman's cat, she went crazy. She tried to kill herself. I found her."

"I'm sorry," Marcus said softly, aching for the child she'd been. It helped explain her trust issues, though, and why she fought so hard to prove men were pigs. "You don't have to worry about me cheating on you. Not that we're dating," he added, before she could protest.

Jillian bit her lip. "I think I know, deep down, that you won't go out with someone else. And that, too, is weird to me. Of all the men in the world I could trust, I never would have placed you on the list. Much less at the top."

His heart kicked into a faster beat. "Why do you think you do?" he asked curiously. "Trust me, that is?"

Her head canted to the side, her cheek practically lying on her shoulder. "Maybe because you've seen the effects of cheating, from the business, from your own life. You know firsthand what it feels like to be betrayed."

His fingers stiffened on the wheel. "I never told you I was cheated on."

"You didn't have to. The look in your eyes when you mentioned your ex said plenty. Men don't like to admit when their lover picks someone else."

"And I suppose women do?"

"No," she admitted. "It hurts and it's embarrassing." Out of the corner of his eye he saw her pinch the fabric of her jeans, twisting. Several seconds of silence passed. "Why are we doing this, Marcus?"

He knew she wasn't just asking about their current topic of conversation, but also about their arrangement, their sudden ease with each other when things could end very badly, very soon and sharing such intimate details about their lives would only complicate matters. "Are we showing all our cards?"

"Why not?" She laughed without humor. "We're about to see each other naked. Again."

"Fine. I don't hate you and I never have. I enjoy spending time with you. I've thought about you since I first clasped eyes on you. I feel like I've wanted you forever. I still don't want a relationship," he rushed out, "but I do want you more than I've wanted anyone in a long, long time."

Her mouth floundered opened and closed and a strangled sound emerged from her throat. He frowned. "Well?"

"Well, what?" she managed to squeak out.

"Show me your bloody cards."

She gathered her composure and crossed her arms over her middle, stretching her T-shirt over her breasts. Her nipples were hard, he couldn't help but notice. He forced his attention back to the road.

"You really annoy me. You drive me crazy, and not always in a good way. I barely know you and for most of the last two days, I've wanted to kill you. But…"

"But," he prompted, teeth clenched.

"I can't stop thinking of you, either. I loved being

with you last night and I hate the thought of you with someone else."

Satisfaction hummed through him. Satisfaction and possessiveness and desire. "Good," he said.

"Good."

"We'll take it a day at a time and we'll tell each other if it stops working."

"Agreed."

"It's all about respect."

Her lips twitched in amusement. "And sex."

"Respect and sex," he said with a smile.

Jillian chuckled, and the sound was so warm and sensual his stomach clenched as an intense wave of desire swept through him. Finally her house came into view, and he eased the car into her driveway. Soon. Very soon he'd have her naked and under him, naked and over him.

He emerged and opened the passenger door for her. Her legs were shaky as she stood, he noticed. Without a word, she trudged up to her porch. Her neighbor was still perched on a rocking chair, watching them unabashedly from her own porch. As he followed Jillian, he waved to the older woman and winked. She blushed.

Jillian unlocked the door and held it open, not looking at him. He swept past her, but still she didn't glance in his direction.

Maybe he was perverse, but he liked her nervousness. It meant she was thinking about him, thinking about what he'd do to her, how he'd make her feel. He might just have to pick a fight with her to work her out of it, though, because he wanted her passion, her fire. Nothing held back.

Turning her back on him, she shut and locked the door.

She stayed just like that for a long while, simply breathing in and out.

"You scared?" he asked softly, because he sure as hell was.

Her back stiffened. "Of course not." She whirled on him, but didn't attack him as he'd hoped. Instead, she sashayed past him and disappeared around a corner. He stood in place for a second, once again surprised by the tidiness and beigeness of her home.

People probably told her she needed to brighten the place with colors. He liked the browns, though. The pristine setting made the things they did to each other seem all the more debauched.

"You getting naked and crawling in bed?" he called.

She snorted. "Hardly. I'm in the kitchen."

Blood heating, he followed the sound of her voice. When he rounded the corner, he spied her in the equally beige kitchen, just as she'd claimed, leaning on the fridge door and pouring herself a glass of white wine.

"Would you like one?" she asked.

"No, thank you." He closed the distance between them, took the glass from her, and placed it on the counter.

A frown tugged at her mouth. "I planned to drink that."

"No alcohol," he said.

Something almost…vulnerable flickered inside her eyes and his chest squeezed tightly. She cleared her throat. "So we're just going to hop right into bed?"

"Of course not." He settled his hands on her waist, bunched her T-shirt until a strip of flat stomach showed. Lean, smooth. He hadn't spent enough time in that area last night and he ached to do so now.

She chewed on her bottom lip. "What are we going to do, then?"

"We're going to get naked, *then* hop into bed." He eased the scarf she wore from her neck, letting the soft material caress her skin before he dropped it on the floor. He looked at the hickeys he'd exposed and experienced a primal satisfaction. "You excite me."

Desire licked its way over her expression, chasing away her nerves. Her posture softened; she curled her fingers around the waist of his pants. "Same rules as last night?"

"What rules?" In three seconds, he was going to taste the pulse hammering at the side of her neck. One…two… He leaned down and flicked out his tongue. Delicious.

Moaning, she tilted her head backward. "No cuddling or…or…that feels good…snuggling after—oh, right there—you just leave."

"I didn't do that last night." He nibbled, biting down slightly.

"But you were supposed to," she said breathlessly.

Normally he couldn't get out fast enough once the sex was over. But he wasn't going to let Jillian use him, then kick him out. "No deal. I'm staying, and you're going to cuddle with me for at least an hour."

"An hour?" She pumped her hips against him.

He groaned deeply, his penis so hard he could already feel moisture on the rounded tip. "Two hours."

"Thirty minutes."

"Three hours."

"Forty-five minutes."

"Four hours."

"Fine." She grinned wickedly. "I'll give you an hour, but I won't like it." Closing her eyes, she rubbed against him again.

He let her pleasure herself for a bit, letting his own need grow and intensify, as well. "You'll like it."

"No, I won't."

"Just for that, I'm staying for two hours. Want to push for three?"

"Fine. Two."

He dropped the shirt's hem and palmed her stomach. Warm, soft. Sweet. She gasped at the first contact. "You turn me on, Dimples."

She arched backward, which caused the juncture of her thighs to cradle his erection completely. He hissed in a gulp of air. The pleasure of that small caress was almost enough to make him come.

His hands slid down and around and cupped her ass. With a single fluid motion, he hefted her onto the counter. Spreading her knees wide, he stepped between her legs.

"Why can't I stop thinking about you?" he asked, the question more for himself. He didn't kiss her yet. He wasn't done talking with her—which was odd. He liked talking with her as much as he liked making out with her.

"Maybe for the same reason I can't stop thinking of you." She grabbed the hem of his shirt and jerked it over his head. The material fell to the floor in a forgotten heap. She splayed her fingers over his nipples, down the ropes of his stomach.

Everywhere she touched, his skin prickled like a live wire. "Tell me your fantasies," he said. One more taste. He needed one more taste before he could utter another word. Leaning down, he laved his tongue over the line of her jaw. Mmm, so good.

A shiver worked through her. "I—I don't know."

"Yes, you do. What do you think about when you touch yourself?"

"I—I don't," she said, and embarrassment laced her tone.

Oh, he knew she lied, but he wasn't upset. He realized in that moment that she'd never told anyone about her fantasies. Never admitted them aloud. He liked the thought of being the first to hear them. The first to do what she really, secretly wanted. "I know you like it rough and hard."

"I do not!" Now she sounded scandalized.

And maybe, he thought, she liked it a little painful so she wouldn't have to deal with tenderness. She wouldn't have to feel softer emotions. That's what he'd been doing, he realized with shock. Numbing himself to everything but pleasure. No emotion.

"You do," he said, "and I do, too. I didn't know that until I met you." But this time, he wanted tender. He wanted soft. He did want to feel. "What else do you like?" He cupped her breast and tweaked her nipple through her shirt. "You can tell me."

"I don't know," she said, panting now.

"Tell me. I just might do it."

"Tell me yours," she hedged.

He brought his other hand into play, cupping both of her breasts but no longer touching her nipples. He dabbled his fingertips around them, making her twist and turn and anticipate his touch.

"Men are easy. We fantasize about making our woman come."

"Uh-uh." She shook her head, black curls flying. "Men fantasize about having two women at once."

"You're all I can handle. Tell me," he beseeched. "Tell me what you've always wanted a lover to do but have never gotten."

She hesitated, unsure. So sweetly unsure. "You'll laugh."

"Swear to God, I won't." He had to hear now. His curiosity was almost as strong as his desire for her. What was making this strong, independent woman so nervous?

"I've never…no one has ever…kissed me. *There.*"

Understanding hit him. He felt his lips begin to curl into a smile, but he forced his expression to remain neutral. Oh, to taste between her legs. He would be the first to do so. More hot, hot blood swelled his cock.

He leaned into her and pressed a kiss into her mouth. Her tongue instantly swept out to meet his. They thrust together, her sweet taste rocketing his desire to a new level. He rocked his erection against her, had to remind himself to breathe, and swallowed her pleasured groan.

Before the night was over, he was going to take this woman in every way imaginable. He was going to make her come with his mouth, with his fingers, with his penis. Tomorrow, she'd have to find a new fantasy. Tonight, he'd give her this one. And, hopefully, a thousand others she hadn't known she possessed.

"Well?" Jillian asked.

"I think that can be arranged."

"You aren't…you won't mind doing that?"

"Mind? I'll love every moment of it. So will you," he said. And then he was kissing her again.

Sweet fire, Jillian thought as she feasted on Marcus's

mouth. Her body was on fire for him. She'd stopped thinking about her dad and his impending marriage. She'd stopped thinking about the consequences of sleeping with her boss, the man she thought she hated but couldn't stop picturing naked, a long time ago.

Right now, he was merely a man and she was merely a woman and only pleasure existed.

He stopped kissing her long enough to work her shirt over her head; then his tongue was in her mouth again and the fire in her blood was growing hotter. Blazing. An inferno.

His fingers worked the back clasp of her bra expertly, freeing her breasts. He meshed his chest into hers and she loved the way her nipples abraded him. The friction was delicious.

"Heaven," he said. The kiss picked up speed and intensity and their teeth banged together as they strained for closer contact.

She was still a little embarrassed that he knew her most private fantasy, something she'd always wanted to experience but never had. Would he actually do it as he'd claimed? Just the possibility excited her, made her shiver. She'd never had the courage to ask another man, but the thought of Marcus's hot tongue flicking against her… "Oh, God."

"Pretty nipples." He jerked her to her feet and worked at her jeans. He had them at her ankles in two seconds flat, leaving her in her underwear, a strip of ice-blue lace.

When she began working at his pants, he stopped her, pulled a condom from his pocket, then motioned for her to continue. She did. He was bare underneath, and his penis jutted forward, long and thick and ready. "You didn't wear briefs and you brought condoms. Do I give off *that* easy a vibe?"

"No, but I'm *that* hopeful a guy," he said and ripped her panties off.

Cool air kissed the heat between her legs.

After he rolled on the condom, he cupped her butt and hefted her up. Not onto the counter this time, but on *him*. Not yet penetrating, though. "Wrap your legs around my waist."

She tried not to let her disappointment show. He wasn't going to grant her wildest fantasy, after all. Should she say something? Ask him why he'd demanded to know, told her he'd love it, if he hadn't planned to see it through?

Not wanting to force the issue, she wrapped her legs around his waist without comment. But he didn't enter her as she'd expected. No, he carried her toward the back door.

"What are you doing?" she asked, confused.

"You have a fantasy. I have one, too." He didn't slow his steady gait.

What? Outdoors? "But you said men only wanted to make their women come."

"That's true." He used one hand to open the wooden door, then kicked open the screen and stepped into the cool evening air. Muted beams of sunlight ribboned all around them; birds chirped happily. "But the little details always change. Like location."

She gripped him tight, holding on as her heart began an erratic dance. "People will be able to see us," she whispered, scandalized. The waning sunlight suddenly seemed like a laser beam, a spotlight. "I only have a chain fence."

"I know. But it's dark…almost."

"Go back inside, Marcus. Right now." He was naked. *She* was naked.

"Are any of your neighbors children?"

"No."

"Then I think I should stay where I am. I can feel how fast your heart is beating. You don't want me to go inside, do you? Not really."

Well… Her gaze circled both of her neighbors' yards. No one was out back. And if luck was on her side, Mrs. Franklin would stay put out front! And yet, underneath her embarrassment, she *was* excited. Anyone could see, anytime. See everything. See the pleasure.

"Someone could be watching from their window," Marcus purred.

A tremor trekked the length of her spine.

He laughed. "I knew it. You, Jillian Greene, are kinky." He tossed her onto the lounge chair she'd placed under the large oak. Its swaying branches dripped emerald leaves, creating a canopy around the chair. The zoom of cars drifted from beyond the house.

He sat at the end and pried her knees far apart. For a long while, he didn't move, just looked at her. "So pretty. So wet."

She gripped the arms of the lounge. "Wh-what are you doing?"

He grinned wickedly. "Deciding where to lick first."

She sputtered for a moment, incoherent. When she'd collected herself, she gasped out, "You're going to do that *here?*"

"Where else?" And then he crawled the rest of the distance and lowered his head, and she forgot about protesting, about her neighbors, about breathing.

At the first flick of his tongue, her hips shot straight into the air. He teased and taunted her clitoris, back and forth, then sank two fingers inside her. She screamed. Right there in her backyard, she screamed and groaned and whimpered at the raw, heady sensation of having a man feast between her legs.

"Better than I dreamed," he said.

An orgasm ripped through her and she bit her hand to hold in the rest of her cries. The pleasure was intense, so intense. White lights blinked in and out of her vision as her entire body clenched and unclenched, clenched and unclenched. She bit down so sharply, she drew blood. It was exquisite. Blissful.

Then Marcus surged up and buried his long, thick length inside of her, stretching her, filling her. So good. So good. He didn't move, just stared down at her. Sweat trickled from his temples. "I think it's safe to say they're all watching now," he said, his voice strained.

And just like that, she peaked again. "Marcus. Marcus!"

"I'd ask if you liked living out your fantasy, but I already know the answer." He rocked forward, hard. "I'd ask if you like the thought of being discovered, but I know the answer to that, too."

She might have laughed. Or moaned. She didn't know. She was having trouble forming proper thoughts. "I… hmm…liked it…hmm."

"I think the neighbor on our left just stepped onto her back porch."

"Oh, God."

"Should I stop?" He pounded forward again.

"No. No!"

His warm breath fanned her cheek and he increased his tempo, slipping, sliding, working deeply. It was too much, not enough.

"Are you sure?" he gasped out.

"Sure. Good. Never stop." If he stopped…if he stopped… He hit her exactly where she needed him, deep, so deep, and she erupted again. She quivered and shook and clung to him, shouting his name.

His muscles stiffened beneath her hands, and he roared his satisfaction, shuddering into her. "Jillian. Jillian, Jillian, Jillian."

"Marcus, yes, yes, yes!"

"Jillian?"

Jillian floated down from the stars at the sound of Mrs. Franklin's voice. She stiffened and stilled. Shit. Shit! Marcus choked back a laugh. At least he was on top of her, hiding her nakedness from view. "Everything's fine, Mrs. Franklin."

"I heard—"

"I'll be sure to spank Jillian for being so loud," Marcus said. He wasn't even trying to hide his smile as his beautiful face peered down at her.

Mrs. Franklin gasped. "Oh! Oh, my."

Jillian heard a door slam shut. She bit back a chuckle and shoved Marcus off her. She ran into the house, her face hot. Behind her, Marcus growled, "Lock me out and I *will* spank you."

She was at the sink, bent over laughing when he stalked inside. Dear God. Her seventy-year-old neighbor had seen her having sex. And she didn't care. What kind of kinky sex slave was Marcus turning her into?

Unabashed by his nudity, he anchored his hands on his hips and glared down at her. His hair was a mess, his color high. His eyes glowed with satisfaction, mocking the anger he was trying to project. When her laughter subsided, he said, "If you think that's going to get you out of cuddling, you are so wrong."

Twenty-One

*Didn't anyone tell you that you wanted to
sleep with me? I thought you knew.*

Ring. PAUSE. *Ring.* Pause. *Ring.*

Despite the throbbing ache in her head, Georgia
cracked open her eyelids. Only dizziness greeted her. She
groaned. Her stomach rolled and her mouth felt like
cotton. *What's wrong with me?*

"Someone kill me," she murmured. What had she done
last night? Wait. She remembered. She'd drunk more
wine, tossed and turned, then finally cried herself to sleep
at sunrise. Wyatt had dumped her. Brent had visited her,
demanding she show him her absolute worst.

Ring. God in heaven, what the hell was making that
noise? *Ring.*

The phone, she realized a moment later. Blindly she
reached out and clasped the receiver. "Hello," she
croaked. Her throat hurt, and she rubbed it, trying to wipe
away the burning sting.

"Georgia?"

She blinked. "Brent?"

"Sweetheart, are you okay? What's wrong with your voice?"

She glanced at the digital clock. Seven minutes past eight. But, but, it was dark outside. It was—eight at night, she realized. She must have slept the entire day away.

"Georgia, sweetie. Talk to me."

"I'm okay." Maybe. "Hangover, I think." She scrubbed a hand over her face, paused, felt her eyebrows—or where they should be. "What the—" Her blood froze in her veins as a memory surfaced.

"I missed you today," Brent said. "Where were you?"

Panicked, Georgia lumbered out of bed and stumbled into the bathroom. Her insides twisted with every movement, threatening to erupt, but she didn't stop until she was in front of the vanity. She flicked on the light, and her eyes instantly teared from the intensity. She blinked them back…and her reflection came into view.

A scream tore from her throat.

"Georgia? What's wrong? What's wrong?"

"Ohmygod. Ohmygod, ohmygod, ohmygod."

"Baby, talk to me."

"I—I…" She looked like a monster. A hideous beast with spikes. She'd cut off her hair, her pretty hair. Clumps of red formed a carpet on her floor tile. And her eyebrows, her perfectly sculpted eyebrows…she'd shaved them.

Georgia leaned over and vomited. She dropped the phone, but heard Brent shout, "I'm coming over."

"No!" she screamed, and dove for the receiver.

"I'll be there in five minutes." He disconnected.

He can't see me like this. He can't fucking see me like

this! Not Brent. Anyone but Brent. Moving faster than she ever had before, Georgia rinsed out her mouth and rushed into her room. She jerked on the first items of clothing she found, a thick pair of gray sweatpants and a white T-shirt stained with red wine.

"Why, why, why did I do this?" But she already knew the answer. In her drunken haze, she'd thought to show Brent he didn't really want her, not for the woman she was.

She whimpered.

She had to get out of here. Where? Where could she go? Jillian! Jillian would hide her, even from Brent. She didn't bother tugging on a pair of shoes as she rushed out the front door.

THEY CUDDLED AND SNUGGLED and Jillian loved every moment of it. She felt cozy, cherished, and could not deny that her body fit perfectly against Marcus's. Who would have thought such a thing was possible? Not her, that was for sure.

She sighed with contentment. She'd never felt more sated in her life, and Marcus was the one who had made her feel that way. It was like he'd reached into her subconscious, discovered exactly what she wanted, exactly what she needed and presented it to her on an orgasmic platter.

"Since you've been inside me," she found herself saying, "maybe—"

"Twice," he interjected.

"Since you've been inside me *twice,* maybe now would be a good time to get to know each other a little better." Wait. That was the opposite of remaining detached. Why had she said that? *Because you really do want to know more about him. You like him.*

"Good idea," he said. "I've been dying to know more about the birthmark on your ass." Without giving her time to protest, he flipped her onto her stomach. "Darker." There was arousal in his voice. "Me likie-likie."

She grinned and rolled over. "Typical male. That's not what I meant by getting to know each other."

"My bad. Let's start with you. Tell me why you're so neat and tidy." He gripped her waist and pulled her more snugly into his side.

She settled her cheek onto the hollow of his neck. The gentle *thump thump* of his heart filled her ears. "You make that sound like a bad thing."

"Not bad. Cute. But your house is color-coded, Jillian."

She liked her name on his lips. Sensual. Seductive. "You've stopped calling me Dimples, at least."

"I like your dimples. They're sexy."

"They're schoolgirlish."

He snorted a laugh. "Tell me that while you're wearing a uniform and knee-high socks and I'll…be turned on," he said, as if just realizing it.

She pinched one of the hard ropes of his stomach.

"Ow. So what's with the tidiness? Your mom's house was clean and subdued, nothing to cause a little girl to grow up to despise clutter and multiple colors."

"Are you a therapist now?"

"Yes." His voice dipped low, husky, and his accent thickened. "Tell Dr. Marcus all your problems."

She chuckled. "I like the serenity of soft, matching colors. I like knowing everything has a place. There's nothing more to it than that, I promise you. Are you saying you don't like my place?"

"I like it just fine. It turns me on."

She almost laughed. "Everything turns you on."

"When it involves you, yes."

If he kept that up, he would melt her. Destroy her resolve to keep things purely sexual. "So what does *your* place look like?"

"I have an apartment downtown. It's filled with boxes, hardly any furniture except for my poker table."

No man liked to gamble more than Marcus, and she found that she liked that about him, his willingness to take risks. "How long have you been in Oklahoma?"

"Long enough to unpack," he said dryly.

"Then why haven't you?"

He shrugged, the action bouncing her up and down. She opened her mouth to tell him she'd come help him unpack, but stopped just in time. Helping a man unpack was a girlfriend's responsibility.

"Why don't you come over tomorrow after work?" he said. "I'll show you around."

She hesitated, even though she wanted to shout, *Yes!* "Okay," she said slowly.

"You can unpack while I take a nap," he added with a grin.

"Ha, ha." She tugged on his hair.

"Ow." He rubbed his scalp. "You're bloodthirsty. I guess this means you're ready for round two."

Yes, she was, but she said, "I need to yell at you first. Get myself more in the mood."

"You don't want to yell at me," he said confidently.

He was right. "All right, smartie. Since you know so much, tell me why I don't want to yell at you right now."

"I have a theory." Suddenly he was all seriousness.

She propped up on her elbow and stared down at him. Her black curls cascaded onto his chest, around his beautiful face. His lids were at half-mast, his brown eyes all warm and silky. "I don't think I want to hear it."

"Too bad. Here's what I think is going on between us." His eyes were intense, unrelenting. "When we first met, you had so much pent-up sexual frustration, you couldn't help but snap and snarl."

"The same could be said of you, then," she said, grinning, knowing now that he was teasing. Sadly, though, his words were true.

"Hey, I'm not going to deny it. It had been a while. More than that, I wanted you and I'd never wanted bait before. I tried to keep you at a distance by being rude. I'm sorry."

Okay. Wow. Sweetest words ever. "How long had it been for you?"

"Nope, not telling." He shook his head. "It's a secret."

"Tell, tell, tell."

"Nope," he repeated, "but I will tell you a different secret. I've never slept with a coworker before. Much less an employee."

Their gazes met and she peered down at him, inexplicably happy. "Never?"

He shook his head. "Never."

"Truly?"

"Swear to God." He held up his left hand, as if he were testifying in court.

Again, wow. The knowledge was intoxicating. She was his first. Well, not his *first* first, but still some sort of first for him.

"Now *you* tell *me* a secret," he said.

Hmm, what should she tell him? She could tell him that she, too, had never slept with a coworker until him, but she didn't want him to know how different he was for her. Finally she settled on, "I wanted to buy CAM from Anne."

All amusement drained from his face. "Fuck," he muttered.

"Yeah. I know." She settled on his chest.

"That explains some of your resentment," he said. "I'm just surprised you didn't stab me in the thigh when you found out I'd bought it."

"I'm not gonna lie. I thought about it."

He traced a finger down the bumps of her spine. "So why didn't you? Buy CAM, I mean."

"I tried to talk to Anne about it, but she always pushed me away with a promise of later."

"Did she ever tell you why she wouldn't sell to you?"

Jillian spread her fingers over Marcus's chest, taking comfort in the *da dump dump* rhythm of his heart. "I went out to her lake house yesterday and asked her. She said she didn't want me to end up like her."

"That's it?"

"Yep. Lame, huh."

"Very." He squeezed her tightly, almost a full-blown hug. "No matter what Anne said, you're damn good bait and your Web site idea was great—and I'm not just saying that because I'm sleeping with you."

"Thank you."

"But I won't lie to you. I'm glad she sold it to me."
Pause. "I, uh, never would have met you otherwise."

In that moment (okay, in a lot of recent moments),
Jillian was very glad she'd met him, too, but that didn't
lessen the hurt of having her dream crushed. "And I won't
lie to you. I still want to run it."

"It's in the red," he said grimly. "We're hurting for
money. Anne had pretty much drained the profits this
past year. It's as if she stopped caring."

Jillian hadn't noticed any disinterest in the company
on Anne's part, but that didn't mean anything. Obviously
the woman was good at hiding things. That didn't make
the news any less shocking, however. She'd always en-
visioned CAM as unstoppable.

"But I'm—*we're*—going to turn it around," Marcus
vowed. "I'm willing to listen to any more ideas you have.
And the others. I'll even do that suggestion-box thing."

"A suggestion box is good." She would have liked
having one for her *own* company. What a sad thought. "So
how did you get Anne to sell CAM to you? 'Cause she
needed the money?"

He hesitated before saying, "Don't be mad, but she
called and offered it to me."

"What!" Jillian jolted up. Anne had called him? Anne
had tossed CAM into his lap? It didn't matter how badly
Anne had needed the money. She should have given
Jillian a shot. Hello, loan.

Marcus tugged her back into his embrace. "She called
me, told me that she was interested in selling and that
she'd heard good things about my firm. I made an offer
right then, she accepted, then later she changed her mind.

312   Gena Showalter

Said it made her nervous to make so many changes in so
short a time. I flew out here, talked to her about it and we
were working out specifics a few days later." He traced
a fingertip over her cheek, then along her jawline and her
nerve endings came alive. "Don't be too hard on her,
okay? Anne really does think the world of you. She suggested I make you second-in-command."

That didn't dull the pain. Anne had never really considered her, yet she'd thrown the business at Marcus. Twice.
"What are you going to do when your cuddling time is up?"
she asked, changing the subject before she started crying.

"I'll be too tired to get up," he said. He gently rubbed
her arm with one hand and toyed with a strand of her hair
with the other, twining the curl around his finger. "You
got a problem with that?"

No. She didn't want him to go. Not now and not later.
Becoming addicted to Marcus, though, and wanting more
from him than sex was not good. "You can't stay the
night," she forced herself to say.

He snorted. "Like I want to stay all night," he said, but
there was no heat in his voice.

"Fine."

"Fine."

They lapsed into silence. It wasn't uncomfortable, but it
did give her mind the opportunity it needed to swirl with
questions. "So…" She couldn't believe she was going to ask
this, but… "You've told me a little about your marriage."

"Yes," he said warily.

"Tell me more."

To her surprise, he didn't stiffen. He continued to
caress her arm. "Why do you want to know?"

"Curiosity." She wished. It was more than that, though, not that she'd admit it. She *had* to know about him and the woman who had claimed his heart. It was suddenly an ache inside her.

"Kayla was…someone people gravitated to. She did everything in her power to make sure those around her were happy and having fun."

Okay. In short, everything Jillian was not. She fought against a wave of jealousy. "That's what drew *you* to her, I'm sure."

"Yeah, but not the way you're thinking. First thing I thought of when I saw her was that if a man couldn't make a relationship work with a sweet thing like that, he just couldn't make a relationship work."

That was more telling than he probably realized and she felt herself relax. He hadn't fallen for Kayla because of love. He'd fallen for the woman because he'd wanted a sure thing, certain success.

That the relationship had failed probably accounted for most of his distrust.

"I'm sorry it didn't work out," she said.

He smiled lazily. "I'm not. First time I saw you, I thought, *get her naked.* I wouldn't have been able to do anything about it if I'd been married."

She chuckled just as his stomach rumbled. "Hungry?" she asked.

"You depleted all my strength, woman. *And* I didn't even get to have dessert at your mom's since you wouldn't let me. Of course I'm hungry."

"Yeah, and I still haven't heard a thank-you yet. So be a dear and fix me something while you're in the kitchen," she added, grinning, her good humor somehow restored. How had he done that? With only a few words, he'd brought her from the brink of unhappiness.

He gave her a mock frown…and pushed her off the bed. She tumbled right onto the floor and landed on her ass, gasping and laughing at his audacity.

"You're up now," he pointed out. "You can fix us both something."

"Perhaps I'll make you *cookies,* since you missed out on them and all."

He studied her grin. "You know, if it would have made you smile like this, I would have eaten your mom's cookies."

She jumped to her feet and turned away before he could see the moisture that suddenly pooled in her eyes. Look at her. Acting like a mushy gushy girl.

"Well, what are you waiting for?" he asked, as if sensing how uncomfortable and unsure she was and wanting to lighten the mood. "Your master has issued his command."

This playful side of Marcus was…more than she'd ever imagined.

He was constantly surprising her today. First by asking her to have an affair with him, then going to her mother's, *then* by coming back to her house, fulfilling her most secret fantasy and sticking around after the loving was done. Now this—sweetness followed by playfulness.

Reaching out, she grabbed the white cotton sheet and jerked it off him. "Get up. If you want to eat, you help fix."

He didn't move. "What are we having?"

"Sandwiches."

"Off each other?" He wiggled his brows. "I bet that's

another fantasy of yours. It is, isn't it?" He leapt from the bed in a single fluid movement. His penis was growing long and hard.

She stepped back, her heart already racing. "You better keep that thing away from me." Her blood rushed hot and needy. She should be tired. She should not become aroused so soon after the last time.

"I'll stay away," he said, "after I've had—"

Ding dong. Bang, bang, bang.

Marcus stilled, frowned. Both of them looked toward the bedroom door, as if they could somehow see outside. *Bang, bang, bang.*

"Someone's at your door," he said.

"I know." Frowning too, she grabbed her robe from its wall hook and wrapped it around herself. "Stay here," she said, walking out of the room. She didn't look back to make sure he obeyed. He was cursing under his breath, though.

Bang, bang, bang. Whoever was out there was determined to get in. Those were hard, fast pounds. A battering of fists. She felt a little panicky at the thought of being caught with Marcus. Maybe she should ignore whoever it was.

"Jillian! Jillian, are you there? Let me in."

"Georgia?" She quickened her step and jerked open the door. Her best friend stood on the porch. The small light hanging overhead illuminated her. Jillian gasped in shock.

Georgia's face was red and splotchy from crying, and her hair—Dear God. Her hair. Someone had cut most of it off to the scalp. What wasn't cut at the scalp hung in chopped locks. Her eyebrows were missing.

"Who did this to you?" she said on a strangled breath. Whoever it was, she'd kill him, take a knife and show the bastard how *she* liked to cut.

"I did it." Georgia stormed inside, her entire body shaking.

Wait. What? "You did this to yourself?"

"You have to hide me." Her green eyes were wild as she surveyed Jillian's home. "I can't let him see me like this."

"Slow down. I'm having trouble understanding you." Jillian wrapped her arms around her friend's shoulders. "Georgia, what's going on? Why would you do something like this?"

"Don't let him in, okay?" She spun, leveling Jillian with a frantic gaze. "He'll come here when he realizes I'm not home."

"Who?"

Before she could answer, Marcus entered the room, pulling on his shirt. "What's going on?" he demanded. Then he spotted Georgia. "Dear God."

Georgia gaped at him. "What's he doing here?" But a second later, she was sobbing and trying to cover her head with her hands. "Don't look at me!"

Helpless, Marcus turned his gaze away and faced Jillian.

"I can't believe this," Georgia shouted, her voice muffled by the hands still hiding her face. "You're sleeping with him."

"Well…" Jillian's face burned.

"What about his rules? What about the fact that he's related to the devil? What about him being a gay cross-dresser?"

Jillian met Marcus's stare, silently begging for help.

He opened his mouth, but no sound came out. She'd never seen a man look quite so out of his element.

Finally Georgia dropped her hands to her sides. "You know what? Don't answer. Maybe it's a good thing that you're here," she said on a hysterical laugh, peering hotly at Marcus. "Now I don't have to worry how you'll react when you see me at work."

"I—I—" he said.

"Calm down and tell us what happened," Jillian insisted.

"Men," Georgia spat. "That's what happened. Men!"

Twenty-Two

I hope you know CPR because you take my breath away.

MARCUS was completely out of his comfort zone. Crying women—Lord, he didn't even stick around when his mother turned on the waterworks. But he didn't want to leave. Georgia was his employee and he felt strongly compelled to make things right for her.

Actually, he felt strongly compelled to make things right because Jillian wanted them right.

"Georgia," he began, but pressed his lips together when she whipped around to face him. Her face was swollen and red, her appearance ravaged.

Several tears slid from her watery green eyes and she roughly wiped them away. "You think I'm ugly, don't you? Well, guess what? I don't care anymore! If you want to look at me, go ahead. I won't try and stop you this time."

"I don't think you're ugly," he answered honestly. There was still something striking about her, even if most wouldn't see past the crazy hair and missing brows to notice it.

"You're beautiful," Jillian cooed. She ran her hand

over Georgia's decimated hair, then patted her back. "You're still beautiful, sweetie, but you have to tell us exactly what happened."

"I'll get us something to drink." Desperate to escape, Marcus strode into the kitchen and downed two beers, one right after the other. Sanity first. Feeling a little more relaxed, he filled a glass with water. He grabbed the hand towel that was hanging on the oven rail. With a prayer for fortitude, he headed back into the living room and handed both the towel and cup to Jillian.

"Thank you," she mouthed, dabbing Georgia's face with one hand and holding the glass to her friend's mouth with the other. "Sip."

Georgia pushed the cup away as the story began to pour out of her with a quiet rage that grew with every word. A boyfriend who'd dumped her, wine, a visit from Jillian's brother, wine, the realization that she didn't want to pretend to be perfect any more, wine, a pair of scissors.

"I'm sorry about Wyatt," Jillian said softly.

"I never cared about him, not really. It was always Brent," Georgia said, shuddering. She laughed bitterly. "We test men everyday and I finally decided to test him and prove that he doesn't really love me. He made me hope and hope is a terrible thing."

"Oh, sweetie. There were other, less-damaging ways to ruin your appearance and test him," Jillian said. "A wig. Makeup. Wash-off skin dye."

"That would have proven nothing" was the tortured response.

"So why did you do this? I still don't understand."

Marcus answered for her. "Desperate people do desperate things, Jillian."

"I had to know beyond any doubt." Georgia wiped her eyes with the back of her wrist. "I wanted to prove him wrong *now,* before I fell any harder for him."

He prayed she wouldn't be sorry later, after Brent saw her. The man might not care about her appearance, but he might take offense at being tested. Marcus shook his head. Bait was never the type to give trust blindly and civilians often couldn't understand that.

Not knowing what he could say, Marcus plopped onto the recliner, content simply to watch Jillian. Wait. Maybe he should just go home. Hanging around wasn't something a casual lover did—especially in the midst of an emotional crisis.

"What am I going to do?" Georgia asked on a shuddering breath.

"Well, we'll get a stylist to fix what's left of your hair. You'll be adorable with punk rocker spikes. Don't worry," Jillian said, but there was doubt in her voice.

Georgia again wiped her eyes with the back of her hand. "What about my missing eyebrows?"

"You can pencil them in. Lots of women do that."

"Yes, and lots of women look like clowns," Georgia countered, more than a little hysterical now.

"Your brows will grow back," Marcus offered when Jillian shot him a pleading look.

"I want to die" was the response. "Just die. Brent's going to leave me and you're going to fire me."

Jillian shook her head. "He's not going to fire you."

"Yes, he is."

"No, he's not."

"Yes, he is," Marcus said firmly, ending their debate.

Both women faced him: Georgia with sad resignation, Jillian with astonishment. He wanted to snatch back his words, but couldn't. *Wouldn't.*

Jillian uttered a forced laugh. "Now isn't a good time for jokes, Marcus."

"Unfortunately, I'm not joking."

A moment passed before she reacted, as if her mind needed time to process what he'd said. Then anger and disappointment darkened her lovely features. At one time, that anger would have aroused him. Now he felt only a sense of loss. He was beginning to prefer her softer side, the side that kissed and licked him with abandon. The side that whispered sweet, hot things in his ear while he was inside her. The side that asked him to taste between her legs.

"Why?" she demanded.

Marcus tangled a hand through his hair. He hated to do this, especially while Georgia was so broken. But he wouldn't lie to either of them and he wouldn't let Georgia carry false hope. That would be crueler than what he was about to say. "There's not a wife on the planet who would choose her as bait. Everyone in this room knows that."

Jillian's eyes narrowed. "I believe I mentioned that she can wear a wig and pencil in her eyebrows."

Marcus shook his head. "Wives will know," he said. "Husbands will know, and neither will pick her. They want the fantasy of what they themselves can never be. They want perfection. The real deal."

"Marcus—"

He cut her off with a sharp shake of his head. "I'm sorry. No matter what you say, my decision will stand. Bait makes money when they're chosen. I'm not doing this to be cruel. I told you CAM is under financial pressure. We simply can't afford to employ bait that doesn't meet our clients' expectations." He paused, then added, "Both of you signed a contract before you began working at CAM. Any drastic change in your appearance is grounds for termination."

That wasn't what Jillian wanted to hear and he knew it. She wanted to hear him say that Georgia would be paid no matter what. Well, he couldn't. And he doubted Georgia would like being seen as a charity case. "I'll pay her severance, but that's all I'm willing to do."

"I'm asking you to keep her on." Her eyes beseeched him. "For me."

He squeezed his lids tightly closed. *For me,* she'd said, as broken as Georgia, and he wanted to give her anything, everything. What next? he mused then. A relationship? Marriage? Those babies he'd secretly longed for? *Too soon,* his mind shouted. *Too much, too soon.* "No," he found himself saying. "I'm sorry."

A moment passed. An eternity. A heartbeat.

Jillian spun on her heel, giving him her back. "I'd like you to leave, Marcus." Her voice wavered, as if she were speaking past a painful lump.

Don't let yourself care. Be glad for this. They weren't a couple and ending things now, before they became any more complicated, was actually a smart thing to do. "Are you sure you want to do this?" The words left him before he could stop them. He remained in his seat. They'd only just come to a truce and he was loath to see it destroyed—despite his need for self-preservation.

Besides, he still desired her. More now than before.

For several seconds, she didn't speak. He knew if he walked out the door he would never be invited back. Things would return to the way they'd been before. They would be enemies. There would be no more kissing. No more sex. No more wacky meals with her family. No more poisoned chocolate-chip cookies.

"Yes," she whispered, facing him once again. There was finality in her features. "I'm sure."

He closed his eyes against a strong surge of regret and panic and need. *What's wrong with you, asshole? Act like a man and leave. You forgot pride once. Don't do it again.* But…

He suddenly felt such a sense of loss that he couldn't breathe. There was a crushing weight on his chest, smothering him. *Killing* him. Things were over. *Things were over.* His panic intensified, storming through him, opening a door in his mind and letting truth flood inside—a truth so palpable he wasn't sure how he'd ever denied it.

Jillian's beautiful, determined face flashed, the wild fall of her black curls and the delectable body encased in that white robe. Deep down he knew he wanted more from her than sex. Always had. She challenged him, excited him and wasn't intimidated by his anger. She met him heat for heat in every way.

She would not cheat on him. She knew the pain of betrayal herself, and there was a tell-it-like-it-is iron core inside her that wouldn't allow her to lie if her affections deviated.

She was the perfect woman for him. Too soon for such feelings? Not so. They'd been there from the first. He'd simply ignored them, then put a different name on them.

He might not have realized he was doing it, but he'd been edging them into an exclusive commitment. A relationship with all the strings he'd claimed he didn't want. They were both wary of romance, but he'd been subconsciously shifting them in that direction. And he wasn't sorry.

"Jillian," he said, standing, meaning to go to her. To make her understand. What did pride matter right now? He'd given it up for Kayla for all the wrong reasons. With Jillian, it was right. So right. "I can't let Georgia keep her job. That's not good business and it's not fair to anyone involved. You have to understand."

"I do understand." For a moment, she looked like she would crumble. Then she stiffened and shook her head. "You still need to leave."

"Jillian—"

"She said leave!" Georgia snapped, jumping into the conversation.

"We were only fooling around, anyway. Scratching an itch, right?" Jillian laughed, the sound strained. "It never would have lasted."

Did she truly feel that way? Maybe, maybe not. Either way, it cut him sharper than a blade because it meant he was willing to try and she wasn't. A muscle ticked under his eye.

"I wasn't just fooling around," he said, but she wasn't swayed. She'd erected a wall between them and he didn't know how to tear it down. Not when he'd spent his entire life trying to build his own walls and keep them up. "I'll see you at work tomorrow." With that, he left, shutting the door behind him.

Jillian wanted to cry. Watching Marcus walk away from her without sprinting after him, yelling for him to stop, *something,* was the hardest thing she'd ever done. She had to remind herself that she was immune to men, immune to their charms and never wanted to get serious.

They were all pigs.

"Good riddance." Georgia collapsed on the couch, burying her face in the cushions.

Jillian's chin trembled. Damn Marcus for showing her a tender, caring side in the aftermath of their lovemaking and causing her to desire all that he had to give, then reverting to the kind of cruel and selfish man that refused to take pity on her friend.

Worst of all, he'd ignored her feelings completely. Just like her dad had done. Just like her targets did to their women. He hadn't really cared about her—hadn't ever *claimed* to care about her. She'd just thought…hoped… Well, better to have seen his true colors now rather than later. Wasn't that what she'd always wanted to tell the women who hired her?

"What am I going to do?" Georgia uttered in a tortured whisper.

"I don't know." Jillian forced her attention on her friend. Georgia needed her now. Marcus, she would think about when she was alone. No, maybe not even then. She felt too raw. "I'll call Brent. He'll—"

"No!" Leaping into action, her friend grabbed her shoulders and pinned her with a desperate stare. "I don't want your brother to see me like this. That's why I came here."

"If anyone can convince you that you're still beautiful, it's Brent." Her brother would not desert a woman simply because her looks had deteriorated. *He* wasn't like her dad or Marcus. He was sweet and kind and loving. Not that she'd ever tell him. He already had a big head.

"He'll walk away from me in disgust."

"You can't know that for sure until he sees you. And isn't that why you did this? So he could see you this way?" As she spoke, Jillian wished the last few minutes had never happened; she wished that she were back in Marcus's arms, laughing with him and dreaming up ways to improve CAM. *Poor, pathetic me,* she thought then, disgusted with herself.

What kind of woman would rather have a man than the truth?

You're just like all the other women out there.

"I can't." Green eyes stared up at her, beseeching her to understand. "I just can't. Not yet. I don't care if Marcus thinks I'm ugly, but Brent…"

"All right." She pasted on a smile, knowing it probably looked shaky and false. It was. "We'll make this a girls' night. Why don't I get you a beer."

Relieved, her friend nodded.

Jillian walked into the kitchen and secretly dialed her brother's cell without an ounce of guilt. Her eyes burned as it rang. Damn it! She rubbed at them to rid herself of the hated moisture.

"Now isn't a good time," her brother's voice suddenly rushed out, slicing into her internal lamentations.

"Brent, it's me," she whispered.

"Jillian, I'm at Georgia's. Something's wrong with

her. I was talking to her on the phone, she screamed and I rushed over. But she's not answering her fucking door. I'm going to break it down."

"She's here."

Except for his panting, deadly silence slithered over the line. "What?"

"She's here. With me."

"Is she okay?"

"She's fine. A little shaken up, but fine."

His breathing became heavier, labored, and she knew that he was running. "I'll be at your door in five seconds," he said. "Have it unlocked."

They disconnected without another word. Softly Jillian placed the phone on the receiver. Looked like Georgia and Brent would get a happy ending. Unlike herself. She swiped a lone tear that had decided to fall. *I'll be okay,* she told herself. *Marcus isn't worth it.*

But what if he was?

Twenty-Three

*Are those space pants, because your ass is
out of this world.*

BRENT RAN LIKE A man caught on fire and the only extinguisher to be found was at Jillian's house. His heart pounded in his chest. Something was wrong with Georgia. He might even have heard her sobbing in the background when he spoke to his sister.

Five houses over, he arrived. His body was tense, his blood boiling with the need to help his woman, to fix whatever was wrong. To wipe away her tears. If anyone had hurt her… Jaw clenched, he flew up the porch. The front door was unlocked, as he'd requested, and he sprinted inside.

The first thing he saw was Georgia, lying on the couch. Her back was to him and a pretty beaded pillow was draped over her head, but he could tell she was shaking. Jillian was sitting beside her, patting her shoulder while staring sadly into the distance.

"What happened?" Brent demanded.

Jillian jumped, as if she hadn't realized he'd entered her home. Georgia gasped his name and scrambled closer to the edge of the sofa. "What's he doing here?" Panic radiated from her and she clutched the pillow tighter to her head. "Leave, Brent. Please!"

Frowning, Brent inched forward. He wanted to touch her, to soothe her, but didn't dare. Not yet. Not until he knew what was going on. "Talk to me, sweetheart. Please."

Georgia didn't say a word.

Jillian stood, looking more vulnerable than she ever had before. "Last night, she cut her hair to test you. *You.* Not Wyatt. They're through."

His first reaction: elation. Wyatt was finally out of the picture. His second reaction: confusion. "I don't understand how cutting her hair could test me."

Bending down, determination falling over her features, Jillian jerked the pillow off of Georgia's head. Georgia didn't erupt, didn't scream, curse or cry. No, she drew in a shuddering breath and rolled to her back, letting Brent see her fully.

He felt like someone had punched him in the stomach.

Her face was a mess; red lines branched from her swollen eyes like a spiderweb. Her hair—mostly gone. Her eyebrows—totally gone. Watery green eyes stared up at him in agony and expectation.

Shit. Shit! *Cut her hair* was an understatement. Most of the silky red tendrils had been chopped to the scalp. There were a few locks remaining and those were in spikes. Gone was the beautiful facade he'd lusted after all these many years. In its place…was the vulnerable girl he'd wanted in school but hadn't been able to have.

You know you want to leave me, her gaze seemed to say. Her chin trembled and she hiccupped.

"You did this to yourself?" he asked quietly.

"Yes." Her voice was tired, scratchy from tears. She closed her eyes, as if she couldn't hold them open anymore. "I did it."

"For me?"

"Partly."

Brent maneuvered around her and eased onto the edge of the couch. "Scoot over, sweetheart."

"No," she said weakly.

"Please."

At first, she gave no indication that she'd heard him. Then, slowly, she inched to the side, giving him room. He scooted toward her, until his hip was touching hers.

"I'm going to bed," Jillian said quietly. She walked away without another word, and he heard her bedroom door snick shut.

"Night," he called. Something was wrong with his sister, but he could only handle one unhappy female at a time. He'd deal with Jill in the morning. For now, he kept his attention on Georgia.

What would drive a gorgeous woman to do something like this? To test him, Jillian had said. To test him…how? *Show me your worst,* he suddenly remembered telling her. His eyes widened as all the pieces of this bizarre hair puzzle locked into place. Testing him, expecting him to leave her.

Over the years, she'd told him countless times that he only wanted her because of her face, her *appearance.*

ise?"

ssed her forehead. "Promise."

LAY AWAKE all night. Once she tiptoed into the to get a glass of water and saw her brother and a snuggled together on the couch. That reminded what she'd been doing with Marcus before they nterrupted. Anger filled her and she'd returned to m, to bed, huffing. Crying.

wanted to strike at Marcus, to hurt him because as hurting.

hadn't chosen her, and that knowledge still hurt. chosen duty and his job, proving beyond any doubt she meant nothing to him. Just what she'd thought wanted, but hadn't. Not really.

nce she'd thought to go to war with him, but then d discarded the idea because she'd feared becoming attracted to him. She didn't have to worry about that . She *was* attracted to him, but she was smarter now. w she knew the consequences of giving in.

Eyes narrowed, she stood. She stumbled to her closet d dressed in a pair of black slacks and a black T-shirt. e jerked her hair into a ponytail, then tugged on a pair sneakers. She grabbed her purse and keys and strode to the living room.

Georgia and Brent were still sleeping, still snuggled gether. Chest aching, she shook Brent awake. He oaned and cracked open his eyelids. A moment passed, nfusion fluttering over his expression. When he iented himself, he frowned.

"Something wrong?"

The little nutcase had ruined her beautiful locks so she could know, at long last and beyond any doubt, that she'd been right.

He wanted to laugh, but didn't dare.

"Well," she said, that one word muffled and defiant.

"Well what?" It was difficult, keeping the happiness out of his voice.

"Do you just want to be friends now?" *That* was sneered.

"Why would I want to be your friend *now?*"

"I knew it." Her lower lip trembled. "I did. I knew you'd say that." She tried to rotate to her side. "You're all the same. Jillian was right. You're all pigs."

He gripped her arm, doing his best to remain gentle so he didn't bruise her, and held her in place. "Sweetheart, you're confusing me here. It's a bad thing that I don't want to be your friend? I've never wanted to just be your friend. I've always wanted to be your lover. And I still do."

Her mouth fell open. "Wh-what?"

"You're beautiful to me, now and always."

Refusing to believe him, she shook her head. "You can't mean that. You never tell me I'm beautiful and you're only saying it now because you're a nice guy. You feel obligated."

He laughed, unable to stop himself this time. "I'm not a nice guy, Georgia, and I don't feel obligated."

"Yes, you are and yes, you do." She still didn't open her eyes. "This isn't funny."

"It kind of is."

"No. It's. Not!"

Maybe she was right—about the nice guy part. After

all, he hadn't pursued this woman the way he'd wanted. If he had, he would have packed his bags and moved in with her—with or without her permission—a long time ago. Instead, he'd let her date Wyatt, the asshole loser he'd dreamed about killing over and over again. Painfully. Slowly.

"I never tell you that you're pretty because I don't care about the outside," he said. "But yeah, I think you're beautiful inside and out. I always have. That doesn't mean I'm too nice to tell you that you look like shit right now."

Her cheeks bloomed bright with color. "You don't have to be rude. I know I look like a mutant."

"A cute mutant. Listen, sweetheart. You can't have it both ways. I'm either nice or I'm rude. Actually," he said after a pause, "I'm neither. I'm just honest. You'll come to love that about me."

"Come…to? So you want to stay around me? You really do love me?" Disbelief radiated from her and, if he wasn't mistaken, happiness, too. The emotion was muted, barely there, but that slight glimmer warmed him inside and out. "Still?"

"Well, yeah." He wiped away one of her tears. "I told you how I love the sound of your voice when you're happy and the freckles you try so hard to hide. But did I mention that I love how you sing songs from *The Little Mermaid* when you think no one can hear? I love that you would die for my younger sister. I love the way you smell, like cotton candy. I love that you gaze down at your hands and twist your fingers together when you're nervous. I love the granny glasses you used to wear and, when I finally get you into bed, you better believe you're going

to wear a pair. I've fantasized abo[...] times I've lost count."

A tremor moved through her, [...] couch shook.

"Lean against the edge, sweethe[...] She obeyed without protest. Inste[...] he stretched out beside her. Her body [...] her scent salty-sweet. God, he'd wa[...] position for so long. Holding her. Soa[...]

"I'm jobless," she said. "Marcus fir[...]

"Good for him." So Marcus was Geo[...] *boss?* Interesting…

"Excuse me?"

"I would have fired you, too. You shaved [...] for God's sake!" He chuckled, but quickly s[...] you, sweetheart, but maybe it's time for a fr[...] everything. The job. Your outlook on life. M[...]

"I think I'm in shock." There was a layer [...] her voice, as if she were finally coming to un[...] depths of his feelings. As if she were finally re[...] she hadn't needed to go to such lengths to test hi[...]

He wrapped his arm around her waist and [...] tight. "Listen up, Scissors. I love you, okay. La[...] hasn't changed that. I want to be with you. I [...] *You.* The woman you are, not the woman you l[...]

Trembling again, she burrowed her head into [...] "I—I don't know what to say."

"Then don't say anything. Go to sleep, sw[...] We'll talk some more in the morning."

"You'll stay?"

"There's nowhere else I'd rather be."

"I'm going out," she said.

Slowly he eased to a sitting position, careful not to jostle Georgia. "Everything okay?"

"There's something I have to do. I'll see you later." She turned and headed for the front door.

"You shouldn't be mad at Marcus," he called. "Georgia isn't."

"You don't know the situation." She closed and locked the door behind her. Outside, muted beams of sunlight fought for dominance with the dark. The air was cool and fragrant with pine and flowers. Blackbirds soared overhead. She had every right to be mad at Marcus. He'd shattered her illusions.

She was going to make him miserable. He could fire her, she no longer cared. In fact, she hoped he did. She wouldn't give him the satisfaction of quitting or let him get out of paying her severance.

Jillian hopped into her car and drove to the nearest supercenter. In the hunting and fishing section, she found exactly what she needed. Her mom had taught her a little trick with some of the more aromatic items hunters used to attract their prey. For the first time in her life, she was putting that knowledge to use.

On the drive to the office—Anne had given her a key a few years ago—her cell phone belted out the song "Crazy." She groaned. She didn't need this now. Still, she dug her cell out of her purse. "Hello, Mom."

"How are things with your boyfriend, Jillian?" were the first words out of Evelyn's mouth.

"He's not my boyfriend." He could have been. Maybe. One day. "I don't even like him." *Yes, you do, liar.* He might have fired Georgia, but up until the end he'd been fun and tender with Jillian.

"I don't believe you."

"How are you feeling today?" she asked, changing the subject before she started crying.

"Good. Happy."

"Really?" Her mom *did* sound happy, and not the forced happy Jillian usually heard.

"You know I get…sad sometimes."

"Yes," Jillian answered hesitantly. Evelyn never spoke to her about the sadness. Never.

"Well, I—" she cleared her throat "—started taking my pills last night."

Jillian almost swerved off the road. Her mom had seen many doctors over the years, had been given many prescriptions, but she'd never taken any. She didn't need them, she claimed. She was fine the way she was. "I'm ecstatic, Mom, but what changed your mind?"

She sighed. "Your lecture really got to me. And you said you would love me no matter how I acted, right?"

"Right."

"Well, I want to act—be—happy."

Wow.

Her mom sighed again. "I need to explain to you about yesterday. When Brittany married Steven, I was upset. But then I realized that she's not like me. She can be happy anywhere, with anyone, no matter what's going on around her. Her life isn't going to be destroyed by Steven, no matter what he might do to her. She's too centered to let a man's actions define her. So I got over it and accepted him as part of our family."

"That's a good thing."

"When I saw you with Marcus, I was more upset than I'd ever been about Steven. Did you realize that? It's just," she said, not giving Jillian a chance to reply, "you're so much like me. You *can't* be happy anywhere, with anyone if things are going badly. Your life *was* destroyed by betrayal once already. I wasn't sure you could recover if it happened again. That's why I never wanted you to let anything—any*one*—into your life. I thought, for you, being alone was better than risking your heart."

Maybe being alone *was* the right choice. And had she heard that first part right? Like her mom? Dear God. Say it wasn't so.

"But you found someone with a backbone of steel," her mom blithely continued on, "and you decided to trust him, despite everything that's happened in your own life. Despite the fact that things could go bad. Well, I want to do that, too. I've never seen you so…happy."

Happy? Ha. If she were any *happier,* she'd drive off a cliff.

"If you can live without fear, after everything you've witnessed, I should be able to, as well."

"I'm glad for you." *But I'm not living without fear,* she almost admitted. Not even close. In fact, she'd never been more afraid in her life. She didn't say it; she couldn't destroy her mom's new outlook.

"There's more." Her mom drew in a long breath, as if bracing herself. She'd probably planned the speech all morning. "When you, Brent and Brittany said I had multiple personalities, well, it hurt. But it also helped me see myself through your eyes. I don't want to be the person who makes everyone around her miserable. I want a life and I want a man."

"Mom—"

"I'm not finished. I'm tired of being alone. Maybe if I get my emotions under control, someone will stick around and love me for who I am." By the time she finished, she was crying. "I'm sorry. The medicine hasn't kicked in yet."

"Oh, Mom."

"No, no. Don't feel sorry for me."

"I don't. I'm just so proud of you."

There was a heavy pause. "Really?" Evelyn asked hopefully.

"Really."

Another pause. Then, of all things, a laugh. "I didn't call to cry or even to talk about myself. I called because last night after you and your—Marcus left, Brent and Brittany spoke to me about you and your dad."

Okay. Seriously. What had come over her mom? She *never* talked about Jillian's father. "What about him?" she asked stiffly.

"I, well, I was wrong to poison you against him. Those are Brent's words, not mine. I just wanted someone to hate him as much as I did, so that my own feelings of hatred could be justified. That came courtesy of Brittany. But this next part, it's all me so listen closely." She cleared her throat. "I knew what I was doing was wrong, every time I told you what a horrible person he was or asked you to stay with me instead of going to see him. Even while I was doing it, I knew I shouldn't—but I couldn't seem to stop. I'm…sorry."

The little nutcase had ruined her beautiful locks so she could know, at long last and beyond any doubt, that she'd been right.

He wanted to laugh, but didn't dare.

"Well," she said, that one word muffled and defiant.

"Well what?" It was difficult, keeping the happiness out of his voice.

"Do you just want to be friends now?" *That* was sneered.

"Why would I want to be your friend *now?*"

"I knew it." Her lower lip trembled. "I did. I knew you'd say that." She tried to rotate to her side. "You're all the same. Jillian was right. You're all pigs."

He gripped her arm, doing his best to remain gentle so he didn't bruise her, and held her in place. "Sweetheart, you're confusing me here. It's a bad thing that I don't want to be your friend? I've never wanted to just be your friend. I've always wanted to be your lover. And I still do."

Her mouth fell open. "Wh-what?"

"You're beautiful to me, now and always."

Refusing to believe him, she shook her head. "You can't mean that. You never tell me I'm beautiful and you're only saying it now because you're a nice guy. You feel obligated."

He laughed, unable to stop himself this time. "I'm not a nice guy, Georgia, and I don't feel obligated."

"Yes, you are and yes, you do." She still didn't open her eyes. "This isn't funny."

"It kind of is."

"No. It's. Not!"

Maybe she was right—about the nice guy part. After

all, he hadn't pursued this woman the way he'd wanted. If he had, he would have packed his bags and moved in with her—with or without her permission—a long time ago. Instead, he'd let her date Wyatt, the asshole loser he'd dreamed about killing over and over again. Painfully. Slowly.

"I never tell you that you're pretty because I don't care about the outside," he said. "But yeah, I think you're beautiful inside and out. I always have. That doesn't mean I'm too nice to tell you that you look like shit right now."

Her cheeks bloomed bright with color. "You don't have to be rude. I know I look like a mutant."

"A cute mutant. Listen, sweetheart. You can't have it both ways. I'm either nice or I'm rude. Actually," he said after a pause, "I'm neither. I'm just honest. You'll come to love that about me."

"Come…to? So you want to stay around me? You really do love me?" Disbelief radiated from her and, if he wasn't mistaken, happiness, too. The emotion was muted, barely there, but that slight glimmer warmed him inside and out. "Still?"

"Well, yeah." He wiped away one of her tears. "I told you how I love the sound of your voice when you're happy and the freckles you try so hard to hide. But did I mention that I love how you sing songs from *The Little Mermaid* when you think no one can hear? I love that you would die for my younger sister. I love the way you smell, like cotton candy. I love that you gaze down at your hands and twist your fingers together when you're nervous. I love the granny glasses you used to wear and, when I finally get you into bed, you better believe you're going to wear a pair. I've fantasized about you in them so many times I've lost count."

A tremor moved through her, so intense the entire couch shook.

"Lean against the edge, sweetheart. I'm falling off."

She obeyed without protest. Instead of settling deeper, he stretched out beside her. Her body was warm and soft, her scent salty-sweet. God, he'd wanted to be in this position for so long. Holding her. Soaking her in.

"I'm jobless," she said. "Marcus fired me."

"Good for him." So Marcus was Georgia and Jillian's *boss?* Interesting…

"Excuse me?"

"I would have fired you, too. You shaved your eyebrows, for God's sake!" He chuckled, but quickly sobered. "I love you, sweetheart, but maybe it's time for a fresh start. With everything. The job. Your outlook on life. Me."

"I think I'm in shock." There was a layer of shame in her voice, as if she were finally coming to understand the depths of his feelings. As if she were finally realizing that she hadn't needed to go to such lengths to test his devotion.

He wrapped his arm around her waist and squeezed tight. "Listen up, Scissors. I love you, okay. Lack of hair hasn't changed that. I want to be with you. I love you. *You.* The woman you are, not the woman you look like."

Trembling again, she burrowed her head into his neck. "I—I don't know what to say."

"Then don't say anything. Go to sleep, sweetheart. We'll talk some more in the morning."

"You'll stay?"

"There's nowhere else I'd rather be."

"Promise?"

He kissed her forehead. "Promise."

JILLIAN LAY AWAKE all night. Once she tiptoed into the kitchen to get a glass of water and saw her brother and Georgia snuggled together on the couch. That reminded her of what she'd been doing with Marcus before they were interrupted. Anger filled her and she'd returned to her room, to bed, huffing. Crying.

She wanted to strike at Marcus, to hurt him because she was hurting.

He hadn't chosen her, and that knowledge still hurt. He'd chosen duty and his job, proving beyond any doubt that she meant nothing to him. Just what she'd thought she wanted, but hadn't. Not really.

Once she'd thought to go to war with him, but then she'd discarded the idea because she'd feared becoming too attracted to him. She didn't have to worry about that now. She *was* attracted to him, but she was smarter now. *Now* she knew the consequences of giving in.

Eyes narrowed, she stood. She stumbled to her closet and dressed in a pair of black slacks and a black T-shirt. She jerked her hair into a ponytail, then tugged on a pair of sneakers. She grabbed her purse and keys and strode into the living room.

Georgia and Brent were still sleeping, still snuggled together. Chest aching, she shook Brent awake. He moaned and cracked open his eyelids. A moment passed, confusion fluttering over his expression. When he oriented himself, he frowned.

"Something wrong?"

"I'm going out," she said.

Slowly he eased to a sitting position, careful not to jostle Georgia. "Everything okay?"

"There's something I have to do. I'll see you later." She turned and headed for the front door.

"You shouldn't be mad at Marcus," he called. "Georgia isn't."

"You don't know the situation." She closed and locked the door behind her. Outside, muted beams of sunlight fought for dominance with the dark. The air was cool and fragrant with pine and flowers. Blackbirds soared overhead. She had every right to be mad at Marcus. He'd shattered her illusions.

She was going to make him miserable. He could fire her, she no longer cared. In fact, she hoped he did. She wouldn't give him the satisfaction of quitting or let him get out of paying her severance.

Jillian hopped into her car and drove to the nearest supercenter. In the hunting and fishing section, she found exactly what she needed. Her mom had taught her a little trick with some of the more aromatic items hunters used to attract their prey. For the first time in her life, she was putting that knowledge to use.

On the drive to the office—Anne had given her a key a few years ago—her cell phone belted out the song "Crazy." She groaned. She didn't need this now. Still, she dug her cell out of her purse. "Hello, Mom."

"How are things with your boyfriend, Jillian?" were the first words out of Evelyn's mouth.

"He's not my boyfriend." He could have been. Maybe. One day. "I don't even like him." *Yes, you do, liar.* He might have fired Georgia, but up until the end he'd been fun and tender with Jillian.

"I don't believe you."

"How are you feeling today?" she asked, changing the subject before she started crying.

"Good. Happy."

"Really?" Her mom *did* sound happy, and not the forced happy Jillian usually heard.

"You know I get…sad sometimes."

"Yes," Jillian answered hesitantly. Evelyn never spoke to her about the sadness. Never.

"Well, I—" she cleared her throat "—started taking my pills last night."

Jillian almost swerved off the road. Her mom had seen many doctors over the years, had been given many prescriptions, but she'd never taken any. She didn't need them, she claimed. She was fine the way she was. "I'm ecstatic, Mom, but what changed your mind?"

She sighed. "Your lecture really got to me. And you said you would love me no matter how I acted, right?"

"Right."

"Well, I want to act—be—happy."

Wow.

Her mom sighed again. "I need to explain to you about yesterday. When Brittany married Steven, I was upset. But then I realized that she's not like me. She can be happy anywhere, with anyone, no matter what's going on around her. Her life isn't going to be destroyed by Steven, no matter what he might do to her. She's too centered to let a man's actions define her. So I got over it and accepted him as part of our family."

"That's a good thing."

"When I saw you with Marcus, I was more upset than I'd ever been about Steven. Did you realize that? It's just," she said, not giving Jillian a chance to reply, "you're so much like me. You *can't* be happy anywhere, with anyone if things are going badly. Your life *was* destroyed by betrayal once already. I wasn't sure you could recover if it happened again. That's why I never wanted you to let anything—any*one*—into your life. I thought, for you, being alone was better than risking your heart."

Maybe being alone *was* the right choice. And had she heard that first part right? Like her mom? Dear God. Say it wasn't so.

"But you found someone with a backbone of steel," her mom blithely continued on, "and you decided to trust him, despite everything that's happened in your own life. Despite the fact that things could go bad. Well, I want to do that, too. I've never seen you so…happy."

Happy? Ha. If she were any *happier,* she'd drive off a cliff.

"If you can live without fear, after everything you've witnessed, I should be able to, as well."

"I'm glad for you." *But I'm not living without fear,* she almost admitted. Not even close. In fact, she'd never been more afraid in her life. She didn't say it; she couldn't destroy her mom's new outlook.

"There's more." Her mom drew in a long breath, as if bracing herself. She'd probably planned the speech all morning. "When you, Brent and Brittany said I had multiple personalities, well, it hurt. But it also helped me see myself through your eyes. I don't want to be the person who makes everyone around her miserable. I want a life and I want a man."

"Mom—"

"I'm not finished. I'm tired of being alone. Maybe if I get my emotions under control, someone will stick around and love me for who I am." By the time she finished, she was crying. "I'm sorry. The medicine hasn't kicked in yet."

"Oh, Mom."

"No, no. Don't feel sorry for me."

"I don't. I'm just so proud of you."

There was a heavy pause. "Really?" Evelyn asked hopefully.

"Really."

Another pause. Then, of all things, a laugh. "I didn't call to cry or even to talk about myself. I called because last night after you and your—Marcus left, Brent and Brittany spoke to me about you and your dad."

Okay. Seriously. What had come over her mom? She *never* talked about Jillian's father. "What about him?" she asked stiffly.

"I, well, I was wrong to poison you against him. Those are Brent's words, not mine. I just wanted someone to hate him as much as I did, so that my own feelings of hatred could be justified. That came courtesy of Brittany. But this next part, it's all me so listen closely." She cleared her throat. "I knew what I was doing was wrong, every time I told you what a horrible person he was or asked you to stay with me instead of going to see him. Even while I was doing it, I knew I shouldn't—but I couldn't seem to stop. I'm…sorry."

Now Jillian did swerve. A car honked at her and she quickly moved back into her lane. "Really, who *are* you? I don't understand why you're saying these things."

"I want to finally let the past go. Maybe you should consider that, too. Bitterness hasn't worked for either of us. Maybe forgiveness will. Now, I have to go. My meds should kick in fully in a few weeks and I want to have my personal ad ready." *Click.*

Jillian stared at the phone in shock—until another person honked at her and she realized she was edging into the wrong lane again. She hurriedly jerked the car to its proper place.

Her mom wanted her to let go of the past, maybe talk to her dad. Brent wanted her to forgive Marcus. Dear Lord. What was the world coming to?

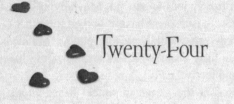

Twenty-Four

If I tell you my name, will you scream it
while I pleasure you?

"JILLIAN."

"Marcus."

Marcus walked through CAM's front hallway, his body on alert. He hadn't expected her to be here. He'd expected her to call in sick or even to quit. But here she was, seated at her cube, looking beautiful, carefree. She was dressed in black, her curls trapped in a ponytail. She didn't glance at him as he passed her, but kept her eyes on her computer screen.

Seeing her—and knowing what she looked like naked—was like a punch in the gut. His blood instantly heated. His muscles—all of them—clenched and hardened. He kept walking, though, and strode into his office, shutting the door behind him. He pulled the blinds closed and tangled a hand in his hair. Shit. He wanted her, so badly. And if things had been different, he could have called her into his office and they could have spent some quality time getting naked. Afterward he would have held her and they would have talked and laughed again.

Sighing, he flipped on the light and moved to his desk, where he plopped down. "Shit," he muttered.

He really did want to call Jillian in here. He wanted to talk to her about last night. About a future. But she would turn him down; he knew she would. And not because she had stopped wanting him. She hadn't. At least, he hoped not. She simply wasn't ready for what he wanted to give.

He'd lain awake last night, thinking about her, and he suspected that she was running scared. He suspected this distance between them had nothing to do with Georgia and everything to do with her own fears of commitment. They'd been getting close. They'd formed a bond. That had to have spooked her. Hell, it had spooked him and— what the hell was that hideous smell?

His nose wrinkled and twitched. He sniffed left, sniffed right. Bloody hell, where was it coming from? He sniffed his armpits. Nope. The office had smelled fine when he'd first walked in, but now… What. The. Hell?

He stood, walked to the window. Opened it. Breathed. His stomach rolled. Holy mother of Christ, it was everywhere. It was like he'd stepped into a horse's ass while holding a bowl of maggots. He gagged. His eyes even teared.

He heard murmuring in the hallway. As fast as his feet could carry him, he raced to the door and jerked it open. He stepped out. Unfortunately, fresh, clean air did not envelop him.

"What's that smell?" Jake asked as he padded down

the hallway. "I could smell it in the parking lot." He fanned his nose.

The rotten stench of hell was wafting from his office, even through the door. "I have no bloody idea."

"Problem?" Jillian stood and sidled around to the side of her cube. She rested her hip against the wall, the picture of serenity.

Joe and Selene entered the building and paused. They looked at each other, then raced past Marcus, holding their noses and peering at him as if he needed a shower as they passed. For a split second, as they crossed his line of vision, he lost sight of Jillian. Then he saw her again, and there was a wicked gleam in her eyes, quickly masked.

Somehow, she had done this. She had stunk up his office.

"I want to vomit," Jake said. He looked from Marcus to Jillian, from Jillian to Marcus. In a quiet voice meant only for Marcus, he added, "I guess you didn't take my advice, after all. You and the little woman still look like you want to kill each other."

"Oh, I took your advice," Marcus said loudly, his voice carrying. "It just blew up in my face. Jillian, may I speak with you for a moment?"

"I'm typing my notes on Saturday's assignment. Could our chat wait?"

"No," he ground out.

She shrugged, the action nonchalant. "Shall we talk in your office, then?"

He *should* make her enter that hellish domain, but he wouldn't be able to stand it. He'd rather cut off his nose. More than the smell, however, he remembered the last time he'd had her inside his office. They'd kissed. Touched. Done exquisite things. The memory already haunted him. "Meet me in the conference room," he said. "Five minutes."

Just then, Danielle and Amelia entered the building. Both were frowning. "Have you seen Georgia?" Amelia asked. Her nose twitched and she waved her hand in front of her face. "What's that awful smell?"

"I haven't been able to get a hold of Georgia," Danielle said, holding her nose, "and she's not home. She was supposed to pick me up this morning."

Marcus looked at Jillian, his gaze pulled by a force greater than himself. Her beautiful lips were thinning with displeasure. "Didn't you hear?" she said. "Georgia was fired."

Amelia gasped. "What? Why?"

"Ask Marcus," Jillian said, her tone flat, devoid of emotion.

Everyone stopped and stared at Marcus. A few of the men straggled into the hallway, too, and stopped to find out what was going on. Marcus felt his blood begin to boil. He'd planned to call a meeting and gently break the news without giving away any details. If Georgia wanted them to know what had happened, she could tell them.

"She needed some time off," he said, keeping his voice neutral. "Jillian. Conference room. Now. Your five-minute reprieve is over." He stalked away before anyone could ask him another question he wasn't yet prepared to answer. He didn't look back to ensure Jillian followed. He knew she would. She wasn't a coward. A human stink bomb, maybe, but not a coward.

He waited for her at the glass doors, holding one open. She rounded the corner, chin high, shoulders squared. After she sailed past him, he let the door close of its own accord. "What did you want to see me about?" she asked sweetly, turning to face him.

He moved toward her and leaned down, getting right in her face. "What did you do to my office?"

She blinked up at him, all innocence. "What makes you think I did anything?"

She didn't deny it, at least. "I have a client coming in today," he gritted out. "You remember our lap dancer from the club? Well, I get to tell her hubby that his wife is cheating. I can't have that conversation in my office if it smells like a sewer."

Guilty color flooded her face—guilt and *arousal,* as if she were remembering the after-hours acrobatics on her couch, as well—and she stared down at her tennis shoes.

"We told each other that no matter what happened between us personally, we wouldn't let it affect our work." Looking at her, being this close to her, was playing havoc with his senses. He could smell her—and it was an addicting, sensual scent that somehow managed to overshadow the stench outside the room.

"That's like telling someone you've fired that it isn't personal, it's just business. Well, guess what." Her tortured gaze lifted, her lashes so long they cast shadows over her cheeks. "It *is* personal to the one getting fired."

"Georgia brought it on herself, Jillian. I think she even understood. You're the only one who can't seem to get past it. Why is that?" He didn't give her time to respond.

"I think you're just looking for a reason, any reason, to keep me out of your bed."

Her eyes flashed with such intense heat, he was almost burned. Almost scorched and blistered. He was very close to wrapping his hands around her neck. He'd choke her or kiss her—he wasn't sure which. Maybe both.

"Just so you know," he said tightly, "you'll watch the meeting with Mr. Parker from my computer. In my office." He paused, hoping she'd say something. When she didn't, he added, "At least have the decency to tell me what it was I was smelling."

A moment passed, then, "Deer urine," she said on a sigh.

His mouth floundered open and closed. "You have got to be kidding me. You put deer urine in my office?"

"That's right." Her eyes narrowed. "What you did to Georgia really stinks, and I wanted you to smell how bad." There was an unspoken *what you did to me really stinks, too,* in her words.

A muscle ticked below his eye. "Do you want me to fire you, is that it? Well, guess what, Dimples. I won't fire you and let you ignore what's between us. If you want to be rid of me, you'll have to grow the balls to quit."

A knock sounded at the door, and they both turned to glare at the intruder. Selene peeked inside. She was frowning. "Mr. Parker is here," she said. "I've left him in the hall. Your office smells like burnt hair wrapped in poo."

"I'll be there in a minute." He scrubbed a hand over his face, suddenly weary. "Just…keep him occupied."

She nodded, gave Jillian a *what's going on look,* and moved off.

"You know, Jillian," he said, drawing out the words.

"You're embarrassed, probably confused by what you're feeling and definitely angry. But I'm willing to wait for you, however long you need."

She raised her chin, appearing confused, hopeful and scared all at once. "I don't understand."

"I was married, you know that, and it failed. I've been running from commitment ever since. You might not have been married, but you've been running, too. One day you're going to stop running and fall. And I'm going to be there to catch you."

Her lips parted and he leaned deeper into her personal space. Their breath blended, their mouths almost touched. "I'm willing to bet that relationships *can* work. If you give yourself to the right person." He left without another word, forcing her to follow.

I'm willing to bet that relationships can work. If you give yourself to the right person.

She tried to block those dangerous words as she watched the meeting with Mr. Parker from Marcus's computer. After a while, blocking them became easy. All she could think about was death. The rank smell of Marcus's office was more than she could bear. She'd had no idea painting deer urine on his lightbulb would cause this kind of stench. Her mom had done it to her dad and her neighbor and laughed about it, but Jillian could not have imagined *this*.

At some point in the meeting—the minutes were blurred together—she stopped trying to pretend it didn't bother her and stood. She walked to the open window and sucked in the cool air. That helped, but only slightly.

All the while, she peered at the computer, watching as Marcus broke the bad news to Mr. Parker in the conference room. When Marcus showed him the video of his wife, sitting on another man's lap, kissing him, the man dissolved into quiet sobs.

Marcus apologized. Jillian wanted so badly to apologize, too, anything to make the man's pain go away, but she could think of nothing. He wasn't a pig, yet his heart had just been broken.

He would never be the same again.

No one was, after infidelity.

Mr. Parker would never trust as easily, never look at women the same way. He'd become paranoid, distrust everything women told him.

For the first time since starting at CAM, Jillian was ashamed. She helped destroy people's lives. Yes, they had a right to know what was going on with their spouse, but was it okay to tempt fate? Would people cheat if they weren't propositioned? Sure, Mr. Parker's wife had cheated without needing bait, but what about the others?

Jillian felt her chin tremble, felt her eyes burn—and it had nothing to do with the smell.

Mr. Parker soon eased to his feet, his legs shaky. He didn't say goodbye, just left with what little dignity he could wrap around himself. When the door closed behind him, Marcus's head sank into his hands. Several minutes passed. Jillian finally left the smelly office and strode into the conference room.

He glanced up at her. "Sometimes the job isn't worth it," he said softly. "My dad would laugh about his clients.

He'd say, 'Be the cheater, son, not the cheated on.' I think I hate him right now."

Jillian sighed, aching for the little boy who had heard such poison. "The urine is on the lightbulb," she admitted. No more war, she decided then. No more anger. How petty that seemed now. Besides, Marcus had been right. She'd attacked him because she still wanted him and was afraid of her feelings.

I'm willing to wait for you, he'd said. *However long you need.*

It's the person you give yourself to that matters.

He'd just broken the news to Mr. Parker with a gentleness and tenderness that had surprised her. Deepened her feelings for him. She sighed again. Without a doubt, she knew it was time to find another job. Maybe as bait, maybe not. But she could not work with Marcus *and* have a relationship with him. She also could not work for Marcus and *not* have a relationship with him.

What should she do? A part of her wanted to fall and let him try and catch her. The fear of hitting the ground, however… No. She couldn't risk it.

"I'm sorry about the lightbulb."

"No problem," he said.

With nothing left to say, she turned. "I'm not feeling well, so I'm going home. I'll see you tomorrow." And then she ran as fast as she could from the building. Trying to escape him. Trying to escape herself.

Twenty-Five

*Great news! I've just received government funding for
a four-hour expedition to find your G-spot.*

BRENT SPENT THE ENTIRE DAY and night proving to Georgia
that the person inside her was all that mattered. He took
her out to eat (in public), to the movies (where he actually
watched a girlie chick flick, just as he'd promised days
ago), then to the Bricktown walkway, where they were
now strolling hand in hand in the moonlight. Redbrick
buildings rose on both sides of them and cars meandered
along the road. The air was cool, the night fragrant.

While she discovered that a man could appreciate her
for the imperfect woman she was, he discovered that he
truly was in love with her. That it hadn't been a fantasy he'd
built up in his mind all these many years. Every time she
laughed, he felt like a god. Like he'd conquered a mountain.

She was witty and warm and so kindhearted she made
him want to be a better man. Actually, she just plain
made him *want*.

He wanted her so badly that he trembled. He wanted to kiss her and wipe away the rest of her upset. Continually he had to remind himself that she'd just gotten out of a relationship. Taking things slow was smart. She wasn't ready for another man yet. Still…

"People are staring," Georgia said.

"So what? If it doesn't bother me that they're staring at my ugly face, why should it bother you?"

She snorted, but a smile hovered at the corners of her lips. Slowly, however, her expression sobered. "You used to run from me in high school."

"Sweetheart, I wanted you even then. Haven't I explained that to you? You were too young for me and I knew it. I also knew that if I was around you at all, I'd make a move."

"Yeah, but you left your own house that night I spilled spaghetti on myself at dinner. That seems a little extreme if you were just afraid of wanting me. We weren't even alone in the room—your whole family was there."

He laughed, he just couldn't help himself. "That's why I ran. I had a goddamn hard-on the size of the Empire State Building and I didn't want my mom to see. Do you know how embarrassing that would have been? Having to explain I was turned on by a girl covered in tomato sauce?"

Georgia's cheeks colored—with pleasure?—as she stopped and faced him. She released his hand, only to reach up and cup his cheeks. Her lips were soft and moist and so kissable.…

"I'll never push you away again," she swore. "I love the way your eyes crinkle when you laugh. I love the humor you find in the most bizarre things. I love that you don't let anyone beat you at board games, even if you have to cheat. Most of all, I love that you see me for who I really am—and you like me anyway. And if, say, you were to make a move on me today…"

Relief and joy swept through him, potent, pure. He closed his eyes against the amazing surge of emotion. Finally! Finally, she was willing to give him a chance. He'd waited so long for this moment, it was surreal in actuality. Like a dream. "Baby, I'm *dying* to make a move. But are you sure you're ready?"

What the hell, he thought before she could answer. He swooped down and claimed her lips. She opened immediately with a needy moan. His tongue swept inside, taking, giving. Enjoying. Blood rushed straight into his shaft. Hard, so hard.

The rest of the world faded away. There was only Georgia, her luscious taste, her soft body pressed against his hardness. Her arms wound around his neck as a tremor slid down her spine. He felt it vibrate into him.

Before he took them to the point of no return, he pulled back. "No more," he said. "I've been waiting for you my entire life, I can wait a little longer."

Her eyes peered up at him, so green they sparkled like freshly washed emeralds. She moistened her lips with the tip of her pink tongue. "I don't want to wait, Brent. I want you in my bed, in my life. Now. Today. Take me home and make love to me."

He experienced another rush of joy. Joy so intense he almost crumbled to his knees. "I'll take you home," he told her fiercely, "and make you mine. Now. Always."

And he did.

THE NEXT FEW DAYS passed in a daze for Jillian. She saw her brother and Georgia several times, but she couldn't stand to be in their presence for long. They were too mushy, too gushy, too much in love. Even Anne was in love. The wily bitch was getting married. Again. She'd sent Jillian an e-mail saying she was flying to Vegas to make an honest man of her "young stud."

"How many times do I have to tell you it's time for you to live?" she'd added. "You're so stubborn, you're probably home alone when you could be out having fun. Life is too short. Let's live it with no regrets."

It wasn't fair. Jillian wanted happily-ever-after for herself, too, she realized; she wanted to forget her fears and grab hold of Marcus, but even though he seemed to want her, too, they both flirted with people for a living. How could she live with that?

While she planned to find another line of work—yep, she was going to move on, no more helping men cheat for her—he couldn't. He owned CAM. He would always be coming on to other women and Jillian didn't think she could stand that, even though it meant nothing. Temptation always, *always* got to a man and Marcus would be tempted on a daily basis.

Still, for the first time in her life, she was truly in love—another realization. Ugh. What a terrible and beautiful and wrong emotion. She didn't know when or how it had happened, only that it had. What she also knew was that love—the cranky bitch—did not conquer all. She might want to forget her fears, but she couldn't seem to do it.

"I hate my life," she moaned to her ceiling. She was lying in bed, and she didn't think she'd get up today.

Her dad had called a few times, complicating things further. She hadn't answered and he'd left her several messages, asking to meet with her. He wanted to get to know her again, see her, hug her, he'd said. He missed his baby, he'd said. He was sorry, he'd said. If her mom could get over the past, why couldn't she?

His wedding was approaching and he wanted her to be a bridesmaid, just as Brittany had claimed.

If she met with him, would she be sending a message that his infidelity was okay? She just didn't know. The little girl inside her, though, wanted desperately to see him again. So many years had passed since she'd even glimpsed his face. How wonderful would it be to let go of past hurts and simply live in the moment?

All Jillian knew was that she was lonely and it was driving her crazy. She was so unsure about everything in her life. Nothing had gone as she'd planned. She hadn't bought CAM. She hadn't remained detached from the men in her life. She wasn't having fun anymore. She was miserable. And she still wanted Marcus.

She sighed. Maybe she *would* see her dad. *You know you want to.* If anything, it would keep her mind off Marcus. Yeah. Right. Like she'd ever stop thinking about him. But if she were to patch things up with her dad, if she were a part of his wedding, maybe she'd finally begin to heal.

Heal…how wonderful that sounded.

The wall clock chimed the hour. Noon. She should be at the office by now. She was too raw, though, and couldn't face Marcus. Not now. Not yet. Another cowardly action, but she didn't care.

Hoping to get his voice mail, she dialed his number. She got the man and his rich timbre made her shiver. It was a voice that would haunt her dreams. "I'm still sick," she told him.

"What's wrong?" he asked.

She heard concern in his voice and it disconcerted her. "I ate poisoned cookies. I'll talk to you later, okay." She hung up before he could respond and dropped the phone on her mattress. It bounced onto the floor and landed with a smack. She half expected him to call back, but the minutes ticked by and he didn't. That…saddened her. And it shouldn't have.

God, she was beginning to act like her mom. Maybe Evelyn had been right when she'd compared the two of them.

"I'm pathetic," she muttered. *He's off-limits.* If she had to remind herself a thousand times a day, she would.

The phone rang in the next instant and she yelped. She practically jumped off the bed in her haste to grab it, but her heart plummeted when she saw it wasn't Marcus. It was her dad. Again. *Ring. Ring.*

Should she answer?

Ring. Pause. *Ri*— She jabbed the "talk" button before she could stop herself. "Hello."

There was a heavy pause. "Jillian?"

"Yes."

"I—I didn't expect you to answer. This is—"

"I know who it is," she said, her voice shaky. He sounded just like she remembered him. A deep, calming baritone that had once soothed her little girl hurts…before he'd brought about the biggest hurt of her life.

"I—how are you?"

"I'm good." Lie. "How are—" she gulped "—you?"

A full minute passed before he answered, as if he couldn't believe she'd asked him that question. "I'm good."

Silence. Obviously, they didn't know what to say to each other.

He cleared his throat. "I, um, well…"

"I hear you're getting married." As she spoke the words, she realized she wasn't upset. Yes, he was starting a new family. But that didn't mean he'd forget about her and stop calling. That didn't mean he was once again choosing someone else over her.

"Yes."

"How's your…fiancée?"

"Christy's wonderful. Her boys are all grown up now and in college. It's just Christy and me in the house and everything's quiet. Too quiet." He drew in a breath, let it out. "I'd really love for you to meet her."

For the first time in her life, Jillian heard desperation in her dad's voice. He even sounded as shaky as she felt.

Her stomach lurched. She'd hated him for so long, but… That silly little girl inside of her was eager, so eager. "I—I would rather meet you first." They were strangers now, so it *would* be like meeting for the first time.

Again, silence. Until she realized he was crying. Quiet sobs, much as Mr. Parker's had been. His tears brought forth her own; they streamed down her cheeks, hot and, she hoped, healing.

"Can you meet today?" he rushed out.

"Yes, actually." Now that she'd decided to do it, there was no point in wasting time and drawing it out. "Can you be at Brandywine Park at...one o'clock?"

"Yes, yes. I'll be there. I can't wait to see you." They hung up and Jillian stared down at the phone. Suddenly nervous, she dialed Brittany's number and asked her sister to bring the twins. Brittany was a stay-at-home mom and eagerly agreed, since the twins often drove her crazy during summer break. Jillian didn't know what she'd say to her dad when she finally saw him.

"You're doing the right thing," her sister said happily.

"I hope so." God knows, all of her other decisions lately had ended in disaster.

Twenty-Six

Wow. You with those curves and me with no brakes…

MARCUS KNEW Jillian wasn't really sick, but he didn't call her on it. It was probably for the best that she wasn't in the office. He was tied in knots. Painful knots. Seeing that woman every day and not being able to touch her was driving him crazy. She made him feel possessive, needy, on edge. And the longer he was around her, the worse it became. She wasn't even sparring with him now and that sucked, too.

He'd told her he would wait for her, but he wanted her *now!*

He'd taken a risk on a woman once and it hadn't worked. For the first time, he was willing to risk again. For Jillian. Anything for Jillian. Everything for Jillian. His heart. His freedom. His life. Just for a chance at happiness. For that brief moment in her arms, after they'd made love, he'd been given a glimpse of something precious.

Something his life desperately needed—but he'd been too afraid to pursue. Then.

He loved her. He did. He'd been a gambler all his life, but he'd been afraid to gamble on that. The stakes had been too high and it had happened too quickly; he hadn't even known her a full week. That didn't seem to matter. He loved Jillian with everything inside of him.

This was why Kayla had left him. She'd felt this…love and intensity and willingness to do whatever was necessary to be with that one person. The person who—God, this was corny—completed you. He hadn't been that for Kayla and she had known it. He'd shut her out because he'd known it, too. He just hadn't wanted to admit it and be a failure at marriage like his dad.

Jillian made him step up and be, well, a man. She never backed down. She gave as good as she got. He smiled slowly, thinking of the deer urine. Kayla had coasted, going along with everything he said until the day she finally snapped and left.

"What's wrong with you, man?" Joe asked.

Marcus blinked and straightened in his chair. His friend was peeking past the door. "Come in."

Joe entered and eased into the chair directly in front of the desk. Jake, Rafe, Matt and Kyle were right behind him. They circled the desk, each one of them frowning down at him.

"What?" he asked.

"You've been an ass for days," Jake replied. "More so than usual."

"I can't stand to be around you." Rafe.

"The girls hate you and that makes *me* hate you." Kyle.

"Thanks a lot. Traitors," he muttered.

The guys shared a look.

"What?" he demanded again, spreading his arms wide. Then, before they could respond, he said, "Each of you now has a case. Go type up your notes or study the photographs. Just get the bloody hell out of my office."

"See. That's exactly what we're talking about," Jake said. "You used to like hanging around us."

"Get. Out."

They shared another look, shook their heads in exasperation and filed out, shutting the door behind them. Marcus dropped his head into his hands. What the hell was he going to do? There had to be a way to convince Jillian to give him a chance, to take a risk on him and stop running.

There had to be a way to catch her, once and for all.

THE PARK OVERFLOWED with children. They flew down the slides, climbed the monkey bars and threw rocks at each other. Sunlight shone proudly overhead, curling fingers of light in every direction.

Brittany had arrived a few minutes before and was pushing Apple and Cherry on the swings. The girls loved it, laughing and begging to go higher. Jillian sat in a swing across from them. It was 1:07, and her dad wasn't here. Maybe he'd changed his mind. Maybe—

"Is this seat taken?"

The familiar voice made her gulp. She stopped swinging and slowly looked up, almost afraid of what she'd find.

There was her father, bathed in the sunlight. He'd

changed. A lot. Deep lines bracketed his eyes and mouth. His blue eyes weren't as bright as she remembered. His curly black hair was now completely gray.

He motioned to the swing next to her and she nodded. "It's yours," she told him, hating how unsure she sounded.

He eased into the black strap. They both looked straight ahead. "Thank you," he said. "For seeing me, that is."

"You're welcome." Suddenly *she* felt like the one who should be thanking *him*. God, she was confused.

"It's, uh, been a long time."

"Yes."

"Too long, I hope." He laughed nervously.

"Yes," she said, surprised that she meant it. Her insides were weeping at the sight of him, at being near him again. When she'd been a little girl, he would sing her to sleep, push her in the swing like Brittany was doing to the twins. He'd loved her, hugged her often. She'd kind of forgotten about those things over the years. But maybe they were the reason she'd felt so betrayed by what he'd done to her mom. To her.

She thought of all the things she'd missed: her dad watching her graduate, his dark looks (maybe even the cleaning of guns) when boys picked her up for dates, a dance at her sister's wedding. He'd been there, but she'd pretended he was invisible. Longing bubbled up inside her.

"I'm sorry," he said suddenly, as if unable to hold the words back a moment longer. "I never meant to hurt your mother and I certainly never meant to hurt you. I loved you. I *love* you. You're my baby."

A hot tear cascaded down her cheek. "Why did you do it?"

He shook his head. "The reason doesn't matter."

"Yes, it does. You picked Mrs. Prescott over your own family."

His eyes darkened with remembered pain. "That wasn't how I saw it at the time. Your mother and I were having problems. Her depression was getting out of hand. She never let you see it because she wanted to be perfect for you, but I had to deal with it every day and I was tired, Jillian, so tired of the fits and the tears. When she left to visit your aunt, it was like a weight had been lifted off my shoulders. Jennifer—Mrs. Prescott—always made me feel important. Like a man. Not a doctor or a therapist or a burden. But a man."

Hearing the torture-laden tone nearly undid her. And hearing his side, she could kind of maybe almost understand why he strayed. Cheating was never okay. After all, he could have just left. But maybe sometimes there were two sides to the story. Everyone made mistakes. Look at *her* life. She'd blamed her dad for her mother's depression, thinking it had all stemmed from him and what he'd done. Not so, she realized now. Her mom had always been troubled.

"I've regretted my behavior all these years," her dad added. "I've wanted to go back and fix it, but…"

Not knowing what to say, Jillian stretched out her arm. She waited, just waited, without saying a word. Tentatively her dad reached out and wrapped his fingers around her palm.

They sat there, holding hands and simply absorbing

each other for a long time. Jillian wanted to sob for all
the years she'd pushed him away, but she held back her
tears. Later, she'd cry later. Right now, she was going to
enjoy her father. A man she'd tried and convicted—then
sentenced—without ever really listening to the full story.

"I'm so sorry, Dad. I never should have treated you
like a criminal."

"You have nothing to be sorry for, baby. You were—"

"Grandpa! Grandpa!" Apple had spotted him and raced
over to him, catapulting herself into his arms. She laughed.

His hand was torn from Jillian's as he wrapped his
arms around the little girl. "Now which one are you?" he
asked with a watery smile. "Peach or Mango?"

She uttered another carefree laugh. "You know who I
am."

Cherry raced over, too. She shouldered Apple out of
the way to get in on the hug. "I'm glad you're here. Did
you bring me a present?"

"Cherry," Brittany admonished. She anchored her
hands on her hips. "We've talked about that."

"What?" the girl said innocently. "It wasn't the very
first thing I said to him. I told him I was glad to see him."

Her dad barked out a laugh. "She's got you there, Brit."

Seeing them together—so happy and at ease—nearly
dropped Jillian to her knees. She could have had this a
long time ago. This love and affection. This *family*.
Because of her stubbornness, she'd lost so many years.

She pressed her lips together to cut off her moan.

Glancing over at her, her dad set the girls aside. He
leaned toward Jillian and wrapped his arms around her.
She vaguely heard Brittany gasp, foggily saw her sister

cover her mouth with her hand, thought she heard the twins giggling about something, and then all she knew was her dad. His smoky-cigar scent. His strength. She hugged him back for all she was worth.

"I love you, Jilly."

"I love you, too, Dad."

"Well, I so did not expect this to happen," Brittany said with a smile.

He kissed the end of Jillian's nose. "You're invited to the wedding. Christy would love it if you'd agree to be a bridesmaid. But if you'd rather not, I understand. Hell, I'd even love it if you were best man," he said.

She laughed, a genuine laugh.

They stayed at the park a little longer before bidding each other goodbye. She received another bear hug and a request to stay in touch—which she promised to do and *would* do. She was also going to take him up on his offer to stand up in his wedding.

Healing felt as nice as she'd dreamed.

She managed to remain calm the entire drive home. No tears, no wild thoughts. She parked and emerged—still no reaction. Mrs. Franklin was outside, saw her, *hmphed,* and strode inside her house, evidently still upset over the sex-in-the-backyard incident. Jillian's chest ached as she climbed up the porch, unlocked the door and stepped inside. When the door closed behind her, she walked into the living room.

She made it to the glass coffee table before her knees gave out and she cried. Her entire body shook with the force of her tears. They were hot, scalding. Her stomach clenched painfully. She'd given up so much, and for what? So she could hold on to fears? Hurt? Pain? Yes, all of those. And she was doing that again now, with Marcus. She hadn't even tried to win his heart.

She was stupid, so very stupid.

The tears continued to pour until she had nothing left. Her nose was swollen and she had trouble breathing. Furious with herself, she banged her fists onto the glass. It shook and there was a small satisfaction in that. She banged again and again and again, releasing all the emotions pent up inside her, unable to stop until they were drained completely.

With her last hit the glass shattered, tinkling like bells in her ears. A sharp pain radiated up both of her arms. Her eyes were swollen as she glanced down at them. Red droplets ribboned from her wrists to her elbows. Flowing, flowing.

The first thought that flooded her mind was that she wanted Marcus. He'd take away the hurt. She pushed to shaky legs, went into the bathroom, and grabbed two hand towels. She wrapped one around each wrist, then she picked up the phone and dialed.

He answered on the third ring. "Marcus Brody."

"Marcus?" She loved him. She did. She hadn't wanted to, but there it was, in all its awful glory. She loved him. Yes, he was infuriating. Yes, he had a smart mouth. Yes, he was as jaded as she was. But he was also tender and passionate and she wanted him in her life, no matter what.

How could you have let this happen? And so quickly? Too late for recriminations now.

"Jillian?" At the office, Marcus straightened in his chair. The client across from him, a young woman who wanted to test her boyfriend of four months, frowned. "What's wrong?"

"I love…my wrists," she said, sniffling.

His eyebrows furrowed together. "You called to tell me that you love your wrists?"

"No, I—" sniffle, sniffle "—cut them, but I can't tell you over the phone. Want to tell you in person."

"You cut your wrists?" Panic hit him and hit him hard.

"I'm bleeding, but that's not why—"

"Fucking hell." How much blood had she lost? "Hang on, baby. I'll be right there. No, hang up and call 911. I'm on my way." He threw down the phone, but it missed the cradle and bounced off the desk and onto the floor.

The girl's frown deepened. "Hey, what's going on? I haven't told you—"

He was already at the door, yelling for Jake. His friend bounded around the far corner, expression concerned. "Take care of her," Marcus instructed, pointing to the girl.

"Where are you going?"

He didn't stop to answer, but sprinted outside and into his car. He made the fifteen-minute drive in six, weaving in and out of traffic. It was a miracle he wasn't pulled over.

Why would Jillian try to kill herself? Why? Was she following in her mom's footsteps? He blamed himself. He should have been more careful with her feelings. He shouldn't have pushed her so hard to accept him. He'd told her he would wait for her, and he would. For however long she needed.

He didn't bother shutting his car door as he emerged, he just raced onto the porch and into the house. When he didn't see her in the foyer, he stalked into the living room. Gaze wild, he looked left and right. "Jillian!" God, where was she? Had she passed out? Concern and fear washed through him in sickening waves. The coffee table was shattered. Had someone attacked her? What if she were—

"Right here," she said softly.

He almost collapsed in relief. She was curled on the recliner, her feet tucked up to her chest. White towels were twisted around her arms. No, not fully white. He could see the crimson stains.

"What happened, baby?" He closed the distance between them and knelt in front of her. She was pale—except for her swollen, red-rimmed eyes.

"I accidentally broke the table."

Thank God. Not suicide. His relief was tangible. "Let me see. Your wrists, not the table." Gently he gripped one of her arms and unwound the cloth. There were multiple cuts, the one directly on her tendon the deepest, but they were already drying. He examined the other arm. It had a few more cuts, but nothing deep. "I don't think you need stitches."

"Good." She exhaled a shuddering breath.

He re-bandaged her arms with fresh towels, then scooped her up and settled into the chair with her on his lap. She instantly cuddled close. "I was scared," he admitted.

"Sorry," she murmured.

"I thought you'd tried to kill yourself."

She snorted weakly. "As if I would ever do something like that. Apparently I'm like my mom, or so she tells me, but I couldn't put the people I love through that."

"You said you'd cut your wrists," he accused.

She chuckled. "And I didn't lie."

Happy to be with her again—and holding her—he tightened his grip and simply breathed in her scent. "I'm glad you called me."

"Me, too."

She yawned and he felt the warm exhalation of her breath. "I went to see my dad today. I hadn't seen him in years and I kind of had an emotional breakdown when I got home. A good breakdown, though." She yawned again. "He told me how much he loves me. I was just so overcome with regret, I hit the table."

"No reason to regret. You have many, many years with him to look forward to." His stomach clenched as longing washed through him. He wanted years with her. He wanted to look forward to them. Thinking she had tried to kill herself… He squeezed her all the tighter.

She sighed, weary. "Will you stay here for a while?"

"Of course." He closed his eyes, sucked in a deep breath. Home, he was home, and there was no place he'd rather be.

"I'm too tired right now, but maybe in a little while we could talk."

"I'd like that." No way in hell she'd be able to get rid of him now. When she woke up, he'd make her understand that they were meant to be together. "Go to sleep, baby. I'll be right here." *I'm never letting you go.*

She curled deeper into him and was asleep a second later.

Twenty-Seven

How would you like your eggs in the morning?

MARCUS AWOKE as something buzzed in his pocket. He slowly cracked open his eyelids. Darkness had fallen. Thin strands of moonlight dripped throughout—a brown room? Confused, he blinked and tried to orient himself.

Jillian was in his arms, on his lap. They were sitting on her recliner. She was quiet, still and warm. Asleep. The buzz in his pocket continued.

Frowning, he dug out his cell and quietly answered. "Yeah?"

"Marcus," Jake said. "I need you to come over to my place. Something's happened."

"I can't." Softly, gently, he kissed Jillian's temple.

"Please. It's important. And hurry." *Click.*

Marcus's frown intensified. He replaced his phone in his pocket, careful not to disturb Jillian. He glanced at her. Her head rested against his shoulder and her expression was soft, sweet. Damn it. He hated to leave her.

He also hated to wake her. She'd been so tired, so despondent. He knew she needed whatever rest she could get. Easing to his feet, he balanced her light weight in his arms. God, he loved this woman.

To think, he was holding the most important part of his life right now. When he'd stopped seeing her as an enemy and started seeing her as a partner, he didn't know. He was only glad that it was so.

He carried her to the bedroom and laid her down gently. She mumbled something unintelligible and rolled over with a sigh. He took off her shoes and pulled the cover over her lower half, then he kissed her cheek.

"I love you," he whispered.

He checked her wrists again to make sure they hadn't started bleeding, then wrote her a note, telling her where he was going so she wouldn't worry if she woke up. He wouldn't leave for anyone except Jake. Jake had seen him through some tough times, and he had always vowed to do the same for his friend, who still suffered some pretty bad days over Claire's death.

Marcus left before he changed his mind. Really, what the hell was wrong with Jake? His friend had never called him and begged him to come by like that.

He sped to their apartment building and this time he *was* pulled over. He took the ticket without protest and hurried on. At Jake's door, he knocked. The TV was too loud and he could hear laughter.

"Jake," he called, knocking again.

A second later, his friend opened the door. To Marcus's shock, he was grinning ear to ear. "Welcome to the party."

Sweet Jesus.

Joe appeared in the doorway and latched onto his arm, tugging him inside. "Don't even think about leaving."

"I thought something was wrong," Marcus said darkly.

"It was," Jake replied. "You weren't here."

"Jillian—"

"Nope. Don't even say her name. You've been an ass lately and it's time you released some of your stress. With someone receptive."

Women were everywhere, he realized. Every color, shape, and size. He tangled his hand through his hair. "Guys, I don't need your help releasing stress. I'm doing fine on my own. Jillian—"

"No, you're not and don't say her name," Rafe said, his arms wrapped around a blonde and a brunette. "It's a smorgasbord tonight, so start filling your plate." The girls twittered at his side.

Kyle walked over, a redhead in tow. He urged her to Marcus's side and nodded. "Now, don't you two look cute together."

Marcus tried to give the woman back, but she latched on to his waist. "Kyle told me to show you a good time." Biting her lower lip, she ran her finger over his collarbone.

He looked away, desperate for escape. Matt stood off to the side, talking with Amelia. When Marcus saw her, he groaned. He and Jillian were still on shaky ground. If Amelia told her about some woman hanging on his arm, it could crack that ground into a million unfixable pieces. Trust was a big thing and hard to win back. Not that he'd done anything wrong, but Jillian was bait and she wouldn't believe that. She would only see the implication.

"Well," he heard a woman say—and it was the sound

of his worst nightmare. He whipped around. Of course she'd followed him. He would have done the same thing. *Should have expected it.*

Jillian stood in the doorway as if he'd conjured her. He tore the redhead from his side and leapt forward. "Jillian, this isn't what it looks like."

"I heard you leave, got up and read your note." Her voice was emotionless, and she was gazing around the apartment. "I didn't have your cell number, so I came here to make sure everything was okay."

"It's not what it looks like," he said again. He reached her just as the music stopped; all conversation stopped, in fact. He didn't care. He'd make a fool of himself if need be. He grabbed her by the shoulder before she decided to run. Thankfully, she made no move to pull away. "Let's go to my apartment. Let's talk about this."

She surprised him by saying, "Okay." But her face was as withdrawn as her tone.

What was going through her mind?

He ushered her out the door and down the hall. No one tried to stop him. He unlocked his apartment and led her inside, to his bedroom. Still she didn't protest. Determined to have his say, he reached under his mattress and withdrew a pair of cuffs he'd purchased with her in mind. Without any type of explanation, he cuffed his wrist, then cuffed hers over the bandage.

"What are you doing?" she asked, confused. Good, a show of emotion.

"Making sure you can't get away. We're going to talk this out."

"Marcus, there's no need."

Eyes narrowed, he tossed the key in the hallway. "Damn it, nothing happ—"

"I know."

Her words penetrated his mind, and he stilled. "You know?"

"I know nothing happened."

"Wait. *How* do you know that? I was holding another woman. Or rather, she was holding me."

"I trust you." Looking unsure, she gazed down at their hands. "And I...love you, so I'm going to trust you, no matter how bad things appear."

He blinked in surprise. "Wait. What?"

"I love you."

Again, what? "You love me?"

"Yes."

Slowly he grinned. "Well, hell, baby. I love you, too."

Tears filled her eyes and she covered her mouth with her free hand. "Really? Even though this happened so quickly?"

"Even though. I think I knew the moment I laid eyes on you. Whether I've known you one day or one year doesn't make a difference to me. I love you so much, and I'm going to sign half of the business to you. From now on, we'll be partners and make business decisions together. Also, I'm moving in with you. And don't even think about telling me no, because we're getting married and married people live together."

The quick flash of joy on her face was followed by concern. "I don't want special treatment on the job, Marcus. I just—"

"Believe me." He held up his hand. "There's no special treatment. I trust your instincts for building CAM. And if I didn't, well, I'd still make you report to me as an employee. You'd just have a different title. Love Slave."

Her lips twitched. "In that case, I accept. All of it." With a whoop, she threw her arm around him and kissed the line of his jaw. "But we have to stop being bait. No more flirting with other people. I want you all to myself."

"Done," he said, happier than he'd ever been in his life. "We've got to have had the weirdest courtship in history."

"Think we'll make it?" she asked, kissing him full on the mouth.

"Absolutely. You can test me anytime you want."

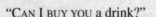

Epilogue

"CAN I BUY YOU a drink?"

Marcus glanced at the woman propositioning him. She was beautiful, the most beautiful woman he'd ever seen—but he knew she was bait. He glanced at his watch, the picture of boredom. "No, thanks," he said, his tone heavy with dismissal.

She ran her fingertip over his shirtsleeve. "Let me buy you a drink, pretty please with a cherry on top. I'd love to get to know you, and one drink won't hurt."

"No. I'm sorry."

"Please."

"No."

She paused, chewed on her bottom lip. "I just moved to Oklahoma City. How's the…weather?"

Oh, damn. The one conversation topic he couldn't resist. Every muscle in his body stiffened. "It's hot. Real hot." He sighed, glanced again at his watch. "All right. Fine. One drink. But we have to hurry. I don't want my wi—mom to find out."

"We'll hurry." The woman told the bartender to bring

them two Fuzzy Navels and turned back to him. "I noticed that you keep looking at your watch. Are you waiting for your wi— mom?"

"Yep. I'm divorced and Mother's been my only source of comfort lately."

"You're divorced?" She leaned in closer to him, fragrant and warm. "Oh, you poor thing. *I'd* like to comfort you."

Unable to resist her a moment longer, he slid his arm around her waist. "That sounds like a good idea. How about we go back to my place?"

Jillian grinned. "Will you do bad, bad things to me?"

"It will be my greatest pleasure."

For the past year, he and Jillian had celebrated their monthly anniversary this way. He always looked forward to it. And it was the only time either of them acted as bait anymore; they'd both given it up and now simply ran CAM. The employees were ecstatic about their partnership because Jillian kept him in line. She'd even brought back spa day. The girls always asked Marcus to join them, citing his need for a Calypso Coral pedicure to match the lipstick he was often spotted wearing after one-on-one meetings with Jillian.

Thanks to their combined efforts and the hard work of the CAM team, the business had reached a whole new level and their financial concerns were a thing of the past. Their sister-in-law, Georgia, now ran CAM's counseling center for victims of infidelity, which Jillian had opened next door. Some of the clients were even hooking up. Marcus grinned at the thought, knowing firsthand that there was nothing like the common bond of betrayal to draw two people together. Georgia and Brent were happier than ever, and they'd become Marcus's new poker buddies.

Marcus had never gotten around to unpacking the boxes in his apartment. He'd moved into Jillian's house right away. She, of course, had made him unpack everything immediately. The beige decor remained, but he'd helped her mess things up a bit by "christening" every room.

Jillian's dad was married now and Jillian had been his best man. Marcus had never seen a happier dad. Or a better-looking best man. Removing that tux had been sexy fun. (Words he'd never thought he would entertain.)

Yep. Love was in the air. His mother-in-law was a new woman, happily dating and no longer trying to feed him poisoned cookies. Anne was happily married to her boy toy and came to visit often, claiming she was proud of the new, improved and willing-to-take-chances Jillian. His men were doing well, as were his female employees. Rule two was a thing of the past, so Matt and Amelia were dating, fighting, dating, fighting. They'd end up together, he thought, once they stopped combating it. Neither one of them had any idea just how good a loving relationship could be. But they'd find out, he had no doubt.

Jake was the only person Marcus was worried about, because the stubborn man still refused to date. One day, though, Marcus knew Jake would find someone else. One day. Love was too powerful to deny.

Jillian had started her Swine Whine Web site, listing the city's most unwanted dates—repeat offenders who were never going to change—complete with a ranking system. Danielle, Selene and Becky had soon taken that over, however, posting pictures of cheating men and women with *Most Unwanted* stamped under their faces.

For his birthday, Jillian had given Marcus a photo of himself with *Most Wanted* stamped across his smiling mug. He'd hung it in his office to show his clients that a happy ending *was* possible.

"Next time," Marcus said to his wife, his love, "I get to be the bait." For now, it was time to take her home so he could get started on those bad, bad things.

"I'm too easy to catch," she said, pouting up at him. "You, at least, put up a two-minute fight."

Grinning wickedly, he paid for their drinks. "Baby, catching you is the best part."

* * * * *

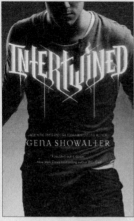

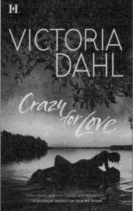

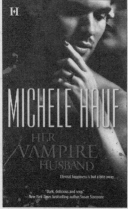

REQUEST YOUR
FREE BOOKS!

2 FREE NOVELS
FROM THE SUSPENSE COLLECTION
PLUS 2 FREE GIFTS!

YES! Please send me 2 FREE novels from the Suspense Collection and my 2 FREE gifts (gifts are worth about $10). After receiving them, if I don't wish to receive any more books, I can return the shipping statement marked "cancel." If I don't cancel, I will receive 3 brand-new novels every month and be billed just $5.74 per book in the U.S. or $6.24 per book in Canada. That's a saving of at least 28% off the cover price. It's quite a bargain! Shipping and handling is just 50¢ per book.* I understand that accepting the 2 free books and gifts places me under no obligation to buy anything. I can always return a shipment and cancel at any time. Even if I never buy another book, the two free books and gifts are mine to keep forever.

192/392 MDN E7PD

Name _____ (PLEASE PRINT) _____

Address _____ Apt. #

City _____ State/Prov. _____ Zip/Postal Code

Signature (if under 18, a parent or guardian must sign)

Mail to **The Reader Service:**
IN U.S.A.: P.O. Box 1867, Buffalo, NY 14240-1867
IN CANADA: P.O. Box 609, Fort Erie, Ontario L2A 5X3

Not valid for current subscribers to the Suspense Collection
or the Romance/Suspense Collection.

Want to try two free books from another line?
Call 1-800-873-8635 or visit www.morefreebooks.com.

* Terms and prices subject to change without notice. Prices do not include applicable taxes. N.Y. residents add applicable sales tax. Canadian residents will be charged applicable provincial taxes and GST. Offer not valid in Quebec. This offer is limited to one order per household. All orders subject to approval. Credit or debit balances in a customer's account(s) may be offset by any other outstanding balance owed by or to the customer. Please allow 4 to 6 weeks for delivery. Offer available while quantities last.

Your Privacy: Harlequin Books is committed to protecting your privacy. Our Privacy Policy is available online at www.eHarlequin.com or upon request from the Reader Service. From time to time we make our lists of customers available to reputable third parties who may have a product or service of interest to you. If you would prefer we not share your name and address, please check here. ☐

Help us get it right—We strive for accurate, respectful and relevant communications. To clarify or modify your communication preferences, visit us at www.ReaderService.com/consumerschoice.

MSUS10R